"Nevin continues his superb American Story series with a fascinating fictional account of the still unresolved Burr conspiracy to steal the Louisiana Purchase. Setting the stage with a host of real-life heroes and scoundrels, he introduces the three primary players in the remarkable drama that almost toppled the fledgling nation . . . Grounded in historical fact and chockfull of intrigue and action, this suspenseful political yarn will draw readers into the tumult and the uncertainty that characterized the early years of American nation building."

—*Booklist* (starred review)

"Another lively look back at the newborn U.S. by a historical novelist who respects both disciplines . . . Nevin loves his political details . . . vivid storytelling about a time as turbulent as it is generally neglected."

—*Kirkus* (starred review)

"*Treason* is a superb example of the historical novel in both plot and execution . . . so convincing that one would like to see an afterword explaining just how far it is historical."

—*Rapport Magazine*

PRAISE FOR *EAGLE'S CRY*

"An intriguing overview of the fractious early days of the American public . . . brimming with personal and political tension, the gripping narrative vividly recreates a seminal moment in the infancy of the U.S. An intelligent, well-crafted drama featuring a cast of authentically rendered historical characters."

—*Booklist*

"A rich robust historical novel of the kind we don't get often enough. Famous men and women spring vividly to life and action abounds. *1812* is a great read."

—John Jakes

"Splendid! History and dreams, men and women who made and preserved us a nation. David Nevin is an author of power and scope."

—James Michener

"Nevin has created a magnificent epic that held me mesmerized."

—Stephen Coonts

"The faded old etchings of battle on land and sea, of statesmen, heroes and villains are now in David Nevin's *1812* brought to vivid life and color and you are there immediacy."

—Gary Jennings

"A brillantly realized chronicle that gives a human scale to the author's panoramic canvas. A considerable achievement and one that transcends genre."

—*Kirkus Reviews*

"Nevin's latest . . . exhibits the best characteristics of the genre: it informs without oversimplifying the subject. Entertaining and very illuminating, Nevin subtly brings to life the War of 1812."

—*Booklist*

TREASON

TREASON

David Nevin

A TOM DOHERTY ASSOCIATES BOOK
NEW YORK

This is a work of fiction. All the characters and events portrayed in this book are either products of the author's imagination or are used fictitiously.

TREASON

Copyright © 2001 by David Nevin

A Forge Book
Published by Tom Doherty Associates, LLC
175 Fifth Avenue
New York, NY 10010

www.tor.com

Forge® is a registered trademark of Tom Doherty Associates, LLC.

ISBN: 0-812-52474-8

First edition: October 2001
First mass market edition: November 2002

Printed in the United States of America

0   9   8   7   6   5   4   3   2   1

For Luci

TREASON

ONE

Washington City, fall 1803

This was the way she remembered it—memories cherished across thirty-five tumultuous years when the world turned upside down and she moved to the center of the nation's affairs—this was her story:

She was born in '68 and that meant she was—let's see—eight when the trouble started. She remembered her father's distress there on the Virginia plantation. He was a Quaker strong in his faith and he held against war. But Millie Esterbridge, who was a year older and lived on the plantation next to theirs, said General Washington would lead the American troops and everyone knew— well, everyone in Virginia—that he was a great man. It would be all right with General Washington in command. Of course, at eight you take a lot for granted, and later she'd marveled at how ignorant they were of war. Everyone, grown-ups, too. At first it had just been the awful splitting between patriots and loyalists, Millie's father selling out and moving his family off to Canada. Later they understood that dislocation and dissolved loyalties hardly mattered against the deaths and the aching widows, the hunger and pain of folks at home and men in the field alike, the men who returned absent arms and legs, their eyes hollowed out like melon husks, and the men who didn't come home at all. Maybe it was in reaction to the war that Pa decided that his faith required him to free their slaves, sell the plantation, and move to Philadelphia, the Quaker center that only incidentally was America's largest city.

She was fourteen when the Revolution ended and the last British soldiers boarded ships lying against the wharves in New York City and went home. General Washington mounted a big white horse and led his ragged troops into the city that the enemy had held so long, and the whole country erupted in joy, bonfires and parades and martial music and speechifying to numb the senses.

The nation was free. There were people who said it would sink right out of sight without British leaders to direct it or war to hold it together, but that made no sense to her. She said so, too, plain and clear, and presently the Quaker elders called to tell her it was unseemly for a mere lass to talk so. But she snorted when the trio departed, austere and unsmiling in their black garb and coarse woolen hose and flat hats—she had a mind of her own and didn't need anyone telling her how to use it.

She was fifteen and then sixteen and when she turned to the mirror she liked what she saw, and from the way young men looked at her and boys stared and Quaker matrons frowned, she came to understand she was not just beautiful but fetching as well. Bright colors weren't the Quaker way but she managed always to have a red ribbon in her glossy black hair or a sash of vivid green on a white gown or the bootlaces of purple silk she once wore, creating a minor stir.

By then everyone in Philadelphia was talking about the way the postrevolutionary government was falling

flat, imploding, no head and no real body, no resources
and no authority, no direction and no aim or intention or
purpose, every state in the confederacy standing alone
and for itself. Seemed we weren't Americans at all but
Pennsylvanians or Virginians or what-have-you. But
shoot, she was both Pennsylvanian and Virginian—and
hence hardly could be one or t'other! By 1785 when she
was seventeen and fresh as a rose in bloom, Pa said the
country was going to ruin and the elders blamed the
slight attention paid the Lord's word, and she thought it
was high time someone did something and wasn't backward about saying so.

And sure enough, as if he'd been listening, General
Washington called a meeting for right here in Philadelphia over to the State House that aimed to straighten it
all out so the blood and pain of the war wouldn't be
wasted. Every day she got out her parasol against the
sun—oh, it was hot that summer of 1787!—and put a
ribbon in her hair and with a half dozen Quaker girls
went to stand along the brick sidewalks and watch the
delegates enter and leave. Ah, frivolity! The girls along
the sidewalk like so many flowers wanting to feel part of
a great day, or at least to be noticed. The delegates
looked toilsome and dour and they danced on the hot
brick because the slippers they wore with snowy silk
hose were so thin. It was said that they were talking
themselves blue, sitting at little tables covered in green
felt while General Washington looked on from a small
dais. He hardly said a word, so it was remarked, but his
stern look held them to the task.

Everyone talked about it on the street and they said the
brightest man in the Constitutional Convention was the
smallest and the quietest, with ideas that thundered but a
voice that could hardly be heard. His name was James
Madison and he was a fellow Virginian. She saw him one
day, pale, wizened, looked old, forty or so, and my good-

ness, you could just see he was smart. She watched him, wondering if he would look up and see her and look at her the way everyone else did, but he walked along with hands clasped behind him, head down, probably thinking great thoughts right before her eyes!

Gossip said that the delegates fought like dogs but by summer's end when blessed fall swept away the miasmic heat they had created a new government. Pa said the Constitution they'd written was a magnificent document that would last into the ages and though it had been threatened a few times it was holding right to this day. This was about the time Pa lost his business and the Quakers read him out of the Society for debt. He went to bed and turned his face to the wall till he died while Ma took in boarders. That was how Aaron Burr came into her life, he a congressman and then senator from New York and a boarder at Ma's house when Congress was in session. Even as a girl she'd recognized what an elegant fellow he was. Handsome, smooth, courteous, usually smiling, he seemed to say that this was how life should be led among men of power. In time she wondered if her own sense of elegance, ribbons and all, had been modeled on the image he presented.

They held elections and of course General Washington took the presidency and she knew everything would be all right. Electing anyone else would have been unimaginable then, though in later years there were plenty of harsh attacks on the grand old man. Everyone said this thoughtless brutality had broken his heart, though he was never one to show pain—maybe to Aunt Martha, but not to the world.

Not that she was calling the president's wife Auntie in those long-ago days or, indeed, anything at all. She was far removed then, jostling on the sidewalks with everyone else to see the parades. John Adams of Massachusetts who'd been a great patriot for as long as she could remember became vice president. Secretary of state was Thomas Jefferson, whom she'd heard Pa denounce often enough when Jefferson was governor of Virginia. Little Mr. Madison was in Congress and everyone said he was the general's right-hand man. But none of this really touched her. What mattered was that the Quaker elders were after her again for those ribbons and the glow in her eyes and the way her figure was developing now that she was in her twenties. That surely wasn't her fault—what should she do, hide in her bedroom?

So when a handsome Quaker lawyer named John Todd asked for her hand she married, had two beautiful babies, and was prepared to be a Quaker matron, biting her tongue and going easy on the ribbons. But when she was twenty-five the great yellow fever epidemic of 1793 spared her and little Payne but took her husband and new baby along with seven thousand others, one out of ten Philadelphians. She'd never forgotten the malevolent horror of that terrible summer, no one knowing where the disease came from or how to treat it, who would be stricken and who spared—and what a ghastly way to die, black vomit spewing, black water bursting from bowels. One matured overnight.

The grief-torn days that followed seemed blurred later; she seemed hardly aware of day turning to night and night to day. And in that terrible period, it was her mother's boarder, Aaron Burr, who came to her rescue. The New Yorker had turned something called Tammany Hall into a political force and was said to be a power in New York City. He took her quietly in hand in the midst of her grief, gentle sympathy mingling with easy practicality. He saw to her business problems, liquidated her husband's law practice and invested the results, saw to funerals and estate and probate matters. She even drafted a will naming him guardian of her child should the terror sweep them again. But even then, she recognized that it wasn't so much what he did as the way he did it. He was smooth and patient, and looking back it seemed that somehow it was his steadfast presence that brought her through those dark days. She owed him a great deal. But she was strong too, possessed of a deep inner resiliency, and gradually her sparkle returned. In time she found herself pondering what life might hold for her next. And Aaron reassured her then in a different way that told her he knew the ways of men and women and of the world: she was a most eligible widow, he said, beauty making up for lack of fortune.

Aaron's elegance, his dress so beautiful, his manner so graceful, to say nothing of that certain quickening in his eyes that produced an equal quickening in a great many women, so the talk went. She well understood the feeling; it wasn't that he was so handsome, though he was, or that his charm was beyond resisting, but all together he produced an undeniable pull. She was grateful that in her vulnerable period he had seized no advantages. Later, as she recovered, she was grateful that in due time he did advance himself, suggesting a willingness to service other needs that absent a husband she might now feel. A bit of nirvana, he said. Somehow, it pronounced her ready to meet the world.

Oh, Aaron . . . She was so fond of him and so definitely not in love with him and held such a clear vision that yielding to the temptation he offered—and temptation probably was the right word—would be to throw away her future that she laughed out loud.

"What," he cried, laughing with her, recognition of failure bright in his eyes, perhaps somehow liking her better for her refusal, "dost thou cast nirvana to the swine?"

"You darling man," she said, "you are a caution." She kissed his cheek and told him to sit in the chair in the opposite corner, and it was then that he told her that his good friend, Mr. Madison of Virginia, had asked to be presented. Presented . . . that had a serious sound.

The famous Mr. Madison, a smallish man somewhat shorter than she, gazed at her like a tongue-tied ox when Aaron brought him around but she found his very hesitations endearing. They were the honest product of obvious inexperience with women. But then, she was none too experienced with men, either—or with the national affairs that presumably dominated Mr. Madison's life, right-hand man to General Washington as he was. And for all his fumbling, when he did open his mouth it was to reveal intelligence of a very high order. He said his friends called him Jimmy. She gazed at him. Jimmy . . . for a man so distinguished? But she didn't voice this—she knew he would hear it as mockery. Jimmy, she said . . . it has a gentle sound. And he smiled. Silence overtook them and she rattled on a bit, and when he rose to go she was sure that would be the end of it. Instead he asked if she would accompany him to a small dinner General Washington was giving the next evening, and to a reception the evening following. He was forty-three and had never married; Aaron had told her his heart had been broken by a callous lass eleven years before and he'd never recovered.

The table of the president of the United States was rarified company for a Quaker miss without experience; she decided that intelligence must take experience's place. Before they reached the main course she had come to understand that she would get just one chance at this level before she was written off. Her solution, reached as she finished the turtle soup, was to keep her mouth shut until she had something to say that she knew she could defend and then say it well. Two such occasions arose before dessert; the second time the general smiled and nodded,

whether to her or to Jimmy she couldn't be sure, and
Mrs. Washington gave her a conspiratorial wink that was
as surprising as it was thrilling.

That spring of '94 there were balls and dinners and he
saw her every day, sitting in her mother's parlor,
anything but tongue-tied. Ideas poured out and she
responded and he accorded her respect, agreeing or
explaining his disagreement. If his heart had been
broken—she didn't inquire—he seemed to have recovered. But when Mrs. Washington—Aunt Martha as she
instructed the younger set to call her—asked if he had
proposed yet she could only answer, No, not yet. I'll
speak to him, the great lady said.

They were married in the fall. She was twenty-six.
The Quakers expelled her for marrying outside the faith
and she bought handfuls of ribbons and wore vivid
sashes and startling turbans—oh, she was bright as a par-
rot! And her husband's spirits opened like a flower and
he laughed and danced though he still was frozen in social groups of any size.

By then the great schism was shredding the government and she was startled to find how bitter and personal
it became.

"I mean," she said, faltering, "you and Mr. Hamilton,
you were friends, weren't you? Together on—"

"Friends?" said Jimmy, as his friends did indeed call
him. "I suppose. When we still saw eye to eye."

They had collaborated on what came to be called *The
Federalist*, a series of cogent papers that as she understood it had pretty well put over the new federal government, gaining the nine states needed to give the new
Constitution effect.

"But Alex changed," Jimmy added, and that was how
he characterized the fight. Alex was a handsome fellow
fully as irresistible to women as they were to him, famous for it, in fact. She remembered an explosive

evening when she had danced with him in one of those intricate quadrilles. It was at a ball the Washingtons gave when she and Jimmy had been married a year or so. The music was gaily rhythmic, the dancers dipping and swirling, and responding to Alex, she couldn't deny that he had a certain magnetic pull. But it seemed aggressive, an invasion that alarmed and then angered her. She was just sorting through these riotous feelings when he said in a low voice, "I wonder that you dare dance with me."

She stared at him. Her face felt hot as it did when she bent over a cooking fireplace. Had he read her mind? Her hand came up—later she realized she'd been close to hitting him—and he added smoothly, "Given that your husband finds me so detestable."

The music ended and his words fell loudly into the sudden silence just as Jimmy, partnered with Hannah Gallatin, stopped beside them. Of course Jimmy had heard and as Hannah gave her a conspiratorial wink he said with a smile, "I don't detest you, Alex. I detest your ideas." All good-humored, but she saw by his expression that he wasn't joking.

"Because I want the economy solid and workable?"

Jimmy hesitated; she knew this was tender ground, because the new nation had been flat broke and a country that can't pay its bills, international or domestic, has little standing in the family of nations. But Hamilton as treasury secretary had put American finances on a sound footing. Jimmy said Alex was a financial genius, which was the more amazing since his only financial experience had been keeping books in a country store in Jamaica, he the bastard son of a minor Scottish nobleman. Hannah patted her arm and went off somewhere.

"No," Jimmy said, "because you want to feed the rich at everyone else's expense."

"Oh, Jimmy," Alex said, carefully smiling to show this was all in fun, "next you'll be prating about the bank!"

"Yes, I will, now that you raise it. Bank of the United States. Functions as a treasury of the nation, doesn't it?"

"Well—"

"It's where government stores its money, deposits taxes collected, disburses as necessary?"

"Exactly—and—"

"And three-quarters of its assets are in private hands and hence the owners of those monies are in a position to manipulate public funds to their own advantage."

Alex's smile was gone. "You will never understand, James. Of course our bank favors the wealthy. Their capital is power and we need them with us, not agin us."

"So you shape law and government and power to their interests."

"Of course—and the bank is a fine example," Alex said, now looking quite self-satisfied.

Then, quite surprising herself, seeing a startled look flash over Jimmy's face, she said, "But won't that build an elite class, the wealthy over everyone else? They hold land, hold commerce, hold politics—they'll have it all, won't they?"

She found herself holding her breath in sheer fright and let it go with a rush. Without a thought she had inserted herself into a complex argument that she was suddenly sure a wiser woman would have avoided. Alex hesitated as if arguing with a woman unsettled him, and then Jimmy said in an easy voice, "She does sum it up well, doesn't she?" She felt a flash of gratitude as he went on, "Control by the 'right' people over the rest of us, that's what you're saying—and Alex, isn't the next step logically to make control hereditary, and doesn't that suggest nobles and princes and such and doesn't that—"

"Damn it all, Jimmy, you can't believe I want a king when we fought a war to free ourselves of a king!"

"I don't think you want a king. But I think your attitude takes us in that direction—"

"Faugh!"

Jimmy colored. "Faugh, my foot! I could see the reality as soon as the debt question came up."

She knew that was a true sore point with Jimmy. At war's end the nation had countless small debts—soldiers' mustering-out bonus, the paper given a farmer for a couple of hogs and a sack of oats, payment to gunsmiths and powder dumps and lead mines, all given on a promise of someday, if we win. Well, now someday had arrived and Alex's plan was to float long-term bonds that would pay these debts all at once and clear the books. Debt management, he called it, and yes, it did make fiscal sense.

But who was holding these slips of paper given throughout the war? Not the soldier mustered out, the farmer for his hogs and oats—no, they long since had been forced by need to sell that scrap of paper to a speculator at a dime on the dollar. Jimmy still got red in the face when he talked of this. He said that piece of paper was a sacred debt of the United States given in honor and taken in the belief that the nation would survive and prosper and honor debts.

But when Alex prepared to pay these debts—and then, quite suddenly as one awakens from a dream, she realized that the music had not resumed and a small crowd had gathered around them. They had interrupted the whole entertainment! She saw Mrs. Washington frowning, the general striding toward the musicians.

And Jimmy cried, voice rising, "I saw it when you rewarded the speculators and froze out the little men, the veterans, the farmers, the small debt holders who'd long since lost their paper. You paid the speculators and devil take those whose suffering had won the war!"

The musicians were lifting their instruments and the general was coming toward them when she heard Alex snap, "Talking of the plight of veterans ill behooves a man who sat out the war."

The first violinist sounded an A and the general had turned and was coming toward the disruption as she saw her husband go pale at this sally. It was his point of vulnerability. Even today his health was delicate and he was often ill. While Alex had been a dashing officer on General Washington's staff Jimmy hadn't been physically fit for the field. He knew that made sense but it still bothered him. As he stood ashen and silent she was moved to a mighty rage.

"Sir," she cried, "surely a man boasting of his war exploits is at his least attractive!"

At which Alex's cheeks flamed deep red and he turned away. She took her husband's arm and turned him into the dance and in a moment the Washingtons passed. The general looked stiff and cool but Aunt Martha glanced at her and with the faintest smile inclined her head in clear-spoken approval.

The next time she saw Alex he smiled and bowed but didn't approach her, and it was just as well. Of course he hadn't been boasting of his exploits, but he had been positioning himself against Jimmy and that had brought up in her a willingness to fight that she found startling—and exhilarating too.

Jimmy didn't say much afterward. He made it clear that he was pleased with her and she realized on her own that he didn't need his wife to fight his battles. Yet things seemed different and after a period of reflection it came to her that she had somehow advanced on that day from the Quaker miss feeling her way to a woman who had legitimated her place in a new world.

But certainly the exchange stood for the schism that was dividing the country. It was philosophical, she supposed, though she didn't spend much time in philosophical musing. Anyway, the basic argument was pretty simple. Are you for entrenched power regulating life or for free people finding their own way on their strengths and instincts? That was simple enough so that left to themselves Americans would have come to satisfactory answers—but then the French Revolution upset all the balances in America.

So it was that on a sunny day in Philadelphia a week or so later she heard someone calling her name as she strolled near the Statehouse. It was a woman's voice, high and urgent with a little note of hysteria. She turned to see Charity Jester almost trotting toward her, wearing an expensive gown of crimson velvet, her pink parasol stabbing the brick walk like a cane. They had been girls together, sharing a primer under some dreaded schoolmaster they both preferred to forget.

Charity seemed to be having trouble getting her breath. "Oh, do you remember that nice Mr. Fournier, Jacques Fournier, I think, he was with the French embassy or some such? Remember how he would smile and correct your French without making you feel a silly goose? He was the count of—oh, I don't know what he was count of, but something, he was somebody, don't you see? And Mr. Jester just learned today that they cut off his head with that terrible slicing machine in Paris. Imagine, murdering a wonderful person in the name of their democracy!"

She stopped, staring, head thrown back, the parasol gripped in both hands. "This democracy business, it's terrifying! I know you believe in it, Mr. Madison and Mr. Jefferson its promoters, I hear the talk, but it'll fool you, it'll turn on you, wait and see! Common folk go mad, give them a chance, that's what France proves. Your followers'll turn on you too, on all of us—you'll see, the ravening mob in the streets, the good people hanging from trees on Chestnut Street. Oh, how can your husband endorse this madness?"

She bristled, ready to leap to Jimmy's defense, but Charity patted her hand and went hurrying down the street as if she feared democracy would consume her right now. But democracy needn't lead to chaos, though Jimmy always admitted that its success did depend on the capacity of free people to control themselves. Frenchmen, breaking out of centuries of feudalism into anarchic revolution had lost that control. But there was a vast difference between France and America; here revolution had been for liberty, there it was for equality. As the search for equality darkened, the nobility was executed in ever greater numbers, Dr. Guillotine's grisly machine snicking and snacking and Guillotine Square slick with blood. Then the Revolution turned on its own, and the Terror began when no one proved sufficiently poor and equal. Finally the guillotine was too slow for the killing ordered and crowds were gathered and taken down by cannon fire or burned alive. The dead numbered tens of thousands. And the mob chanted slogans that once had defined American patriotism and democracy.

No wonder Charity Jester in her fine gown was terrified—so was everyone else possessed of wealth and position. These pressures led to a seismic shift in American affairs that was itself revolutionary. Until now there had been no parties; leading men simply stepped forward to take the reins. But the growing schism led automatically to two parties evolving into the two-party system. The old-line wealthy elite were Federalists, personified by Alexander Hamilton. For the moment they had the government and were turning toward coercion and control of the little man, driven by the fear that what they saw in France must follow here. Opposing them were Democrats, first called Republicans, then Democratic Republi-

cans, soon shortened to the Democratic party. Thomas
Jefferson led, Jimmy provided the intellectual power,
and her old friend Aaron Burr of New York was a rising
star. They stood for the little man, and the tighter and
meaner things became under frightened Federalists, the
stronger the Democrats got.

And she, stronger and more confident each year, marveled at how often great events and national movements
and crucial decisions turned on the same human emotions that children in a nursery will exhibit—rage, fear,
greed, hunger. . . .

Thomas Jefferson was Jimmy's best friend and the
three of them were often together. She liked Tom no matter what Pa had said. He was clever and witty and very
gentle, an innately decent man. His mind ranged all over
the place with bewildering speed and she often stopped
trying to keep up. Yet in the end she thought Jimmy had
greater weight, which was another reason she rather resented the deference he showed Tom, only a decade his
senior. Settled in marriage now, she handled herself well
and people listened to her with real interest.

Things were changing rapidly. General Washington
retired to Mount Vernon. John Adams succeeded him.
Tom had stepped down as secretary of state and was at
his estate at Monticello. Jimmy left the Congress and
they returned to the Madison estate, Montpelier, in sight
of the Blue Ridge Mountains. Living in a mansion in
which Jimmy's family made her welcome, she nevertheless had a full taste of life in a house not her own.

The national atmosphere darkened steadily. Rank fear
seemed to guide Federalists as if they saw hordes of
common men advancing on them. Laws became abusive.
Every time she and Jimmy went to Philadelphia, still the
capital though the new capital on the Potomac would
soon be ready, things became more volatile and danger-

ous. And then Congress passed the Alien and Sedition Acts.

On one of their Philadelphia trips she went on to New York with Hannah Gallatin to visit Hannah's family. New York was booming, soon to overtake Philadelphia, she was sure. Aaron Burr gave them dinner and a tour, bursting with pride. Then, afternoon shadows lengthening, she and Hannah strolled down Broadway.

They were near the Battery when they heard hoofs clattering. A wagon fitted with benches and bearing a half dozen men in dark coats stopped across the street before a print shop. Carrying oaken clubs the men jumped out to kick open the shop door.

The two women stood frozen, gazing across the street. They heard shouts and a crash within the shop and then a scream. An upstairs window popped open and a woman leaned out.

"Jeremy!" she yelled. "Come quick! They're after Paw, they'll smash the press—"

The press? A sign hung over the door, *The Peck's Slip Tattler*. A newspaper! The men were constables after an editor who'd spoken out of turn.

A dark-haired young man in breeches and buckled shoes and a white shirt with bunched sleeves burst from a next-door tavern, dashed into the shop, and was knocked senseless by a constable's club. Then a skinny, gray-haired man in his fifties was led out with hands bound behind him. Crying and cursing at once, he stepped over his son's inert body. Two stalwarts hurled him facedown into the bottom of the wagon. When he sat up the side of his head was bloody.

The woman in the window poured invective on the constables, their ancestry and parentage, their sexual proclivities, their dietary habits. It was thrilling no matter how rough, for in the most direct way at her command this woman was making her stand. But without even looking up two of the constables took sledgehammers from the wagon, strode into the shop, and from the sound were beating something to pieces.

"Goddamned scoundrels," a tall man in a sailor's cap snarled. "Busting up poor Jethro's press. The only man in New York with the guts to tell the truth, pin the tail on those donkeys in Philadelphia, damn president don't know his right hand from his left, and here they are smashing Jethro's press!"

He stood poised on the balls of his feet, fists clenched. "You know why they want to crush Jethro, don't you? 'Cause the truth scares the shit out of them!"

At which the leader of the constables turned with eyes red and club poised, and said, "Maybe we'll take you too, you seditious son of a bitch!"

The man in the cap laughed. "Try the Alien and Sedition Acts on me, will you? Well, you can kiss my arse!" With another loud laugh he turned and fled into the warren of streets that led to the east-side docks.

"I expect we'd better walk along," Hannah said, voice trembling. It was deeply disturbing—this was the Alien and Sedition Acts in action and it was sickening. It had become a crime to criticize the government. Speak your mind on the capabilities of the president and look for the constable to snatch you from the tavern and into jail you went. Troublesome aliens who arrived under the illusion that democracy meant democracy were easily deported. Print a letter in your newspaper that said the government was a donkey and draw a couple of years in prison, your press destroyed.

They walked on, neither speaking, and it struck her suddenly that her view of everything had changed. A slightly abstract view of politics had shifted in her mind to something visceral and direct. "It's all real, isn't it?"

she said to Jimmy on her return. "This printer, editor, this Mr. Jethro, doubtless still in a cell somewhere, probably in the same bloody shirt—"

Of course she had known that politics affected people's lives but never again would she see issues only in the abstract.

"What about the First Amendment, free speech, free press?" she demanded of her husband.

"Oh, yes," he said, "violates the Constitution, all right. But who's to stop the Congress? The Supreme Court is powerless, scarcely functioning, really. Government can do as it pleases."

"That's outrageous!"

"Well, maybe it'll make common folk see the danger."

One could hope, anyway. The Federalists were squabbling among themselves while Democrats were coming on strong. The election of 1800 was nearing and Tom was making a serious push against John Adams, while Aaron Burr stood for vice president. Adams had New England, Jefferson the South and West; they counted on Aaron for New York.

Not long before the election she bumped into Aaron by chance on a Philadelphia street and let him give her tea in a sidewalk café. He was remembering life in her mother's boardinghouse and the day he had brought Jimmy to call, and what an innocent naïf she was then. Well, she was a far cry today from that long-ago Quaker miss. And the times had changed with her. Imagine— through Tom they might sit in the august General Washington's seat yet.

With a little smile that she took as introduction to a witticism he added, "Though it might just as well be me."

But he wasn't joking and she said rather sharply, "No one sees you there, Aaron."

"Oh, I don't know," he said, all geniality. "Try that in New York—you'll be surprised. There's little sentiment there that I am in any way inferior to the sainted Virginian. Stranger things have happened, you know."

She snorted. "Horse gives birth to a goat, that would be stranger."

Something sparkled deep in his eyes, and he said with what she saw was utter seriousness, "You underestimate me, dear girl." It unsettled her; Aaron had a profoundly devious mind.

So the election of 1800 came about and the Democrats won with the help of New York and poor John Adams was sent home to Massachusetts with a broken heart just as the government moved into the new capital on the Potomac.

It was no less, as Tom put it, than a second revolution! The people had turned from the old way to the new, from privilege and control and coercion to the belief that free people could find the self-control to govern themselves. Magnificent!

And then Aaron sprang his dirty trick. For a terrible few weeks he seemed in position to carry out what she had first taken as a bad joke—with Federalist help, to exchange places with Tom and make himself president, Tom vice president.

She was enraged at this sudden scandalous turn. My word, Aaron seemed to be confirming the Federalist fear that the agony of France must play out here. Charity Jester's worst dreams ready to unfold—Democrats attacking each other before they even took office! Oh, but she was far from Ma's boardinghouse now. She watched the country boil toward civil war, Virginia and Pennsylvania preparing militia to march on Washington to enforce the Constitution. Responsible Federalists began to back off. Hamilton put country before politics and argued for Jefferson over Burr as a man of quality. More Federalists abandoned Burr and his dream collapsed.

So the crisis passed, and with it her anger. For after all,

she could see that this really had just been Aaron being Aaron—greed and cavalier willingness to strike for the main chance was an indelible part of his nature. That and his pride and his unshakable confidence—he would have made a good pirate.

Democrats remained enraged and so did Jimmy. But Aaron had been a real friend when she needed one and that she could not forget. And wouldn't, and that was that. Anyway, it was settled after a few alarming weeks, and no great harm appeared done. Things went on, Aaron as vice president presiding over the Senate with his usual panache, graceful and smiling. Really, it struck her as a triumph of democracy that it had responded to crisis with such vitality.

But she saw that Tom and Jimmy intended to punish Aaron, strip him of power and deny him victory's rewards. She knew he'd assumed that once it was settled they'd all be friends again. Punishing him struck her as small, unproductive, even dangerous. Of course they shouldn't trust him—he always would be drawn to the main chance. But to strip him of power and position, bare him to the world as a shattered man—quite aside from the cruelty, she saw no profit and much risk in that.

Jimmy remained adamant and finally it became one of those subjects best left alone in a marriage. But in the act of differing from her husband, of questioning his judgment, she realized that in some subtle way she had come of age.

Now Tom was president—she had decided that "Tom" would do perfectly well—and Jimmy was secretary of state and they were presiding over a great success. The people loved them and Federalists crept around like whipped dogs. By this time they had moved to the new city on the Potomac and built a handsome home of brick, three stories with cupola and porte cochere. It stood a few blocks from the President's House where Tom, the lonely widower, pressed her into service as official hostess. She took over presidential entertaining, and invitations to the mansion became wildly sought after; the town was still a social wilderness, few congressmen brought their families, and everyone was hungry for a kind word and a good meal. Jimmy was at the heart of everything as secretary of state, but she felt she wasn't far behind him, so central to Washington affairs did her dinners become.

Her ambitions grew. If Jimmy succeeded Tom—and who would be better?—she would be the president's wife. Her social mastery would matter more than ever and she would be in a real position to complete this magnificent mansion. It was glorious on the outside, if a little boxy, its yellow sandstone walls painted white, but it was scarcely finished inside and in desperate need of decoration, which she quickly found that Tom intended to ignore. But just wait!

Year by year, adventure by adventure, she and Jimmy grew closer; once she had amused him and then she pleased him and then she interested him and now he depended on her. When they were apart they were equally stricken. He was a darling man.

And then a terrible whisper came up the Mississippi from New Orleans. Napoleon intended to reclaim the province of Louisiana from Spain, to whom France had surrendered it long before. Napoleon? Napoleon Bonaparte, dictator of France, the most powerful man on earth? He who had whipped the British to a standstill, who controlled most of Europe and obviously intended to rule the world? He wanted Louisiana?

Yes, as a matter of fact, the whole vast territory, New Orleans to Canada along the Mississippi and westward to the Stony Mountains. The day he took possession

Jimmy's dream of a continental nation would be dead. But Napoleon wouldn't stop there. Soon he would want American territory too, Appalachians to the Mississippi, including the new states of Tennessee and Kentucky and Ohio. The United States would be left hugging the Atlantic shore. And it would kill the new democracy, voters would cast the new form into the dustbin.

Yet how could the embryo nation stand against Napoleon's eagles? Only by subordinating itself to Britain in return for a Royal Navy blockade to seal the coastline and starve French troops. But subordinating itself to Britain, a Federalist dream, would destroy the new democracy just as quickly.

So they must make Napoleon see that he could not win *before* they reached that point. What could she do in this crisis? She could stand by, and she understood how important that could be. When Jimmy talked all night of possible approaches, she listened. When he went silent she awaited his return. When he drew his chair to the window and stared into the dark she draped a blanket over his shoulders. She fed him and cosseted him and fussed over him; one day he told her—voice casual but eyes fixed on her—that he doubted he could get through this alone. That was worth a very great deal to her.

Two years passed without French response. They had done all they could and Jimmy drew up a proposal to the British that would save Louisiana but destroy the new democracy. And then one day as they took tea with Tom in the mansion the message arrived: Napoleon Bonaparte had offered to sell all of Louisiana to the Americans! We had asked for the city of New Orleans or the right bank of the river or even a square mile above New Orleans on which the American flag could fly as guarantee of free trade on the river. And Talleyrand had said, what would you give for the whole?

The whole? The country rocked with joy. Negotiations finally settled on $15 million and the deal was done. Jimmy told her poor Albert Gallatin, treasury secretary, was horrified at the price—and Hannah told her later that Albert muttered in his sleep—but Jimmy said someday it would be regarded as a great bargain. It saved the new democracy—that was bargain enough for her.

Oh, the vast and wonderful change—the nation more than doubled in size, its future as a continental nation assured, the threat of Napoleon removed forever. And she had changed with it. She was thirty-five years old and she had grown up too, faced tragedy and been made stronger; she had entered national life as an innocent and grown wise in experiencing democracy's birthing pains. She had focused ambition and she felt complete as she had not at any time in her thirty-five years; and she supposed that is what maturity meant.

But more immediately, she grew uncomfortable with the wild celebration of the vast purchase. Everyone said Tom was a genius for mastering Napoleon and with sublime contradiction said how lucky that the Frenchman decided to sell. And with growing outrage she began to ask where in all these salutations was credit for her darling little husband, who had taken on the most powerful man in the world in hand-to-hand combat and won? While he, modest man that he was, generous and decent, his voice light, his manner quiet, watched credit being taken by 'most everyone when it was plain to her that he and he alone had stood as Horatius at the bridge. Carefully she sharpened a fresh quill and unfolded a clean sheet of vellum and began to write:

Mr. James Madison, Esq.
Sir: Permit me to inform you that in the opinion of all right-thinking Americans the credit for the late, great

*triumph of Louisiana rests squarely on your shoulders,
as did the weight of the equally great campaign that
achieved the triumph. And who, dear sir, should know
this better than the undersigned?*

> *Your loving wife,*
> *Dolley P. Madison*

★ ★ ★ ★ ★

Two

Washington, fall 1803

Captain Julius Caesar Barlow, United States Army, came down the merchant brig's gangway onto the dock at Annapolis with his traveling case in his hand. The day was cool and bright and he was in a hurry, already ten days overdue at the State Department and still fifty miles away. He was a tall man with a lean frame, but deceptively strong. Yellow hair grown much too long spilled from under a slouch hat, and while he wasn't old, you didn't get to be a captain in today's army at a tender age.

He answered to Jaycee Barlow, which name he was ready to back up with his fists out in the paddock with everyone and anyone who found humor in his birth name. He'd only been a day old when Ma and Pa hung the name on him—he'd asked Ma about that—and what the hell could he have done at a day's age to warrant such a trick? But Ma said it was because they foresaw great things for him, and he let it go. What the hell. Pa had worked himself to death on the little farm in the Virginia hills down the road a piece from Mr. Madison's huge plantation—Mr. Madison had five thousand acres if he had a five-dollar gold piece—and what did it matter now? He thought of poor Ma, strained and graying, the smell of hickory smoke always in her hair. Her smoked hams and bacon and cheese, later joined to his military salary, had kept the family alive for years. But any fool could see it was a time for caution when his given name came up.

Down the gangway with case in hand feeling squeezed by calendar and clock. He'd come from a frontier post in Indiana Territory, carefully pointed logs set deep in the ground to form a stockade that you sure as hell needed out in Indian country. Everything was delaying. He'd come across the northern route to the Hudson and then down to Manhattan Island to board this Annapolis-bound brig. The skipper spoke a passing vessel off Philadelphia and learned that the great purchase was complete, the country doubling in size. That was only middling news in Barlow's view—seemed it solved all the problems, so what would there be left for him to do? He might get to Washington and be told to go back to Indiana!

The idea dampened his spirits so he cast it aside. Now, sea legs giving way to land legs, he stepped along, lithe and quick as if on a trail, threading through boxes and barrels and bales of northern manufactured goods feeding the agricultural South—

"Look out, dumb-ass!" A stevedore with arms like hams shoved him aside. He had a glimpse of a load swinging overhead and plummeting to fall with a loud bump where he'd just been and the urge to clout the stevedore passed.

"Why, thankee, brother," he said.

The burly man half smiled. "Didn't want my dock bloodied up," he said.

Captain Barlow got directions to the Washington stage and set out along cobbled streets crowded with

carts and carriages, here and there a horseman on a
good-looking beast, the warm aroma of fresh manure in
the air. He stepped around a dead hog that was beginning to fester, passed a saddler and a tailor shop, a hatter
with his produce stacked in his window, a tavern with a
wooden sign that seemed to feature a hog, the smell of
stale beer billowing from its open door. Then, up ahead,
drawing a small crowd, a strange procession wended
down the hill.

A boy walked in front, limping. He looked scarcely
fifteen, hands bound, a rope around his neck—like a
goddamned dog! He was crying, tears coursing down a
freckled face innocent of beard. Behind him, holding the
rope, came a burly bo'sun in Royal Navy uniform—
British damned navy seizing men right here on American
streets! Like they hadn't heard about the Revolution, figured we were still colonists at their beck and call. And
just behind the bo'sun came a pimply ensign not much
older than the prisoner. Arrogant-looking little bastard,
the ensign, that was the thought Barlow remembered
later. As they passed he thrust out a foot. The boatswain
went down with a crash, the rope flew from his hand, and
Barlow yelled "Run!" just as he swung the case into the
ensign's face.

So there was the ensign flat on his butt with blood
pouring from his nose, the bo'sun roaring up, the prisoner hurtling down the block hands still pegged behind
him, tripping, going down, rolling up and disappearing
around a corner at a dead run. Then, too late, Barlow saw
they had an escort, an Annapolis constable in a black suit
and a flat hat with a truncheon like a marlinespike in his
hand. It was like being stuck in jelly, ensign leaking
blood and tears on the cobblestones, bo'sun up and coming, constable closing from the other side—and then
with his face set hard under that black hat the constable

stepped aside and jerked his thumb in the direction away from the waterfront and Barlow went up the hill at a dead run with a death grip on his case.

An hour later, safely on the Washington stage and beyond the grasp of Annapolis law, he could relax. British press-gangs operating openly in American ports—it was outrageous. He had heard lots about it but this was his first experience and it left him both shaken and enraged. He was a soldier, after all, and his basic thought was, We'll have to fight them. Show 'em the Revolution was real. They said they were after their deserters, and maybe that frightened boy was one of them, which wouldn't have mattered to Barlow anyway, but probably he was just a likely-looking sailor lad they wanted to press into service on one of their hell-ship frigates where life must be like torture, judging from the desertion rate. Press-gangs were everywhere, stopping ships on the high seas with warrants for this deserter or the other but taking pretty much as they chose.

As darkness fell and the stage lurched to a fifteen-minute stop at a stage inn for a dinner of beans, salt pork, and whiskey, Barlow's pleasure in the memory of that ensign bleeding all over his pretty uniform began to fade. The closer he got to Washington the more out of place he felt. He was a soldier, quite capable of disciplining a company or knocking someone on his butt if needed, but what did he know of diplomacy? Mr. Madison, now, would he have taken it upon himself to break up a British press-gang? Intervene physically? Not very damned likely! Barlow was going to be a fish out of water. I mean, he told himself sternly, these men are educated. Sophisticated. They've been everywhere and done everything and know just about all there is to know. Wouldn't be running the country, otherwise. And he, a plain old rock-'em-and-knock-'em soldier was going to fit right in?

The Barlows had lived down the road from the Madison manor house, and he and Mr. Madison had had a few friendly encounters when he was home on leave. But out on the far frontier, he had slowly come to conclude that he wanted more than life on a military post. The congressman from his district would retire soon; Captain Barlow might make a dandy replacement. But first he'd need experience, so he bethought himself to ask a favor: could Mr. Madison use a clerk and allow Captain Barlow to make himself useful while learning the ways of Washington?

He remembered how Charlie Smithson had jeered. Charlie commanded Company D and was a canny fellow. "You ain't a diplomat, for God's sake. Sitting around drinking tea with your finger cocked—you'll never make it where folks pussyfoot about kissing each other's bums while preparing to stab their backs."

"Oh, I don't know," he'd answered, "isn't that what we do in the army?" Charlie had damned near fallen in the fire, he'd laughed so hard, admitting Jaycee was right. But still, the closer to Washington the more uneasy he felt. A clever quip was one thing, sitting down with men who ran the world was another. Quite another!

In his only civilian suit, decorous black, pantaloons tucked into well-brushed boots, he presented himself at the State Department. It proved to be a rather shabby little brick structure adjoining the President's House, itself a boxy-looking place that stood among a little cluster of buildings beyond which there appeared to be wilderness. He heard a shotgun bang in the distance, bird hunter in the swamp that lay between the mansion and Capitol Hill. Was this even a town? It didn't look too fancy, anyway; maybe he'd be all right.

"Captain J. C. Barlow, reporting for duty."

A tall and austere man wearing a very plain suit rose from a desk at the front of a big room. "I'm Jacob Wagner, chief clerk, and you will be answering to me."

Wagner! God, everyone knew about him, the old Federalist who'd been chief clerk under Secretary of State Pickering when the Federalists were in power, and there wasn't a madder dog among Federalists than Timothy Pickering. And Mr. Madison had kept him on! Infuriated the radical Democrats—Barlow was second or third cousin on Ma's side to John Randolph, a bigwig of some sort in Congress whose rhetoric could peel the bark off a tree, and more than once he'd heard Mr. John carry on about this Wagner infidel. And here he was in the flesh!

He clicked his heels and bowed. "Yes, sir!"

"Ah, Captain . . . Mr. Barlow . . . what the devil do people call you?"

"Jaycee, sir."

"I see." The older man smiled faintly. "Then Jaycee it'll be. Now, sir, this is not the military. No saluting. Heel clicking at a minimum. Courtesy without standing at attention . . . you get the drift?"

"Yes, sir."

"Very well. We're short of clerks. You'll make six, but two are ill, so you're needed." He frowned, gave Barlow a measuring glance and scooped up a sheaf of papers. "Here—the secretary may want this, another communication from our squabbling team in Paris, Mr. Livingston and Mr. Monroe. He's with the president; hustle over to the mansion and put it in his hand." Jesus! Just walk in the president's house and pass the papers! All his doubts came rushing back. He didn't know how to do this!

A brick walk circled to the front of the mansion and it did occur to Barlow that Ma should see him now. The big building looked much better up close, bright-painted columns glowing white in the sun. He cut across the lawn that three sheep seemed to keep nicely mowed, doing a little quickstep to avoid their droppings. What a startling change such manicured surroundings were from the Indiana frontier.

A surly guard yanked a bell pull. Presently a young man with a pleasant face appeared and said he was Isaac Coles, the president's secretary. He said he would deliver the message.

"My orders are to put it directly in the secretary's hand." He felt momentarily more comfortable, a note of command in his voice. But Coles merely nodded and led the way up a long flight of marble stairs and across a wide traverse hall with a frayed carpet. Water stains marred the walls, meaning a leaky roof. Coles stepped through a door, then returned to gesture him in.

It was a long, oval room that was beautiful of itself though somewhat marred by shabby furniture with stained and worn blue cushions. He was surprised— Ma's parlor at home was more gracious than this. The blue drapes hanging by the three windows at the far end were bunched carelessly and one appeared to be torn. Late morning sun beamed through windows that over-looked a stretch of what apparently was pasture for several cows. Beyond the meadow was rough brush and in the distance the Potomac was a silver line. The roof leak must be worse here, for walls and floors alike were stained by seeping water.

He had a confused impression of several men at the far end of the room, a steward circulating gleaming Champagne flutes on a tray. Good God—the tall man with rusty hair shading to gray, that was the president! He felt like the youngster tossed in the pond, told to swim or drown. The president was looking out a window and talking with surprising volume. Barlow heard a slight note of anger in his voice though he wasn't speaking angrily; it was the note you heard in barracks-room talk well before the fight really began. Then he saw Mr.

Madison, handed him the papers with a murmured greeting, and was backing out when Mr. Jefferson said, "Well, who's this?"

Mr. Madison introduced him as the new clerk and a former neighbor. What now? He felt the center of attention, exactly what he hadn't wanted. This was going to be a disaster.

"Franklin Barlow's family?" the president asked.

"Franklin is a cousin, sir. We're the poor relations."

God—he must be rattled. When had Jaycee Barlow considered himself poor relations to anyone? But before he could say more the president had given him an appraising look, and said, "Well, have a glass of Champagne. Much to celebrate—Congress approves the Louisiana Act and Baring Brothers agrees to put up the purchase cost against United States bonds."

The steward presented the tray and, unsure what he should do, he took a glass and after an awkward moment backed to a wall by a small but good table. Behind him hung an indifferent view of General Washington on horseback, the beast's head too small, its rump too large. Girandoles were spaced on the walls and several lamps not lit stood on small tables. Chairs and a couple of sofas were scattered here and there, polished wood frame and stained cushions, but the half dozen or so guests were standing. Platters of what looked like cheese and meat with stacks of fresh bread tended by a couple of stewards stood on side tables with unopened bottles of Champagne and a big tureen of whiskey punch.

He realized that Mr. Madison was telling a story on Napoleon that was producing chuckles, though he noticed a darkening in the president's expression. It struck him suddenly that they had been here for some time and had been drinking steadily—flushed faces, muscles at the mouth gone slack, smiles of false elation, unmistakable signs when you knew them. He studied the guests.

The big man in the blue coat with brass buttons, ruff of gray hair, probably was the navy. He recognized the secretary of war, Henry Dearborn, a fat man with red face and bright eyes, cup of whiskey punch held awkwardly with a plate that he steadily emptied. Mr. Madison finished his story to laughter that seemed to delight him.

But suddenly the president jerked a drape closed to block sunlight pouring through a window, and again there was that suggestion of anger. "Well told, Jimmy," the august man said, "but there are serious things afoot." It was a reprimand and smiles vanished. Mr. Madison's face closed, the look of youthful pleasure gone. He started to speak, stopped himself, then said mildly but clearly in defense, "I thought it a decent little story that matched the occasion."

"Oh, doubtless, but it's just so ironic, here we are, celebrating the great purchase—"

"What's ironic about that?" Dearborn rumbled. "It's a magnificent acquisition—does us credit as a people."

"Yes," the president snapped, "and its dangers match its magnitude."

A small man in a fine black suit said in a heavy accent, "I expect the president refers to the irony of unintended consequences." Barlow was feeling more at ease or at least comfortably unnoticed, and he turned with interest. Black hair circled the gentleman's shiny dome but the accent told the story. This would be the clever treasury secretary, Albert Gallatin, who had maintained Alexander Hamilton's financial wizardry even as he bent it in democratic directions. Federalists hated him for his success while radicals denounced him for not shattering every hint of Federalism. He was Swiss, his accent often nearly impenetrable.

"Exactly, Albert," Mr. Jefferson said, sighing. "Face down a great danger only to find more waiting." He made it sound a complaint. "We were so focused on making Napoleon see he couldn't hold Louisiana—but it's almost as if he tricked us in response, dropping the whole thing in our laps. Yes, it's a magnificent acquisition and long-term it almost certainly removes any doubt we'll be a continental nation, but digesting the whole thing at once? Short-term, you understand. What—was any country ever doubled in size in a pen stroke? Since the beginning of civilized time?"

What an interesting idea! Barlow glanced at the president with pleasure. Think about it—doubling size could change everything, all the balance, the very fundamentals of their lives, all the thinking that had guided them. Mr. Madison said as much, his apparent dislocation of a moment ago vanished.

The president lowered himself to a long settee. A frayed blue cushion fell to the floor and he muttered angrily, reached for the pillow and slapped it into place so hard that dust rose. Barlow looked at him cautiously. Dark pouches bagged below his eyes. He talked in a low, discouraged tone, ruminating over their troubles. The men stood quietly, holding their glasses; had the rapid turn in the room's atmosphere surprised them? Or was this just the way great men did business?

He felt more and more an intruder—he didn't belong here—but there was no way to leave without drawing attention, and he stood quietly. The atmosphere was steadily darkening, as when you're at a friend's quarters and he and his wife quarrel. The president sat hunched forward, his long frame folded upon itself, elbow on the settee arm, forehead on his hand. His voice held that troubled note, sometimes dropping to a murmur that men strained forward to hear. At the same time that core of anger persisted, as if he felt tricked or imposed upon in some mysterious way. But now Barlow saw it was reciprocated in the other's expressions, like when the colonel took a load on and had the urge to talk and you had to stand there, like it or not.

Everything was different, he was saying. Horrified by the infusion of new territory, all Federalists could see was that it would dilute New England's share of political power in the Congress. Anyway, Democratic success was infuriating to men who had always insisted that Jefferson and Madison winning the election in 1800 had been an ugly accident to be corrected at the next election in 1804. And here it was late 1803 and the people were in the streets cheering the administration's triumph.

But the radical Democrats beat just as loudly on the opposite door. With a start Barlow heard them discussing his wild-eyed cousin Randolph, who apparently led the abusive wing of the party. It seemed Mr. John was trying to force an extreme version of democracy that would eliminate 'most everything about the federal government except its name. With the popularity of Louisiana, he was saying, why not? Give that idiot his way, the president said now, and the people would turn to the Federalists in a flash. He lifted his forehead from his hand as if for emphasis and glared about the room, looking for disagreement. When their gazes met for an instant, Barlow had the feeling you get when you meet a bull in a pasture and realize you're pretty far from the fence. Americans, the president said, head turning to and fro, are centrists. They think and operate from the center, and neither the extremes of Alexander Hamilton nor of John Randolph would appeal for long. Barlow had never thought of such a thing but saw immediately that it was true.

The silence held when the president paused. The men stood watching him. They all seemed to be drinking whiskey punch now. Dearborn stood by the table eating with his fingers from a plate. That tension of anger threading through the talk seemed reflected in their faces. It was polite and modulated, but it turned out that great men at work or at play were captive of all the emotions you'd find in any common barracks room. *That* was a revelation!

The president wore an angry mask, cheek propped on his hand. The others, watching him, matched his expression. Suddenly it struck Barlow that none of this was new to these men. What fascinated him was stale to them—the president was telling them what they already knew! Yet you heard his rising anger in his snappish voice, his didactic tone. His face seemed pale, features set, a hollowness under the eyes. Could he be ill? For a moment he looked on the verge of heaving; you saw that sometimes, liquor going against the gut there in the officer's mess, open bottle on the table, someone swallowing furiously as others jumped away. . . .

Look at the impact of doubling our size, he was saying. The British act like rabid foxes. They had figured that Napoleon's North American plans would keep him too busy to attack again on the Continent. Now, free of New World ambitions and fueled with new American dollars, he already had plunged back into European war and was giving the British fits. And the view in this room, which Barlow couldn't doubt, was that they were taking their anger out on us. They were trying to force us into alliance against France, seizing our merchant ships on flimsy excuses and kidnapping our sailormen from ships and even from our streets, while we resisted in every way short of war.

Given that Barlow might be a wanted man in Annapolis right now, he decided to keep his own press-gang experiences to himself. The president lurched on to Spain, which was talking war, though frontier experience with the Spanish said it always was hard to separate bluster from intent. Still, they really were furious at France taking Louisiana and selling it to the Americans. They had counted on Louisiana to block rapacious Yankees from their own rapacious gold mines in Mexico. Now, with the Spanish empire dying and Americans in Louisiana, what would save its gold?

America believed Florida and Texas were part of the purchase; Spain seemed ready for war over the very notion. But you never could tell. Barlow knew from Spanish officers in St. Louis that the weaker their nation the more arrogant their manner. This had led him into delicate situations. He remembered one little popinjay— well, never mind.

But then, listening, he heard a startling new wrinkle. While technically France had resumed ownership of Louisiana, so far it was a paper transaction, physical transfer of authority not yet made. So Spain still was in control—suppose it simply refused to surrender New Orleans?

He saw, however, that this was not new to anyone else in the room. The president was patronizing them. Watching their irritation, he thought this was something to see, great men in high position boiling with the same emotions you'd find in a frontier officers' mess or a roadside tavern in Maryland. They were just people, after all.

But now the talk shifted to New Orleans itself and for the first time he saw that they had been celebrating a negative—Napoleon would not build an empire on the Mississippi—but had given little thought to the positive, and this is what the president in damned clumsy fashion was growling over. Now that the Louisiana Territory was ours, what would we do with it? Listening to them talk of New Orleans, he saw that they knew nothing about the place.

And Barlow did know because he'd been there. He hesitated, then emboldened by the display of emotion just witnessed, scribbled a note on a blank page of his notebook and passed it to Mr. Madison. But silence fell over the room as he moved. It was as if they had run down and awaited something new. Barlow felt suddenly conspicuous. The president was staring at him in a way that suggested his tenure in Washington might be short.

"Captain Barlow tells me he knows New Orleans," Mr. Madison said, not offering much cover. "Perhaps he can advise us."

"Knows" was an overstatement, "advise" an invitation to trouble. His note had said nothing of the sort. He'd been a first lieutenant then and Major Jennings at Fort Massac had installed him as a hand on a passing flatboat and sent him undercover to gather information on the Spanish army. How many troops, their quality, their morale, their artillery, estimates of their invasion capacity if they came here, their defenses if we went there to throw them into the sea? He had quickly discovered that as men the Spanish soldiers were like men everywhere, but as combat infantry they were weak, untrained, their hearts not in soldiering.

In a soft tone in which Barlow read danger, the president asked him when he was there.

"Three years ago, sir. Went down as crew on a flatboat."

He started to explain further but Mr. Jefferson's voice, quiet but commanding, cut through. "I see. And how did you find New Orleans?" The tone was neutral, neither pleased nor displeased, waiting. Barlow quieted a momentary spasm of nerves. They were just men, after all. But his hands were shaking.

"First, it's a finished city." He stopped to quiet a tremor in his voice. "And it's somehow surprising after a thousand-mile float where you see naught but Indian villages and the occasional trapper's dugout scraped from the bank. Then you start seeing habitation, then hunters, then skiffs laying out trotlines for catfish, then houses, and then you round a bend and there it is, like seeing the Promised Land, so to speak."

"So you liked it?" Voice offering no encouragement.

"Well, yes, sir, it's pretty. Narrow streets, brick-and-plaster houses fronting right out to the street, balconies and trellises all about." He was talking faster than usual, nervous, and he carefully slowed himself. "Huge cathedral on the big square along with the Spanish army compound, ships from all over tied up at the levee, ten to twenty when I was there. It's a world port, comparable to Baltimore. Warm, sultry, music in the streets, and unbelievable flowers. Maybe what Paris would be like in the summer."

"And the people? Did you like them too?"

"Start off, they was just totally French—shook off forty years of Spanish rule like a dog shaking off water. I tried to like them, but they sure don't meet you halfway. Not a tenth of the way. They acted like they hated Américicans. But maybe you can't blame them—about the only Americans they see are boatmen, and they're a rough crowd."

He thought that over. Rough, all right. When a flatboat landed, the men wanted whiskey and women and didn't keep it a secret, though that wasn't fair either.

"It's a long float, you see, eight weeks or more, and then the walk home, six hundred miles on the Natchez Trace, and that just gets you to Tennessee. So you can see they'd be looking for fun when they hit New Orleans. And I guess New Orleans folk think that's the way all Americans are."

"What about local Americans?"

"Not more than one or two, I don't think." Actually, there were a few but that wasn't a story for here.

The president was watching with a hard expression, as if Barlow had violated some tenet. His voice had a harsh note as he asked, "So how will they react to becoming Americans?"

"Be a bitter pill for some, I expect."

"Think they'll resist?"

The question was startling and immediately Barlow saw that like everyone else he had been looking at the purchase through American eyes. It wrenched his mind around. Take at it as folks there might, bundled up and sold without a word to a country they had no use for. . . .

"Yes, sir, you put it that way, they might. Well might. It's a happy sort of place, you know, you feel like there's music all around even when you can't hear it, those big bright flowers, the bouillabaisse in the eateries down by the levee . . . but the people aren't to be taken lightly. French to the core, arrogant to Americans, insular, too proud for their own good, see their sleepy town as the center of the world. Didn't strike me as men very open to new things, new ideas. Still, they're men of power, too, tough and strong, and you'd want to think seriously before you crossed one." More than once he'd had to stifle his tongue and pull his forelock, playing the humble deckhand.

Could they resist? "Yes, sir, I reckon, give them a leader to pull them together."

"So they impressed you, these people."

Barlow hesitated. "Yes, sir, I guess you could say—

"How long were you there?"

"Three weeks or so. Enough to look around."

"Flatboat crews spend a month there with nothing to do but drink and whore?"

"No, sir—"

"You're a soldier, aren't you?"

"Yes, sir. Captain, Company G, First Infantry, on detached duty."

"Then what were you doing on a flatboat?"

"Sir, Major Jennings—"

"You were sent down, to investigate the place. Isn't that it?"

"Yes, sir, the major put me aboard a flatboat as crew-man—"

"So you could sneak into New Orleans."

Just a minute, now. Barlow took a deep breath. "I don't believe 'sneak' is the right word, Mr. President. I was on a military—"

"With orders to sneak into New Orleans and look around."

"On military reconnaissance, yes, sir."

"A spy, in other words." Mr. Jefferson spat the word out.

"Yes, sir, assessing the enemy. In an undercover role."

"Spy . . ." the president said. "It has a dirty sound. Like reading others' mail. Gentlemen don't stoop to that. I suppose nations must spy, but I don't like it. . . ." His voice trailed off and Barlow read open contempt in his expression. Already feeling exposed and very alone, Barlow now felt his temper fraying. The man had never served in the military—governor of Virginia during the Revolution and none too heroic when a British column approached, if the stories could be credited, then diplomatic posts abroad where perhaps gentlemen didn't read each other's mail, Barlow wouldn't know about that. But when the others were looking at you over musket barrels?

All this in split instants in the gathering silence, his temper fraying—

"Sir," Mr. Dearborn said, "gathering information on enemies or potential enemies is well within military practice. I'd say the captain is to be commended."

"That's all very well, Henry, and may indeed be so. There are various dirty jobs we ask—"

Dirty job! "Sir," Barlow cried, voice cracking with anger and with the sure knowledge that his new position in Washington, now an hour old, was already finished, "I examined enemy defenses, morale, training, infantry armament and artillery, offensive and defensive capacity, all under direct orders from my superior officer to whom I delivered a written report, I suppose available to you in War Department archives." He struggled for a deference but then the dam broke. "I will say openly, sir, it was not a dirty job and I will not accept that characterization!"

And he stood there, waiting for the roof to fall in and crush him, and he decided he didn't give a damn.

James Madison felt like standing and giving his clerk a hurrah. There was a tough capability about Barlow, and Madison felt he had handled himself well in a trying situation for which he'd had no experience. And the president had been quite impossible. Tom was no military man—as always, Madison had to add that neither was he—but no one questioned the right of an army to collect intelligence on an enemy.

No, something was wrong with Tom. That ugly reprimand for an innocent story—why shouldn't a small man with a small voice be pleased by laughter and applause? He was good with small groups and tongue-tied before large. Applause was tonic . . .

Something wrong, though, perhaps bad news from Virginia, more likely a migraine headache taking hold. The president haunted the mails from Virginia—Dolley said he was rigid with fear, though as with physical pain, he held emotional pain in fierce privacy. His youngest daughter, Maria, was close to term with her second child. The first had nearly killed her and this one promised to be worse. There had been such losses in that family—he had never recovered from his wife's death in consequence of childbirth and four of his six children had died. Now one of the last two was in great danger; bringing a new life into the world was precarious business.

But Madison had suspected migraine when Tom began lamenting chronic problems with Britain and Spain and the Federalists. Such talk patronized his cabinet members and they were clearly irked, if unwilling to protest. And then, stoutly laced whiskey punch exacerbated everything. No one was drunk but neither was anyone, including Madison, entirely sober. Migraine often took Tom by surprise, sending his mood plummeting before the pain started. Now that Madison considered it, jerking the drapes against light, sudden pallor, attitude deteriorating—those were clear signs. When the pain arrived even laudanum could do no more than dent it. Dr. Rush's best nostrums helped very little. The only treatment was to lie motionless in a dark and silent room and wait it out.

Now, his interrogation of Barlow apparently forgotten, Tom lurched to his feet, fist pressed to his forehead. Madison took his desperate expression as an appeal, and said softly, "Yes, sir, we all can agree these are tremulous times—"

"We could agree with that before the lecture," Albert Gallatin said, an angry snap in his voice, ready to take on Madison as he wouldn't the president. Tom looked one to the other, surprised, just becoming aware that it hadn't gone well. Moving cautiously as if sight and balance were uncertain, he set down his cup, murmured an excuse, and walked out.

There was a long silence. Then Benjamin Stoddert said, "What the hell—is he ill? Or drunk?" Stoddert was a big, bluff man with ruddy cheeks who was leaving the government after years as secretary of the navy.

"Ill," Madison said sharply. "Migraine headache."

"He looked wobbly."

"Migraine affects eyesight," Madison said. "Nauseates, too—he'll lie down in a dark room."

"Sick or no," Stoddert said, "he had no call to read us

a lecture." He looked at Madison. "Nor you neither. That business about the British stopping our ships, that was a slap at the navy. No other reason to hammer what we already knew."

"Same with the army, Dearborn said. "Lecturing us like schoolboys."

But it was Gallatin who seemed most deeply stung. There was brilliance in Albert, in his grasp of high finance and complex mathematics, but in general as well. But like many brilliant men he was impatient, easily bored and irritated. Not a good mix for politics. "Anyway," he said, "we didn't speak of the real danger—the only one we reasonably could have affected." Angrily he jabbed a finger at Madison, his bald dome flushed scarlet. "I mean Aaron Burr," he said. "A dangerous man, like an attack dog that's been abused."

At once Madison's composure fled. The session too long, a sick president, too much to drink—and then he's to be blamed? "Abused?" It was a shout torn from his throat. "What the devil do you mean? Explain yourself, sir!" His normally soft voice sounded a satisfying bellow in his ears.

Gallatin took a step back, startled, then stepped forward, the red suffusing his face darkening. "Abused, that's what I said. By you and the president, though I helped too. Of course he put the democracy at risk, but there's an irrationality in the president's hatred."

Madison struggled for his voice. "We should trust a man who betrays, who would destroy everything for his own gain?"

"Don't lecture me, sir! We've had quite enough for one day. Now, I share your anger—but I fear we've created a monster."

"No! He's self-created."

"So?" Gallatin's voice was calm again, anger gone, and Madison was irritated anew when he realized that in calming himself Albert had seized the initiative. "What does it matter who created it—I just think we made it hard." He sounded patient and wise, and Madison couldn't help fretting—it had been Gallatin's angry view that had set off the whole exchange in the first place. Now, Gallatin said, "He never saw he'd done anything wrong. 'Just politics,' he said to me once. 'It's all a game.' I took it that games have prizes and when one comes your way you seize it if you can. But the president—well, I remember inauguration day, you weren't there, Jimmy, but when it was over and everyone milled around, I saw Burr go up to Tom with a big smile, put out his hand and start making the expected talk—honored to serve, together they can make great medicine for the nation, and so on. And Jefferson gave him a faint smile that seemed to drip contempt, touched his fingers, and dropped them as if they smelled, and turned his back. Turned his back! God, you should have seen Burr's face. White as a sheet. It was brutal."

"And in this sudden conversion of yours, we should have done what?"

Gallatin, his recovery of his own temper absolutely maddening, said in superior fashion, "That's mean-spirited, Jimmy, putting it that way. Not like you at all. I'm speaking temperately." Yes, Madison thought, he'd given Albert the high ground, his own temper having overcome his usual control. Before he could get past this thought Albert added, "What might we have done? Killed him with kindness, perhaps. Kept him close where we could watch him. But we froze him out—that empty vice presidency." How odd, Madison thought—it was like hearing Dolley's words spoken aloud. Of course, she was partial to Burr for good reason but she also was wise, he had to give her that. He was struggling to regain his own composure, which somehow Albert's cool and quiet demeanor made more difficult.

"Looking back," Albert said, "maybe it wasn't wise to cut him out of what he believes are his just desserts. So he's going back to New York to run for governor and figures that will put him in position to swing a big stick in the party."

"I don't care—"

"No, that's not the point. I hear from New York that Hamilton can arrange his defeat. Alex detests Burr, you know." Gallatin had married into a big, intensely political family in New York and probably knew what he was talking about. "So see it as Burr will—he gives us New York and swings the election, we squeeze him out and throw him to the dogs, he returns to New York and is whipped again—and what has he got left? But he's a man of great capacities—brilliant, able, a powerful orator—with nowhere to go. Tell me that's not dangerous, Jimmy. If he wins in New York he's just a problem, but if he loses he's your original loose cannon. How can he recoup but at our expense? That's our real danger. And you and I helped make it."

Madison was calming. Maybe handling Burr without gloves had been a mistake, but Tom wasn't open to forgiveness. But then Gallatin ignited a new fire. "Remember," he said, "Mr. Burr is very close to General Wilkinson."

Now Dearborn, slumped on a sofa nursing a cup of punch, heaved himself up with the cup tumbling to the floor. "Just why shouldn't the vice president be friendly to the uniformed commander of the army?" He was a hopeless Wilkinson partisan.

Gallatin glared. "Because two men of unsavory reputation have the strength of ten for malefaction."

"General Wilkinson's unsavory?"

"An odor of treason should make him so, I'd think."

"That is foul, sir, foul. Unproved gossip. Wilkinson would call you out for such loose talk."

Suddenly danger loomed. Both men drinking, both flirting with deadly ground. Madison was jolted out of his own small irritation. Quarreling over that fat scoundrel of a general! He jumped up. Time to go, he said, hurrying them. Slowly, with the sort of rumblings a bull makes to show who owns his pasture, they went spilling down the stairs.

As the room emptied Madison turned to see Captain Barlow still standing by that dreadful picture of the big-rumped horse. The captain had a drawn expression. "You'll want my resignation, sir?"

"For that little contretemps? Not a model for how to address a president, but no, you won't hear more about it."

"But the president—"

"Believe me, he's ill and he won't want to revisit today."

They walked in silence and were at the State Department building when Barlow laughed quietly. "After I wrote you I almost wrote again to withdraw the request. I got to thinking, important men here, the president, cabinet members, senators and such, they'd be so far above me, they'd know so much and have such skill they'd laugh me out of town. They'd be . . . special, somehow, they'd see everything on a vast scale. . . ."

"Not plain men, you thought? Hardly human?"

"That's it. Well, human, of course, but at such a level—and yet, today—"

"Pretty damned human today, you're saying?"

"Yes, sir, I thought so."

"Good. Keep that in mind, Captain. Great men have position and ideas and command authority, granted. But they come with all the emotions that every man on the street possesses, sometimes even more, in that power magnifies emotion. They have all the hopes and dreams and rages, all the jealousy and pettiness, all the ambitions and hungers that possess any man and every man. What separates him at the top from him on the bottom is narrow, a percentage point or two; what joins them is the rest—call it their humanity."

Barlow smiled. "I think I'll like it here," he said.

★　　★　　★　　★　　★

THREE

Washington, fall 1803

"I like my letter," Madison said. The morning was mild and they were walking from the house on F Street, he to his office, she to the mansion that she must make ready for a vast open house celebrating the purchase. She had given him the letter the night before when he had returned tired and discouraged to pour out his dismay at the clash with Tom. Her hand found his and squeezed and they walked hand-in-hand.

In fact he was not getting much credit for Napoleon's decision to sell. It was all Tom's doing, or Napoleon's, or the work of luck and good fortune and for many, a beneficent God whose aim was for the young United States to lead the world to democracy. But not Madison's doing. He didn't care so much about the world but above all he wanted to shine in Dolley's eyes and her letter had said he did.

Her hand was warm in his. She seemed to breathe life into him; she said it worked both ways, but he knew hers was the greater giving, for he had been ossifying into prematurely despairing old age when that providential squirrel made its move. He blessed the creature that at the precise instant had dropped a nut from a Philadelphia chestnut as she strolled on the bricked sidewalk with other Quaker women. The nut struck her shoulder and she cried aloud with music in her voice that transfixed him. It sounded so *happy*—only later did he realize that she made herself happy through sheer will. She had been in widow's weeds and he had followed as closely as he dared until he spied a friend who could identify her.

Madison was a man, he knew now, who needed a woman, and until he saw her that day he had passed much of his life alone. A small man, often ill, constitution never strong, his voice soft, his manner gentle, his nature shy, his only force was in his intellect. But the power of thought, the joy of study, the mentality to seize issues, absorb and integrate and then command them, the sheer exciting fascination of ideas—ah, there he towered, and about that he had no doubt. His position in the life of the nation was secure. His had been much of the brain power behind the Constitution—not all, certainly, but much. When President Washington was struggling desperately to integrate a nation that seemed bent on disintegration, he had turned often to Mr. Madison.

But books and ideas and position in the councils of power make cold bedfellows. Years before there had been another girl, sixteen or so, scarcely half his age. Awkward and shy, he had proposed, she had accepted, and things were coming along, though looking back he could see that he had spent more time talking to her father of politics than talking to her of love. He guessed he'd loved her; how could he know now? A frequent visitor was a student not much older than she; he leaned on the piano as she played and sang romantic ballads while making what Madison termed sheep's eyes. Then her letter came, callous and unfeeling in its utter casualness, though now he could see that he hadn't made enough impression to warrant more. Yes, she had agreed to marry him and all that, but she'd thought it over and decided to marry the student. She hadn't even bothered to seal the letter properly—rather than wax she'd used a bit of bread dough. Bread dough to seal a letter that broke his heart!

That had proved to him that women were not for him, he lacked the touch, he was too shy, he didn't understand women, neither did he need them, a man couldn't have everything—and such empty feelings had sufficed until the day of the fortunate squirrel that had acted by the hand of God or at least of fate in hurling the nut that led to the laugh that caught the man. Oh, Jimmy! she would cry at the thought, and then that ringing laugh.

Years of ice shattered as in the spring thaw. The friend who identified her had clapped his shoulder. Eligible widow, eh? Charming-looking piece, I must say. Talk to Colonel Burr . . . I think he lives in her mother's house. Boardinghouse, you know . . .

Within the hour he had tracked Burr down. Burr was still a congressman then and New York senator later, as Madison remembered it. They'd been friends since their days at the great college at Princeton, though Burr had been only thirteen when he entered college; Madison had supposed Burr's father having started the school accounted for this admission leniency but found later that no, he had simply crashed through the entrance exams with real brilliance. He remembered every detail of that day he'd first seen Dolley. Aaron had regarded him with the tolerant amusement of a man who knows women toward one who doesn't. But sure enough, he had taken the palpitating suitor around and presented him with a ringing endorsement that made him out to be quite a fellow, lively and bright and witty, with a splendid future. It had been almost embarrassing, and then she had given him a slight smile that had the intimacy of a wink, and afterward they had chuckled together.

Well, Jimmy, his friends said, maybe you waited over-long but then you did yourself proud! He took a boyish pleasure in their surprise and, yes, admiration, the dunce about women who had speared the prize. And every year it seemed to him that love deepened and took on new and richer dimensions.

But one thing you had to say: Aaron had been gener-ous and kindly that day, and that wasn't to be forgotten.

She had known the letter would please him; he hungered for her praise, with which she was generous but not lav-ish. They walked more slowly, enjoying each other's company, she amused as always by his conceit of a squirrel as instrument of happiness. When they parted she saw he thought of kissing her and then thought better of it, outside the State Department building, in sight of the guard at the mansion, and she was relieved in one sense and disappointed in another.

That guard, at the north entrance that everyone used, gave her a vivid smile as she approached and leaped to open the door. His name was Dumster and to most peo-ple he was as sullen as his name sounded, slapping a cudgel in the palm of his hand. But she had found that a smile, a quip, recognizing him as a man of significance at the president's door, had unlocked a remarkable cheer-iness. It amused Jimmy; when he was alone Dumster of-fered unspoken disdain but when Mrs. Madison was with him, no courtesy was too great.

Later she would see the president's chief steward, Mr. Lemaire, and discuss menus and drink for the three to five hundred guests she expected, but now she hurried up the marble stairs to examine the rooms. Jimmy had said the oval room in the center, scene of yesterday's con-tretemps, looked awful. When she stepped into the room, which was magnificent in concept and design, she was appalled. Drapes drawn haphazardly, one torn, walls streaked and parquet floors stained in the shape of old puddles, residue of a leaky roof even though Tom had ordered the roof repaired. The room had a dingy, soiled appearance, furniture haphazardly tossed about, cushions sagging and soiled, with two still on the floor, a half dozen vile paintings of which one featuring General Washington on a horse with a huge behind was the worst, but all of them must be off the walls and hidden if not burned before she put their guests through this and the adjoining rooms. She could cover the worst of the wall stains with American and French flags and all manner of bunting, and she could borrow carpets from private homes to cover the worst floor stains . . . but really! This was just disgraceful.

The president chose this moment to stroll in, looking sunny and chipper. "Good morning, dear Dolley," he almost caroled.

"My," she said, "you're looking well."

"Feeling it, too. I was quite under the weather yesterday—one of those huge headaches coming on. But then it faded in the night." Without a change in tone he added, "Maria managed to take solid food. The mail came in last night."

It took Dolley a moment to grasp that he meant he'd heard from his daughter's sickbed. "That's wonderful, Tom. We pray for her." He nodded, turning abruptly away to look from the window.

Now or never, she thought. "Tom," she said, "really, we'll have the whole city, everyone who matters and many who don't, through these rooms at the open house. For goodness' sake, we simply must make this house as decent on the inside as on the outside. This is a disgrace! This is a great building—you more than anyone know how great it is—but truly, my heart bleeds to see what should be a center of the nation's soul in crumbling disrepair!"

But his warm expression closed down and soon she was sorry she'd raised the point. He went over the reasoning again—he was cutting government expenses to the bone. The Federalists had run up a tremendous public debt, in the forties of millions. Did it purposely, he said, to make big interest payments to the wealthy who loaned the money and to give them control far beyond that of a single man with his single vote, which he saw as the basis of American citizenship. That was why he had cut the army and navy in half, for goodness' sake. The debt soon would be paid in full, and then, well, we might think about the mansion.

"But this is my dwelling place, too," he said. "How can I demand sacrifice everywhere, then pay public money to beautify my own quarters?"

It was an argument that didn't persuade but which she couldn't win, so she let it go and he went off to his office. But it was pointless penury in her view and she doubted there would be any public remonstrance over a magnificent building treated with respect. Yet the need and his rather cavalier rejection of the obvious filled her at once with sadness and with powerful ambition. As things stood now, Tom controlled everything and she had only an invited role in the mansion. She served as hostess in the absence of a presidential wife. That had evolved into real duty; she found herself overseeing official entertaining, which proved to be very hard work with no real authority. She must accept or reject menus, check wine supplies, round up plates and glassware from all over town, borrow servants from private homes, be sure the washtubs were set up below for immediate washing for reuse of plates, glasses, silverware—overwhelming detail. This was all right, too, she liked enter-

taining, liked to see people find joy in what she had
arranged. But her only authority was what the president
delegated and that did not include redecoration.

But Tom wouldn't be in the office forever. He talked
constantly of wanting to go back to Monticello and see to
his architecture, his scientific agriculture, his ranging in-
ventive mind, his connections with men of intellect and
science here and in Europe. One of these days he would
decide not to run again. And who would succeed him?
Who better than Jimmy? In her view he was more the architect of the second revolution that brought the new
democracy than was Tom, though it had been done in
Tom's name and of course he got the credit. That was all
right, but as in addition she felt that her husband was the
author of the great purchase, so he equally was the logical successor to Tom. And then she would have the power
to act and command and then she could give this building
the commanding position in the hearts and minds of
Americans as a whole that it held in her own now.

Yes! That would solve all problems. But she was
schooled in politics now and she knew that many a circumstance could unravel what seemed practically or-
dained. And then, dismayed, she thought of one primed
to do just that. Gathering her reticule, tossing her cape
over her shoulders, she hurried out.

When Madison spied his wife turning down the brick
walk from the mansion toward his office he felt a flush of
pleasure. He was amused by how pleased he was to see
her after only an hour apart. You are in love with your
wife, he told himself, and chuckled. Yes, by God, he
was! He watched her from his window, walking briskly,
that blue gown he liked moving with her hips, burst of
lace at the bodice, the diamond he'd given her the day
they wed glinting in the hollow of her throat. She had

protested that this was hardly the Quaker way even as she held it to her throat with trembling fingers.

But when she swept in he saw something stern in her expression as if she had had to nerve herself to come. "Jimmy," she said as she seated herself before the plain table he used as a desk, "I'd like to invite Aaron to the open house."

He gazed at her. Aaron Burr . . . the president detested him but Madison's feelings were more complex. Still, for his own personal gain, Aaron had been willing to shatter everything for which they had worked and fought. He had challenged or at least put at risk the second revolution, as they called it, because it broke the trend toward elitism in favor of common-man democracy. In Madison's view, putting noble work at risk was an evil act and damnably hard to forgive. Dolley's feelings ran deeper with more memory and more pain, granted, but look—it was Aaron's own actions that had put him beyond the pale.

"It's an open house, isn't it? Why an invitation?"

Friends and enemies alike would flock to the open house. No one would pass up a party in this social desert where occasional buildings were separated by forest or cornfields.

"But he won't feel welcome," she said.

"Dolley, that's because he won't *be* welcome."

"But that's not fair, Jimmy. I know you're still angry, but he is the vice president and he should be there."

"The president doesn't want him there, you know, and it is his home. No one will eject him, but—"

"I had hoped you would ask the president."

"Me?"

"I had hoped you would. You're a kindly man, Jimmy, really—don't let yourself be hard. Of course Aaron was wrong, but we can't hold it against him the rest of our lives, can we?"

Was that so much? He valued her ideas and advice and normally leaped to accommodate. But this? Forgive a man who had put the very future of the country at risk for his own gain?

"Let me think on it, sweetie," he said. He sat pondering after she left. Where had Aaron gone wrong? They hadn't been close for years but Aaron had always been a likable fellow—one of those genial, elegant men, witty and generous, able but more clever than wise, whose company can be a pleasure. But over the years as his own mind and spirit toughened Madison had found that such men often were flexible to a fault, self-serving, weak in conscience, and inconstant despite their charm. And in the end after they had climbed the heights together Burr had proved himself just such a man, an opportunist at heart, empty, conscience stunted, forever grasping.

Alexander Hamilton insisted that Burr had no core to stand as guide between right and wrong. Still, it was Burr who had pretty well pushed Alex aside to bring New York into the democratic fold. It was he who had made an obscure social club called Tammany Hall a political power strong enough to swing New York. Madison remembered the Burr of their youth, sleek, handsome, the aura of revolutionary war hero still glowing, and glowing the brighter in that Madison's health and overall weak constitution had kept him from the military. Of course all this was long before the meeting with Dolley. Looking back, those were innocent days when they were full of hope and dreams and yes, faith that they could create what was unknown since classical times, a democracy to stand strong among the kings and czars of modern times. They were all friends then, united in persuading Americans to accept the new Constitution. But that was long ago.

In those days Burr had a talent for mimicry and a sense of fun. Madison could still remember his antic little charades, Hamilton presented to the queen of England, Hamilton snuggling up to General Washington, Hamilton meeting a new woman and making a profound leg, Hamilton faced with a conundrum. And it was true, there was always that stiffness about Alex, that yearning for rigidity and order and his liking for the upper classes. Burr had a whole scene of Hamilton with the common man, washing his hands, holding his nose, eyebrows raised to his hairline, shuddering, backing away.

So much water under the bridge since those palmy days . . . though Madison could see now that Burr had put his finger on a basic truth. Hamilton did fear the common man as possessed of mob instincts who would throw truth, honor, stability to the winds in pursuit of his own selfish ends. Poor Alex! The turbulent 1790s with their wild shifts in thinking and then the Terror in France drove him to his own destruction. More and more clearly Alex wanted government of the good, the wise, the right people, their goodness and wisdom and rightness demonstrated by their acquisition of wealth. But that wasn't what Americans wanted, and the Democrats arose to articulate their dreams of a common-man democracy.

Which led, in turn, to the great temptation of Aaron Burr. Go back to drafting the Constitution—Lord ha' mercy, Madison was there, had a big hand in it, and with all the others let the great anomaly slide by unnoticed. Blithely the drafters, including certainly himself, had not considered the possibility that the body politic would divide into parties, one trusting of the common man to control his own destiny as a free man, the other quasi-monarchical, looking to authoritarian government that would keep the common man in his place.

No, they had simply assumed that leading men all with the same ideas would be advanced for the presidency. He with the most votes would be president, the runner-up vice president, ties to be decided in the House.

But of course parties did arise and that led to tickets. In 1800 Jefferson, with Aaron Burr standing as vice president on the Democratic ticket, won the election, seventy-three electoral votes against Adams's sixty-five. Then, viewing Jefferson and Burr as a team, president and vice president, Democratic electors gave seventy-three votes to *each* man. But under the old terms of the Constitution, soon to be repaired so the situation could never arise again, each man with seventy-three electoral votes meant a tie even though no one had voted for Burr for president. So the election would be settled in the House—and the House was still passionately Federalist.

Madison had anticipated this peril. To defeat it, a single elector in a single state must give Burr one vote less than that given Jefferson. He planned to accomplish this in Virginia. Then there would be no tie and hence no problem. But as Madison saw it now, Burr had *wanted* that tie to arise. He wanted a chance to push Jefferson aside and seize the prize himself. And he knew that the man most likely of all to sense the danger and take steps to cancel it was James Madison.

So he sent a man to Richmond, a rat-faced fellow in Madison's memory, to threaten a still greater danger— war between North and South. The quarrel between the sections was real and deadly. It had nearly torn them apart when they were writing the Constitution, turning on the slavery question and the South's insistence on maintaining the institution. In the end, living with slavery was the price for havingthe Constitution. This clash was a real issue, all right; Madison knew the American nation was anything but a happy, cooperative family. So he had to listen.

This sleek creature with his yellow hair greased down was somehow ominous, David Gelsen his name, mouthing on and on over the insults he said Virginia had offered Burr in the last election. It hardly seemed an insult, but in fact Tom and Aaron had formed a losing ticket in 1796, and while Virginia had given Tom all its twenty-one electoral votes, it gave only a handful to Burr.

"Sorry," he had told Gelsen, "Colonel Burr just isn't popular in Virginia."

"But that won't do now," Gelsen had barked. "Democrats won the presidency because New York swung their way, and we—Colonel Burr—did the swinging. Now, sir, I am here to tell you that we will no longer tolerate Virginia's hostility, its rule-or-ruin mentality, its disrespect."

Oh, Madison remembered that talk well!

"Look, Mr. Madison," the oaf had said, "you plainly don't like me and I don't like you one whit more. Probably you think I'm vulgar and aggressive—"

Madison remembered coloring: it was exactly what he had been thinking. "Well," Gelsen had said, "way I see it, your fancy manners, your high-and-mighty pose—why, hell, you're as false as a lead dollar, all that gentility lived on the backs of black men. What the hell kind of democracy is that?"

That strike so close to the truth had infuriated Madison but before he could respond Gelsen swept on. "Two promises: First, we've arranged for votes to be withheld in the North, and second, we'll split the party wide open, you insult our leader again."

So . . . Virginia gave Burr equal votes. So did every other state. No votes were withheld despite Gelsen's promise. The result was the tie they had feared all along. Jefferson and Burr—which would be president? When, remember, *no one* had voted for Burr as president. What had been a clear-cut electoral victory, Jefferson over Adams, by this unhappy accident now would be left in the hands of radical Federalists in the old House who burned with fury at having lost the election. A Massachusetts congressman whose name he couldn't remember had stopped Madison on the street a few days later.

"Haw!" he bellowed, "a fine mess of pottage you have, my friend. Your evil man from Monticello is finished and so are you!"

Stung from his usual calm, Madison had snapped, "You try to stop us and the people will throw you in the garbage pit!" And then, controlling himself, he had added more moderately, "Anyway, Mr. Burr will step aside and that will settle it. You'll see."

But Aaron had not stepped aside. He hadn't done the right thing. And in his silence the Federalist move to use him or use the imbroglio to appoint a caretaker leader from their own ranks had strengthened. They all swore—and believed, Madison didn't doubt—that this internal fight among Democrats before even taking office was the start of the predicted collapse à la France—the terror and blood in the streets would be next. This was the real damage Aaron had worked, offering their enemies a wedge that could have been fatal.

Well . . . they had come closer to civil war than Madison ever wanted to see. Virginia and Pennsylvania mobilized militia to march on Washington to block the theft of government. Not until then had reality struck the old party and patriotism prevailed. The nation had come perilously close to shattering. And their quondam friend Alexander Hamilton had shown his inherent stature—despite all their quarreling and fury over the years, in the end he had stood for his country instead of his party. His voice urging fellow Federalists to vote for Jefferson despite his politics because as an honorable man he was much superior to Burr had been a major factor in the ultimate Federalist decision to back off after thirty-seven ballotings and weeks of agony and declare Jefferson the president, Aaron the vice president.

What still struck Madison as amazing was that after all this Aaron had supposed there would be no consequences for having tried to steal the election. Even more disturbing, Dolley seemed to suppose the same thing, asking insistently, where is the profit in retribution? But it was too late for Aaron to reform himself as loyal lieutenant. He would serve as vice president but would he given no duties beyond what the Constitution gave him, sitting on the dais as president of the Senate, voting to break ties. Over the next years they had frozen him out, stripped him of every fragment of power, appointed none of his people, given him no share and no say in the administration, treated him as if he didn't exist—they had made him a laughingstock. Yes, it had been brutal. Jim Ross, the Federalist senator from Pennsylvania who had helped persuade Napoleon that he had no future in America, put it clearly. "I'd say you emasculated him— cut his nuts sure as gelding a stallion colt."

When he came home that night he saw she had read his face. He shook his head. "You know he would misread an invitation as a bid for rapprochement."

She gazed at him in silence that grew more and more uncomfortable before she said, "It feels like a mistake. He's going back to New York to run for governor. I suppose he'll win—you know his strength in New York. And then he'll be a legitimate figure to succeed Tom. And I want *you* to succeed Tom. I want us to live in that mansion. I want to make it what it can be, should be—I want it part of the American heart, iconic, like the flag itself, as no other building possibly could be. I don't want Aaron to push you aside."

Passion made her voice vibrate. He gazed at her. Sweet and kindly, but she was tough, too, often more practical than he. Sometimes he couldn't tell if her ambition was not more for herself than for him. Odd and interesting— she saw as danger that Aaron would be elected in New York, and Albert Gallatin saw as danger that he wouldn't be elected. Two knowledgeable people, both wise, saying plainly that Burr was a dangerous man.

"What do you think we should do?" he asked.

"Make him ambassador to France, or Russia, or Spain—something, anything that gives him a way out, that saves face."

"You don't think it's too late?"

"Probably it is—but even the offer would ease some of the sting."

But he knew Tom would never do it and that was that.

"Aaron is more capable than you think." Her voice was a whisper. "And more dangerous. He's not overburdened with conscience, you know. And he won't just vanish. . . ."

FOUR

Washington, fall 1803

As Aaron Burr saw it, he had been the victim of a political plot to deny him the fruits of victory. They sought to crush him to block an inevitable ascent to the highest office. It was he who had given them the original victory—without New York there would have been no second revolution, as the sainted Mr. Jefferson liked to term it, and without Burr there would have been no New York. Fate then threw up the strange conundrum that Burr had seen was inherent in the Constitution, the tie that pitted two men of the same party against each other. It wouldn't happen again because they were amending the Constitution to correct the anomaly, but there it was, a fait accompli, placing them in the hands of their enemies.

Throughout, as Burr reminded himself often, he had acted with perfect propriety. The Virginia cabal expected him to fall on his sword, immolate himself on behalf of Saint Tom, the holy voice of freedom. But flinging himself under the hooves of Virginia was not Aaron Burr's style. Yet there was nothing grasping in his character, as he had proved by his gallantry in this crisis. Presented a great opportunity, courted by Federalists, the prize dangled before him, he had done nothing. No promises, no deals, nothing! Or almost nothing. Talked to a few friends, letters here and there as courtesy might require, defending as the need arose his positions as less radical than those of Mr. Jefferson, making it plain as was his duty to himself that he was a factor to be considered. What he did not do was meet Virginian expectations—he stayed engaged and awaited the outcome.

In the end the vote turned against him. Well and good. He accepted the verdict. As vice president and logical successor he would be loyal and helpful. He would be vigorous for the administration's greater glory as preface to his own future. And then, in public, at the inauguration itself, the new president cut him to the bone with the world watching. Disgusting!

Ever since they had abused him. Cut him from every vestige of power, every privilege of the vice presidency, denied him any voice. One public humiliation after another. Occasional dinner invitations proved meaningless. He sought a few appointments in New York for his lieutenants and was denied while Jefferson and Madison aligned themselves with his chief enemies at home, old Governor George Clinton and his serpent of a nephew, DeWitt. He was left with nothing beyond the duty the Constitution prescribed—president of the Senate with a vote only to break ties. It was clear that he would even be denied renomination to this meaningless office; they were pushing Governor Clinton into that spot, assuming he could deliver New York—and would be too old to aspire to the highest office.

Oh, it was plain as day—they sought to destroy the man who could block the rise of James Madison. Jimmy was a fine fellow, a friend as Jefferson never had been, but now he was in ambition's grip. But as president? No one doubted his intellect, but where was the vigor to mount a horse and unsheathe a sword and lead a nation to glory? Could you imagine little Jimmy lifting the masses with the thunderous oratory that came naturally to Burr? Obviously they must drain the strength of the real leader if so timorous a man were to have a chance. A plot, then, from the beginning.

But they should have known better than to pick a fight with a fighter. Burr waited, but a fury burned in him day and night. Revenge was sweetest when it took the form of justice, and nothing was more just than righting the wrongs done him and destroying the hopes and dreams of his enemies. And the time was close now.

On the dais overlooking the somnolent Senate the sheer vigor of his thinking filled his veins with thunder and he leaped up, passed the gavel to a sleepy senator, and went hurrying along the marble halls, clerks making way, guards bowing. He paused in the rotunda for a quick mug of ale, ignoring members of both parties clustered around food stalls, and bolted out into fall sunshine to walk briskly, swinging his silver-knobbed stick. As he walked, contemplating the fate of his enemies, his mood continued to improve. Yes, by God, let them learn the cost of traducing Colonel Aaron Burr!

He had a couple of free hours before General Wilkinson appeared at his rooms in Mrs. Simpson's house. They would dine on a fat duck that the good Mrs. Simpson should be preparing even now. With it they would have a couple of bottles of a really fine Madeira that he had procured recently. Washington was a work in progress, which he enjoyed watching as he stepped around piles of wood and brick, stone stacked on timbers, mud holes into which a little gravel had been tossed, the Capitol not half-finished and likely to be years in process. His stick clicked against paving blocks in rhythm to his rising spirits.

Then in the distance he saw two women approaching, the swing of their long skirts, the slenderness of their waists suggesting youth and beauty. He drew himself up and when they were close he saw to his surprise that it was Dolley Madison and that friend of hers, what was her name? She'd been married to Carl Mobry, the shipping figure, and he understood that after Mobry's death she took over the business and was succeeding so far. Imagine a woman running a fleet of ships crewed by a rough cast of men! What was her name? Darnelle, Dahlia—no, Daniella, that was it. He seemed to remember that Mobry had found her in New Orleans. They called her Danny and she was a damned fine-looking woman. And his old friend Dolley, in her thirties now and not so fresh as when he'd known her as a young widow, but still fine. He felt a faint stirring of regret; perhaps he should have tried harder. . . .

He bowed over their hands, taking a moment longer than necessary with Madame Mobry's firm hand in his.

Still, he couldn't resist a thrust, and he said to Dolley, "And how is your good husband? Still fuming at his old friend, I suppose."

"Well, Aaron," she said, "he's quite busy, you know."

Neat! She had skewered him nicely and to turn a moment's confusion he said to Mrs. Mobry, "Mr. Madison is a little hostile these days, which seems poor recompense considering that I brought them together."

"So I understand," said Danny Mobry, the faint smile, the edge of irony in her voice delighting him. Danny . . . a nice name for a woman who really was very pretty.

But he seemed to have stung Dolley, for she said with some asperity, "Well, what could you expect? Behaving as you did."

"In fact, Dolley, I behaved with perfect propriety." He glanced at Danny. "She refers—"

"I remember it perfectly, Mr. Burr. I was there."

"Indeed she was," Dolley said. "She and I worked together to defeat you."

He chuckled. "Defeated by two beautiful women. That does ease the sting. I should have been more gallant." He let his smile fade as he looked at Dolley. "More seriously, the fortunes of politics threw me into parity with Mr. J. Was it incumbent on me alone to step down?"

"Of course. No one voted for you for president."

"But we don't really know that, do we? Equal numbers voted. Do you suppose New York electors are so dedicated to Mr. J? Should the North have no voice? I remember when Jimmy and Mr. J came to see me in New York—you know about that?"

"I've heard it described."

"Yes . . . in 1792, seeking cooperation. Frankly, Dolley, I've never felt less than either of these gentlemen. And would Jimmy have asked my intercession with you if he'd felt so superior? Then later, after we'd all fought the good fight and the people turned to us—and New York, remember, was decisive, and I assure you New York would not have been ours without me—then suddenly I become quite inferior to the noble leader from Virginia."

He paused a moment for effect, then added, "And finally, dear Dolley, what did I do that was so vile? I said nothing. I did nothing. But I could have encouraged the Federalists—they had the votes to put me in. I could have made arrangements, agreements, and they were willing, some of them, at least."

"Hamilton wasn't," Dolley said. "I don't think Alex would have let you become president."

"Ah, yes, Mr. Hamilton . . ." The rage that lay below his smile these days came boiling up. He tried to throttle it but saw in her eyes that he had failed. He leaned on his stick with his head bowed for a moment, then looked up with a fresh smile. "Sorry. It does anger me. Alex seems to take joy in calumniating me. We've known each other for years, tried lawsuits as co-counsel, saved men from the gallows by working together. Yes, he's a Federalist and I'm a Democrat, or was, but I never hated him. Yet the things he says, the things he does, do hurt me to the core. . . ."

Then, straightening further, "I don't hate, you know. But Jimmy does—I think he hates me."

"He doesn't—"

"And Mr. J—I admit if I were going to hate, he would be high on my list, but I've always been fond of Jimmy. I was fond of you, too—I'd never have presented him if I'd thought him less than worthy."

"No one questions that, Aaron," Dolley said.

"Yes, but my point is that I did nothing to influence the outcome."

"Well," she said, putting her hand on Danny's arm, "we both remember those days very well—we were busy heading off civil war."

"Civil war! Oh, Dolley, please, I hardly think—"

"Oh, yes, and you know it! And all you had to do was withdraw, just state that you wouldn't serve."

He smiled. "Dolley, Dolley—isn't that asking too much of any human being?"

A look of disgust flashed over her face and he knew he had made a mistake. Before he could shift to cover it she said softly, "That man you sent down to threaten Jimmy with sectional war if Virginia slighted you on electoral votes—that was part of the plot, wasn't it? You were looking for a tie."

"Certainly not! We had arranged for Democratic electors in the North to withhold votes from me."

"Democratic electors in states the Democrats had a chance of winning?"

Oh, she was quick. He remembered Matt Davis guffawing as they instructed electors who wouldn't be serving since they were from states Jefferson and Burr couldn't possibly carry. All right! So he wanted the tie and plotted a little to get it. Wasn't that politics, after all? But he didn't have to answer her and he hastily shifted ground. "Am I invited to your big open house?"

She hesitated, something uneasy in her expression. "It's an open house. No one is invited per se."

"But will I be welcome?" She stared, wordless. "Or will I be asked to leave?"

Again that—not a tremor, really, but some concern— and he guessed there had been talk about this. Then she said evenly, "You'll be as welcome as all the others."

He bowed. "I'll be there." Again he held pretty Danny's hand a moment longer than necessary and he walked on well satisfied. He had slipped a dangerous question and a pretty woman had responded to him. Danny had hardly spoken, yet he knew she had reacted, and sometimes sparking reaction was as good as conquest. Though he might look to that later, too.

One odd note in passing. Early in the conversation Dolley had remarked that Danny had just brought in one of her ships from New Orleans, and he had said casually that his old friend General Wilkinson with whom he was dining this evening had often described New Orleans as a delightful city. At the mention of Jim's name a certain shadow had crossed Danny's face, though she had said nothing. Interesting . . . Jim had been running flatboats to New Orleans for years on the side from commanding the army, and Burr knew his reputation was dubious in some quarters. Now, walking along, he stored the thought. He liked Wilkinson, though he knew that many people didn't. Sometimes Jim seemed to revel in his enemies, an attitude Burr could well understand. Still, it was a note to remember.

———

Yet as he walked on his mood began to shift. There had
been something in Dolley's eyes that had been kindly
and sweet. He shouldn't have picked at her about
Jimmy—his quarrel with her husband wasn't with her,
and of course she would defend him. No, it was when
he'd asked her about the open house. At that instant she
was reaching out to him, he was sure of it, not as woman
to man but as—

Yes! That was it, that sympathy, that caring warmth
for his feelings . . . and there flashed into his mind a recurring image of his own dear mother. His walk slowed
as emotion welled. As sharply as day becoming night the
boulevardier swinging his cane—the image of himself
he liked best—faded into the darkness of vulnerability
and pain and loss. His mother had been beautiful, he was
sure of that, and kind and sweet and she'd loved him
without reservation, even then he'd known nothing he
could do would ever dampen the warmth in her eyes. He
was sure of all this, though sometimes he wondered how
much was real and true and how much a picture he had
constructed out of his own hungry need. For she had left
him, too, abandoned him when he needed her most, and
sometimes he felt something like hatred for her, hatred
that of course he squelched and denied. For everyone
told him then that her death was a tragedy that he must
find strength to endure. Love and hatred intertwined with
the terrible impermanence of life. He was two and a half
years old.

Now, of course, an adult himself, he understood that
that inexplicable application of God's impenetrable motives, yellow fever, had swept her away with his father in
one terrible swoop. Yet at another level it was beyond
fathoming and it was betrayal, if not by her then by life
itself. For years he had cried himself to sleep. Why
would God take her? She was Jonathan Edwards's
daughter—why would God seize the daughter of the

greatest preacher of all time, as he was widely described? And take her husband, Aaron Burr, himself a famous preacher of the gospel? A family tragedy . . . but he could never quite shake that feeling of betrayal and with it waves of rage and need all intermingled.

He and his sister went to live with an uncle who was piety itself and believed piety demanded a hard hand, and after a while the boy toughened and stopped crying himself to sleep. When he was ten he ran off to the docks in New York City where as a poor and homeless orphan he landed a berth as cabin boy on a brig bound for Le Havre. They were ready to sail when here came his uncle helling down the dock with the law in trail.

He was bright, he saw that plainly, and if denied the seafaring life then books must lift him to independence. He worked hard and at the age of eleven decided he was well equipped to enter the College of New Jersey, which his father had made into a powerful institution. It was the senior Burr who had moved it to Princeton, where it had taken such hold that town and college alike were called by the same name. They *owed* him, he informed the startled trustees; they told him to go home and study more. He did; a man (as he now saw himself) who wants and is willing to work can hardly be denied. Two years later he demanded not only admittance but admittance at the third-year level; granted a start at the second-year level, he sailed through with time left over to form a whist team with Madison, then an upperclassman, which kept them both in pocket money for years. Oh, yes, his association with Jimmy was of long-standing, and Jimmy had been sickly even then.

Waves of sadness still swept around his mother's image, which took on grandeur beyond what any human could support. He understood this, obviously she had been flesh and blood and doubtless she'd had her weaknesses, her angers, her failures of perception—grant all that and it still made no difference to his vision of the golden aura enveloping her memory.

He finished Princeton, read for the law, and rushed to join the army when the war began. He made Benedict Arnold's great march to Quebec, the starvation march as the men who were there called it; began as a cadet and arrived a captain, aide to Arnold and then to Richard Montgomery, into whose command Arnold placed his men. They took Montreal and raced on to the walls of Quebec and what a difference victory would have made! But atop the walls a bullet killed Montgomery at the instant of triumph and the American attack broke and failed. With aching heart Burr did his best to recover General Montgomery's body for burial with honors, but the general had outweighed him by a hundred pounds. After forty paces with the body on his back he fell and the redcoats came swarming down the walls. In the end he left his dead general and fought his way back to his lines. It hurt, leaving that great man; it hurt today in the memory of it.

He went on to command a regiment through enough combat to last a man a lifetime. He drove it day and night until at last his health collapsed. Lieutenant Colonel Burr; he had earned that rank with honor and honesty, and of all the titles that had come since—officer of the court and senator and vice president and, he was sure when that title came, president—Colonel Burr would be the one he cherished and demanded as by right.

Then the great transition in his life that stilled some of the pain of old. He met Theodosia and everything was different.

Mrs. Theodosia Prevost, American-born wife of a British officer, mother of two sons in their teenage years and two daughters. She was a full ten years older than Burr. Major Prevost was off with the British army; she maintained the family mansion in the New Jersey countryside and made it a watering post for officers of the American Continental Army. That her husband was a Briton and an enemy was just one of those things. There were rules attached to visits to Mrs. Prevost: you must first be brought and introduced by someone she knew and welcomed, and then she must specifically invite you to come again. Absent these tests, your reception would be frosty indeed. But pass them and you were welcome whenever you reined up the long circular drive to her house, and if you bore a shank of beef, a side of bacon, a half dozen bottles of Madeira, that too was welcome but not required. All manner of officers visited; Burr fell in love.

She was smallish, her hair dark, her complexion dusky, her eyes big and liquid and warm, not truly beautiful but possessed of a beauty that everyone recognized. Her warmth, that infinite sense of caring, the unqualified approval in her expression seemed to him a miracle, coupled as it was with intellect and learning of a range to match his own. She was charming beyond any imagining and he needed her in a way that went straight to his heart. No distance was too great, no detour too far to bring him past her house and find him time to stop. He was handsome and dashing, his very appearance seemed to excite women and his conquests were legendary, but this was the woman who mattered. She mothered him, of course, balm to a tortured spirit, and people said that was her attraction, but Burr knew better. When her husband took fever in Jamaica and died she and Burr married and in due time she gave birth to a daughter whom Burr insisted on naming Theodosia. Yes, she mothered him . . . she was a mothering woman.

But even then cancer was advancing on her, slowly but with devastating insistence. It became worse and worse. She was more and more often bedridden. Two more babies came; both died. It was tragic, yes, but they were happy. He would always have that. Burr was active in law practice, in the state legislature, in the U.S. Senate, and wherever he went he outlined Theodosia's problem and begged doctors for a new cure or even new hope. Neither was forthcoming. She was sweet, generous, kind, comforting—she helped him hold his life together—but twelve years after they married she was dead. He was devastated; he and little Theodosia shared their powerful grief and grew closer still; his daughter became the mainstay of his life.

The year he was elected vice president, Theodosia married Mr. Alston, whom Burr expected soon to be governor of South Carolina. His son-in-law welcomed him into their married lives with an open heart which Burr (with much pleasure) suspected Theodosia had made a condition of agreeing to marry. Burr wrote her constantly, sharing his life with her, seeking her advice, bombarding her with instructions for her own improvement and for educating the gorgeous grandson she gave him; without Theodosia life would be empty indeed.

But then, life was a study in loss and irony. Since his youth women had opened to him as flowers and he had plucked them as a man plucks blossoms in a garden, admiring the sheer joy of them even as he knows they won't last. But the earliest memories of his life were of loss and the crowning blow of his life was the loss of the only person who had ever set that first loss aright.

Aaron Burr was strong, forceful, a man of power who knew how to grasp it and how to use it. He scorned fear, he enjoyed risk, he was physically hard and he was a dangerous man to cross, a man to make great marks on the world. But much had been taken from him and deep-rooted pain also drove him, infusing all that he did—pain and loss that a woman's caring eyes could lift into the open like a wounded cry.

Well, then, pacing along, had he been so wrong when the great chance struck him with a near blinding vision? The talk with Dolley and the ranging memories it triggered had disturbed him more than he liked. He felt oddly vulnerable, not like himself at all, and he needed to refocus control before seeing Wilkinson. This was a weakness that he was sure old Jim would discern in an instant and by sheer instinct turn against him, like a dog that scents fear.

They had brutalized him, demeaned him, made him a laughingstock among men whose response was like so many sharks sensing blood. What did they hold against him? That he had not stepped back, pulled his forelock, yielded to the Virginian. Well, suppose he had played the good soldier, withdrawn, demanded that the prize be awarded to Jefferson. He would be the much-honored vice president instead of the pariah, an important part of a successful administration—and he would have had a straight path to succeed Jefferson.

Or would he? Would Jefferson ever step down? Who knew? The Constitution put no limits on presidential service. Would he step aside for the New Yorker? Madison, now, there was a man with a lean and hungry look; who was to say he wasn't the Cassius of this administration, at least as far as his old friend Aaron Burr was concerned? One look told you Madison had been positioning himself all along to be the next president whenever Saint Tom decided to step down. So suppose Burr had pulled his forelock against all his instincts—you still had to wonder if there wouldn't have been some new circumstance to put him where he was now. Just had to wonder . . .

Against all his instincts . . . that was the key, wasn't it? It wasn't in his nature to step back from opportunity. Drive ahead, seize the grail, make it his own—that was Aaron Burr's way and it had been from the beginning.

He remembered rounding up stragglers during the war, sometimes he'd have to put a pistol barrel under a man's nose, but he got them, all right, every one of them older than he, and he formed them and threw them against the enemy and by God, they'd done well, too. And they felt better about themselves, you could see it in their faces. When he turned them loose a lot of them didn't want to go.

That was his way. Maybe wisdom said back off but Burr was a plunger and he liked it that way.

The duck was superb, a handsome big bird done to a turn. His spirits were restored, the boulevardier returned. He could always thrust away the old pain but it was like masking a toothache with laudanum—you knew it was still there, only hidden. Still, a good bird assuages one in other ways. He would have to compliment Mrs. Simpson, perhaps get her a flacon of scent . . . which, naturally, he really couldn't afford. But then he really couldn't afford a handsome suite when everyone else in House and Senate had a room or shared a room in a boardinghouse. But Aaron Burr was an elegant man, a student of Lord Chesterfield's letters to his son. Now, there was a man, the elegant British nobleman, who knew how to live! And here in the rude United States, far from fashionable London, Aaron Burr held up the flag. A Chesterfieldian gentleman . . .

When had he begun slipping into debt? His law practice had been lucrative but then politics took more and more time and with politics came power and with power came men eager to see him over any financial embarrassment with open-ended loans. He made it a point of pride to execute a note for every dollar he borrowed but they never carried a closing date and with a few exceptions he had repaid none of them.

Elegant dress, membership in fine clubs, handsome homes that befitted a man of his stature, lavish gifts for his darling Theodosia—all this took money. He considered himself a patron of the arts and enjoyed underwriting impecunious artists and writers whom he felt had something to offer the world of culture and deserved encouragement. It was surprising how little it took to keep some poor devil alive so he could practice his art in peace. Of course, when you multiplied that by ten or twenty, it did add up. But there always were more men of substance willing to send around a thousand in gold, have your note ready. . . .

He sipped the wine, watching General Wilkinson eat, feeling a sudden hollowness in his own gut. Superb wine, by the way, came fully up to the merchant's claim—and should be superb, at the price. But that was the thing, he had more or less lost track of his debt, tens of thousands, certainly, though now he couldn't really say exactly how many tens of thousands. For a man of power there was always more. But now . . . the administration emasculating him in public, denying him even the trappings of counting for anything despite his title, which itself had become a mockery. Emasculated . . . if the men holding his paper ever felt Samson's locks were completely shorn and decided to call his notes . . . He stopped himself. He refused to think of debtor's prison. He would die there—it must never, never happen!

"So, Aaron," Jim Wilkinson said, "how do you see your future unfolding now?" Burr started; had his expression betrayed him? "Excellent duck, by the way," Wilkinson added. "I've always admired your capacity to live well."

A compliment within a taunt; that was General Wilkinson for you, probably the reason so many people disliked him. Burr enjoyed him despite the occasional barb, perhaps because Wilkinson's angry, cynical, deeply suspicious nature rather matched his own, though there was a roughness in the man too, nothing like Chesterfieldian elegance. He'd spent most of his life on the frontier and it showed. Been a big mule in the Kentucky Conspiracy at one time, too, days long past now.

His pretensions toward the elegance that came so naturally to Burr did make him faintly ridiculous. They were near the same age—indeed, Burr had known him rather well during the Revolution when they both were on General Washington's staff. Wilkinson had been pasty-faced even then, running to fat at a time when Burr, lean as a wolf in those days, had sought out combat. Burr had heard the bullets whistle while Wilkinson was moving paper from one office to another. But that was all right; in Burr's eyes Wilkinson had always been more a political than a military figure.

His career mirrored that. He'd established himself as a trader and a political figure in Kentucky after the war, engaged in the slippery tobacco trade with the Spanish in New Orleans. Eventually he returned to the army with enough political pull to land a berth as second to the chief of staff, Major General Anthony Wayne. It amounted to a bad joke that Burr appreciated immediately. Wayne was a fighting general, beloved of his men, called Mad Anthony for the ferocity with which he had battered the British. He gathered fighters around him and he made his men proud. Wilkinson, on the other hand, personified the political general of which Wayne was the antithesis. At once the natural-born plotter began undermining the fighter and was well on his way to unseating him when the latter took ill and died, leaving the way open for the plotter to slide into his shoes. Underhanded, of course, but Burr considered army command as political as it was military and felt Wayne should have been able to hold his own. It was too bad in a way—Wayne had been a great figure in American military history—

but it also meant poor Jim had been living with calumny ever since. And with rage of his own—he'd had the political weight to get the command but not to get the rank that normally went with it. He remained a brigadier, fuming and furious.

Over the years he had let himself go somewhat. He was still a rather handsome man with sandy hair and increasingly round countenance that reflected to those who looked carelessly a kindly and even an innocent impression. He had added much fat and his girth combined unfortunately with his taste for fancy uniforms made to his own design with extravagant epaulets and flashes of color into which he fitted himself like a sausage in its casing. Burr had supposed until now that a uniform was a uniform but it struck him as nicely independent that a general should design his own to set himself apart. Jim's girth didn't help, though; when he wore his saber it tended to stick out behind like a rooster tail.

Actually, on strength of appearances alone, he was a little ridiculous but when you looked into his eyes you saw nothing at all ridiculous—nor innocent. Wilkinson was a dangerous man, quick, clever, duplicitous when necessary, skilled at turning the other cheek until he could deliver swift and deadly retaliation. He hadn't climbed over bodies to the highest command by following a gentleman's rules. Mad Anthony Wayne had been honest and direct, a fighting man as Wilkinson never would be, but it was probably well that he died before he could fully engage his subordinate. Burr would have put his money on his devious friend.

"What a good fellow you are," Wilkinson went on, holding his glass toward the light to admire the color. Burr was uncorking the second bottle. "Able, superb political instincts, capacious of mind, grasp of the large view—and how disgracefully they abuse you, my dear friend. As, I might add, they do me too. We are victims together."

"Oh?" The wine was sweet on Burr's tongue, its fumes strong in his mind. "I don't think of you—"

"Held to this miserable rank, sir. Brigadier! When every leader of the army was a major general. Wayne was a major general—am I less? The rank is mine, and they deny me. Just as they deny you—oh, don't pretend, Aaron, it's to your honor, as it is to mine, that such men should abuse us."

He went on in this vein for some time. Denied the rank, denied the honor, and the money—did Burr know that a brigadier's salary was a pitiful $104 a month? Thank God he still had trade connections on the Mississippi, cargoes running to New Orleans, to supplement this niggardly sum. Burr restrained a smile, remembering now that rumor gave Wilkinson a good deal more connection with the Spanish than mere favorable trade conditions. Spanish gold in his pocket, he sharing American secrets, which technically probably would be treason but in a part of the world that didn't matter much. And after all, it was only rumor, doubtless kept alive by his manifold enemies whom he liked to say were jealous bastards who held his trade success against him. Still, he always added, he reveled in his enemies for a man can be measured by their ranks. What's more, the day of their destruction would come, Burr could bet his last dollar on that. For—and here Wilkinson's voice dropped to a whisper—he had dreams of a scale that soared far beyond their meager grasp.

But then, as if he might have said too much, he waved a hand impatiently, and said, "Well, enough of that. My destiny will unfold as it does." His eyes brightened. "More importantly, what of you? I sense my old friend is at a crossroads. I know you well, Aaron; you're not a man to take abuse and soldier on with a smile. I know you have plans to correct inequities that must rankle your soul. Tell me."

Burr smiled. "I suppose you do know me, Jim. Yes, I do have plans that will, as you put it so nicely, 'correct inequities.' You understand that New York controls who will be the next president of the United States?"

Wilkinson's eyes opened wide. "Jefferson is very popular with this Louisiana business; I'd have thought—"

"Oh, he'll be reelected next year, no doubt of that; no, I refer to 1808. Everything will be different then."

He talked on with enthusiasm, the level of the second bottle steadily lowering, the ravaged duck pushed aside.

In essence it was a simple equation but there were subtle complications and ramifications that delighted Burr and were sure to engage so devious a mind as Wilkinson's. But the overarching fact was that New York was the largest state after Virginia and it was crucial to the new Democratic party. That it had gone Democratic in 1800 had put Jefferson in office; how it went in the future would determine the future. And the rank and file there were furious at the treatment given their native son. Now, it happened that the party machinery had fallen into the hands of that weak old fool, Governor Clinton, who was propped up every morning and made to perform by his ambitious nephew, DeWitt Clinton. Jefferson and his little handmaiden, Mr. Madison, had been courting Clinton, supposing he could deliver New York.

All this calculated, you see, as if Aaron Burr simply would go off and die somewhere to everyone's convenience. Well, in fact, Colonel Burr intended to return to New York, reestablish himself, reclaim his power, and take over the state. The governor's chair would be open and Burr's popularity had never faded, so his operatives there informed him constantly. He was stronger in New York City where the origins of his power lay, but he was strong in Albany too. Party machinery would be in the Clinton faction's hands, but Burr had cast the party aside in his outrage. He would run and win as an independent.

Then four years to consolidate his power and collect New York Democrats in his hand again. He would control New York while in 1808 New York would control Democratic chances. Ipso facto, Aaron Burr would dictate the next president. He might designate a worthy figure or he might take it himself, but the one sure thing was that the next leader would not be a Virginian.

This prospect was so lovely that he talked on and on as the Madeira level sank. Then he noticed Jim's eyelids sagging. Enough, enough. He poured the last of the wine, and more to signal that they were done than out of interest, he said, "No more about me, now. Before we finish I must hear about what's next for you."

Wilkinson's eyes popped open and he took up the glass with new relish. "I'm so happy to hear your plans, Aaron. Crush your oppressors, that's the ticket. I knew you would find the ultimate revenge."

Burr smiled. "You do have a way of casting things, Jim."

"I care about such things, sir. Care about justice, about propriety, decency. I resent its denial, to me and to a man of great worth. Is it any wonder that I dream?"

Well, it was Wilkinson's turn. "Of what do you dream, my dear general?"

"Of the West," Wilkinson said instantly and Burr saw this had been in his mind all along. "I leave next week for Fort Adams to take immediate charge of the troops with whom we'll enter New Orleans and take control. Five hundred men."

"That many? Do you expect trouble?"

"Perhaps. The city is volatile, it well could go out of control. Ultimately, however, it will be the star of the West. You know, Aaron, you should take a closer look at the West. You need to educate yourself in this vast and wonderful area, so as to equip yourself for—" He broke off with a self-conscious laugh and then emptied his glass.

Still, as if fascinated, he continued, "You should go there, Aaron. You would find a paradise. Full of strong people, rich fields, vast forests, a river network coursing like veins of gold, all athrob with trade for which the world awaits—it's no accident, you know, that the French hungered for it. But they were fools." He twirled the glass in his big fingers. His reddened cheeks were shiny. "Fools because they imagined they could bend those westerners to their will. Easier to get a mule to co-operate. The western American would never be French-man nor Spaniard, believe me. But what he will be is the progenitor of a new nation."

Now Burr's eyes popped open. This was interesting. He watched Wilkinson's slow smile. "You're surprised," the general said. "But reflect—do present leaders have the courage to defend? I think not. They're in thrall to Federalists and those idiots hate and fear the West. West-erners know this. You'd be amazed at the spirit of revolt burning there—revolt against the East. But you would be stunned by how sparsely populated it is, miles and miles of prime land occupied by a mere handful of Indians, awaiting men who know how to put it to use.

"And New Orleans—beautiful city, a sophistication level unknown in this rude country. You asked if I scent trouble there—well, I can promise you they are enraged. They're French, you know, forty years of Spanish rule has barely touched their Franco-centric nature, and they were overjoyed when it seemed Napoleon would take them back, return them to their native heritage, don't you see? Then, just like that, he peddles them to the Ameri-cans, whom they can't stand—of course they're furious and ready to fight. They won't, not right away, but they are cavaliers, you know, men of pride and power. In the end they will want their own country. . . ."

He shrugged with a muted little chuckle. Sweat stood on his upper lip and he wiped it with his napkin. "That's the point, you see. It's an empire, anchored to the sea by a beautiful city and a people who yearn for independence. This administration will never have the courage to defend it." He gave Burr an appraising look. "If you were president, if that should come in time, yes, you have the plain guts and the skills to hold it. But no one else, not another soul in America. It's an empire lying fallow; it only awaits the man who has the range of vision to lead it to its natural future—independence. That man, supported by military force, can know greatness."

He paused, as if to let that sink in, and Burr heard a coarsening note in his voice. "Florida and Texas— clearly ours by terms of the Louisiana Purchase. But will this administration have the courage to demand it, take it if Spain resists? I doubt it. And yet Spain is weak, its empire is moribund, it has only handfuls of soldiers in the Americas. Opportunity that cries out to be grasped."

Wilkinson's lips were parted, his breathing heavy, his gaze fixed on Burr's eyes. "An empire . . . for remember, just down the road a thousand miles or so lies Mexico, vulnerable, defenseless, its mines pouring out their golden stream." A long pause. "Mexico yearns to be taken as a woman hungers for a man . . ."

Then he relaxed, smiling. "You should go west, Aaron. See for yourself. Drift downstream and absorb possibilities."

"Perhaps I will," Burr said slowly. The talk had stirred something deep in him. But he shook his head: he had crossed a bridge and was a new man with new plans to rule a nation. Still . . .

Wilkinson, as if recognizing this shift of thinking, stood to go. His voice was light and yet somehow charged as he said, "Remember, Aaron, the West is a plum waiting to be plucked and Mexico is the pot of gold at the end of the rainbow."

He shrugged into his coat and clapped on his hat. And

said, easy as a feather in the breeze, "Well, old friend, I hope New York works out as you expect."

Even the possibility that it should disappoint him plus the note of doubt he heard in Jim's voice brought a draft of icy air into the room. "You question my chances?"

"No, no, not really. It's just that I hear Hamilton is striking hip and thigh. But I have faith in you, Aaron."

Burr lay awake long into the dark night, the wine heavy in his head. Hamilton . . . well, he would take care of Hamilton. But empire . . . God, that was a stirring thought, moved into a whole new range of possibility. Trust old Jim to come up with something grand. That would be king of a whole different order, wouldn't it, not running every four years, not worrying about the public as one ruled by edict and off with the heads of those who objected. . . . Eventually he drifted off, crowns of Mexican gold spinning in his mind.

FIVE

Washington, fall 1803

She was nervous, always was when one of her huge entertainments started. So much could go wrong at an open house, things certain to arise to confound you. A familiar tremor ran through her chest. It was here-we-go, never quite ready, a dozen things still up in the air, guests pouring through the door, too late to worry now. All right! She straightened her shoulders, adjusted her gown, affixed her smile, and bore down on the latest of the entertainments for which she was becoming known.

Guests flowed into the oval room, turning eagerly to the waiters, whose trays held Champagne and Madeira and whiskey punch as well as a wide assortment of the savories and canapés that Chef Julien was turning out at top speed in the scullery below, bellows keeping the ovens glowing. She had stripped the best homes in Washington of a dozen servants dressed in formal livery to supplement the regular staff. A contented murmur soon became a roar.

It was a little after one in the afternoon; the party would run well into darkness. She saw the president stroll into the oval drawing room; receiving lines had gone the way of Federalist pomp in the Jefferson administration, but still, he was the president and there was an inescapable formality as he moved in a little cluster with his cabinet, Albert Gallatin of treasury, Henry Dearborn of the War Department and the others. She saw Jimmy lagging a little behind with that glum look he took on when with relative strangers. How could he lose so completely the cheerful conviviality he presented to small groups of friends?

She knew her open houses were important and went far beyond mere social contact. Where else could junior congressmen and senators, to say nothing of clerks, judges, military officers, and men of affairs in Washington who were trying to make a city of this village on the Potomac get to hear the president's thinking straight from his mouth? She watched Tom move from group to group, never pausing long but never leaving abruptly, very much in command, cabinet members bowing, chatting, Jimmy somewhat morose but obviously trying.

The multiple rooms through which guests spread looked better now, partly because attention was focused on people, on food and drink, on the nervous clamor of conversation with the eager, sweaty scent of ambition strong as musk. But her efforts had worked wonders too, banners, drapes, flags from France and the United States linked on this great transfer of territory celebration. She could see all its faults but she had worked desperately, less to hide flaws than to draw attention away from them. Inside finishing was rough, there was no help for that, and the ceremonial hall on the east end where Mrs. Adams had hung presidential laundry was still unfinished. Tom planned wings for the building because he considered it too small for its grounds, architect manqué that he was. But the interior—well, that was a battle she wouldn't win with Tom, nor would she ever subject herself again to his patronizing explanations of finances. But he would deal with the outside because he liked building things while if she were just free to deal with the inside—and again she felt that stirring of ambition that marked her as surely as it marked everyone else in Washington. Unseemly it might be but certainly it was there.

Mr. Lemaire, the chief steward, appeared in a doorway, his dark eyes alert, and in a moment snapped his fingers to direct a servant to an empty glass in a congressman's hand. Etienne had come from France to take charge of domestic arrangements when Tom became president, while she was designated the widower president's official hostess. Tom in his diffidence had done nothing to clarify the inherent conflict, so with their first big banquet in preparation she had gone down to the kitchen and taken Mr. Lemaire head-on. A bit of blood was shed, in French and in English, and when it was done there was no doubt who would control. Of course, that was long past now; they had become friends and she often interceded with the penurious president to get the chief steward what he felt a properly staffed house must have. Now he came quickly to her side.

"A success already, I believe, Madame—they are eating like hogs, if that is an appropriate American expression."

"Quite appropriate," she said, watching a congressman balance a half dozen savories on his left arm and snatch them up with his teeth between droughts of whiskey punch. With Etienne beside her, impeccable in black suit and white cravat—he was a handsome man a little shorter than she with brown hair falling to his shoulders—she hurried to the state dining room where sawhorse tables held crystal bowls of Champagne punch and whiskey punch. A silver tureen with a silver ladle stood beside the latter; it was full of clear corn liquor to spike the punch for legislators who wanted drink to match their temperaments. A man with a corkscrew was opening Madeira and she heard Champagne corks pop. Trays of polished glasses were rotating up from below where a black woman who was touched by the furies and couldn't speak intelligibly but was the soul of goodness was at her washtubs. Dolley congratulated Etienne as some budding crisis drew him off.

She drifted from the big dining room through the rectangular drawing room beside it to the fine oval room with its blue furniture. The sun was shining and some guests were on the terrace, which offered a magnificent view of the Potomac beyond the swamps. She saw Maggie Smith and her husband whose *National Intelligencer* was an administration mainstay. There was Sam Smith, an old friend and ardent Democrat now representing Maryland in the Senate, deep in conversation with Senator Ross of Pennsylvania, who had supported them on Louisiana, Federalist though he was. Mr. Bayard of Delaware who'd played such a part when Aaron tried to steal it all was examining a painting with a skeptical eye. There was a stir at the door and she turned to see the tall, emaciated John Randolph, that strange but brilliant Virginian who more or less ran the Congress from the chair of Ways and Means—and she saw he had brought his dogs! Beautiful hounds—she was enough of a countrywoman to know a good hound when she saw one—but at a party? It was disgusting—more and more people were doubting his sanity these days and she could see why.

Ned Thornton, the handsome British chargé, bowed. "Would it be impertinent to observe that you are clearly the most striking woman here?"

She laughed. "An acceptable impertinence, my dear sir." She wore a gown of lime green silk with milky pearls and a turban of the same lime green, and had spent hours in preparation. Ned was always pleasant though he listened too much to Federalists who assiduously courted the British. From an occasional undiplomatic glint in his eye she suspected he held Americans in general contempt. But what else could you expect in this day and age from a Briton reared in the ruling classes?

"You seem unusually ebullient today, Ned."

"Yes, for I am going home. Ordered to return to London." But his expression went suddenly somber and he sighed. "A patriot wants to be close to the action and my country faces terrible peril—the insane ambitions of a man who wants to rule the world."

She didn't answer. She had no position and yet had come to find herself a quasi-official, so to speak, and she had learned to mind her words. Whatever fear and outrage Britain might feel for France and vice versa, the U.S. was determinedly neutral.

As if understanding that he'd overstepped, Thornton's public smile returned as he said, "But I will miss these soirees given under your hand."

"We'll miss you, too, Ned."

"You're too kind. But my replacement carries ambassador rank and that certainly will please Mr. Madison."

Indeed. It rankled a bit that Britain had thought no more of us than to give us a young chargé. A full ambassador would be a welcome change and certainly our due.

"Yes," Ned said, "Mr. Anthony Merry. I look forward to present-ing him."

She smiled. "Mr. Merry. May he live up to his name."

Again that glint in his eye. "I'm told his nickname in the Foreign Office is 'Toujours Gai.' "

But the glint had warned her. "An ironic description?"

He gave her a quick look—and blushed! He'd outsmarted himself, and left little to look forward to in Mr. Merry.

She heard the president's voice behind her. "Ah, Ned, you come to help us celebrate our magnificent acquisition. Half a continent, my dear fellow—changes everything, eh?"

A loaded comment, Dolley knew. For all the Americans' bluster and all the dire consequences they had said would befall France on the Mississippi, they really had just been trying to make sure that the river couldn't be closed. No one had given a thought to the vast range of uncharted country that lay beyond the river and reached at least to the mountains said to tower far to the west. Of course, Mr. Jefferson was saying in deceptively casual fashion, everyone knew that American settlers ultimately must sweep west to the Pacific and dominate the future, but Meriwether Lewis and Captain Clark now in winter camp on the Mississippi ready to march at spring's first thaw gave the matter fresh immediacy. Mention of the young explorer called her sister to mind for an episode involving them both and just then Anna came into the room with her husband-to-be and hurried to Dolley's side. "You'll see," Mr. Jefferson was saying, "Meriwether Lewis will shape the history of this century. He will make us a continental nation."

"I'm sure American destiny is grand," Thornton said quickly, "but my sovereign would insist that I remind you that Great Britain is the dominant power in the West. Spain barely holds California. In the end, the western coast of North America will be British, an extension of Canada."

Mr. Jefferson laughed and clapped Thornton on the shoulder. "Oh, Ned, I fear you're becoming a tease. Our own claim is stronger than Britain's, by far—our own Captain Gray sailed the merchant brig *Columbia* into the dominant river and named it for his vessel. When Captain Lewis crosses those storied mountains and comes down the Columbia a new era will be born."

Thornton's mouth flew open but before he could speak the president said smoothly, "Come, come, dear friend, we mustn't fall into debate on so festive an occasion. You must tell me of your successor, but first I understand that little mare of yours has foaled. All went well, did it?" And he led the chargé off arm-in-arm.

"I thought he was going to give his western lecture again," Anna said. Both men had bowed when she approached and she had given them a neat little curtsy. "Do you remember that dinner?"

"When he raved about the West until the dessert was spoiled? Indeed I do. I remember you flirting with Captain Lewis, too."

Anna gave her a wise smile and didn't answer. The captain was still the president's secretary then and Dolley had grown fond of him. But he was no match for her clever little sister, and she had a vague feeling that Anna had taken advantage of him. But now he was set for a march to what might be glory or might be his finale. Everyone was painfully aware that Lewis and Clark and all their men might disappear forever.

Danny Mobry drifted by as Anna turned to greet someone. Danny said she would leave for New Orleans within the fortnight. She was a tall, handsome woman, her hair a cap of black curls, Irish by ancestry but a New Orleans girl born and bred, which explained her lingering French accent.

"You'll be the toast of the city now that it's American," Dolley said. "You can explain the newcomer's habits."

A shadow seemed to fall across Danny's face. Of course nothing was easy for a woman trying to run a shipping business in a man's seafaring world, but Dolley saw there was more to it than that. "Explain the Americans?" Danny said. She looked more lonely than ever. "The people there may not react very well." Then her expression changed and she stepped closer. Her voice fell to a whisper. "We must talk, Dolley. Not here—but New Orleans can turn into a great danger. A disaster."

"Oh, Danny—"

"Listen to me, Dolley. I'm not a fool. You've called on me more than once and I've served my new country. I'm telling you, New Orleans is much more dangerous than anyone seems to think." And she added, "Who else can I talk to?"

All right; Danny had earned her voice. She'd had a powerful role in upsetting Aaron's ugly plans and in the midst of the drama had watched her husband die on the rotunda floor even as the final vote that gave Jefferson the election echoed in the air. And the messages she had carried to an uncle in New Orleans who controlled much of the province's trade had certainly been helpful in Jimmy's triumph over Napoleon.

"All right," she said. "Sunday afternoon around two."

A loud crash—from the corner of her eye she caught the image of a burly man backing into a waiter, the tray tilting, the glasses sliding, cascading in a shaft of sunlight, crashing . . .

"Etienne," she called, clapping her hands.

As that small disaster was corrected she saw Aaron come into the oval room looking as if he couldn't imagine his presence causing anything but pleasure. Splendidly turned out, as always, in a dark gray suit that obviously was of London wool and cut to the latest design, lace ruffles and cravat in snowy linen, sheer white hose of fine silk, sterling buckles—she wished again that she could get Jimmy to pay some attention to fashion. Wearing those black suits that looked as if his father had worn them—following fashion, he said, was following frippery.

"You look beautiful," she said.

"Now, now," he said, "you had your chance with me."

"And thank God I didn't take it."

He laughed, and then, something warm and kindly in his tone, said, "You've come a long way, dear girl, and you radiate happiness. Jimmy has done well by you and I congratulate you both. He and I have our differences, but what are they, after all, in the face of true love and happiness?"

She smiled. "Gracefully said, sir."

Then, spoiling it, he added, "Though you might have gone further with me." In fact, all he'd offered her was the opportunity to go to bed with him.

"I've gone far enough to suit me, Aaron."

"Sorry," he said. "That just slipped out. But I was thinking, Jimmy won't follow his good friend into this house."

"We'll have to wait and see, won't we?"

"Oh, I suppose, but the point is, I'm going back to New York. I'll have a hand to play, and then—well, may the best man win."

She smiled. "Then Jimmy should have no trouble."

He laughed out loud. "Touché, dear girl. I should know better than to joust with you. Anyway, you're as beautiful as ever and I congratulate you on a happy marriage."

Oh, my, she did like Aaron! For Jimmy honor stood unmovable as a mountain; for Aaron it slipped and slid, but there was no denying his charm. She watched him go striding about the room bowing and shaking hands as if he were the guest of honor. The president and Jimmy too, if truth be told, had shown something vengeful and not to their credit in humiliating Aaron, transgressor though he was. Perhaps they had increased the danger, too. Their courtship of Governor Clinton was another humiliation made public. But Aaron might yet have a real voice in 1808. She remembered the old political maxim: you never know who may come back to haunt you.

General Wilkinson strode into the room. She didn't like Wilkinson, who would be leaving shortly for New Orleans to receive the vast province for the United States. He was gross and obsequious, his round and

smiling face at first cheery and boyish but on closer expression dissipated, the expression in his eyes sly. And
that uniform! Fancy to a fault, it hardly suggested the
democratic air Tom sought to project. There were rumors of his being too close to the Spanish—indeed, that
he was in their pay. Jimmy told her not to listen to gossip, but she rather liked gossip—it added such interesting dimensions.

Just then in an odd intuitive flash she had a strong impression that Wilkinson and Aaron purposely avoided
each other. Aaron had been in an opposite room and entered from that side as Wilkinson appeared. They might
have collided but each turned sharply away. Strange and,
she supposed, meaningless. Then, interesting again, she
saw that the general's turn had brought him directly before Danny. He bowed, she nodded, they passed on and
again, her expression of distaste so marked that Dolley
thought she could not have mistaken it. New Orleans
currents must run deep.

Etienne Lemaire appeared beside her. "The Champagne is almost exhausted, Madame. Shall I—"

"Let's let it run out, Etienne. They'll have to go home
sometime and maybe that will start them." She followed
him into the state dining room to make sure the whiskey
punch was in good supply, knowing that that was what
most men in Washington wanted to drink, with plenty of
corn liquor on the side to intensify its impact. When she
returned to the oval room she saw Aaron deep in conversation with Danny Mobry. Danny's strained look seemed
to have passed. Ah, me; Aaron did have that effect on
women. She hoped Danny knew what she was doing in
encouraging Aaron, and then decided that was foolish.
Danny was a widow in her thirties and if she chose to
dally with one of the most charming men in America, so
be it.

But the next time she was close to Danny she whispered, "On guard, dear; he'll break your heart if you give him a chance."

Danny laughed. "He is a charmer, isn't he? I might just get carried away and give him that chance."

"Don't say you weren't warned."

There was Mr. Wagner in his shabby suit with an untouched Champagne flute in hand. He was alone and looked somehow forlorn and her impulse was to go speak to him. But he was always cool to her as if the very presence of the secretary's lady was an imposition, so he could be lonely alone.

She saw the new clerk, Jaycee Barlow, looking at General Wilkinson with an expression that was somehow frightening, so bleak and hostile and full of a raw urgent force did it seem. Then she remembered that he was a soldier, and she had heard that the rank and file hated Wilkinson for his cruelties and his posturing. She understood that but it also struck her that she wouldn't want Barlow for an enemy.

A few minutes later she found herself at the clerk's side and he seemed a different man. He bowed deeply and asked immediately if he could get her Champagne. She shook her head and asked how he found Washington.

He hesitated, looking about the room, then gave a brilliant smile, and said, "Exciting. Vivid. Very different from Fort Massac, certainly, very different."

She remembered Jimmy saying that Barlow wanted to enter Congress from Virginia. "How does politics strike you now?"

"Very well, thank you, ma'am. I think I might fit right in. Seems rather like the army. The maneuvering, I mean. This, though, this is spectacular—" He threw out his hands, palms up, widened his eyes theatrically and laughed, and immediately she saw a charm that had nothing to do with looks.

She set off on her rounds but caught occasional

glimpses of Barlow talking to another woman—he seemed to have met everyone or at least every woman there. Presently she saw him deep in conversation with Danny Mobry. Both of them looked surprisingly serious and then Danny exploded in laughter and Barlow stood with his arms crossed, watching her and smiling.

She saw young Mr. Adams, the new Federalist senator from Massachusetts, slender, handsome, features sculpted as if from clay. She wondered how such a face would weather the years; certainly his father, the former president, fine man though he was, offered no beauty of countenance. Perhaps his mother, visage sharp as a blade today with a temper that seemed to match, had been a youthful beauty. Dolley's heart warmed to Mr. Adams—he had arrived too late to vote on the Louisiana Purchase but announced that he supported it and would have voted for it. Since every other Federalist had voted nay, John Quincy's statement brought much pleasure to Democrats and strident outrage to his fellow Federalists. Timothy Pickering, former secretary of state and now the other Massachusetts senator—he'd been instrumental along with Alexander Hamilton in destroying Mr. Adams's presidency—was saying everywhere that John Quincy Adams's would be tarred and feathered in Boston for his apostasy.

Then with some consternation she saw Mr. Pickering himself in the state dining room lading corn liquor into his whiskey punch. He was a tall, angular man, no longer young, with a long pendant nose and what appeared to be a habitual scowl. He took a pull on his glass, pursed his lips, and then ladled in more. And turned in her direction, Mr. Adams's direction. Collision became inevitable and she saw that pride would let neither avoid it. She saw Adams's back stiffen. Pickering's face contorted and his lips moved in what she was sure was a snarl.

Quickly she stepped close and in a low and intense voice said, "Not here, gentlemen, not here."

Adams, instantly abashed, bowed, and said, "Oh, madam, we do apologize."

"Speak for yourself, young man," Pickering snapped. "I apologize to no one in this house or of this persuasion." He spun on Dolley, his cheeks gone startlingly red. "Mr. Adams has destroyed himself in supporting Mr. Jefferson's insane purchase."

"That is enough, sir!" she said sharply.

"And you, madam," his voice rising, "doubtless you imagine you and your husband will reside in this house, but I assure you it will not happen. Louisiana will be the destruction of the Democrats and it will be up to the great Federalist party to right the ship of state and bail it out and set it on course."

Pickering's tall frame went well with his striking face; he had the gleam of a fanatic about him and headed a Federalist division that dreamed of splitting off New England into a new country under British protection—secession. She forced a smile that she knew was strained, and said, "On the basis of courtesy rather than power, I demand not another quarreling word. This is a party, gentlemen!"

Pickering wore one of the old wigs now going out of fashion. He bowed. "Very well, madam," he said. "I believe your comments are well taken."

Democrats had their own extremists of whom John Randolph was the leader, that strange man with his dogs. She spied him in the oval room, the dogs beside him. He made constant trouble with his demands that the most extreme Democratic rhetoric be carried out to the letter. But Tom and Jimmy hadn't been elected as extremists—they held policy toward the middle, which suited most Americans, keeping Federalist institutions that proved useful but bending them toward opening that included everyone—*good God*!

One of those dogs had just urinated on a chair! Lifted

his leg and sent a golden stream onto the cushion and puddling down to the carpet. It was just too much!

"Mr. Randolph," she said, closing on him, "please remove these animals immediately."

Startled, he goggled at her. "Eh?" He towered over her, his body thin as a sapling, his once handsome face so emaciated as to seem a skull. He was said to be ill in body and head and was famous for his vituperation though she knew he was too much a Virginia gentleman to use it on her.

"That dog just wet the chair," she said.

"Oh, no. He wouldn't do such a thing."

"I saw him! Here—" She seized his hand, pressed it to the wet chair. He snatched it away as if burned.

"Well, dogs will be dogs."

"Let them be dogs elsewhere. Now!"

He stiffened. "Where my dogs are not welcome, I am not welcome."

"Remove them or I'll have them removed."

He glared at her. "Very well, madam," he said at last. "But I see you consider yourself a significant figure in this house. I advise you not to let it go to your head—I can assure you your husband will never occupy these halls. His policies are obscenities, blasphemies, worse than the droppings of my dogs. You'll see—with this magnificent purchase the Democrats will be so strong that the people will cry out for purity of party. Trimmers, Federalists-in-disguise, men fearful of their own shadows will be out in favor of a real Democrat! And you, madam, will be out with them!"

"Remove your dogs, Mr. Randolph," she said.

Arms clenched across her chest, she stood looking from a window at cows moving slowly up toward the barn, trying to control her anger and her breathing. At last, with a deep breath and a sigh and a fresh smile, she turned back to the mob and to her great pleasure saw Benjamin Latrobe across the room rubbing his fingers along the inside of a window frame, his expression thoughtful. A somewhat round man about her age with artist's eyes, he was an architect from London with a flare for interior design; he was central to her plans for the house and she had grown fond of him. But before she could join him she saw Sam Smith, the burly Marylander, glaring at a fellow senator of the Federalist persuasion whose name she'd forgotten. Then, tilting forward, he jabbed the other in the chest, and boomed, "Well, by God, I say Florida and doubtless Texas too are part of the Louisiana Purchase and by every right, we should have them! That's what the Mobile Act means, sir—we assert our dominance over Florida at least as far as from the Mississippi to Mobile."

It was unfortunate party talk, and sure enough, here came the natty little Spanish ambassador, the Marquis de Yrujo, who had married Sally McKean, daughter of Pennsylvania's governor and one of Dolley's oldest friends. Sally seemed much in love with him, which surprised Dolley because he seemed a blustering little popinjay to her. As luck would have it he was close enough to hear Sam bray and rushed to assure him in ringing tones that Florida belonged to Spain now and forever, as did Texas. "The Mobile Act amounts to a declaration of war on Spain," Mr. Yrujo shouted. "I assure you it will be so regarded!"

Oh, my. Of course the purchase included Florida, as the Mobile Act proclaimed, but Jimmy said there was no chance we would push it—we were too busy for war with Spain. But naturally Sam blew up and in the exchange of pleasantries it began to seem it would be pistols on the lawn. Eventually Sam steadied and Sally led the popinjay away.

Breath slowing, Dolley turned back to Mr. Latrobe. He smiled when he saw her; he shared her passion for this great house and could see its potential for magnificence.

"You see, madam," he said, hand on the window frame, "this must be reworked entirely, stripped and re-painted, with new cabinetry work, too, insets and so forth. And then, delicate offset colors, cream or the palest gray-green to soften the sharp white, which itself could profit from a touch of cream. . . ." She loved such talk, and my goodness, if she and Jimmy ever lived in this house, what they could do. She and Mr. Latrobe.

Madison had retreated to a corner where he stood watching the crowd, the Champagne in the glass in his hand scarcely touched. There was Dolley circulating, checking, charming, always smiling, a quip or a greeting for everyone. He liked to watch her, that free, easy, fresh spirit. She did, in fact, seem to know everyone and surmounted the political differences that unhorsed so many alliances, let alone friendships. Apparently she'd had some trouble with John Randolph and he had been about to intervene when he saw John leaving with those damned dogs. He rather hoped she had thrown the troublesome Randolph out—what he deserved for bringing those animals.

Abruptly the British envoy, young Mr. Thornton, appeared beside him. They chatted a moment on his posting home and his replacement, who sounded a bit of a mixed bag. Then, subtly shifting position so that his back was to the room, his moving lips not visible, he said with an oddly tentative note, "I—well, I've enjoyed America. I know you feel I'm too much with Federalists—"

"Find them comfortable, I don't doubt, their aristocratic tendencies and all."

Thornton chuckled. "Yes, sir, more or less. I—well,

would you forgive the impertinence of a bit of advice?"

What in the world? "Of course," Madison said.

"Off the record?"

Madison nodded and the envoy's voice dropped lower still as he said, "Then, sir, I urge you to take the war now resuming in Europe utterly seriously. It will be a fight to the death and Britain will never give in. If the French cross the Channel we will fight from house to house, hedgerow to hedgerow, we will never yield. So, you see, we will do whatever we must to whomever we must— whomever!—and it would be very wise not to step in our way at this moment when civilization hangs in the balance before the barbarian's war machine."

The bluntness of this outburst was startling. Madison knew the war in Europe was proceeding on a whole new scale. Past wars had stumbled on for decades, but this had a new ferocity. It had started with terrified monarchs in neighboring countries moving to squelch the French Revolution just as enthusiastic revolutionaries decided to carry their vision of equality to the masses in Europe by force, set them all free and give them the French manner.

Out of fighting that raged across Europe the Corsican military genius Bonaparte had risen to seize power in France. He had introduced numerous and commendable social reforms in the midst of police-state rule—none of which was any of America's business—but now he did seem to hunger to rule the world. Already he was preparing to name himself emperor of most of Europe. Yes, both sides had paused in 1801 in a makeshift peace, but that had proved to be mere breathing space as war ignited again, coals tossed on dry tinder. Abandoning his Louisiana dreams had, among other things, left Napoleon free to pursue the conquest of Europe.

"Everything depends on our navy," Ned said. "So it will never accept desertion and will never give up the right to stop ships and search them for its deserters. Never."

"But you take our citizens too. Ten to one, our people against actual proven deserters."

"Yes, but we return them when shown they are bona fide Americans."

"After they've given years of service under the most brutal conditions."

A long pause. "This is unofficial, remember," Thornton said.

When Madison nodded, the Briton said, "You're right. It is a hard policy. But it is essential to our survival. So my point is that like it or not, it will get harder. Much harder. My guess is that soon you will see increasing restrictions on trade, more seizures of cargoes that we deem contraband, and the definition of contraband will grow steadily wider. . . . In other words, Mr. Madison, be ready for dangerous times."

There was a long moment of silence. Then with a slight bow, Madison said, "Thank you, Mr. Thornton."

Such a conversation demanded an immediate report to the president. By chance, Dolley joined them as he finished.

"Well," Jefferson said, "they're putting relations on a whole new footing. So short-sighted—they can't win their war without our trade."

Yes! Madison had lived with this conviction for twenty years. It was all so clear to him, and equally so that the British were simply too arrogant to grasp the reality. Blinded by arrogance—and little America must suffer on that account. Someday . . .

"Suppose we send Jim Monroe over to London to make these realities clear to them?" the president said. "He's doing little enough in Paris, I must say." A late arrival on the Louisiana matter, he'd been there ever since squabbling with Robert Livingston, the regular ambassador, over who deserved credit for the purchase. At least sending him to London might ease a tiff that was becoming embarrassingly public.

"I'll write him," the president said. "Let him try to make them see, they simply must end the impressment outrage. Stealing our men—criminal kidnapping, no lesser word will do. You'd think they were Barbary pirates!" He looked across the room, shaking his head. "They're so contemptuous—we're still just errant colonials to them."

There was another long pause. Madison kept his silence. Dolley's mouth opened and he raised a hand to quiet her. Then he heard Tom say, voice so low it was almost inaudible, "Sooner or later we'll have to fight them, you know. We can't accept their abuse forever, no matter their reasons."

"Try trade sanctions first," Madison said.

"Of course. But you know, Jimmy, they've never understood and I don't know that they ever will. So it will come to fighting."

"Later rather than sooner," Madison said. The Royal Navy had six hundred capital ships and one or two new ones came off the ways every week.

The president gave a crooked smile. "On your watch rather than mine, I hope," he said. "Which in fact might begin next year. Your watch, I mean."

Next year? Madison stared at him. They'd had no formal discussion on his standing for reelection in 1804 but everyone had assumed he would run again and possibly into the future as well; there were no rules except General Washington's precedent of two terms. Still, the president made no secret of his hatred for this service. His mind was so vastly capacious, running in so many directions, that public posts with all their mundane demands weighed on him. It had been his slowness in accepting President Washington's invitation to run the State De-

partment that had crystallized the old gentleman's dislike for him, which Jefferson had reciprocated fully.

But this sudden remark shook Madison "No, sir," he
said sharply. "You must run next year, it's what everyone—"

"Oh, bother everyone!" Tom cried. "I am so sick of
this gilded cage. My daughters need me—or I need
them—and how long is it to go on? Monticello needs
me—I have incredible plans for it. Do you realize how
much of my life I've given to public service? I'm getting
old, I want to savor what's left . . ."

But it wouldn't work. Madison knew this by instinct,
not withstanding a sudden surge of hidden ambition that
left him somewhat breathless. He shook his head. Tom
was still the personification of the new democracy and
the public saw the Louisiana Purchase of which it approved so raptly as solely his work. Were he to step
down now anything might happen. At last Tom threw up
his hands.

"All right, I'll run again but believe me, never again.
In 1808 it'll be up to you because *I* won't be here."

Madison didn't answer because he couldn't. Part of
him said he wasn't presidential material and another part
demanded, Who the devil could say any such thing? Of
course he was prepared. The intensity of his feeling embarrassed him—in fact, shamed him. But he knew the
feeling was real. Then, oddly, he saw the same fire in his
wife's eyes though she didn't speak. It were almost as if
she couldn't, as if she were frozen in some intensity of
feeling, and then she saw some crisis developing across
the room and whirled away.

No more was said about the presidency; no more
needed to be said. Madison stood beside his tall mentor
and they watched the circulating crowd. Aaron Burr
seemed in high style, his dress perfect in a way that
Madison couldn't imagine imitating, his manner exuding

charm, his laugh light and easy, his supply of quips and gallantry seemingly inexhaustible.

"Look at him," the president said. "Buzzing about like a bee visiting one flower after another." Then, with no change in tone, he added, "Albert thinks Burr is our greatest danger." It was the first reference he had made to the harsh cabinet meeting. In the same meditative tone he added, "I should think the British or the Spanish or the Federalists might be so considered, but Albert was very strong on his point. What do you think, Jimmy?"

Madison watched Aaron with his smooth assurance, that obdurate quality, sort of a sense of potential waiting to burst into the open—glittering intellect was not his strength but the capacity to seize the moment and lead the charge he had shown in the war were just as striking today.

"Yes," he said slowly, "I think he well could be. . . ."

Six

Washington, fall 1803

Madison was on the Hill seeking a clarifying sentence in a bill soon to go to the vote in the Senate. That settled, he knew he should pay a courtesy visit to John Randolph, the Ways and Means chairman on the House side to whose rapier tongue the Speaker had more or less abdicated. There was a chill in the air this morning and he carried his coat slung over his arm and had donned woolen hose with his plain black suit and low boots against the mud. He had considered and rejected the idea of wearing a wig for the sake of formality. Seeing Randolph was always tedious and to fortify himself and perhaps delay the moment he paused at a tea stand in the rotunda. The proprietor had his pot over a charcoal brazier on a cart and had set up a three-sided counter of boards, corners anchored by towering racks of cakes.

He took the hot cup with its fragrant steam, refused the dollop of whiskey naturally offered, looked at the cakes, which a couple of flies were exploring, and decided against and sipped his tea with easy contentment. Then several congressmen whom he knew slightly—all had been at the open house—called for tea and to give them room Madison stepped around the corner of the counter, past the cake stand.

"Good morning, Jimmy."

Startled, he recognized the voice before he turned. Aaron Burr.

"Why, Aaron—I didn't—didn't—"

"Oh, Jimmy, I'm likely to pop up in all sorts of unexpected places."

Madison felt off balance, stumbling. What had Aaron meant? If anything. It had been a long time, years, perhaps, since he'd talked substantively to Burr. What was there to say, after all, when cutting him from power had said everything?

Aaron brushed cake crumbs from his waistcoat. He clicked his cup on the counter and the proprietor hastened to refill it. "Here we have refuge from tedium," he said lightly. "High though the honor is to sit as president of the Senate, listening to the endless drone of little men is weariness personified. John Adams in his vice-presidential term, you'll recall, infuriated everyone by insisting on entering the debate. But I restrain myself—having already infuriated everyone who counts."

The man was playing with him and Madison felt strangely tongue-tied.

"And you, Jimmy? You're well, I take it? I spoke to Dolley at her open house—her charm does grow year by year, don't you agree? I congratulated her on a happy marriage."

"It has been happy," Madison said.

Abruptly Aaron drained his cup and set it down with a click. "I must be off, Jimmy. Duty calls." He laughed, low and sardonic. "But I expect we will have many encounters in the future. I am not in the least finished, you see."

Madison was left alone at the tea counter, cup growing

cold, pondering the genuine menace he had sensed in Aaron's words.

"Well, Mr. Madison," John Randolph said, voice rising, "welcome to Capitol Hill. Thank you for doing me the signal honor of looking in on me, actually standing here in my very own office, lowering yourself to my level, sunken reprobate that I am." He was on his feet, and he snatched up the whip lying on his desk and flexed it in both hands. His three hounds stood alertly, a growl starting deep in the throat of the one nearest Madison. Randolph's voice rose to a near scream. "You understand, I'm the more honored, the more flattered, the more prepared to grovel in gratitude for this mark of forgiveness only a fortnight since I was ejected from the executive mansion! Hurled out, sir, my poor innocent hounds with me, bade never to darken the great man's door again. And so soon, so wonderfully soon, here you are in supplication for some favor the need for which should have been considered before the wanton brutality that hurled me into the street—"

He paused, gazing owlishly at Madison. "Or did your lady not inform you of these events?"

As always, Madison's patience was wearing thin. "My lady told me your dog wet a chair," he said.

"Wet? Wet? What do you mean?"

The last of Madison's patience went. "I mean your dog pissed on a chair and Dolley didn't like it and threw you out. Or threw your dogs out and you went with them."

Damn it all . . . Madison had sworn he wouldn't lose his temper and immediately had done so. Maybe the encounter with Burr had unsettled him, but sooner or later Randolph managed to light off most everyone. Always thin, now he was becoming emaciated, Madison thought.

He was a tall, awkward Virginian, his every move clumsy and stumbling, and his once handsome face now was ravaged by who knew what inner demons. He was famous for his vitriol, his rages, his slashing rhetoric. But some of the success they all shared so far was due to Randolph's ability to push crucial legislation through Congress. Still, there was more and more talk that he was going mad and none too slowly at that.

This might have been of small consequence except for his leadership of Democratic extremists who wanted purity of principle without the slightest compromise. Over on the Senate side Sam Smith, their old friend from Maryland, was showing signs of this infection too. It was ridiculous and dangerous, Madison felt. Americans didn't want extremes of left or right, to use the new French term; they were moderate by nature and tended toward the political center. Yet Randolph's force and rhetoric had some of the appeal of the revolutionist storming barricades for his convictions. It could pull in otherwise balanced moderates, and that made him dangerous. This self-generated anger seemed to grow day by day.

"And did your lady also tell you that I gave her fair warning—enjoy the power that you seem to feel managing social frippery bestows on you, power that you abuse against innocent dogs that have no sense of your petty little rules—"

"You feel that dogs should piss where they please, John?"

"Dogs, sir, are dogs. They run true to form because they are honest, which is much more than I can say about Democrats as we know them today. As you and the sacred Mr. Jefferson run them. Caviling, compromising, kissing the enemy's posterior, more Federalist than the Federalists, tail tucked firmly between your legs as you lick the hands of John Adams and Timothy Pickering in vain hopes that they will pat your anxious little head. But they will not, sir! They will never warm to you, lick their boots as you may—that vile creature Jacob Wagner . . . Timothy Pickering's man! And he still has Pickering's collar around his neck! You still defend him!"

Ah, God, here we go again. Jacob Wagner had been chief clerk when Mr. Pickering was secretary of state and busily undermining poor President Adams. A complete picaroon, Randolph had howled from the beginning, by which he meant an advocate of Mr. Pickering in all respects. Of course keeping the highly professional Wagner would mean a ferocious fight with the radicals but the issue went to the heart of the new democracy. The vote in 1800 that put them in office had been cast not so much for Democratic party theory as against Federalist extremes, the vile Alien and Sedition Acts, the insistence on a large army and navy with no enemy in sight. Americans wanted government to hold to a steady, sensible course. So he kept Wagner on duty, fight though it meant.

"John," he said now, trying to keep his voice even, "how many times must we go over this? The Federalists packed government with partisans; are we to be no better than they? And yes, you make complaint of Albert Gallatin at Treasury, but in fact he kept some of the Federalist mechanisms that Alexander Hamilton invented because he found they were necessary. Now, Mr. Wagner, he's been a devoted officer—"

"Of course, of course," Randolph shouted, "because you abandon your own people to follow the Federalist line in hopes they will love you, of course Wagner is happy to seize you by the nose and lead you down that path—"

"Damn it all, John," Madison cried, "nobody leads me—"

"Ah, so it is not Wagner who's the villain—then it

must be your own pusillanimous fear of combat, fear that the big bad Federalists will eat you up!" He was pacing now, the dogs wheeling and turning with him and glaring at Madison as the obvious cause of their master's upset, he flexing his whip—

Crash!

The whip slashed across the desk and papers flew as he shrilled, "Well, let me tell you sir, to the extent your argument ever had any merit—which I deny—today it is empty of weight. Today we are in a new era, an era of great success, an era in which the Democrats can do no wrong." Abruptly his voice fell to a cajoling note. Leaning against his desk, he essayed a smile that gave his emaciated face a death's head look.

"Don't you see?" Again that ghastly smile. "The Louisiana Purchase proved the party's worth, proved its leadership capacity. Who else could have managed that? Federalists with their subservience to Britain? Would Napoleon ever have dealt with such toadies? French eagles would have been marching up the Mississippi this moment if the Federalists had been in charge and you know it!" His voice was going shrill again, the smile vanished as he tapped the whip against the desk like an angry metronome.

"Oh, James," he cried, "you and that gutless leader of yours have success in your hand—and you fear to grasp it. In the people's eyes you can do no wrong. Now is exactly the time to seize opportunity and strike for the true democracy, the true principles that we all stand for. Or, sir"—voice dropping ominously—"that honest Democrats stand for, believe in, those who are not traitors to a magnificent cause, those who don't let fear hobble all their decent impulses." He was pacing again, the big dogs wheeling nervously.

"Discharge that evil malefactor, Mr. Wagner, at once! Today, sir! Shut down the bank—it is a vile manifestation of Mr. Hamilton's mad desire to control everything. As for Mr. Gallatin, hang him from the nearest tree if that's what it takes to wrest this nation's finances from his snakelike coils!"

Radical Democrats saw the Bank of the United States, functioning as the treasury and yet principally owned by private investors, in the same evil terms today that Madison and Jefferson had used at the beginning. But the trouble was that once in power themselves, they had found that the bank stabilized the American economy in a way that was essential to prosperity.

Yet in howling after the bank Randolph had put his finger on the crux of the radical position. What the extremists wanted was a reduction of federal power with weight shifted back to the states. It was the fight over the Constitution all over again. The most radical of them, Randolph and Patrick Henry and many patriots, including James Monroe, if somewhat more moderately, had fought against a constitution that must leach power from the states. As the bank stabilized the national economy it thwarted the radical dream of returning most power to the states.

Then, his manner changing with theatrical suddenness, Randolph flung down the whip, dropped into his chair, tossed a leg over the edge of his desk, and gazed at Madison over tented fingers. One buckled slipper dangled from a toe. "Now, sir," he said, "enough of this folderol. What's this I hear that you're sending Mr. Monroe from Paris to London? Perhaps to favor that vile New Yorker, Mr. Robert R. Livingston, may he rot in hell as he tries to steal credit for the triumph in Paris from our fellow Virginian? Or are there darker reasons?"

Madison fought down sheer rage. Good God! Didn't he have enough problems with Monroe and Livingston at each other's throats without John Randolph complicating—

"Darker reasons, sir! So I suspect and so do all right-thinking Democrats disgusted by the sniveling servility of an administration that fears its own shadow! Now, sir, you should understand that we are coming to stormy weather. Those of us who truly care about democracy have waited patiently for you and your weak-kneed leader to take the initiative and we've waited long enough! From this moment on I put you on notice—and please convey this to him who quakes in his boots at sight of a Federalist—we will drive you and flog you. We will give you no rest. And we will demand an accounting for this dispatch of Mr. Monroe to London. Why, pray tell, such a move?"

Madison was still struggling for control. "You understand the British are stealing our men, seizing our ships, doing their best to inveigle us into their world-range war with France? We need a treaty that—"

"Treaty! With the perfidious British? Don't try my patience, sir—I'll split my gut with laughter! The British will never give up impressment, and what does it matter? Bothers New England shippers, but who cares about them? Federalists to a man. Anyway, they're coining money with their ships, that's why they pay wages that attract British tars to desert. Let them choke on their fat profits, they need nothing more. It's all false, false, false!"

"What the devil do you mean, John?"

"I mean, it's a trick to destroy Mr. Monroe's reputation and deprive him of his triumph in Paris."

Madison stared at him; it was too ridiculous to answer.

"Yes, sir—snatch him from triumph and send him on a fool's errand that must fail. Thus, sir, destroying a competitor."

"Competitor?"

"For the presidency, sir! Don't play innocent. You know that Mr. Monroe is a true believer in the democratic cause. I don't doubt he's heartsick at your surrender to Federalism. Yes, when the time comes you'll find him a voice of power ready to rally Democrats everywhere to the true cause!"

He smiled again, more than ever a death's head. "Which is what I meant when I warned your lady not to raise her hopes of residence in the great house—you, sir, will never occupy those quarters. I know your plan, your hope. Let the great man run one more time, then slide in yourself. But no! It is not to be. Mr. Monroe, warrior of the revolution, successful governor of the largest state— yes, we will bring him in with drums and cymbals, flowers strewn in his path. And I warn you, sir, the party will understand if you set him up for failure now—and the party will make you pay."

Such theatrics! Madison didn't doubt they were serious and dangerous and yet they didn't really exude threat. Nothing like the cold menace he'd heard in Aaron Burr's voice. He stood and gazed down at the gaunt man sprawled in his chair, hounds panting beside him.

"John," he said, "it's remarkable to see so brilliant a man playing the fool. Good day, sir."

SEVEN

Off the Eastern Shore, fall 1803

A breeze was kicking up whitecaps on Chesapeake Bay. Sunlight glittered on flying spray as Captain Mac crowded on sail, the very set of his back radiating pleasure. Danny Mobry leaned against the taffrail, grasping some of what Carl had felt when wind thrummed through rigging and sails cracked like gunfire. God, how she missed him. Should she buy this ship? It was an overwhelming decision. The square-rigged vessel was long and lean, quite unlike conventional wide-bellied merchant craft, newly built, paint and brightwork glowing. She was designed to trade capacity for speed and speed was just what Danny needed in the new circumstances of the New Orleans market. Captain Mac spun her about and they ran up the wind, tighter and tighter, spray flying and starboard rail awash, till Danny felt a shiver of fear. She glanced at the wake boiling in a long stream of bubbles behind.

"Look at her point up," Captain Mac shouted, "I never seen nothing like it!" Later, approaching the builder's wharf, he said, "She'll make up in speed what she lacks in capacity, and pointing to the wind like that she'll run up the river to New Orleans faster'n anything we have."

Everything depended on New Orleans. Carl often had talked of the immense potential in the American West, fertile, beautifully forested, vast areas still filling with people in transition from hunting to agriculture, how it would explode when the Americans finally popped the cork out of the bottle. It was a little frightening to hear the Spanish, who had loomed all-powerful in her girlhood, referred to as a cork awaiting popping, but after her years in America she understood. Now it was popped, the Spanish and the French were going, and surely that meant opportunity for her—but opportunity without danger is rare, and uneasiness quivered at the back of her mind.

How terribly long ago, it seemed now, the day when Carl Mobry had nosed his ship up the Mississippi and into the bayou to lay it alongside the ramshackle pier her father had built. She was Daniella Clark then, named for Daniel Clark, whom she called uncle, the powerful Irishman who'd made himself the merchant prince of New Orleans and then passed his empire to his heir, the second Daniel Clark. That icy gentleman with whom her relations were prickly to say the least, had made himself more French than the French. Carl Mobry was very American, big, bluff, hearty, voice booming and crashing until he'd seen her, and then he'd gone quiet and he'd bowed and murmured something. Half-afraid, half-thrilled, she had known by instinct in the absence of experience that something momentous was going to happen.

While Carl made up a cargo of hides and fur and what little raw sugar was available in those days, he courted her with the single-minded intensity that she found later he brought to anything he wanted. And he left no doubt that he wanted her. It set off something wild and explosive in her, too; shy on the one hand, anxious to plunge on the other, she'd yielded in a fortnight and the priest had married them. They danced all night and friends from miles around staged a chivaree to end all chivarees. When they'd all recovered the crew slipped the lines and the ship stood down to the river. She clung to the rail and watched home and family and all she'd known in her sixteen years vanish as they took the first turn on the long run down to the sea. Carl put his big arm around her shoulders, and whispered, "You'll see, little princess. You'll love America—and New Orleans will always be here." She could remember now how she'd looked up at him through tears and tucked herself against his reassuring bulk.

Fifteen years had passed and twelve had been glorious. She did love America; everything seemed to blossom in the light of freedom just as Carl said. He had owned a small merchant fleet then—he was twice her age—and it had grown to a dozen ships by that awful day when his heart exploded and big, powerful, masterful Carl Mobry fell to the floor in the Capitol rotunda at the very moment the House of Representatives turned thumbs down on Aaron Burr's challenge and delivered the presidency to Thomas Jefferson.

Oh, the agony! He was her life and her joy and in a moment he was gone. She found herself the owner of a dozen ships crewed by men who had never taken orders from a woman. But almost as if he'd foreseen this day Carl had made her part of the business, privy to its intricacies; now the company was his monument and she would neither sell it nor allow anyone else to run it. But there was a much larger issue, too; under the law everywhere, were she to marry, her husband would be the legal owner of her business, and that she could not tolerate. A husband absorbing Carl's business? Never!

But what a fight she'd stirred with her determination

to run her firm on her own! Still, the very need to fight and be strong had seemed to fill the jagged tear in her life and she'd entered it gladly. Half her captains quit and all the merchants who had shipped regularly with Carl refused to risk their cargoes with such a perplexity as a woman in command of rough-handed sailormen. Now, three years later, she was alive but still vulnerable, her fleet reduced and her only real customer a rum distiller in Boston whom the rum cartel had frozen out of the Jamaican sugar market. She could deliver Louisiana sugar heretofore not used commercially that other shippers scarcely understood, and her distiller dealt with her gratefully. It had saved her life but it still was a slender reed.

Clinch had an occasional cargo for her, too, and even more important to her bruised feelings, he seemed to trust her; Clinch Johnson, an odd fellow with a hand in many businesses who somehow had become her friend just as she was discovering that friends were scarce. Odd in appearance and in manner as well, he was a decade her senior, plump and florid with tufts of yellow hair standing out in cowlicks from each side of his square head like little horns. His suit was usually stained and always tight and buttoned rigidly to the collar. When he spoke, which wasn't often, his voice rose scarcely above a whisper. But he smiled readily and she'd gotten used to him. In fact, he was easy company and she came to realize that she liked to talk things through with him. He never told her what to do—that would have ended it all—but he had a way of cocking his eye at the horizon and offering an observation that made good sense.

Now time was running short. American ships would be flocking to New Orleans and she must be there, for as a native she had invaluable advantages. Her command of the French language said New Orleans, not Paris or Marseilles. She knew the bayous, understood life on the river, knew the old families. But at the same time she was American, her English now almost without accent, her business entrenched in the nation's new capital, the nation's leaders her friends. Clinch said there weren't a half dozen Americans who knew New Orleans as well, so insular and guarded had the Spanish kept it.

But to make her move she must have ships available and she certainly wouldn't jeopardize her sugar run. Clinch knew of a shipper who'd failed just before taking delivery of a new vessel from an Annapolis shipwright, Simon Mason. It was available at a knockdown price— twenty thousand dollars.

Now, the vessel gliding toward the wharf, she saw the builder pacing anxiously. He cocked a foot on a bollard as the lines flew over. She swallowed, instinct telling her she must decide now. What would Carl say? Her hands were shaking.

Mr. Mason was tall and not much older than she, slight in build, anxious in manner, worry lines etched in his face. "Like her?" he called impulsively, and she nodded and then wondered if that had deprived her of a bargaining point. But immediately, too eagerly, he offered her a deal—he had keels laid for two more and she could have all three at a price of seventeen-five.

"He's a better builder than businessman," Captain Mac whispered. "She's a good ship. I been over her stem to stern. Deep in the bilges. Man builds good in the bilges, he builds good everywhere. And I never seen one to point up so. Cut days off that river run—get you out of English Turn twice as fast."

English Turn . . . the bête noire of ships running a hundred fifty miles up the river to New Orleans. You made that horseshoe loop against the current only when the wind was just right.

DAVID NEVIN

She was looking over the edge of the cliff. Then she took a deep breath and jumped. "Forty-eight thousand for the three."

"Done, yes, ma'am, thank you ma'am."

Clinch nodded in that slow way of his. It was the next day; she'd taken the night stage. Clinch was gazing out the window of her office on the pier, watching two dogs circle one another.

"See them pups?" he said. "You watch. Smaller one, he's going to jump the big one. Grab the advantage. Early presence in New Orleans, getting out of English Turn ahead of others, that sounds like advantage to me . . ."

Before she could answer there was a snarl and a sharp yelp and then the larger dog fled, the smaller in noisy pursuit.

She felt good. Carl would be proud of her.

The Louisiana Purchase, so she told Clinch, healed another tear in her life as it united her new country with her old. She loved the new, but vestigial clamors of the old came unbidden to her mind—the melodic patois French, the warm and usually scented air, the vast river draining a continent past her doorstep, the laughter and shouts and the click of dice around the marketplace, the floating food odors, the narrow streets of blank-faced houses, plain and austere but opening onto gardens with fish-filled pools, and beyond, handsome rooms with polished tile floors where hospitality was generosity itself.

Now, suddenly, it was American. A new commercial orbit would arise. New Orleans would boom on the trade of the West with Spanish restrictions removed. But her romantic memories hardly fit the new reality. The America she knew was oil, the New Orleans of memory water, and now they must mix. She knew what people there thought of Americans, of whom they had seen only roistering boatmen. They were proud, unduly proud in her view, to say that forty years of Spanish rule had scarcely dented their Frenchness. Now in a finger snap they were to become Americans? Explain the new to the old, Dolley had said. But it was vice versa, too, the gap of knowledge and acceptance equally wide on both sides. Somehow she must show Dolley this reality.

Then just as the papers were signed on the first ship, *Carlito* to be burned in black across its stern, a public sense of trouble in New Orleans broke into the open. Enraged by the Louisiana sale, insisting that Napoleon had promised to return the province if he ever gave it up, the Spanish were full of threats. Rumor said they were moving troops into Florida and Texas preparing for war. Spain wasn't very strong, granted, but strong enough to field an army bigger than the American army. Anyway, Spanish officers in New Orleans had not actually completed the transfer to France and still controlled the province. Suppose they fought to keep it? Where would that leave Mobry Shipping with three new ships for which she'd have no cargoes if war barred her from New Orleans? And what of the sugar runs on which she depended? She had stretched her credit to the limit, bankers always reluctant to back a woman. She had an idea that Clinch might have had a hand in their taking her paper, but he didn't say and she didn't ask.

Still, Carl had never balked at risk. He said it was the wine of life. Neither did she think it would disturb him that she was sailing to a lover. Life had run hot in him; he'd want no less for her. Yet there was a danger in Henri Broussard of New Orleans—she wanted him too much and was too lonely when she was away, which she was most of the time. He had been an ugly little boy when she was a child; he insisted that he'd been in love and it had broken his heart when Carl came and spirited her away. Said for years he'd imagined plans of revenge that

would reclaim her. So when she returned to New Orleans
to reestablish the business that fell apart when Carl died,
she found that his urgent, liquid French swept her back
to childhood and at the same time stirred something very
powerful deep within her. Looking back at the intensity
and vigor he had presented on her first trip as a widow
she saw that it had only been a matter of time before attraction and loneliness overcame her and she invited him
into her *pension* and then into her room and then into her
bed. But he wanted a wife and she would not marry and
give away the business Carl had built and left for her.
And so they were at swords' points, attracted and re-
pelled, angry as often as they were loving. Several times
she had decided to forget him, but there was a force in
him that drew her back. She told herself to be calm but
when she thought of him waiting in New Orleans, loneliness and desire throbbed in equal measure. Had from the
first, when she'd noticed the hair curling on the back of
his strong hands and quickly looked away.

But Henri was merely a troublesome worry; New Orleans and the American reaction to it had become a matter of life and death to her business and hence to her.

"I bought a new ship," she said to Dolley Madison.
"Three of them, in fact."

"My goodness! That's wonderful. Must mean you're
doing well—over the hump, so to speak."

"I will be, I think, I really do—if things go well in
Louisiana."

"And you're afraid they won't." It was statement, not
question.

"Yes . . ."

It was Sunday afternoon a little after two. They were
in Dolley's little study off the main salon where she kept
her desk with its piles of correspondence, her needle-

point and crochet baskets, stacks of novels arrived from Paris, many still in shipping boxes. A half dozen paintings and drawings hung on the walls in no particular order. They were by various artists of varying quality dealing with rural scenes in the Virginia plantation world, black folks cutting hay, an old man with his dog tending a flock of sheep, a racehorse preening with jockey on his back. It struck Danny that what these paintings said was that for all Dolley's cosmopolitan polish, some part of her still turned to the comfort of her girlhood on a long-ago plantation. As Danny still oriented to the banks of a bayou that flowed through swamps to reach the Mississippi.

She drew the comparison, nodding toward the pictures, but Dolley responded with a bare and noncommittal shrug.

"Well," Danny said, suddenly uncomfortable, "be that as it may, I do know the country of my girlhood as you know the Virginia tobacco country, and I'm finding that people here know Louisiana no better than they do the moon."

"They'll soon be learning, I suppose," Dolley murmured.

"Doubtless," Danny said, voice more tart than she'd really intended. "The question is whether they'll learn in time."

With a newly stern set to her mouth, Dolley said, "I think you'd better say what you mean." Dolley was ultra-sensitive to any criticism of Jimmy, and since she considered Jimmy the core of the government, any questioning of government action. Now she said, "Obviously you've come with something on your mind in hopes I'll pass it along, which puts me in an unattractive position to start. So say it, but don't expect a great deal from me, I warn you of that going in."

My, Danny thought, we are high and mighty today.

They were old friends; Dolley's first husband had been Carl's attorney. When yellow fever swept him away it was Danny who dried Dolley's tears. They had seen each other through much turmoil and she didn't feel she needed a sharp tone just now.

"Dolley," she said carefully, "just listen a bit. These are serious matters." She sketched out the people of New Orleans as she knew them, a friendly, humorous people filled with music and laughter but very proud and highly volatile. Pistols were the weapons of duels but sabers, broadswords, machetes, dirks, sword canes, and skinning knives were common tools of warfare along the levee. Bronco boys rode alligators for sport and sometimes the odor of alligator musk from the swamps across the river swept into New Orleans with a pungency to leave one gasping. Jean Lafitte and his brothers and his men were on the streets and welcomed in New Orleans society. And that society, its reverence for the titles of nobility, the elegance of its balls, the excellence of its dinners, rivaled anything to be found in New York and Philadelphia, while Washington was not even in competition. They were sophisticated people, French in language and outlook, Spanish in terms of their governance these forty years, the combination giving them a taste for intrigue, an awareness short of cynicism, perhaps, but highly conscious of human frailty and every man's capacity for self-delusion when it was to his advantage.

"They sound quite striking," Dolley said. What she meant, Danny read, was *Let's move this along.*

"Perhaps pride is the dominant trait," Danny said. She was choosing her words. "Proud of their French heritage, which Spanish rule hasn't touched. Proud of their sophisticated ability to get on with Spanish masters while yielding them little indeed. Firm in their belief that their language is more noble, their culture more sophisticated, their life more charming, their city more beautiful—that, in short, they are the center of the world. In their ignorance, they don't know Americans, and from this, they don't like Americans, and indeed, hold them in contempt."

She saw anger rising in Dolley, and added, "I know, I know—but I am telling you how they are. They didn't want to be American, didn't ask, didn't vote, nothing. They awaken one morning to find they are the newest citizens of the bustling, aggressive country to the north at which they've always sneered."

"So?" Dolley said.

"So I've come to tell you that I believe handled with tact, caution, attention to their attitudes and beliefs, it all may go well. It can go well. The people there are adventurous—treated well, they'll respond to their new country with its wonderful democracy and personal freedoms. But Dolley, you're not treating them well."

"In what respect?"

Danny shriveled a little at the coolness of tone and then lurched on. She understood General Wilkinson headed the army and must be on hand, but Dolley should know that he was held in contempt in New Orleans, where he visited frequently for ostensible trading ventures and often was drunk. The governor sent to take charge, William Claiborne—

"He's governor of Mississippi Territory close by," Dolley said, "and he's said to be competent."

"Not by people in New Orleans. He's young in a society that honors age and he speaks no French. How is he to talk to them?"

"I suppose it will work out."

"Yes, perhaps—but Dolley, much more important, to make them citizens against their will but deny them the rights of citizens, this is a recipe for trouble."

"What rights?"

"Those of a citizen. Self-government. The right to

vote. The right not to be taxed without representation."
She raced on. "I asked Jimmy at the open house. He had
asked me if I thought they would resist. I said no—
they'll be thrilled to enter the Union as a new state with
all a state's rights and privileges, elect congressmen and
senators—and he broke in to say none of that will happen. Do you know the government that is planned?"

Dolley nodded.

"So you know—you appoint this governor who
doesn't speak the language, he names a governing council of his own choice, it promulgates laws but he can veto
them at will and his veto can't be overridden, he can discharge any or all of the council members the moment
they displease him and then just rule by fiat for as long as
he likes—good God, Dolley, that's just what they've had
under the Spanish military. They're insular, you know,
but not so insular they haven't heard the glories of American democracy shouted to the heavens. You take them
over against their will, make them citizens but deny them
the rights of citizens, and you expect them not to make
trouble?"

Dolley's expression looked frozen. "You're getting
into areas that don't concern you," she said.

"They *do* concern me! I'm taking ships in there, I'm
known as "the American" now, they'll turn to me—or
on me—"

"Yes," Dolley's voice sharp now, "you have business
concerns, I understand that. But there are bigger fish to
fry here than any business—"

"No! That's not right, not fair. You *owe* me insight on
where I stand, where New Orleans stands."

"Owe?" It was a warning that Danny deeply resented.

"Yes, owe!" she shouted. "My husband died on the
rotunda floor while we were fighting to win the presidency for Mr. Jefferson over Burr. You weren't there,
you were down on the plantation waiting for Jimmy's

father to die, but I was there. And Carl was. And over the noise, all the shouting as the dam against Jefferson broke, I heard him calling me and turned to see him going down. And all he said was, 'It hurts, oh, it hurts!' He didn't have time to know he was dying, didn't have time to tell me he loved me, to hear me tell him I loved him, he was gone, gone—"

She was crying openly now, tears streaming, voice clogged, not giving a damn about any propriety. "So don't tell me I don't have the right to ask any damned thing I want to ask! And in New Orleans, too, you sent me to persuade my uncle to go to Paris to tell the traders there they'd lose everything they'd invested in New Orleans if Napoleon triggered war, and do you think it was easy? He the leading trader, a power whose word pretty well tends to be law in New Orleans, proud as a peacock, stubborn Irishman-cum-stubborn Frenchman who looks on America as vulgarity personified—I stood there in his study and clubbed him into submission with logic, and if Zulie hadn't chimed in on my side it never would have worked. No one but that wonderful woman could have swung him around. Dolley, I've *served*, and don't you tell me I haven't, don't tell me I haven't the right—"

Dolley was furious. Standing here in her own study, her pile of French novels awaiting her pleasure, being harangued—yes, doubtless Danny did have the right, but that didn't mean—

She stood with her fists clenched and caught a glimpse of herself in the mirror, anger making her face harsh as rough-cut stone, and it struck her she never wanted to see herself looking so. For a moment this increased her anger and then she caught herself and turned to stare from the window, fists opening, breathing slowing, getting control of herself. Yes, Danny did have a right if anyone did. And yes, she was desperately trying to keep a business alive as a woman in a climate that considered a woman's place solely in the home or in the fields and did everything it could to impede her. Yes, if riots started in New Orleans, if it tried to resist Wilkinson's troops, if it succeeded with Spain's help in breaking away, all that Danny Mobry had fought to preserve would be gone. And men everywhere would say, See, women can't run things, can't give seamen orders, women belong in the bed or the home or the fields.

But what could she say? She knew exactly why Tom had wanted to put such tight restrictions on self-government in New Orleans. Jimmy had explained it, his loyalty to Tom keeping him from even hinting whether he agreed or was just following orders. These were people who had never had self-government and couldn't really be expected to understand that self-government depends on the self-control of the citizenry. Look what happened in France only a decade ago—the country New Orleanians call their own even if they've never been there. Democracy was strangled by citizen excess within a year.

How could we be sure it would work? And what could we do if it didn't? In other words, the American leaders were afraid, though she didn't say that to Jimmy, it being pointless to agitate him when nothing could be changed. But those were the questions, and she couldn't really disagree. Nor could she tell Danny in so many words that her people weren't to be trusted. She tried to explain gently, watching anger build in Danny and feeling steadily more uncomfortable herself.

"It wasn't that we didn't trust the people there," she said. Of course, that was a lie. It was exactly that we didn't trust them. She saw a cynical expression settle on Danny. "But you have to admit, they have little to no experience in democracy. How could they, under a French and then a Spanish king, soldiers in control of the daily aspects of their lives, what they might and might not do laid out by royal decree, no one asking them their opinion. Then suddenly they're free, they vote as they please, they want this and that, they order—"

"They go mad, in other words. Think the whole world has changed."

"Well, something like that. Wouldn't they?"

"Why would they? They're not fools. And the soldiers would be there to control elements that went out of control."

"Well, I'm sure it won't be for long. Give them a little while—"

"A month, you mean? Or two?"

"Uh . . . you see, it takes time—"

"A year? Five years, ten?"

"Surely not that long, but you see, until they prove themselves—"

"Why must they prove themselves? They didn't ask to be Americans. We got them, now we say you must prove yourselves."

"But look what happened in France—"

"Dolley, really, I love this country and I love its democracy—look, I can tell you or anyone else or everyone that I think the government is all wrong and no knock will come in the dark of the night. But what I hear you saying, you're afraid to offer it to any beyond your accepted crowd."

"No, I—"

"You're saying the end justifies the means. You fear repercussions in Louisiana so it's all right to deny freedom."

"I am *not* saying the end justifies the means," Dolley shouted. Then, hesitating, since that was exactly what she was saying, added, "Well, maybe for a little while. Maybe it's necessary once in a while. . . ."

"I think your own philosophy is at fault," Danny said, voice now soft, almost gentle. "The end doesn't justify the means, at least in this situation it doesn't. There is no reason to expect trouble if the people are given freedom, certainly not trouble beyond what Wilkinson and five hundred troops could handle. But in denying them the freedom you take for granted, you offer them deadly insult, you tell them they are too stupid or too venal to live as you do, they must prove themselves to reach your ennobled state. I believe this sets up much greater danger, and down the road a year or two—or even sooner—you may have trouble that will dwarf any excesses of freedom you might find now."

Dolley couldn't—wouldn't—give Danny the real answer. Tom simply had been afraid to risk passing freedom to those who had never known it. That was all there was to it, and Jimmy hadn't tried or hadn't tried very hard to dissuade him. A mistake? Perhaps. A fallacy of logic or philosophy? Perhaps. Likely to cost them down the road, as Danny feared? Very possibly. But there it was.

As she saw Danny out she said she would pass this on to Jimmy. And she would, but she knew it would make no difference. Things take on a life of their own. Tom was afraid and he was both an admirer of France and a veteran of French culture, having lived in France at least a decade. Was he right? Was Danny right? Who could say? In the end things are simply done and someone always finds a mistake in one way or another. But the essence of governing is deciding, and this decision had been made.

Maybe Danny sensed this without being told. As she stepped off the veranda she said in a small voice, "Wish us all well, Dolley. We'll see rough days ahead."

★　　★　　★　　★　　★

Eight

Boston, fall 1803

When John Quincy Adams became the senior senator
from Massachusetts he seemed to have driven a wedge
between himself and his family. Between himself and his
father, really; the others didn't matter so much. His
brothers' opinions could be readily dismissed and his
mother tended to be critical anyway. But he treasured the
bond of intellect with his father.

Now his support of the Louisiana Purchase had
brought it all to a head and though the trip from Washington to Boston meant jolting over frozen ruts for a couple of weeks each way, he knew he must go. That Boston
newspapers and fellow Federalists were attacking him
wasn't important; the editors were asses and fellow Federalists were scarcely better. But now they were calling
him a faithless son who toadied to the very men who had
cast his father into oblivion. That he must counter.

Of course losing to Mr. Jefferson three years before
had been a brutal blow to the old man. Fussy, often tedious, usually argumentative, too fond of instructing others, John Adams nevertheless had served his country

well. He found the final repudiation nearly unbearable and the family rallied around him.

But, as the son reminded himself on the lurching, shuddering trip north, his own career had shattered unnoticed in his father's ruin. He had spent a decade abroad as an American diplomat; it was his insightful reporting that allowed his father to sidestep the war with France that Federalist radicals sought, for which you'd think the people might have shown a little more gratitude. In the fury of defeat his father had ordered him home. If he'd been left in place he thought President Jefferson would have reconfirmed him, for they were old friends; in years past, when the two families were still close, Mr. Jefferson had served as informal mentor to the young John Quincy as they walked the streets of Paris together. So with a new wife and child, young Adams came back to the dubious prospect of earning a living in Boston where ten years of diplomatic experience were worth approximately the breath it took to ridicule them. He opened a law practice though he hated the lawyer's life and began making the quarrels of common men his own, he who had dined with kings and prime ministers and whose reports had averted war. It meant skulking about courthouse halls angling for business, all under the strain of appearing both a gentleman and an eager attorney. Then politics beckoned . . .

But the Adams clan was disillusioned with politics. A people who would repudiate the greatest man in America didn't deserve an Adams. Of course this was fine talk but John Quincy noted that the family wasn't hustling across the common in hot pursuit of a citizen not at all interested in paying his bill now that his cow had been recovered. The family barely forgave him when he was elected to the state senate and was horrified when he campaigned among fellow senators for election to the United States Senate. His brothers wouldn't speak and his mother was cold. He found that a constraint he had not surmounted had arisen between him and his father, some native New England reticence barring him from forcing it into the open. But now, thundering along in a rattling, jouncing coach, breath frosting, a cape clutched to his shoulders over his coat, he knew he must have it out.

At Boston he rented a livery horse, but riding to Quincy he let the horse slow to a walk. At a stream he dismounted and sat on a stone as the horse cropped grass. Presently it broke wind and the gassy odor struck Adams as metaphor for his own hesitations, and he mounted and rode on. His mother opened the door. She hugged him but he sensed reserve as well. Louisa, little George, the baby—were they all well?

"I've come to talk to Father," he said.

"Well, it's about time!" Then her tone softened. "I'm glad you've come; he needs to see you." All at once he saw how hard this had been for her, her nose sharper, her face under the white lace cap more lined, and he put his arm around her thin shoulders and whispered, "I love you, Ma."

"Oh, go on with you," she said, but her smile told him how he'd pleased her, and her voice softened as she knocked on the study door, and said, "Here's Johnny come to see you, dear."

His father clasped his hand and drew him into an embrace. But when the talk proved aimless John Quincy blurted, "I've decided to support the Louisiana Purchase."

"So I understand."

That was no help. "Do you disapprove?" he asked.

"Mr. Jefferson had no choice—Napoleon on the Mississippi is unthinkable. Your position is quite proper. Federalist opposition shows the bankruptcy of their thinking."

All this was delivered in quick bursts absent the

warmth of old. John Quincy swallowed. "The Federalists are saying—"

His father snorted. "They can't see beyond their noses. Nor can Mr. Jefferson. I see endless trouble ahead. A nation doubling its size overnight—can that fail to disrupt? Countless unknowns—will the people of New Orleans rebel? They didn't ask to be Americans; mariners touching here tell me New Orleans folk were delighted to go back to France and they detest Americans. Will some pirate come out of the swamps—the notorious Lafittes, perhaps—and lead them to fight for independence? Split off the whole West, not just the new possessions, and make a new country, Cincinnati to New Orleans? Odd if we had to fight for what we thought we'd purchased, eh?"

"General Wilkinson is going there with five hundred men."

His father gave him a sardonic smile. "Wilkinson, now. Just the man. He's already quite familiar with New Orleans."

"The rumors . . . taking Spanish gold for years."

"None provable, though. Twice I was ready to cashier him but the evidence collapsed. And he fights like a cornered ferret when he's challenged. Thoroughly nasty man."

John Quincy cleared his throat. "So your concern about the purchase is whether the people there—"

"More—it shakes the whole country. It certainly worries people here. When that vast territory fills with voters, why, New England will be but a tail on the dog and will have about that much say in directing the dog's nose. The new will orient to the middle states and the South, slave country, not to the manufacturing Northeast. Incredibly dangerous, in other words, but not taking it would have been worse. Thank God we could buy it instead of fighting for it."

"You know the Federalists are attacking me on this?"

His father laughed. "You expected otherwise?"

"All right," he said, laughing too, "I didn't. But they act like mad dogs. Timothy Pickering blackens me wherever he goes. You know how he is."

"Unfortunately," his father said. Pickering had led Alexander Hamilton's attack on the elder Adams that in the end had helped assure Jefferson's election.

"Pickering is a scoundrel." His father's anger boiled over. "Consider his attacks an inverse measure of your worth."

That was well and good, but his father remained cool and remote, so he said, "They're saying obscene things, you know." He sighed. "God, there's such hatred—I know politics is full of strong feelings, but this implacable hatred seems new."

John Adams sighed. "Compounded of rage and fear in equal measure, leavened with surprise."

Surprise? They'd had years to get used to the change in government. As had, for that matter, his father. But as if he'd read the son's expression, the father said, "They never believed it could happen; this late they're still reeling. And fear, yes, because with the world turned upside down who knows what disasters may unfold. And, curious though it sounds, rage because the Democrats *haven't* done all the terrible things predicted. It's like a betrayal—everyone knew they were insane sycophants of the French, addicted to mad dog revolution, everyone was sure they would destroy the country, and here they've kept the old Federalist establishment in good shape, changed it only slightly, everything going smoothly, and now with the nation agog over this purchase, Mr. Jefferson appears sure of reelection when all along Federalists assumed it would be theirs after four years of Democratic ruin. You see? The Democrats betrayed them by not falling into the ruin Federalists predicted for them. Of course they're furious."

He laughed for the first time, throwing his arms over his head and stretching. "So Timothy Pickering's great hope comes down to none other than John Randolph of Virginia."

The radical Democrat who kept the House in turmoil with his volatile explosions? "I've met him now," John Quincy said, "and he seems a bit mad."

"More than a bit, I'm sure. Democrats are terrified of his tongue. Canny as the devil, with an unerring sense for opponents' vulnerabilities—and I hear he hates Jefferson more than he hates Federalists. Sees Jefferson as Judas betraying the Democratic revolution by his restraint. Keeping the bank when they'd talked of abandoning it. Refusing to shatter the economy. Holding federal power when they wanted all power returned to the states. Keeping Federalist officeholders in place—that galled the Democratic radicals the most, denying them the spoils. They're Pickering's hope—if they can wrest control from Jefferson and Madison they'll drive their party into the ground."

"And if they don't, what then?"

"Oh, many things could sink this administration. Revolt in Louisiana. The Lafittes or some other mad adventurer peeling the West off into a new country. What do you suppose Brother Burr will do now that Tom and Jimmy have ruined him—roll over and play dead? Suppose Great Britain forces us into the fight against Napoleon. This expedition to the Pacific, Lewis and Clark—suppose they're wiped out, disappear, never come back? Suppose Britain decides to defend its interest in the Pacific Northwest—do we want to fight Canada? Or a naval disaster after the Democrats have gutted army and navy in behalf of their low-cost-government philosophy. But with the likes of Mr. Pickering as his opposition he's probably safe. Why, Pickering's extremism might keep Mr. Jefferson in office all by itself—now, that would be a jest!"

But this levity struck John Quincy as offensive. He wasn't observing from Olympus, he was on the front lines where things were real, and he said rather sharply, "Secession is no jest, and Mr. Pickering is talking seriously of separating New England. Link it with New York in a new country—they'll support Aaron Burr for governor there because they think he'll give them the state. Now, that's serious business, Father."

"Well, I'd never support secession. I want the nation intact. I love it even when it rejects me." For a moment pain shone on his father's face and then with obvious effort he cleared his expression, and said, "But it's only twenty-seven years since the whole adventure began. Fifteen years since the Constitution. Thirteen since General Washington first became president. We changed government then; we might again if the majority in the nation stood against our interests."

"My God, Father, is it that real?"

"For many in New England, yes. Look—the new far west territory will enhance the West we already have, Kentucky and the others, and all the people who will rapidly be filling it will cleave to the middle and southern states, probably advance slavery across the continent, in time leave our little states as appendages with scarcely a say against an overwhelming majority."

"But New England would find market for its manufactures."

"Well, the market would be there in any event. And New England could control its own destiny."

"You sound—"

"No! I'm telling you the painful reality. Mr. Pickering is not so outlandish, not in New England terms."

This was more like the give-and-take of old but without the old warmth. "Well," John Quincy said slowly,

"I've taken a position on this Louisiana question and I'm catching the devil for it. I'd feel better if I had your support. . . ."

His father shrugged. "Of course you do."

Damn it all, they were getting nowhere. Abruptly, he decided. "Now, sir," he said, "I've come a long way to discuss real things and so far we've touched nothing a couple of letters couldn't have handled."

"Well, son, what do you want?"

"I want to know what disturbs you so. You're cool as a cucumber and have been since I stood for the Senate. Does it really disturb you as it seems to Mother—do you demand that I limit my career on the basis of yours?"

The older man colored at that but said only, "I suppose I was a little hurt when you announced for the seat."

"Like Mother, then."

Rather sharply his father said, "I was hurt when I lost and your mother is a tigress in defending me, but I don't hold with all her views. But I would have thought that you'd have discussed it with me as we've discussed so many other things. I'm not a fool in politics, you know, or inexperienced. But, no—you appear to consider me a worn-out old man so obsessed with his own defeat he wanted to drag everyone down into the pit to suffer with him."

John Quincy felt New England reticence slipping. He lowered his head to guard against moisture in his eyes. So that was it! He reached blindly and his father took his hand. "Other way around, you see," he whispered. "If you had objected I couldn't have borne to go against you. That's all—I feared you would say no, and oh, Father, I *did* want to escape that law practice. And I do feel my life has been built around public service and that's what matters to me. I belong in the public arena—I know that now. So I want—I suppose I came here to ask—I want your blessing."

His father's grip on his hand tightened and then in a moment both drew back self-consciously and cleared their throats almost simultaneously, and then both laughed. "Come," his father said, "we must tell your mother."

★   ★   ★   ★   ★

NINE

New Orleans, December 1803

Danny Mobry's swift new ship, *Carlito*, made the run up the Mississippi to New Orleans in record time. But the riverfront was alarmingly deserted. Her resources were stretched to the limit and she was depending on the business boom in New Orleans she had supposed would follow the purchase. But where were the chains of flatboats coming down stream heavily laden with raw goods for the world market? Where was this business?

They tied up within sight of the cathedral's twin towers. She sent a message to Henri, then waited on the quarterdeck in the golden light of the evening sun. Fishermen were unloading on narrow wharves flush to the levee. A grizzled man cleaning fish hurled offal aside and gulls and seabirds snatched it and fought for dangling prizes in midair with screams of fury. The odor of alligator musk drifted across the river. The familiarity warmed her heart and yet she saw clearly that this no longer was home. Her parents were dead and the plantation was her brother's by primogeniture. Washington was home.

It was near dark when Henri appeared in a polished cabriolet drawn by a handsome black gelding. He ran lightly up the gangway and for a moment she feared he would kiss her in public, and then was disappointed when he didn't. He gripped her hand, as lean and handsome and strong as ever. Alarm at the somnolent riverfront lay in her mind but she didn't want to think about business on this first night.

"Let's walk a bit," she said, and they climbed to the levee promenade, paved with crushed shell and lined with small orange trees. It was a favorite place for strolling lovers; vendors offered glasses of lemonade and little cakes, a languid fan waved over them occasionally, driving off flies. This walk was rich in memory with its view of the river on one side, of the cathedral square on the other. When she had arrived on her first return to New Orleans after Carl's death she had sent word to her uncle. Henri, also a distant relation, whom she dimly remembered as a boy, had appeared as messenger. Walking beside Henri tonight she remembered how the sheer physicality of the grown man had struck her that first night. A year had passed before she led him into her room, but she had felt it from the beginning.

But tonight, by the time they sat down to a supper of waterway cuisine that raised more memories, she knew he was different. He'd always been tense, perhaps a bit driven, which matched her own nature, but this was more. As he touched his glass to hers and murmured, "Welcome home, *chérie*," she identified the difference—it was anger, far below the surface but real.

"What is it, Henri?" she said, her voice cast low.

He gave her a weary, frustrated smile. "Is it so obvious? Oh, I suppose it's this outrageous situation we have through no fault of our own. We were so close—so close! After forty years in the Spanish wilderness we were returning to our home, our roots, our people. The French prefect had arrived to accept the transfer, Monsieur Laussat, Pierre, I might say, we have become very close. No finer gentleman ever lived; can you imagine how he feels, his whole world snatched out from under him? He had such plans for New Orleans—he went over everything with me for guidance on how it would be received—"

He touched his small mustache, which she suddenly realized she'd never liked, and gave her a crooked smile. "Quite an honor, you know—he assured me I would be a chevalier within a year—and then, the Americans!"

"Oh, Henri . . ."

"We are French, Danny, don't deny it—French!—the most cultured, the most noble, the most eloquent people with the most beautiful language in the world. Yet we are handed over to the barbarians without a word to say about it. You've seen the rabble the flatboats bring each year, whoring like madly rutting beasts, drinking themselves insensible."

He raised a hand to stop her protest. "Oh, I know they don't stand for *all* Americans but I've been up to Nashville and Louisville and I'm confident these boatmen represent the majority. You can't deny that."

"I can, actually."

He waved this aside. "Mr. Clark will lose influence, wait and see. The old guard French will have nothing to do with these rabble newcomers. Already Clark is seen as too close to them, American consul and all that, going to Paris for them. Why, it was betrayal of his own!"

"Do you confront him with that, Henri?"

He frowned. "There is no reason to." He popped a fat oyster into his mouth and raised a finger. "But it's not over yet. Monsieur Laussat has taken permanent quarters and the Spanish officials aren't leaving. The American regime may be as short-lived as it is unwelcome."

"I wouldn't count on that," she said.

His eyes glittered. "But of course, I forget. You are one of them. An American."

She controlled her temper. "I'm an individual. Aren't you, after all? Are you one of something?"

"Yes, I am. I'm one of the Frenchmen of New Orleans who is outraged to be made subservient to people whose crudity knows no bounds. Already they are flocking into New Orleans hungry for future spoils, ready to take over. A fellow named Livingston from New York City, my God, he's been here three months and he's into everything, doesn't waste a moment. Nothing decorous about him, I can assure you. You understand, things should be done at a certain pace—but these Americans rush out to make their deals while gentlemen are still addressing the formalities."

It was all going wrong. She didn't want to talk politics, she wanted him to murmur in her ear the ancient song of man and woman. She put her hand on his. "Please, let's not quarrel."

His eyes widened. "No, of course not. I'm so glad to see you. . . ." He talked on in this vein, but something had gone out of the evening and she answered mechanically. When he took her to the *pension* he entered her room as by right when she had anticipated the romantic moment of leading him in. He made love to her in a direct, almost aggressive way that was far from the dream she'd held of this reunion.

She was crushed, but then it struck her there was more to his anger than politics.

"All right!" he snapped. "I want a *wife*." They talked for an hour there in the dark. Marry him. Mother his children. Live on the plantation. Run her business from there. It would work, he wouldn't interfere, he'd swear on his mother's grave. Yes, there was the dilemma. Henri was strong and aggressive—the law would make her business his, and sooner or later he would take it. He would say that circumstances had changed, invalidating his oath. But she would not give what Carl had built to any man. Eventually he slept but she lay long awake.

Zulie was her sparkling self, a black-haired infant suckling furiously on her huge breast perfecting her glowing look, madonna of the bayous. When the baby boy was done he went instantly to sleep and Danny was allowed to hold him, murmuring into the tiny shell of an ear, feeling the familiar drag of pain and regret for all that was not to be.

Madame Zulime des Granges, a fine-looking Frenchwoman well into her forties, the widow of a French count, was Uncle Daniel's mistress and had an earthy sense for matters of the bedroom. Once Danny had asked why she didn't marry Daniel since they had lived together for years, and she had laughed. Well, as for sleeping together, her late husband's family had no objection since it kept her out of trouble, and after all, they recognized that a woman needs a man, a point to which she felt Danny should pay more attention. But as for marriage, it seemed that if monarchy returned to France her grown son would be a prince and of course, a prince's mother has obligations. Danny still remembered Zulie adding with a deep, resonant chuckle, "So, my dear, Irish seed plowed into a French seedbed—its ecumenical, international, and highly satisfactory."

"But do you love Daniel?"

"Do I love him, does he love me? We make love, my dear. Isn't that enough?"

"Well . . ."

"Danny, of course I love him. But that doesn't change

the realities of our lives." Then, adroitly shifting the subject, she asked if Danny had seen Henri. When she nodded a look of amused complicity swept Zulie's face.

"And he took good care of you? Worked out the kinks of long absence, I trust."

Danny nodded, feeling her own face flame.

"How many times? Thrice, I hope. Thrice is best—soothes and smoothes—"

"Zulie! Really—"

The older woman laughed. "You're too much the American, darling girl. Too stiff in these matters." Then, her point well made, she asked, "How did you find Henri?"

"He seemed . . . angry. . . ."

"Oh, these men. They're so important—take themselves so seriously. Your esteemed uncle is beside himself with rage."

"Mr. Clark? But he's not even French."

Zulie chuckled. "I see Henri has been assuring you of the superiority of all things French, a near obsession in New Orleans, which I happily don't share. But your uncle's rage is over the failure of the Americans to name him governor."

"You mean he expected—"

The nursery door opened and Clark walked in, obviously having overheard. Her uncle, as she called him though technically he was a cousin, was twenty years her senior, an austere and she thought dangerous man of unshakable nerve who wielded controlling economic power in New Orleans with a strong hand and an icy manner. A smallish man, not much taller than she, he was feared in New Orleans. She knew she irritated him; a woman in business was unseemly, a woman with economic power of her own an aberration, a woman who drove a hard bargain but made it too attractive to turn down. And then when France was ready to reclaim Louisiana it was she who had threatened him with ruin if he didn't follow the directions she brought from the Americans—it was too much! So he'd gone to France and seen his business friends and warned them this was serious and their losses could be high, but thereafter Danny had sensed that edge of malice.

Now as he stepped into the nursery he was flushed with anger. "Of course I expected! Who is better qualified, who did more to bring about the sale? Do you suppose the great Napoleon was cowed by their infantile threats? No—great men speak the language of money and that is the language I spoke. I have it on excellent authority. Louisiana was a disaster for the Americans and no one in Paris paid the least attention to their mouthing until I arrived and talked to men who could whisper in the great man's ear in language he understood. Oh, it's beyond denial—I made my move, and voilà! It was done!"

Danny was shaken by this display of insularity in a man she respected. Then he whirled on her, his expression supercilious. "Ah, then, my dear niece, welcome. You have come as advance representative of the hungry hordes of Americans who will descend upon us to strip us like so many locusts. You arrive early with the Spanish still in control and business flat. Unfortunately for you and your brethren, it will stay flat. I shall be most surprised if the Spanish vacate—they're enraged, you know. And their control will be triply tight. You'll see. Zulie, have her join us at dinner tonight. Now good day, madam."

Zulie retrieved the baby, tucked her breast back into her gown, and said with a placid smile, "Poor Daniel, he does get into a temper. Can't blame him, really. He feels betrayed."

Well, Danny thought, so did she—she'd heard the old malice in his tone. But what mattered was his estimate that business would stay flat.

"He's right about that," Zulie said. She peered at Danny. "The Spanish won't go away and American trade won't come till they do. But you, you're fixed, you have your sugar. . . ."

Danny left feeling she'd been hit by a runaway horse.

The evening at her uncle's house brought nothing to encourage her. She went with Henri—neither mentioning the night before—to find Clark's house on rue Royale filling with the powers of New Orleans. They were in a big bright room with birds singing in bamboo cages, mirrors glittering in mother-of-pearl frames, sperm-oil lanterns with cut-glass chimneys all ablaze, a spray of peacock feathers in a stone vase standing alone on the mantel of polished ebony.

But the guests grumped and growled, mouths turned down—they had been tricked, abused, cheated, and worst of all, ignored. Sold without notice into a lowly culture, and now they were to be denied the democratic joys the Americans trumpeted, like servants supping on gruel in the kitchen while the guests were at table over a joint.

Servants presented Champagne in crystal flutes and trays of shrimp and marinated squid and savory cheeses. Danny remembered a few of the guests from girlhood—sagacious old Bernard Marigny de Mandeville with his curling white mustaches, his lady beside him now quite old; Jacques Villere, who headed the militia; General de Flaugeac; Jean Dauquin, whom her father had admired—but most were newcomers or had faded from memory. The women stood in a little group with Zulie.

Neither Spanish nor French officials were present; apparently they were in seclusion, nursing ravished feelings. The transfer to the Americans was a few days away.

Henri stood with a group of men. Several turned in her direction and she sensed they spoke of her. Henri's hands extended, palms down, as if he were refuting them, but then his hands rolled upward, classic symbol of the dismissive shrug. Just then he caught her eye and colored.

Zulie walked her about the room, reminding everyone of her family connection. All were polite, none cordial. Her New Orleans roots might improve her chances for business but to these people she had joined the enemy.

Monsieur Marigny bowed over her hand. "I remember you as a little girl—I knew your father well. A fine man."

"Thank you, Monsieur."

"And your husband. I dealt with him and found him always sensitive to the realities."

"I am trying to follow in his footsteps."

He frowned. "So I understand. Perhaps you'll succeed. But—well, I am told you know the American leaders. I pray you will tell them what a desperate mistake they make in the insult they offer us."

"Insult?" But she knew what he meant.

"They want our city. They want our river, our trade, all our possessions—but they don't want us. Why else would they deny us participation in the nation they are forcing us to enter? There can be no reason but that they don't trust us, don't like us, don't want to know us. They want only to use us. To think we can't understand the nobility of their democracy slaps our faces. Perhaps we felt a tentative if uneasy acceptance, but that vanished when they denied us citizenship. When you return you must tell them that."

"I already have."

He gave her a keen look. "And?"

"No answer."

"You see!" His smile was triumphant. "They will never be welcome in New Orleans."

A tall man in his late thirties, clearly an American, walked in with a gorgeous woman and started toward them. Marigny sniffed, fixed the newcomer with a stare, then turned and walked away. "My, my," Zulie said. "I see Monsieur Marigny left his manners at home. He does that sometimes." Well, Danny thought but didn't say, that described most of the guests. She watched the new couple with growing interest. The woman was about Danny's age and gave an instant impression of assurance and authority. The man moved with equal authority and yet with an odd physical clumsiness as he strolled from group to group. The supercilious curl of his lip might have been only their shape, for his manner was warm and rather loud as he shook hands and clapped shoulders, oblivious to or ignoring a proper French disdain for the overt manner.

Zulie said the woman was Madame Louise d'Avezac, lately of Santo Domingo. She was a widow who had lost husband and two children when Creoles were massacred in the Haitian revolution. The American, obviously much in love, was Edward Livingston. Watching his manner, Danny understood Henri's disdain; Henri would have many more chances to be offended as Americans came.

It seemed that Mr. Livingston, who'd been here just three months, was the former mayor of New York city. There'd been some scandal there involving a theft of funds and he had restored the loss from his own pocket, resigned, and come here to repair his fortune in what he said would be an explosion of prosperity. Zulie added that he was the youngest brother of the Robert Livingston, who had arranged the sale of Louisiana, which connection brought him no great affection in New Orleans.

If this or anything else disturbed Mr. Livingston, he didn't show it. Danny studied him over the rim of her glass. He too had come for opportunity, and he had less connection than she; perhaps her quest was not so feckless. His French was atrocious; Madame d'Avezac coached him quietly and occasionally questioned him in English, then told him the correct form instead of telling his listeners what he was trying to say. A wise woman.

When he was presented to Danny she was surprised to find him courtesy itself—and then she realized it was American courtesy, open and direct, and it swept her back to the drawing rooms of Washington and Philadelphia. A wave of nostalgia for the new society so different from the old shook her momentarily.

At table the same message of anguish and anger flowed through the talk, delivered in swift, liquid French quite unlike the Parisian model. The accents and inflections pulled her back toward the talk around her father's table, but the content was very much of today. The guests seemed dislocated, their world disintegrating. They rang the changes of their grievances: where would it all end?

Commerce was dead. The Spanish closing the river in a fit of pique the year before had shattered everything. Americans upstream sent no goods for fear of seizure. The river was soon reopened but the French intention to reclaim Louisiana sapped the confidence of shippers in Tennessee and Kentucky. Turmoil, trade dead, weak merchant houses failing, suicides—a dismal time. Danny listened in dismay; where could she fit? Then Monsieur Marigny led them in an effusion of fresh fury over the Americans denying them an equal place in the American structure. Second-class citizens! Mr. Madison should hear this, she thought. If their new country didn't trust them, why should they trust it? Of course they turned on her, hurling their anger down the table. Each barb came with dark looks at her. Henri didn't defend her; he seemed embarrassed but perhaps more for himself than for her.

Abruptly Monsieur Dauquin said, "But lo, let us remember that in our midst we have a newly arrived American, once one of us, now one of them—perhaps she will honor us with explanation."

Silence. Henri was examining his plate. "Well," she said, "Monsieur Dauquin is right—I have been away. And on returning, I find that manners in New Orleans must have gone into terminal decline. I can't imagine a dinner in Philadelphia or Washington where a woman would be so badgered. But in any event, you ascribe too much to me. I don't make American policy."

A man with gray mustachios whose name had escaped her snorted, and muttered, "Certainly not . . . a woman . . ."

"Then why do you harangue her?" Zulie snapped.

After a silence, a small man who had arrived late fixed them with a droll look, and said, "We speak of trust, but in truth, would we want to be trusted by a country that trusts James Wilkinson to command its army?"

When the laughter died, Monsieur Dauquin, not at all abashed, said with a wicked grin, "And this governor to be foisted upon us? Monsieur Claiborne? Governor of Mississippi Territory—a wilderness! I have had dealings with this person. How to describe him? A Spanish piece of eight, cut it into eight bits, cut each bit into eight, and one will make Monsieur Claiborne!"

She saw that the gibes had shifted the mood and heard a new tone enter the talk. Spain, someone said, intended to reclaim Louisiana anyway—and France would stand by regarding with amusement Americans being euchred out of their funds and still denied the river.

"I have it on the best authority," General Villere said. "Spain will never accept Americans positioned to threaten its empire. The barbarians already are demanding Texas and Florida! Obviously Mexico would be next."

"Mexico worries the Spanish sick, and it should," her uncle said, surprising her. "It's practically defenseless. I've been twice to Vera Cruz, once a good fifty leagues inland, and I assure you it's ripe for the taking. Why, a thousand men could march from Vera Cruz up to the Valley of Mexico in twenty days' time!" His eyes gleamed. "And the gold pouring from the mountains—my God, the man who took Mexico would own the world!"

The reverent attention given that image of gold opened Danny's eyes. She had an international perspective now, and she saw that these people weren't really French or Spanish or American, they were a breed of their own, like the pirate Lafitte out of Barataria Bay down on the coast who attacked only Spanish vessels. She heard a subtext vibrating below the surface—if pressed, they too could be pirates. Throw the Americans out and stand on their own feet like men. France or Spain or both would welcome the move—and support it. Hinting revolution; she found it frightening. Give them a leader who could lift their hearts and stir their souls— she realized Mr. Madison and Dolley and all those careless, complacent people in Washington had no idea of the risk their cavalier manner was creating. Risk that could sail her—and perhaps her new country as well— straight into disaster.

When they left the table she sought out Louise d'Avezac and quickly saw they could be friends. Soon Livingston joined them. "Wasn't ignorance on parade tonight?" he said. "But that business about Mexico—that was interesting. A thousand men . . . think of it."

William C. C. Claiborne, new governor of Orleans Territory, appeared as wary of New Orleans and its people as they were of him. He arrived the day before the transfer, a slight and rather pallid young man who stood with shoulders hunched, his glance shifting rapidly as if he feared being caught looking at anything in particular.

Word that he'd come swept over the city and it seemed that half the population found excuse to stroll slowly across the Place d'Armes and around the Cabildo hoping for a glimpse of him. Danny couldn't stay away. To her surprise, she found her uncle seated on a bench watching the crowd, his eyes bright and knowing. She joined him and they sat in silence. He gave a raw chuckle when Claiborne appeared at a doorway, then ducked back so rapidly he collided with General Wilkinson in his gaudy uniform.

Danny knew Wilkinson by his dubious reputation, in New Orleans as well as Washington. The few times she'd seen him had done nothing to improve on that. He bowed and scraped to people with connections, but his eyes were cold as stone. Dolley considered him odious but when Danny asked why they kept him Dolley had darted one of those wary looks—same old story, leaping to defend Jimmy—and said she really didn't know. Because they didn't have anyone else, because he had strong political connections, because they already were working great change and to have cashiered the army's commander without specific cause would have disrupted further—Dolley had shaken her head and Danny changed the subject.

Claiborne's head popped out and withdrew, Wilkinson again behind him. "Dangerous man," Clark murmured.

"Claiborne?"

"No, no—he's a typical small-scale Tennessee countryman—I dealt with him as governor of Mississippi Territory. Stubborn and dense, qualities that don't go well together. Dauquin was right the other night. But

Wilkinson is a different cut. Rotten person—lazy, treacherous, duplicitous, self-serving. Been coming here for years, you know, as soldier and as trader. He poses as a buffoon, he's often drunk or seems to be. The only obvious reason to respect him is that he has five hundred troops in bivouac two miles away. But that far underestimates him."

"You told me once he was close to the Spanish."

"One long romance. Been feeding them information on the American military for years. Keeps them alarmed so they're willing to pay him, don't you see? I hear he's getting two thousand a year in gold—double what his own army pays him. You'd think that would disturb the Americans, wouldn't you?"

He gave her a wicked grin, baiting her, which she ignored. "Keeps the Spanish alarmed about what?" she asked.

"That the Americans plan to grab Mexico."

"Do you think they do?"

"Of course." He smiled and an image of how Jean Lafitte might look as he boarded a ship flashed across her mind. "All that gold? No one can resist it."

Cannon boomed on the Place d'Armes and guns on ships in the river echoed the salute. Spanish soldiers temporarily sworn in to French service presented arms, steel helmets under feather clusters gleaming in winter sunshine. Wilkinson stood before a handful of American troops; he'd left the bulk in bivouac. Nearby were four companies of New Orleans militia, each unit in a different uniform. Danny, standing with Zulie and Mr. Clark, watched Henri sitting a bay mare before his troop.

The French prefect shouted from the Cabildo balcony to a couple thousand people in the plaza. They stood motionless and silent as the elegant French phrases washed across the square. Monsieur Laussat saluted the people of New Orleans. The great Napoleon had paused in deciding the fate of the world to study the best interests of the people of Louisiana and had concluded they lay with the Americans. He commended them to their new government and urged them to go with God.

There wasn't a sound as the oration ended. She saw no smiles. The French flag started slowly descending as an American flag rose on a new pole set beside the old. The two flags paused at equal height. Laussat pronounced the colony passed. The cannons roared again and the flags moved, one up and one down. Danny watched the Stars and Stripes snap and roll in the breeze. A handful of Americans waved their hats and cheered. They made a small tinny sound and soon fell silent.

Governor Claiborne stepped forward and looked across the plaza. Straighten your shoulders, for God's sake, Danny thought. Straighten up, speak up, make them glad—

He didn't. He stood with that curious slump, shoulders turned as if for flight. He spoke in English, statements short and abrupt. They should all be honored to join a great republic and he was sure they would prosper together. Cooperate with him and he would cooperate with them. Work out the future together. His voice carried scarcely halfway across the big plaza and most of the audience was gone before he finished.

Mr. Claiborne came down to the plaza and looked around uncertainly. Monsieur Marigny led a group of notables forward. He carried a symbolic key on a red pillow and made a graceful speech. Soon it became evident that Mr. Claiborne understood no French. Louise d'Avezac stepped forward to translate, but Claiborne took on an irritated, impatient look before it was done. When Marigny finished Claiborne handed the pillow to someone behind him and bowed perfunctorily.

Then, obviously on impulse, Louise stepped forward and Danny heard her say, "Sir, it will all be so much easier when you have mastered French. It would be my great pleasure to volunteer to coach you in the nuances of our language."

Claiborne smiled, as men will to a beautiful woman, but shook his head, and said rather sharply, "Thank you, but that will not be necessary. I have no intention of learning French. The United States is an English-speaking nation and Orleans Territory now is part of the United States. All business will be conducted in English. Citizens who lack the language of their new country should set about learning it immediately. Good day, madam." With another perfunctory bow he retreated into the building.

So the province passed, the American flag flying, the new government installed. Danny sighed; the new governor could not have found a better way to alienate those he must govern than to refuse their language. Clouds passed before the sun and gloom settled on the plaza. She saw Livingston and Louise D'Avezac hurry away. The Place d'Armes was nearly empty when Clark presented one arm to Zulie and the other to her. It was a bad beginning.

"D'you see? D'you see now?" Henri seemed beside himself with excitement. Apparently he'd stabled his horse and come directly to her rooms, still in the odd uniform his militia unit had adopted. "That oaf! That fatuous fool! This is to be our leader, this dropping of a dog, this *merde* that any civilized society would toss into an ashcan. But the Americans send him to rule and abuse us."

They sat in wicker armchairs at the open double doors leading to the balcony. She heard horse's hoofs below, the crunch of iron tires, the cry of a peddler. A woman was laughing and Danny felt a thrust of pain and in that moment realized she herself was no longer in love. Something had died.

"Well," she said, "the new governor did seem obtuse."

"Obtuse? Obscene is the word you want."

"Really, Henri—that goes too far. He's not—"

"Did you hear Monsieur Lassaut's splendid speech? Did you hear the nuances?"

"What nuances?"

"That France still cares, that there still is a future, that we are not alone."

"I didn't hear that."

"You weren't listening. He was subtle—a French characteristic that you seem to have lost—but to the knowing ear it was clear that France would welcome the spirit of revolt that now boils in New Orleans."

"Revolt? What do you mean?"

"Danny, Danny, you've been gone too long. New Orleans is full of cavaliers who won't accept such an oaf as Mr. Claiborne as their ruler for very long." He broke off, staring at her. Then, "Have you heard of the Mexico Association?"

"I've heard chatter about taking Mexico."

"Far more than chatter, darling. You know about the gold there? That riches beyond reckoning await the men who have the strength and courage to make it their own?" He touched his little mustache, a gesture she realized all at once both stood for the man and raised her hackles fiercely. "I might add that I am one of the leaders of the group. I can promise you that great change is afoot—today's little ceremony is anything but the last word."

She stared at him. A freebooting attempt to take Mexico from Spain and loot its gold? A plot to take New Orleans? A plot against the whole West?

"For God's sake, Henri, that is dangerous talk. You are part of the United States now—"

"Never!"

"—and they're not going to let—"

"They'll have nothing to say about it. Spain will support us. They already are enraged at losing Louisiana, at the insane demands of the Americans for Florida and Texas as well. If we seize New Orleans they'll support us—and Monsieur Lassaut makes it clear there would be no opposition from France. Wouldn't that be a capital joke—Napoleon takes the simple Americans for sixty million francs and we keep Louisiana anyway!"

"And are you the leader who will gallop at the head of this phalanx?" He hesitated, coloring. He wouldn't be the leader, she knew by instinct. He was too small a man, though he did have a certain power. She thought of him at the head of his troop in his fine uniform. He touched the lapels; she thought the uniform reassured him somehow. He had won that position, and yes, she saw he could be a powerful lieutenant.

"I seek nothing for myself," he said. His eyes shifted away as he added, "But given the gold in Mexico there would be plenty for all." And she saw immediately that that was the key—it appealed to everyone—to delusions of grandeur and convictions of destiny, to patriotism, to the eternal hunger for wealth and power. That's what made it so dangerous, she thought with a sense of surprise. Something for everyone. And on such fertile field a leader will be drawn as a fly to honey.

She rose. "I think it's time for you to go, Henri."

"Eh? What? I thought we would dine and then—" His glance flicked to the bed.

"I'll dine alone—at the *pension* table."

He gave her a steady look, cold and mature. He stood, looking down at her. "Very well," he said. She had cast the die and saw he understood it.

"I will bring the sugar manifests in the morning," he

said. He had been arranging the sugar cargoes that her ships carried to the Boston distiller.

"I would be grateful if you would continue as before."

"As a business arrangement," he said.

"Yes. As a business arrangement."

He gazed at her another moment, then nodded briskly. "Perhaps it's as well," he said.

That night she sat a long time in the wicker chair by the open doors to the balcony, listening to the sounds of New Orleans in the dark. Laughter and shouts and passing carriages. And then, later, the sound of a woman crying.

It was very late and the night had gone still as a graveyard before she slept.

"Ended it?" Zulie frowned. "No, really, you mustn't. He's a good boy, worth keeping. As men go, you know."

"No," Danny said, "it's finished."

"My dear, really?"

"He hates Americans."

"Well, well, many here do. You just have to accept that, darling girl."

"But Zulie, he talks of plots, of revolt, of seizing Mexico, of all sorts of treasonous—" She broke off, for Zulie's expression had changed radically.

The mischievous twinkle was gone. Quite coldly, Zulie said, "These are not matters to be spoken of. They are not women's affairs and should not be."

"But—"

"No buts, Danny. Do not speak to me of such things. Do not come into my house and speak to me of such things."

Danny stared at her. Nearly a minute passed. Well, Danny thought, that told her what she needed to know.

At last she said, "Let's ring for brandy. Somehow I need something stronger than tea."

When she reached her *pension* she found a note from Louise inviting her to tea. She arrived to find Mr. Livingston there.

"What a way to start," she cried, taking a cup from Louise.

Ed Livingston was smiling. He seemed to take everything lightly. "Bad, I suppose," he said, "but it doesn't make much difference. Would they have liked anyone who wasn't French?"

"Ed*vard*," Louise said, "you know the failure to be French is the greatest sin!"

"Ah, darling, how fortunate that Americans are a positive gumbo, everything and anything in with the spices, English and French and Dutch and Spanish and Irish, a bouillabaisse of a people. You'll fit in perfectly, you see—you might as well surrender and marry me."

"Ed*vard*," she said, glancing at Danny.

He chuckled. To Danny he said, "I'll win her over, you'll see. There's a great future in New Orleans and we'll all be part of it." Then, talking in his easy, fluid way, he laid out a vision that shook Danny with its exciting hope.

"The American West is fermenting like cider in a bottle." He glanced at Louise. "Wait'll you taste cider from good New York apples, sweetheart." She rolled her eyes and he laughed. To Danny he said, "Fermenting cider, it'll blow the stopper right out of the bottle. And New Orleans is the mouth of the bottle and the Spanish were the stopper and it's a right good thing that my big brother bought the place because before very long our people would have blown out the Spanish stopper on their own. And to milk the analogy a little more, the cider pours out through the bottle's mouth. All the West's exploding prosperity'll flow right through New Orleans and we'll all grow rich beyond our imagining, and what do you think of that!"

He said he'd come downriver by keelboat, stopping often and renting horses for cross-country travel, and he'd found the West amazing, never seen anything like it, he'd supposed it was wilderness but while doubtless there was plenty of wilderness, still everywhere he looked he saw explosive growth. The spirit and confidence was infectious, every crossroads aimed to be your next metropolis. And indeed, growth was right before your eyes, new brick buildings even in small towns, places that started with a single lane stretching up from the river now boasting a grid of streets. Decent inns in the larger towns. New land broken to cultivation, stumps of the forest still standing. Court systems functioning, elections well certified and secure. Cincinnati, Louisville, Nashville all starving for capital so long as the stopper was in the bottle but capital would follow in a rush with the river clear.

"Oh, Ed*vard*," Louise whispered, "can you be so sure?"

"Sweetheart," he said, and Danny saw he'd been talking to Louise all along, not to her. "Can you conceive what my brother's purchase means to the United States? Doubles our size, makes the immediate West secure, means we'll be a continental nation. Means everything west of the Mississippi clear to the Stony Mountains will flow through New Orleans. Think of it—that brown water out there, it's Stony Mountain runoff as well as Appalachian, rainfall two thousand miles apart."

It anchors American democracy, he said. All these Frenchmen talking of democracy as a spent force because Paris blew up—we'll prove them wrong, for now we have the weight to assure success. You'll see, he told

Louise, these same men will glory in democracy once they understand its strength. Why, even now they were angry because the country hadn't given them full representation. He laughed. "There at Clark's house, they think I'm too American, gauche, vulgar, too friendly, too open, don't dance on punctilio's point—but just wait'll American prosperity makes this a great international port instead of a sleepy Spanish outpost, you just wait, sweetheart!"

Louise laughed and shook a finger at him. Danny thought she would have kissed him if they'd been alone.

There was one of those silences when everyone is a little embarrassed. It gave Danny her opportunity. "I've heard it won't stay American long enough to appreciate American virtues."

He sobered instantly. A stern look swept his face and she remembered that he'd been mayor of New York City, no small post even if Philadelphia was larger, and that he came from the powerful New York Livingstons. This was a man of experience.

"Well, it's volatile—far more so than Mr. Claiborne or the general suspects. And generally, they don't like us. There's constant talk of seizing the city, defying America, and so forth, but they were peaceful today." Then a sudden thrust. "You've been talking to Henri Broussard, I take it?"

It set her off balance. She hesitated, then agreed.

"Henri leads one faction. Not strong enough to act alone but a nucleus that could fester into something real, I suppose. Spain would support any move to hold Louisiana and France would be amused and certainly expend no capital on our behalf."

"Have you heard of the Mexico Association?"

"Certainly. I may join it. Aims at the liberation of Mexico. You know revolution is incipient there now?"

"No . . ."

"Appears to be true," he said. "Everyone who comes out of Mexico says the priests are leading a liberation movement that must explode." He shrugged. "We might help that along."

"And seize some gold?"

"Presumably they'd appreciate liberation." He smiled.

"I sense an independence movement."

"Well, they're bruised. Offended. Big mistake to deny them a role in our democracy. Of course they're hurt. Bumped their dignity." He shrugged. "But no one's beating the drum to raise the troops."

He smiled brightly in a lightning shift of mood. "Tell me something quite apart—is that greyhound ship of yours as fast as she looks?" In a flash she saw why Louise had invited her.

"Faster."

Livingston said upriver shippers were holding cargoes till the dust settled in New Orleans, but he had persuaded an old friend to send down a load of cotton. He had a buyer in New York waiting to transship it to London and speed was of the essence. The load would be here in a day or two; they had been waiting for the transfer of authority to the United States. Could Danny deliver that load in forty days?

"In less," she said.

"Suppose we say a bonus for every day under forty, a penalty for every day over."

She hesitated. Many things can delay a vessel and she was on a slender margin. Still . . .

"I have two sister ships building, equally fast," she said. "And my connections in New Orleans certainly exceed yours."

"But you're an American, too," he said. "You understand time or you wouldn't swap space for speed."

"So," she said slowly, "melding American ways with New Orleans ways will be the key to this glowing future you see. Are we discussing a single cargo or a business connection?"

He glanced at Louise. "You were right, she's smart." He extended a hand to Danny. "Let's do business."

"When your cotton's aboard, we'll sail within the hour."

And she would return to loneliness.

★　　　★　　　★　　　★　　　★

TEN

New York, early 1804

Aaron Burr was feeling at home. Walking the crowded streets of New York again, stepping around dead animals, rapping snouts with his stick to clear his way through hogs that roamed the streets cleaning up offal, holding a perfumed handkerchief to his nose as necessary, he drank in the ambiance of the streets. Along the waterfront he found vessels docked in tiers against the piers showing a forest of masts, stevedores shouting, handcarts rumbling, merchants under the sheds shouting their wares, old friends darting out to clasp his hand. He paused by his old Wall Street office, occupied now by another attorney with a huge vulgar sign.

These were the streets where he once had worked magic—and now had returned to do so again. Reactivate the boys of Tammany, the street runners and the vote humpers and the hungry editors and the boys skilled in nosing out families in trouble and dropping a little rescue on them with the admonition to the man to vote right. Smiling and confident and polished, shaking hands on every corner, Burr had come home for vindication and restoration and, ultimately, revenge.

But was that really right, revenge? The word had jumped into his mind but it was as if some ill-shaped dramatist had seized his story—no, revenge was a cruel word, demeaning, not at all a gentleman's way. Burr had a clear view of himself. He wouldn't use the word *noble* with its note of conceit but neither would he dispute another who applied it to him. Nothing of the Chesterfieldian gentleman in revenge. And Burr was profoundly and universally a gentleman—and as such was well above so petty a concept. But perhaps a little recompense for the abuse he had suffered; that was within the gentleman's code.

He felt he knew himself well. He was impetuous. His nature was to seize opportunity and make it work for him. Both qualities had carried him far in war. He had a certain political genius, which he felt at root was based on having a clear view of what he saw as man's natural cupidity. He was decisive, capable of action in a moment when he saw his interest or his advantage. He was proud, a man who would brook no slight and yet was never quarrelsome—a gentleman in short.

He felt profoundly abused by Jefferson and Madison. Did he regret seizing his chance to challenge Jefferson, which began with arranging the situation? In the sense that it proved costly since it didn't succeed, perhaps, but no remorse. He had acted within his fundamental nature and within the nature of politics as he understood and practiced it. Politics was a rough game; why did the Virginians suppose Tammany Hall worked so well? It was Tammany in the end that put Jefferson in office. Without Tammany, no New York; without New York, no Jefferson. So who the hell were they to take a superior attitude?

Sometimes he wondered if he had an unusual need for success, for triumph, for the love that the people lavished on a man who succeeded in politics. He had so little other love, that is. Women, of course, yes, he could pick and choose, but that was empty too. Listening to them simper, seeing the naked need in their eyes, wives fluttering their eyelashes and sliding tongue between their lips when they met him, the sheer tediousness of those who couldn't understand when it was over. He was approaching fifty and while he was still more than capable, the driving needs of youth had passed.

But women were not to be confused with love. Love went to the depths of one's soul and was precious. Of course, he no longer mooned over mother and father swept away in the yellow fever epidemic, he understood disease isn't personal. And yet there was a feeling he'd been abused that he couldn't quite put aside in the death of his darling Theodosia, the terrible malignancy growing in her body even as they wed. They had been profoundly happy despite living in the knowledge of certain doom that was only postponed. And then the cancer took her and left him alone.

There had been a maturity and strength in her that he had found comforting and stabilizing. Like a mother too, and he had needed that. His daughter showered him with love on which he relied as a drowning man relies on a plank. But she had her own life, she'd married and gone to South Carolina and given him a gorgeous grandson. Now she was far away and he rattled around the big house on his country estate at Richmond Hill up Manhattan Island like a solitary pea in a pot. Often he fled its empty echoes for the town house on Fulton Street down in the heart of things where the sound of passing carriages in the night told him he wasn't alone in the world.

He felt that in some new way he was on thin ice. It wasn't that he had any doubt he'd win the election and all that went with it. Rather it was the growing recognition that this time, for the first time, he *had* to win. To his dismay, he was finding it impossible even to contemplate the possibility of losing. At the very thought tears tended to start and he could feel his face about to crumple. It got so that he could not even allow the errant thought in public lest he lose control. This frightened him for it was so different from his usual confidence that he could handle anything and no man could undermine him.

Well, it was just that he had been so battered. The abuse over the tie vote; the sterile vice presidency so rich in title, so empty in fact; the humiliating ejection from the party he had served so long; the relentless abrasion. Even stone can be worn down by wind and water. Yet God knew he had done nothing to advance himself. The fight in the House had raged for weeks and he could have intervened at any point. Federalists and Democrats alike were open to deals, but he made no moves. Alexander Hamilton attacked him but he didn't respond. A gentleman, he waited for fate to take its course.

And then in the end it was the sanctified Mr. Jefferson himself who'd struck a deal! Burr had not a moment's doubt of this. Jimmy denied it, but Jefferson had talked widely of his plan to keep Federalist measures like the Bank. Burr thought it was pure sophistry for Madison to insist there was no connection and hence no deal. He expected Tom to so insist—he'd have done the same under the circumstances—but Madison was supposed to be an intellectual big mule and here he danced to sophistry's tune. So they secured the presidency—and immediately set out to destroy the only man who could block little Jimmy's ascent.

Alexander Hamilton was the great puzzle. Alex had been a friend, or at least, an associate. They had tried lawsuits together, as co-counsel and as opposing counsel. Burr was confident he'd won most of his contests with Hamilton, but that was the nature of law and politics. It wasn't personal. But throughout the battle in Congress Hamilton had pounded Federalists to choose Jefferson over Burr as a man of probity and character. Did Alex harbor a mysterious hatred? More than once Burr had inquired but there was never an answer. He had parsed out word by word what Alex had said and found the man obscenely clever at going far enough to make his meaning clear but stopping short of the challengeable. Didn't say a lot for his courage, calumniating a man in sanitized language, but Hamilton was a sly fellow.

So Burr had been abused; now he must have a single blazing victory that would correct wrongs and betrayals on all sides. He would stand as an independent and emerge in control of New York and then watch both parties vie to lick his boots. Then the presidency would be his to take or to dictate. He might stand as the controlling hand behind the scenes but more likely would be in front. A man who can bring a vast crowd to tears and five minutes later to laughter is a man to be feared in politics. And sure enough, tidal shifts were already under way. Several Federalists invited him to dine and talk and soon were pledging their support. He listened in silence, concealing his surprise at their effrontery, and let them depart Fraunces Tavern believing that if he wasn't exactly with them, still he more or less approved. So much in politics, especially dangerous politics, can be handled with a smile, a raised eyebrow, a reminder of one's reliability. No one asks you to take a pledge in blood.

A leader of the group that invited him to dine, a fellow named Woodson who liked to be called Woody, slowly worked his way around to the Federalist plot to split New England off from the United States and tuck it under Great Britain's wing. It seemed that Timothy Pickering, who led the splinter group for secession, never passed New York without spending a few days in Woody's home talking dreams. The New England men thought their chances of success would be much greater if New York joined them; what did Colonel Burr think of that? What Burr thought was that here was opportunity. What he said was that these were interesting if dangerous ideas and ones that would bear much consideration.

"But not," Woody said, "to be rejected out of hand?"

"No interesting idea should be rejected out of hand," Burr said, and sure enough, that satisfied them, though in fact it told them nothing. Woody then went on at length that the problem was this mad acquisition of the West, which certainly must dilute northeastern political weight in the Union and could do the Northeast no earthly good.

Hamilton opposed secession but Woody said he wasn't listened to as before, and added, "I suppose you know he says harsh things about you, Alex does. Bad blood there?"

"On his side, evidently. Not on mine."

Afterward it was their emphasis on Hamilton's attacks that lingered. Why did Hamilton hate him? Burr had reviewed the question dozens of times without finding an answer. It seemed that no end of people hated him and wanted him destroyed, as witness the abuse of the last few years. The list of his enemies seemed to grow and grow. He needed the victory that now lay in sight and the power that went with it. Everything would be different then. . . .

Big, growly, rough Matt Davis could hardly contain himself. He spilled out his story with shouts of laughter and Burr had to admit that the situation was truly delicious.

"So I go to Albany like you said, and sure enough, state Federalists are holding their nominating caucus at Spottswood's Tavern. You know the place?"

"Log structure, if I recall, barnlike but comfortable."

"That's it. Well, I know old Spottswood and I get him to show me where they'll meet, and sure enough, there's a cabinet in the room and when I open it I see it's one of those that goes through the wall, the other side opens in the next room. So right away I rent the next room. Naturally I don't say a word to Spottswood, but soon as he's gone I wedge the cabinet door on their side so it won't open and then I drill some little holes. So the next day, they meet with great secrecy, guards on the doors and everything, and I open my side of the cabinet and I hear everything they say! Oh, but we foxed 'em!"

"Wonderful," Burr said. "So you learned . . ."

"Well, the Federalists, they're feeling mighty beat." It was plain that Davis didn't intend to be rushed. He was a beefy man who concealed his sharp intelligence and education under a coarse manner that tended to deflect much inquiry. And in the end, Burr had to admit the story was worth the wait. The caucus met to name a Federalist candidate for governor. The Democrats had already nominated a nonentity named Morgan Lewis, a jurist of some sort. Alexander Hamilton was chairing the meeting and he said that the weakness of Morgan Lewis gave Federalists a heaven-sent opportunity to name a powerful candidate.

Davis laughed, a drop of spittle flying, and said, "So someone name of Woody up and nominates you! I nearly fell out of the cabinet when I heard that! And Alex, he starts sputtering that Woody is out of order 'cause you aren't even a Federalist. And you know, he said a funny thing—that he heard you would listen to secession talk. Then a bunch of 'em were yelling, I couldn't make it all out, and then this Woody, he hollers the only reason they wanted you, you could whip Morgan Lewis. Then someone else or maybe the same man, I could hear but not see, remember, hollers for the floor and moves they go without a candidate. Y'see? So they can vote for you! Someone took a voice vote and must have been three-quarters was on your side."

"How did Alex react to that?"

"Like to tore his britches he was so worked up. Pacing and shouting, voice fainter as he moved away, finally he comes to my end of the room and he leans right on the cabinet and he's shouting right into my ear. Oh, Aaron, it was rich! Hell, I can hear him better'n the people in the room. And he like to went crazy—saying they'd dishonor the party, that you were a Democrat in sheep's clothing, only reason you're independent, the Democrats stole your footing—"

"Which is a lie," Burr said sharply. "I left the Democrats to become an independent."

"Aaron, it seemed everyone in the room knew that."

"What else did he say?" Matt looked momentarily puzzled and Burr snapped, "Did he speak of me personally?"

People were using his name pretty loosely these days and he was weary of it. He saw Matt come alert. "No," the big man said carefully, "just political stuff, how you were a Democrat at heart and all that. . . ."

Burr's heart slowed. "So where did it leave us?"

"In the catbird seat, that's where. Alex, he went on and on, and after a while it was just him, no one answering, seems like they were just waiting for the vote. Then they banged through a resolution to name no nominee and urge Federalists to vote for you and everyone went to cheering."

There! That clinched the New York gubernatorial election. He felt a wave of elation so heady it was like too much rum. Burr knew that he ranked high with the Democratic rank and file and could count on drawing at least half their votes even as an independent. Now Federalists would vote for him too because they certainly wouldn't vote for the Democrat. And another thing . . . He'd readily admit he was human enough to relish the image of Mr. Hamilton in a fury, abandoned by his own party.

A letter from New Orleans: Wilkinson had received the province from the French and was standing by. Apparently the administration already was in trouble there. The governor, whom Wilkinson called Wee Willie, was all at sea, Frenchmen throbbing with rebellious spirit cutting circles around him, his blunders making everything worse. What was more, it looked as if France might reclaim the province on some flimsy excuse and Spain was threatening war over American aims at Florida and Texas. With fools in Washington and fools there, Wilkinson stood alone as the only stabilizing influence and wasn't sure how long he could stomach such taradiddle. It all cried out for a man of vision.

Only to his trusted old friend could he say such things—but then, he said, only a man who had suffered as had Burr from pygmies momentarily in high places could really understand. Good old Jim! And there floated unbidden into his mind Jim's terse remark at their last meeting. Burr had seen something burning in those canny eyes as his old friend whispered, "Remember, Aaron, the West is a plum waiting to be plucked and Mexico is the pot of gold at the end of the rainbow."

That thought kept coming back—but his pot of gold was here in New York City. He gathered his troops at Richmond Hill, his hundred-acre estate on the Hudson well north of the bustling city on the tip of Manhattan Island but well south of the farming village of Greenwich. Just being here gave him a soothing, peaceful feeling of well-being. He had to smile to himself—he liked fine things, good wine though he was abstemious, cartons of the latest books from London and Paris, the company of artists and writers whom it was his privilege to assist in their pecuniary misadventures. He was a Medici of the arts without, sad to say, Medici resources. Richmond Hill was just the sort of place he needed and, yes, that he deserved.

That he no longer could afford it was simply the price of public service in a democracy. But then, so he reminded himself to maintain his cheery attitude, America was changing rapidly anyway. Specifically, New York City was marching up Broadway and the Bowery and soon would engulf first Richmond Hill and then Greenwich Village itself. So he was selling now to an immigrant chap from Germany named Astor. Gross man, John Jacob Astor, thought only of money. The fellow intended to turn the hundred acres into five hundred building lots and doubtless make a fortune; he'd had the temerity to chide Burr for not doing the same, and Burr was too polite to take note of the gulf that separated them. Burr was a gentleman, and gentlemen didn't grub coin by selling their homes piecemeal.

Still, win the election and all would be well. Power makes its own rules. The campaign pace grew frenetic. Peter Van Ness arrived each dawn to put the leader's thoughts into sparkling prose. A tall young man with pale eyes, corn-silk hair, and no sign of a beard, he was bright and handy with words. For friendly newspapers he poured out answers to the billingsgate spewing from the attack papers that looked to Mr. Hamilton for direction. Hamilton claimed he was too busy to direct his editors and Burr said the same thing. That a paper friendly to Burr had printed in riotous detail Matt Davis's account of how the humiliated Alex lost control of his party was none of his doing, Burr said with a smile. He told everyone to ignore newspaper chatter but knew some of it always sticks.

Burr couldn't campaign for himself; the candidate must stand above the hubbub, seeking nothing but willing to answer the people's call. Still, moving about the state, introduced wherever he went by local agents, he found frequent forums where, speaking not for himself but for a common good, he renewed his old capacity to dominate a crowd. It was magic the way he could swing men from tears to cheers and have them ready to charge the barricades.

Tammany Hall was spreading the word for Burr. Matt Davis was out from dawn to midnight guiding his troops, a dozen hearties who spoke the people's language and had ready funds for barrels of beer and elaborate free lunches at voting rallies. Burr had captains in every sizable town.

Matt had a talent for concealing his real intelligence. Had a way about him, too, walk into Tammany and get everyone in line, tour the city's bars to set up rounds on the house, lift his own tankard in loud salute, the drinks a courtesy from Colonel Burr who counted them blood brothers and their vote his due. And if it was necessary to break someone's face, Matt knew about that, too. Political campaigns need discipline.

A rumor was running, nothing you could tie down, that linked Burr with secession. Alex was mouthing at dinners with friends, speaking clearly but carefully. There was talk of treason, but Burr was comfortable. He knew he'd kept his own skirts clean. Van Ness, a tedious idealist at times, sought assurance that Burr didn't intend to split up the country and Burr had to explain to him that in politics the best policy was to keep everyone guessing. Peter said he'd have supposed one would support what one felt was best for the country. Burr let his expression discourage such tittle-tattle.

Day by day, he prowled the docks, letting the boys see him in his fine broadcloth suit, his impeccable hose and silver-buckled shoes and silver-headed stick, always a gentleman but salt of the earth and unfailingly happy to see his friends on the docks. Shake hands, give 'em a little speech, man to man—oh, he set himself no airs. He'd walk from his town house on Fulton Street, circling mud holes and offal, past houses mostly of wood, two or three stories, many brightly painted and new given the fire after the British left, here and there a fine building of brick. Along the East River, under the rows of sheds he saw cotton bales and wood piles and barrels of rice and flour, hogsheads of sugar, chests of tea, puncheons of rum, pipes of wine, boxes and cases and this and that scattered, groaning carters staggering off in every direction, and to the owners of all this diversity of goods he managed to find something to say that made it clear he understood their particular problems and that their lives must naturally improve when he entered office.

And there one morning he collided with Simmons McAlester to whom he owed—well, just how much money he couldn't say at the moment, but a lot. Sim was admiring a towering vessel ready to sail on the flood.

"Aaron, my friend," the merchant cried, pumping Burr's hand. "Ain't my baby a beauty—*Bowery Queen*, off to Whampoa up the Canton River, back in a year with tea and spices of China worth the cost of the vessel and crew's hire once again! No wonder I can afford to keep you in comfort the way you keep all those scribblers and paint whackers and fiddlers who never earn a bloody cent, eh?" He laughed and slapped Burr's shoulder, the sort of unpleasant intimacy one must accept from those from whom one borrows. God, but he would like to be free of debt, free to tell the Simmons McAlesters of the world to go straight to hell! Instead he smiled.

"But Aaron," Sim said, "I see Hamilton's sheet snarling at your heels. A problem?"

Burr shrugged. "Seems foolish to me. Last spasm of

an embittered man. What can he do when his party tells him to go whistle in the wind? No, Sim, I'll win and the Virginia crowd will learn to mind its manners. I won't forget my enemies, or"—he fixed McAlester with the look that had transfixed so many juries—"my friends."

"Among them, you know I stand in the foremost ranks."

"Aye—you have been a good friend." He put the slightest emphasis on the past tense.

"And I am today," McAlester said quickly, "and will be tomorrow. Now, let me ask you—campaigns are expensive and leave you no time to practice law. Would a little—"

"Well, now that you mention it—"

"Shall I send over five hundred?"

"Or even seven . . ."

"I'll make it a thousand. Dash off a note in that amount and my man will pick it up."

"You're a prince, Sim. I'll have the note ready—and believe me, I won't forget."

"I know you won't, dear boy. Friends to the end!"

Voting lasted three days and the results took another week to drag in from around the state. As the reality became clear Peter Van Ness turned green and threw up in a wastebasket. He carried the basket out to dump it in the alley and he was crying. Burr felt as if he'd been punched in the chest and for a time wondered if he might be having a prolonged heart attack. And thought a heart attack might not be such a bad idea at that, given this disaster for which he was totally unprepared.

Morgan Lewis drew nearly thirty-one thousand; Burr had scarcely twenty-two thousand. He had been beaten. Not just beaten—he had been smashed, crushed, destroyed, humiliated, degraded. Something must be wrong, it made no sense. He locked himself up in Richmond Hill and saw only Peter and Matt, whom he sent out to probe the meaning. Was it theft? Error? All to be rectified the following week?

It was Peter with his instinct for figures who dug out the truth. It turned—again!—on Hamilton. It was Hamilton who had stiffened the Federalists against him when he was tied with Jefferson. Thwarted him then, thwarted him now—it was too much! It wasn't even that Hamilton had conspired against him or even been especially active, and somehow that made it worse, made him more culpable. He had simply talked. Yes, Hamilton had discredited himself with many Federalists but many others still looked on him as the leader.

What had happened, then, was that for every Democrat who swung away from Morgan Lewis to vote for Burr, a Federalist following Hamilton's lead had crossed the lines to vote for Lewis. Federalists voting for a Democrat! Such was the passion that Hamilton could instill in his followers. But it destroyed Aaron Burr and there was nothing he could do. Nothing. This man whom he'd never harmed had demonstrated the implacable hatred of a small man for a giant, sowing the conviction that Burr was a duplicitous man without principles who would sell state or nation for his own gain.

He sat at his desk, the gold coins Sim McAlester had sent over stacked on his blotter. They mocked him. He stayed inside with blinds drawn, unable to face the public that had repudiated him, that had drunk his beer and laughed in his face and turned thumbs down like any Roman crowd leaving him to the lions. He would meet sneers, laughter, fingers pointing, ridicule, he would be a man of pretension slashed off at the knees. What now his fine suit, his silver-headed stick, his condescending good cheer on the docks? He could not go forth a beaten man.

And then, outside he would meet McAlester and all

his debtors whose attitudes had shifted overnight, he was sure. His hand shook as he stacked and restacked the coins. McAlester had a drawerful of his notes. Dozens of other men held his notes. Peter had totted it all up once but Burr had thrown the figures away—he couldn't bear to look at them.

A man who'll be governor, who'll choose presidents, who probably will *be* the president—what does it matter if you take his notes? They're worth more in your hand than as cash. But a man destroyed? What sensible man of business wants such a pitiful fellow's notes? Call them and be done with it. His breath was short and ragged. He slapped the coins with the back of his hand and scattered them on the floor. He was facing debtor's prison and in debtor's prison he would die.

The sale of Richmond Hill closed; it would satisfy but a sliver of debt. After dark he shifted to the Fulton Street house. Van Ness and Davis and the others brought him news, which boiled down to the world getting along fine without Aaron Burr. He felt forgotten, diminished, shrunken. His creditors made no move but he knew they were out there, firelight flashing against the eyes of waiting wolves.

With the magnitude of the disaster came rage that settled to a coal that burned and burned in his heart. It was beyond quenching, nor did he try. It was to be nurtured, it was his when all else was taken, it became his measure as a man. Day by day it became more clear that someone must pay. Not necessarily Hamilton but not just anyone, either; it must be someone who mattered. The dueling field came ever more often to mind, sun bright and crisp, air cool, checked butt of the pistol solid in his hand, the summons to the ultimate, the weapon bucking, satisfying jar clear to his shoulder, everything boiled down to this deadly moment, everything settled and done, the awful pain eased, honor restored, everything put at risk, taking life or surrendering it . . . *settling* things.

He waited, watching through his minions, and then the answer came in a copy of the Albany *Register*. There he found a letter from a Dr. Charles Cooper of Albany to one Andrew Brown, who appeared to be an Albany merchant. Presumably Brown had passed them to the *Register*'s editor. The letters described a dinner at the home of Judge John Tayler of Albany at which Hamilton had been a guest. Cooper quoted Hamilton as saying Burr was a dangerous man and then added words that riveted Burr's attention: "I could detail to you a still more despicable opinion which General Hamilton has expressed of Mr. Burr."

There!

There could be no weaseling from this. Hamilton had a talent, in Burr's view, for saying things that fell just short of actionable. Twice he had stepped over the line and each time had hurried to remove the sting before the words became public. But this was far over the line. "Despicable" . . . no man of honor could allow such a statement to pass and still live with himself.

"Please, Aaron, don't let this get out of hand," Van Ness said. "'Despicable' is one of those ambiguous words, who knows what this Dr. Cooper really means by it. Let's go slowly here." His long face was troubled; Burr saw compassion and sorrow in his pale eyes and somehow that increased his fury. By *God!* he would not be an object of any man's pity.

His letter, which he told Van Ness to swallow his objections and deliver to Hamilton, was short and direct. It cited Cooper's statement and asked Hamilton to acknowledge or deny that he had uttered "a still more despicable opinion."

The answer, delivered in two days, appeared to Burr just the sort of equivocating nonsense you could expect from a blackguard who attacked behind one's back. Van Ness thought it reasonable; this infuriated Burr and he was ready to throw his old friend out until he remembered how few real friends he had left.

How, Hamilton asked, could he respond to so general a statement? Tell him specifically what was said and he would affirm or deny without delay.

"Let's ask the doctor," Peter said. "Maybe what he thinks is despicable is just plain old political comment."

"Bah! He won't get in the middle of this—next thing he knows he'll be facing pistols himself."

"Aaron," Peter said, "listen to me. I told Hamilton if he would just say he could remember nothing in the conversation that would justify the doctor's construction, that would settle the matter. I'll get it in writing, we'll publish it—"

But no—that would not suffice! Once again the man who had calumniated him would walk free, leaving Aaron Burr alone, broken, humiliated, to be cast into the dust, kicked into the gutter like the hogs and the dogs that died in the street. Oh, no, it would not do!

His next letter, which Peter carried, shaking his head in disapproval, demanded "a general disavowal of any intention on the part of Mr. Hamilton in his various conversations to convey impressions derogatory to the honor of Mr. Burr."

"God Almighty, Aaron," Peter cried. "*Any* conversation? Over what, the last twenty years? He's attacked you politically for years; I've heard you say things about him, too."

"Peter," Burr said, "if you're on Mr. Hamilton's side, then I erred in giving you the honor of acting for me. I think it's time to declare yourself."

Peter's pale face reddened. "Sir," he said, "I am your friend and I've proved that many times. I'm with you in this, too, but I'd rather not see you put your life at risk."

What life? What life did he have left after all that Hamilton had stolen from him? He put both hands on Peter's shoulders. "My dear old friend—I must do this. I must. Tell me you will see it through with me."

Peter was back within the hour. He said Nathaniel Pendleton was acting for Hamilton now. Burr knew Pendleton, a lawyer and a pleasant young man. No hostility was implied in Pendleton's acting in a matter of honor, as there was none in Van Ness's role. Peter said Nat had reported that Hamilton was prepared to say that his talk with Cooper had been entirely political and he did not—here Peter read from a note in his own handwriting, "did not attribute to Mr. Burr any instance of dishonorable conduct nor relate to his private character."

"And you told him?"

"On your instructions, Aaron, I told him that might once have sufficed but would no longer."

"Good," Burr said. "Good."

A July sun came up hot and glaring on the day of the duel. A rowboat carried Burr and Van Ness across the Hudson, oarsman sweating on the sweeps. They would fight in New Jersey to give a slight clothing of legality to their meeting. Dueling was against the law but everyone ignored that; to hide behind the law to avoid a fight was a clear sign of cowardice. New York authorities could ignore what happened in New Jersey while New Jersey could ignore what a pair of New Yorkers might do.

They landed on the Jersey shore under the towering Palisades and climbed halfway up to a ledge. It was long but narrow, utterly private, no way down from above, nor up from below except the single path and that accessible along the shore only at low tide. There would be no interruption. It was seven in the morning. Looking across the river they could see Manhattan Island wooded and deserted, about two miles north of the village of Greenwich. They were cleaning sticks and rocks from a level patch when Alex and Nat Pendleton arrived. Dr. Hosack was with them but he held at the boat so if called he could testify he'd seen nothing.

Burr stood carefully apart, as did Hamilton, while Peter and Nat reviewed the plans. He didn't look at Hamilton; it was too late, too much said and done, all cast in stone. Nat won both coin tosses; he would choose his man's position and he would call the duel. They loaded the two smoothbore pistols together; Hamilton had provided them as was his right. Each took a .544 ball—oversized, to Burr the balls looked nearly as big as walnuts. He looked away and let his eye wander; the Palisade cliff to his right, the broad river below, beyond it the long, narrow island, the city in the distance. Downriver he could see the roof of Richmond Hill; the German already was stripping timber to make way for his building lots. He sighed and a great calm came over him; he was doing the right thing and if this was how life was to end, it would be a good ending, in defense of honor. Gulls were flashes of white near the river's surface and high above a pair of hawks wheeled on rigid wings. He thought of Theodosia and her beautiful little son who called him Gampy, whose little hand clutching his finger could almost make up for the slings and arrows of the world. Almost.

Nat Pendleton placed them carefully. Alex was ten paces off, slender and elegant as always, looking quite calm. They were facing each other. Neither acknowledged the other. Peter put the pistol into his hand. He closed over the checked butt, his finger caressed the trigger and pulled away. It was a nine-inch barrel of solid brass, the London maker's name, Wogdon, cut into the metal. Nine inches; a killing barrel, hard to miss with so long a weapon. But it was Alex's choice. He held the weapon close to his face and pointing at the sky, the heft good and right. Pendleton had placed Burr with his back to the light, presumably to make him a better target. There was glare and presently Hamilton put on a pair of spectacles, the better to aim, so Burr assumed.

The sense of calm was overpowering. He was at ease, he had confronted his agony and was dealing with it, and if death were a minute away or fifty years off he would meet it in peace. He had made his stand.

"Are you ready?" Pendleton's call.

"Yes."

"Yes." He saw Alex match his own turn into the duelist's stance, standing sideways to minimize the target, right foot twenty-four inches ahead of left, gut drawn in, pistol held to deflect a bullet from the shooter's head even as it delivered its own killing ball.

The ready call, the answering affirmatives, hung in the air for a shadowy, quivering moment and then Pendleton, voice gone high, cried:

"Pre-*zent!*"

He was steady, suddenly supremely confident, and he brought the pistol out to level, saw Hamilton's body squarely centered over the sights and felt a rush of exultation so savage and pleasurable as to be nearly sexual. And he squeezed smoothly down on the trigger, felt it give as the hammer fell, felt the pistol buck, through the smoke and roar saw the blue blossom from the other's pistol—

Hamilton turned, the pistol fell from his hand, he gave a single loud cry and fell on his face.

Burr shook his head, looked around, looked at his own pistol and dropped it on the ground. Hamilton had fired and missed. He started toward the fallen figure as he might toward someone struck by a cab in the street, no clear sense that he'd had anything in particular to do with it—

Van Ness spun him around. They started down the path. Dr. Hosack was climbing up and to Burr's great surprise when they were near Peter produced an umbrella, which he opened and held before Burr's face that Hosack might not see him when they passed. Then they hustled on down the steep path and found the boatman waiting to push off and it was over, over, over—and Burr had no idea how he felt, none whatsoever.

It was incredible . . . perfectly outrageous. The city of New York acted as if there had never been a duel before, as if murder had been committed. Peter and Matt Davis and Sammy were in and out in relays with bulletins from the crowd. Information ricocheted across the city. How Burr's ball had smashed liver and lights in Hamilton. How the great man had looked up with a gentle smile as Hosack approached, and said, "This is a mortal wound, Doctor."

How for many minutes he had seemed dead, and then, lying in the bottom of the rowboat returning him he had revived and murmured that he'd lost all feeling in his legs. How he'd thought only of his wife and daughters, giving noble instructions to break the news to them slowly. How a friend had seen his boat land at Greenwich Village and had ushered them into his house. How surgeons skilled in gunshot wounds had been summoned from a French frigate in harbor and had concurred that nothing could be done. A priest gave him absolution. How his daughters stood by his bed and he shut his eyes to stop his tears at sight of them. The heaviest doses of laudanum could not ease his agony.

And who had done this terrible deed? That wretch

Burr. That villain, that scoundrel, that evil man who'd never been up to any good. Rumors flashed across the city. Burr had practiced, firing for two hours daily. He had wrapped himself in silk, believing it would deflect bullets. He had laughed and shouted in triumph when Hamilton fell. On the battery a mob burned him in effigy.

Hamilton died the next afternoon at two. His pain had been excruciating, death a welcome release. Flags flew at half-mast. Naval vessels fired minute guns, the solemn thumps a minute apart like a giant drum beating out the nation's sorrow. His funeral cortege was a mile long and the streets were lined with weeping mourners. That wretch Burr was on everyone's lips.

The wretch cowered in the house on Fulton Street, the door locked, the blinds drawn, Matt and Peter slipping through alleys to his back door with their hateful reports. Burr could not understand it. Duels were commonplace, fatal often enough to make this one not unusual. It was a *duel*, for God's sake, not some back-alley ambush. They had stood in the sunshine ten paces apart, each with a loaded pistol, each taking his chance. One bullet struck, the other missed; it could just as well have been the other way around.

Just a duel . . . but the city carried on as if it were the tragedy of the ages. A grand jury was empaneled, a murder indictment demanded. Then a new eruption. It was revealed that the noble Hamilton had said he would throw away his first shot to give Burr time to reconsider. Despicable, if true, Burr muttered. Pendleton announced Hamilton's intention and said he had fired by accident when Burr's bullet struck him. Peter insisted Hamilton had fired and missed; he revisited the ground and found Hamilton's bullet imbedded in a tree twelve feet above ground. Each side insisted that proved its point. But Van Ness went into hiding, afraid to walk the streets.

It was so incredibly unfair! Burr had acted out of

honor and with perfect propriety—and he was being pilloried, his enemy glorified. It was exactly as he'd been treated for years now, acting always with propriety within his rigid honor code, and always his enemies traduced him without mercy, Jefferson and Madison and the Virginia crowd, and now New York—and Hamilton, striking him even in death!

The grand jury, denied a murder charge because the event took place in New Jersey, returned a felony indictment for issuing a challenge; a grand jury in New Jersey prepared an indictment for murder. It was closing in, all rigged against him. On the eleventh day after Hamilton's death Aaron Burr caught a night packet to Perth Amboy, hat pulled low and using a pseudonym. From there he took a rapid stage to Philadelphia and went to the home of his old friend Charles Biddle, into whose family dear old Jim Wilkinson had married. A few days later a friend traveling under a false name arrived to say that New York's governor, that same Morgan Lewis, was preparing extradition papers to have Burr hauled back in irons.

And he was off again, southward toward Maryland and Virginia and the Carolinas, flying from New York ruin with Wilkinson's words booming in his brain, the West an empire awaiting an emperor, Mexico the pot of gold at the end of the rainbow. Address me, he told his darling Theodosia in a hurried letter, by my pseudonym—Mr. R. King.

He wasn't finished yet.

ELEVEN

Washington, summer 1804

On one of those hot, humid days when Dolley Madison couldn't wait to escape to Montpelier she heard a carriage crunch into her yard. From a third-floor window she saw Maggie Smith being handed down the steps, and called, "I'll be right down." And, of course, she thought of Aaron Burr. It was in Maggie's—Margaret Bayard Smith's—drawing room she had warned James Bayard that he flirted with civil war, he being Maggie's uncle or cousin or something. As Delaware's sole congressman he had had the deciding vote when Aaron tried to steal the presidency. Federalists dreamed of setting aside the election and Dolley had come privately to lay out what would happen: Virginia and Pennsylvania troops would march to forestall a coup. Coup? Mr. Bayard sputtered at that but it made the point, all right. Clicking down the steps, seeing Maggie in the foyer below strangely pale with her husband's paper, the *National Intelligencer*, rolled in her hands, the recurring thought came, yes, Aaron was wrong, made a terrible mistake, but still and all, Jimmy had been too hard on him, breaking him politically when even with his flaws and ambition he had value—

And then, like a blow to her body, Maggie's cry, "Have you heard? Oh, Dolley, Mr. Hamilton is dead."

Dolley stared at her, knowing somehow what was coming.

"Aaron Burr killed him," Maggie said.

"Oh, my God . . ." Her knees went watery and she sagged slowly till she was on the polished floor, legs curled under her.

"A duel?" she whispered. But of course, a duel—that damnable election in New York! She understood how much store he'd put in that, what expectations he'd assigned, his utter confidence that day they talked on the street that New York would reward him. And then it all had gone wrong and he'd been crushed—

Alexander Hamilton dead? Scanning the paper, Maggie gave her the horrid details. Alex's gallantry now magnified in death, how he'd lingered a day in agony, how the noble man had said he would throw away his first shot, how he hated dueling but Aaron harried him until he had no choice, how his last thought was for daughters and wife, how Burr had shot him down like a dog, how mourners had lined up for blocks and mobs hung Burr in effigy and Burr fled the city under cover of night—

Oh, God, it was too much!

"Poor Aaron," she whispered.

Disapproval swept Maggie's face. Coolness in her voice, she said, "Mr. Burr? It's Mr. Hamilton who's dead."

"Oh, I understand," Dolley said. "I understand too much." She extended her hand. "Here, help me up, there's a good friend. And then, forgive me, but I'm going to go lie down."

Tears streamed down her face. She bade Maggie

good-bye and slowly went up to the bedroom and took off her gown and fell on the bed in her chemise. The slow leakage of tears continued. Presently she shivered despite the weather. She drew a sheet to her chin.

Alexander Hamilton dead. Slender, vibrant, strong, a current in him that focused your attention and made you want to agree, to earn his approval, see his smile. He was a great man, he and General Washington and John Adams and Tom and her own darling little husband, great men all—how different the country would have been without them! The general gone, John Adams finished, now Alex cut down in his prime. By Burr. They had been friends once, Aaron and Alex—her tears were not really for Alex but not for Aaron either. She cried for the pain inherent in living, the way fate set courses from which there was no turning, the cruelty of inevitability.

He and Aaron were so alike, each immensely attractive to women with consorts everywhere, conquests for which Alex's long-suffering wife forgave him time and again. He was on the other side politically and could be as harsh as anyone else, but in person he was funny, scintillating at the dinner table, gentle in manner, swift and witty when challenged, cutting when challenged hard. Still, you could catch an underlying contempt in his voice when you listened carefully, even when he was at his most charming. Perhaps there was something cold in him, too. Razor-edged intellect so far surpassing that of most people was a gift; he shouldn't have used it to humiliate. He was a great man and of towering intellect but not without blemishes.

And Aaron . . . poor Aaron. Yes, he'd dug his own grave, he shouldn't have tried to steal the presidency or wanted so much from the election or yielded to rage, yes, yes, yes—but so much had been taken from him, too, all his bright dreams turned to dross. She liked Aaron Burr and he'd been a good friend to her, but that wasn't it.

Rather, she understood him. He burned with need and it was his flexibility, his liquid sense of ethics that could be adjusted so readily to attain his ends without lessening his warm self-approval that made him his own worst enemy. And now he was alone, indicted for murder, wanted in New York and New Jersey, disgraced, running south ahead of the law. Alone, the crowd abandoning him, dreams canceled, hopes dying with Alexander Hamilton's last breath . . . Yes, Maggie was right, it was Alex who was dead, but it was a sort of death for Aaron too. He would pay and pay across what was left of his life.

Then, her breath catching in her throat, a shattering new thought—in the end, Aaron could blame Jimmy for his ruin. He would never blame himself. Never. Probably he hated Tom, but they had never been friends. Betrayal comes from friends, from those in whom you have invested some measure of love and who then turn on you. He might well see Jimmy in exactly that light.

Young Mr. Pendleton had made public the negotiations preliminary to the duel. Both letters and his verbal encounters with a Mr. Van Ness representing Aaron were spelled out in detail in the *Intelligencer* report. It took but a single reading to see how narrow and remote had been the offense and how relentlessly Aaron had forced the issue. Bruised by loss, feeling oppressed, Aaron had wanted to strike out, make someone pay. Alex plainly had tried to avoid the issue but Aaron had given him no room for apology or even explanation, instituting new demands as old demands were met. Aaron wanted to fight, wanted to kill; she could see him now, willingly accepting the possibility of losing his own life, pressing on and on. That would be his way—he was a freebooter at heart, a swashbuckler for whom risk was a pleasure. Alex was a man of brilliant intellect who looked upon risk as risk and saw no reason to take more than necessary. Of course he had tried to avoid risk for a manufactured quarrel in which the direct statement he had or had not made was never even identified—a deadly quarrel over a single adjective and that delivered by an unidentified individual who had no part in the proceedings! But it was so plain: Aaron was a fighting man and Alex wasn't. And, what really mattered, Jimmy wasn't a fighting man either.

But Aaron was destroying himself. His mad maneuvers to seize the presidency, his horror at the collapse of his dreams in New York, now a desperate man running into the wilderness ahead of indictments for murder. Whom would he blame if not himself? He would have no trouble seeing Jimmy as the betrayer, and little more in persuading himself that all his troubles could be laid at Jimmy's door. A challenge can always be contrived. She knew that if Jimmy were pressed hard enough, he would not refuse to fight. And in the depths of her soul, she knew that if they met on the dueling field Aaron would kill her husband.

It was a calamity visited upon the nation, the vice president of the United States killing the leader of the opposition party. The news struck Madison a near physical blow. Of course it was just a duel, personal, there can hardly be anything more personal than a quarrel that leads to a duel, everyone should understand that. Certainly that was the position they must take—but in truth he knew this might have set back by a decade the nation's efforts to take its place in the family of nations with full respect, position acknowledged, rights established under international law. It was little enough respected now, Britain stealing its seamen with impunity, France sneeringly talking of undoing the Louisiana sale, Spain openly threatening war, the British and Spanish ambassadors supping constantly with the opposition in their host country. Now he knew the cry would go up that the barbaric Americans are shooting each other down like so many street curs.

Mentally he turned up his hands; maybe it was just another obstacle in a long campaign that he had every intention of winning. But there was a personal side too. This would strike Dolley a brutal blow. He went home early and found her lying down. She had been crying. She gazed at him wordlessly, and all at once, surprising himself as much as he obviously did her, he blurted, "I suppose you blame me."

But that that was foolish, born out of his own uncertainties and perhaps a touch of guilt, for Aaron had sought forgiveness and found not a shred of that godlike quality in James Madison, not a bit.

She sat up. "Oh, Jimmy, you don't think that, please."

He sat on the bed. "Sorry," he whispered. "Self-focus out of hand. But I—" He started to say he couldn't help it, but he thought that wasn't true and he'd do well to keep his mouth shut. So he held her and she put her cheek against his and presently she went to sleep and he sat there thinking.

Alex and Aaron . . . perhaps they'd been too alike, each too powerful to tolerate the other in his sphere, so perhaps there was an inevitability here that could not have been foreseen. Alex insisted that Burr had no core structure nor guiding inner essence. Still, you had to remember that it was Alex who had been pushed aside in New York when Burr made Tammany Hall a political power and snatched New York's electoral votes. It was Burr who had put Alex into the angry minority.

He remembered the young Burr, sleek, handsome, profoundly self-assured while still a boy at Princeton, then later the aura of Revolutionary War hero glowing, this well before the meeting with Dolley. Looking back now, those seemed innocent days when they were full of faith that they could create what was unknown since classical days, a democracy to stand strong among the kings and Cossacks of modern times. They were all friends then. Madison and Hamilton had been—well, not close, exactly, but comrades-in-arms supporting the new Constitution.

But then the French Revolution, the seminal event that was shattering Europe and changing monarchical expectations, started collapsing into anarchy and terror. Probably Alex's yearning for authoritarian government started then. American democratic government was just starting. The Bank of the United States that Alex designed was working well—so well we still had it long after Federalists had been retired. You could see Alex swell with importance in those days, his bias to the well-born and the wealthy growing stronger, perhaps from some of his own inner yearnings and fears. Good old General Washington, God bless him, had spent his life working his way to the top of that class, starting poor and landless, rising on sheer ability; he had tried hard to be balanced but gradually he tilted Alex's way.

Dolley stirred and Madison adjusted the shade to dim the light pouring into the room. The seismic shift was starting then. Madison and Jefferson had made a horseback tour of New York and New England, botanizing, they called it, and certainly Tom was off his horse to examine and sketch every new plant he saw, but they talked politics too, and no one gave them a warmer welcome than Aaron Burr in New York. An odd point, Tom, Aaron, Madison himself, were of the elite that Alex sought to empower. He remembered Alex furiously angry one day shouting, "Class doesn't impress you because you already have it!" Again, when Madison listed the virtues of the common man, Alex glared and said,

"The naïveté of the well-born. You can afford the benign view."

"Well," Madison remembered saying, "your everyday American, I say he's inherently decent, honest unless sorely tempted, trustworthy as voter or as juror."

"You've seen too little of the brute world," Alex had answered, patronizing a little. "Out of broader experience, I say he is not to be trusted, he's selfish, he'll sacrifice the large and the whole for his immediate interest or even gratification, and above all he must be controlled."

"No!" Madison had been having trouble with his temper. "Free men can govern themselves very well. You'll see."

"If I have my way," Alex had said, "they won't be given much chance." There was no humor in his voice. Then as if fearing he'd gone too far, he'd added, "Now, see here, Jimmy, I won't have you characterizing me as undermining our government. The Constitution is mine, too, and I'd do nothing to subvert it. We're a republic, the people can vote us out whenever they choose. All we're talking about is interpretation of the Constitution. Nothing in it says that government can't pass laws to protect itself and keep a tight rein on boors and louts who lack the inner means to control themselves. And I say it's essential that government do just that."

"And I believe free men must be free to vote their will, and on that basis I suppose we must fight it out."

So they settled down to fight the philosophic issue. But Alex did put the country ahead of philosophy, when Aaron tried to seize the presidency from Tom, and again, when Aaron tried to resume power in New York. Each time, note, Aaron had been the loser. Yet Alex's views had darkened. Madison had seen a recent letter in his distinctive hand. Alex had become so disillusioned that he could write of the nation's "real disease, which is DEMOCRACY." Capitals for the evil—which he himself had helped create. He must have been full of pain and pessimism. Poor devil . . .

And Aaron had proved his dark side too in that opportunistic grab for a presidency. Still, Madison had to wonder if his own vigor in stripping Burr of power had all been selfless. Was there no touch of revenge? No political jealousy, no rivalry in succeeding Tom, no fear of Tammany and New York?

No, he told himself sharply, the man had brought them close to civil war—how could he be trusted? But just the same, having to convince himself again left an ugly taste. And now Hamilton with his financial genius was dead, and Burr with a certain genius of his own was a wanted man with all his prospects destroyed.

Still, remember the sharpness in Burr's eyes, mysterious and unreadable. What would he do now? Roll over and die? Hide on his daughter's plantation in South Carolina? Aaron Burr? Not likely. He remembered Albert Gallatin saying Burr was a dangerous man—and now the truth of that statement had a new and quite visceral reality. For now, wounded but not dead, he would be more than ever dangerous. They had not heard the last of him, and what came next might be real trouble.

Dolley stirred and her eyes opened just as he was deciding this was a thought with which he need not burden her. Not now . . .

★　　　★　　　★　　　★　　　★

TWELVE

New Orleans, summer 1804

It was past midnight and Brigadier General James Wilkinson, commanding, United States Army, was in his carriage crunching along a roadway of crushed shell that ran alongside the river, returning with a sense of high satisfaction from Madame Gratiot's establishment. A good dinner with a fine wine, quiet atmosphere among genial men who were painfully cordial whether they liked him or not—one of power's pleasures, he thought, was the way men who resent and fear you pull their forelocks and pretend to be friends—and afterward a session with Eva Marie. There were a couple of new women, a stunning mulatto newly arrived from Haiti and a high blonde who said she was from Paris, but Eva Marie knew the tricks that got the general going—he didn't exactly need them, but they did help—and he had stayed with the tried and true. Now he smoked a good cigar from Cuba as his carriage wended toward his quarters.

Houses appeared along the river road, an occasional horseman, here and there men on foot certainly up to no good at this hour. He locked the carriage door on the inside, making sure the window glass was in place. His driver was a husky trooper named McClanahan overcome with gratitude for the sergeant's stripes the general had granted him and he kept a cudgel handy, but tonight the general had dispensed with his usual guard, four horsemen riding ahead, two troopers clinging to the rear of the carriage. He didn't like to advertise his presence at Madame Gratiot's; all the best men were there but they were discreet about it.

As they passed into the narrow streets of the city, houses flush to the property line with blank faces that hid who knew what deviltry inside, a century-old city showing its patina of sedate age, he was thinking with mild arousal of Eva Marie's charms and so was quite unprepared for the explosion of noise and the howling mob of men that came bursting through swinging doors. He saw in a moment that they were passing a famous trouble spot, Monsieur DuBois's ballroom, if that was the right word, where a weekly quadroon ball was held, drawing dusky women and excited men of all stripes and classes. The mob poured into the street carrying the fight from inside and individuals attacked each other with howls of rage, screams of gutter English and obscene French, Americans, and French natives of New Orleans at it again.

The carriage lurched to a stop as the mob surrounded it and the general felt a shiver that started at his eyes and ran straight to his bowels. He checked the carriage door again to be sure of its lock and shrank back into the seat, trying to place himself out of sight. Breath rasping, he half drew his saber and then as if it were hot he thrust it back into the scabbard. He had his pistol but now realized he wasn't sure of the load, and to draw but not fire, that would be worse—

Machetes from the cane fields were flashing outside, men ducking and twisting. He saw a Frenchman backed in a corner holding everyone off with a rapier, men in ruffles and lace with dirks snatched from forearm scabbards ready to kill. A tall man in buckskin moved a shiny fighting knife in tight little circles daring anyone to come on, and just then a little man in a seaman's round hat slashed his knife arm with a machete swung from far overhead and he screamed and the knife fell and he crawled away, the little man slapping his rear with the flat of his blade and shrieking with laughter. And then someone knocked the seaman down and kicked his head, the machete flying away.

A terrible face appeared at the carriage window, an awful demon clinging to the door, screaming and pounding on the window, and when the glass broke the general felt his time had come. Then the face disappeared and the loudest noise was his own rasping breath. He beat on the carriage roof with his stick, telling McClanahan to drive on and run down anyone in the way but then from the opposite window he saw McClanahan pulled from the box and beaten to his knees. Three men were kicking him. Then the carriage lurched forward. He opened the eye window and saw one of the rioters astride the lead horse whipping the beast into motion, the other horses ready to follow.

As the carriage hurtled away he had a quick impression of two troopers, the regular patrol, approaching at a run. Thank God! But as if they didn't see the carriage they stopped before the mob. One began beating the pavement with his stick and the other bawled, "Sergeant of the guard! Sergeant of the guard!" Then the carriage swept away, rocking furiously on mad turns. The general thought of jumping out but God knew what perils would await him there, broken bones and broken head against the worn cobbles of the streets, and with lips quivering he waited for the carriage to go over with a smash—

And then realized it was slowing. He looked again. The rioting rider was gone, the horses were slowing and stopping of their own accord, panting. He opened the carriage door and peered out cautiously. The street was deserted. He and his carriage were alone. Fearful the horses would start again he managed to reach the step onto the box without touching ground. He looked around and realized he had no idea where he was. Then it struck him that he'd never handled a four-horse team. Suppose he started the horses up, could he—

"Sir, sir, are you all right?"

The general turned with a sensation of absolute joy and saw the sergeant of the guard followed by a half dozen mounted troopers coming at a fast trot. Immediately he jumped down from the box and caught the near horse's bridle.

"Don't be ridiculous," he snapped. "Of course I'm all right. Don't be a fool!" Suddenly he was enraged. "What took you so long? Where have you been? DuBois's place, that's where—"

"Yes, sir, we went there first, those devils took off like birds when they saw us, left a couple half-dead in the street, we flung them in a cell—"

"Well, goddamn it, you took your own sweet time in looking for your general. I won't forget that, Sergeant."

"Yes, sir."

"You'll be lucky, you keep your stripes. What about McClanahan?"

"They beat him pretty good, I'm afraid, sir."

"Damned fool—let himself be pulled off the box. Well, here, here, let's get on with it. Put up a man to drive, the rest of you follow on, let's get moving!" He glared at the sergeant. "Do I have to take care of every goddamned thing?"

———

"Trouble again at DuBois's last night," Governor Claiborne said. Wilkinson saw that Wee Willie was chewing his yellow mustache again, never a good sign.

"The usual," the general said. "I broke it up quickly enough."

Willie stared. "You were there?"

"On my rounds, you know. I called the guard and made sure they cleaned it up."

"I'm impressed. I didn't know you made regular rounds."

"Irregular, you might say. I like to keep my eyes open, turn up when least expected, you know. Does soldiers and civilians alike a world of good to know the top man has his eye on them, eh?"

"The usual, you said?"

"I had the sergeant of the guard interrogate the scoundrels. Seems the Americans wanted Tennessee reels and the French wanted gavottes. Same old story."

"Good God. Fight to the death over a dance tune. They're all barbarians, especially these Frenchmen. Nothing wrong with good Tennessee tunes—after all, this is America now, whether they like it or not."

"And they don't."

"I know that! And I don't give a damn and neither should you."

"I don't know that I do," Wilkinson said, putting a note of danger in his voice and starting to stand.

"No, no," Claiborne said quickly, "I didn't mean to imply—I'm a bit on edge, I suppose. This constant squabbling and trouble. This anger. Americans feeling they're the new inheritors come to take possession and get rich overnight, French feeling they've had city and country stolen, French saying the Americans should adjust immediately to their ways, Americans saying who the hell do these Frenchmen think they are, they don't like the United States let 'em go elsewhere . . ."

Wilkinson, who had heard this a hundred times, held up a hand. "Just human nature, Governor, and probably not important. A few nights in the *jusqado* judiciously applied will settle most of 'em down."

Claiborne sighed and looked down, chastised.

"More important, I think, is the spirit of revolt running." He watched Claiborne's eyes jerk open. Such talk always alarmed the governor.

"Have you heard something?" Claiborne whispered.

"The talk seems louder. This American, Edward Livingston, left New York under a cloud, you know, and I don't give a damn if his brother is ambassador to France, he's got his fingers in everything—practically taken over the Mexico Association."

"Mexico Association?"

"Talkers in the main, I think." Actually, he thought they showed considerable promise if some clumsiness in matters of conspiracy and plotting, and in fact, they did talk too much. "They dream of seizing Mexico, you know."

"Well, God Almighty, we can't stand for that!"

"Can't stop talk, and we'll pinch 'em if they move. Point is, American aims are clashing with French aims, and these French bastards, there's no one more arrogant in the world. Not an ounce of loyalty to the new nation, they'd love to see France return or Spain resume control or declare themselves independent and take care of the Americans with machetes."

"That's just it," Claiborne bleated. "It's terrible." Then, rather irrelevantly, "They insist I learn French."

Wilkinson laughed. "Who could learn such a through-the-nose language? And why should you? Be a sign of weakness if you tried."

"You think so?"

"Absolutely—and if you tried you'd be bound to mangle the language at first, and then they'd ridicule you."

"That's true, isn't it? Where would American dignity be then, people laughing in their sleeves?"

"Or in your face."

"Yes . . . do you think that's why they pester me about French, so they can ridicule me?"

"Wouldn't surprise me. Then Lassaut and Morales still hanging on, they encourage New Orleanians to believe they're soon to be rescued from us American devils." Lassaut was the French prefect who had turned over the province, Morales the Spanish intendant who'd been in charge until the transfer.

Claiborne was chewing his mustache again. "I have no instructions to remove them."

"Doubtless it would make things worse to try."

In the same uneasy voice Claiborne continued, "From the tenor of the messages from Washington, I think we've given up any idea of taking West Florida by force. Or Texas. That should ease things, don't you think?"

"Um . . . yes, certainly." This had taken Wilkinson by surprise and he needed a moment to digest it. Then he said, "In addition to Lassaut and Morales, I suppose you know Folch is back again."

"Folch?"

"Vizente Folch, governor of West Florida."

"Spanish, you mean?"

"Spanish, yes. No idea what he's doing here. I thought I'd go see him."

"Why would you do that?"

"Spanish army is building up in West Florida, according to my information, perhaps in Texas too. I intend to let the governor know if he tries to use those forces he and they will come to a very dark end."

Claiborne brightened. "Good idea. But see him privately, just the two of you, so we can deny it if Washington objects."

"Yes, sir," Wilkinson said briskly. "Excellent advice."

When he left the governor was by the window looking disconsolate, chewing on his yellow mustache.

He strode smartly along the street, swinging his stick, left hand resting on his saber, watching men doff their hats and step respectfully out of the way. Wee Willie was unchanged, seemed to learn nothing, gain no strength; he had a dictator's power and was afraid to go out his door.

Of course New Orleans was a hotbed of intrigue, ready to explode—the general was an old hand at intrigue, he could show these local folks a few things. But there would be no revolt, not until a leader came along. A man whose voice could ring to the rafters and lift men to exaltation, so that they hungered to storm the barricades. Not the general; Wilkinson knew himself well. At intrigue, negotiations, maneuver, guile, he was without equal, but the capacity to inspire would never be his gift. No, what was needed here was someone with a golden tongue and deep insights into the ways of men and politics.

Someone, in short, like Aaron Burr, a man of real power. Someone who when a man thwarted him had no compunction about shooting him down like a dog. The news of Aaron's duel had come the week before and Wilkinson had seen instantly that it would destroy him. You couldn't kill a man like Hamilton and get away with it. Aaron should have understood that and found another way to take his revenge. With some attention to detail, for instance, he could have put Hamilton into debtor's prison and disgraced him. Instead he killed him and made him a sanctified hero for all time. And ruined himself.

Which was fine. Aaron had been locked into his New York dream but now it was time to dream on a scale measured in hundredweights of gold! So he walked along musing on the ways of fate. It might take Aaron a little while to perceive the reality but then he'd come along like a dog following a piece of meat.

And strolling, hand on his saber hilt, he said out loud, "I *own* the son of a bitch now. He's mine." He laughed, thinking of the fine old adage, all comes to he who waits. And the general had been waiting a long time.

"Honorable sir: I will call upon you at ten this evening and wish to see you alone; should you find this uninteresting, please return a note by my messenger."

There, Wilkinson thought, that should tweak the Spaniard properly, a nice mixture of authority and courtesy, subtle reminder that the visitor was off his own and on the general's ground.

With lingering regret he set aside his uniform and wore black with buckled shoes, a freshly charged pistol under his coat his only weapon. When his carriage stopped before the governor's hotel a well-dressed aide stepped from the shadows and bowed deeply. The general acknowledged the lackey with a curt nod and followed him up two flights of stairs, trying to avoid puffing on the second flight. A door gaped open; the governor was waiting. Wilkinson let the flunky announce him, then strode boldly through the door to find Governor Folch poised in the middle of the room. The governor was a tall, slender man with a dueling scar prominent on his right cheek. He wore black velvet with silk hose and silver buckles on his shoes with an effusion of lace at throat and wrists and he bowed with just the right blend of courtesy with equality.

A second man stepped forward dressed in even finer fashion. A flash of irritation at this violation of his terms vanished as the general recognized the Marquis de Casa Calvo, a Spanish commissioner who was hanging on in

New Orleans for no apparent reason after having effected the transfer of Louisiana from Spain to France to the United States. Señor Casa Calvo might be most useful.

The governor poured an excellent Spanish brandy and offered an innocuous toast to which the general responded with an equal lack of color, wetting his lips but not swallowing. This was no time to have alcohol in his brain.

Then, amenities done, the governor put a harsh note in his voice as he said, "I'm glad you chose to call, General, because it allows me to inform you most emphatically that American threats to Florida are intolerable. They demean us but demean even more those who make them." His English was heavily accented but fluent. "West Florida is not to be considered part of Louisiana—and I might add that the transfer of Louisiana to *los Estados Unidos* is itself the height of illegality, and many of us feel that His Majesty should be about reclaiming it immediately. France made solemn covenant to return the province if possessing it no longer fit the first consul's plans. But no—quite illegal, sir!"

In fact, as Wilkinson well knew, such agreement as there was had been an afterthought, by the Spanish commissioner and by the French; he could imagine the laggard Spaniard saying, Oh, by the way, and the Frenchman with the arrogance of the powerful waving a hand and saying, Certainly, certainly, as he hurried to dinner.

But this was as good an opening as any. "From the tenor of what you're saying, I take it that you'll be surprised when I tell you I agree with you."

"You do?" Folch said. "That does surprise me." Wilkinson saw Casa Calvo smile. The dueling scar on Folch's cheek was suddenly livid, and he said, "Then you should understand how serious we are. To mince no words, we are ready for war. A battalion has arrived from

Cuba and more are coming. Texas is being reinforced as well. American filibusterers will be dealt with summarily." He paused. "Do you understand me, sir? By firing squad! We will show no mercy."

Wilkinson smiled. "Exactly the right course, sir. More than justified by my country's excesses."

There was a long silence. At last Folch said, "This is not the attitude I expected. Do I scent a Trojan horse at work?"

"I think we should hold up now and hear what the general has to say," Casa Calvo said. His voice was soft but very confident. It was the first time he had spoken and Wilkinson saw immediately that Folch considered him a superior.

The general smiled warmly. "Of course, you are suspicious as a wise leader must be. But clearly you are unaware of how long I have been a friend of Spain." From the corner of his eye he caught Casa Calvo's nod. Then, portentously, his gaze boring into Folch's eyes, he said, "A full twenty years ago I pledged fealty to Spain and it has never wavered. My reports have furthered Spain's interests again and again. For officials here—and for the captain general in Cuba—I have repeatedly reported American aims on Spanish territory and I have headed them off as well. My dear governor, America is unalterably your enemy, but at the same time, Spain has no better friend that General James Wilkinson."

Folch glanced at Casa Calvo, who nodded and smiled. "Secret Agent number thirteen, if I'm not mistaken," he said.

"Quite so," Wilkinson said.

"You have rendered us great service, sir."

"*Gracias.*" To the governor, "I think this makes clear you can trust the information I bring you." He waited a beat. "And the guidance I can offer you." Another beat. "I could warn you when danger approaches, alert you when threats are false, keep you a step ahead of your enemy. Make no mistake, sooner or later the United States will attack. Of course I would know about it at the start, and I could head it off or I could alert you if it couldn't be held off."

"Could, you say," Folch said.

"Well, certainly, I would want to feel my loyalty and help were appreciated."

"Tangibly, I expect."

"Is there any other form of appreciation? Let me be frank, Governor. These many years ago when I took my oath of fealty to Spain I was promised as a Spanish agent a stipend of two thousand dollars a year in gold. That was duly delivered for a number of years, but then it stopped, with just dribbles since. Now, sir, as I reckon the books, your payments to me are in arrears in the amount of twenty thousand dollars."

That was a stretch, but faint heart never prospered at the dice table. He let the amount sink in, then said, "As commanding general of the United States Army, my value is greater. Now I believe four thousand a year in gold would demonstrate Spain's appreciation appropriately."

"My God, General, twenty now and four each year, that's a fortune," Folch said. "I don't even have such funds in gold."

"Very well." Wilkinson stood. "You're not interested. Fine. I've served you well but for no real appreciation, it turns out. Now, to be blunt, you will discover American plans when you are attacked. But so be it." He turned to the door.

"One moment, General," Casa Calvo said, breaking a long silence. "Don't be hasty—an unfortunate American trait. You must know that in the Spanish world there usually is a way to work around problems." He tented his fingers and leaned his chin against them; he was a small-ish man with round cheeks and a small mustache and a shock of black hair that fell over his forehead.

He thrust the errant lock back in place, and said, "Your information obviously is of great value. Twenty thousand in gold, well, that is a large sum to be raised at once, but it is in my immediate power to deliver twelve thousand tomorrow morning and the rest in timely fashion. And accept your four thousand requirement for the future stipend."

"In gold," Wilkinson said.

"In gold. Satisfactory?"

"Most satisfactory, Señor. Because it demonstrates the value my adopted nation of Spain places on my service."

He saw a faintly contemptuous smile flash over the Spaniard's face and regretted the fatuous remark. Recovering, he said, "In appreciation, I will give you some advice, put it on paper later, but run through it now."

He held up a hand, ticking off fingers. "First, build up your forces in Florida and Texas. Be prepared for attack and it probably won't come. Your former officials are still here. Good—keep them here as long as the Americans will tolerate it. They can keep you abreast and they keep the Americans guessing. I can tell you that our officials are profoundly uneasy at their presence but feel it would show weakness to order them to go. That uneasiness can pay you rich dividends."

He put on a serious face. "The United States considers New Orleans and the navigation of the river to be vital, so were you to seize either there would be real resistance. But the rest of Louisiana, all that lying west of the Mississippi, you should reclaim that immediately and hold it as buffer against attacks on Mexico. There is in some quarters in America, I'm sorry to say, a hunger for Mexico and its gold that approaches a mania. You need not only Texas but all to the north of it as a buffer from which you can sweep American adventurers. You'd have no great trouble in seizing the land west of the river— American forces there are physically weak and disloyal to boot, so no great resistance could or would be made. Politically you would find much weight on your side in the United States—many in the East are opposed to Louisiana anyway. They'd never countenance war to preserve a stretch of country they didn't want in the first place."

He expanded on these points for fifteen to twenty minutes. Finally, running down, he made a show of searching his mind for anything else. "Oh, yes, an exploring party is setting out from St. Louis now. Small, headed by an America officer, Captain Lewis, Meriwether Lewis, said to be aiming at anchoring the American claim on the Pacific Northwest. Now, sir, I can tell you that Captain Lewis's real aim is to map the terrain in order to descend on Spanish holdings at Santa Fe." He saw them blink at that; the Spanish were desperate to keep Santa Fe for its gold and for the fur trade that flowed in from the North. The very mention of Santa Fe was enough to put them into panic.

"So," he said, "I suggest you send a series of patrols ranging north from Santa Fe. Seize these men and hold them in a dungeon and who will ever know? I would place cardinal importance on this move in order to protect your holdings."

Ah, God! Back in his carriage he slapped his fat thighs in sheer joy. Twelve thousand dollars in gold, and plenty more to shower upon him after that! Plans began to form. He would put six thousand of it in sugar, explain it as one of his old tobacco shipments paying off at last, sell the sugar in Kentucky at quadruple the price—and hide the other six thousand in gold inside a sugar cask for the ride north. He had a half dozen men there he could trust to receive it and hold it for him. Oh, what a blessing this had turned out to be!

Suddenly he was hungry, thirsty, he wanted a drink, by God, he wanted a woman!

He rapped on the ceiling and opened the eye window that let him speak to the driver.

"To Madame Gratiot's, Sergeant." McClanahan had a huge black eye and he'd needed help to get up on the box; broken ribs, apparently. But he was afraid if he let anyone else drive the general he'd never be returned to his soft job.

Wilkinson settled back on the seat as the carriage lurched into the turn. Yes, a private celebration, two doubles of good Kentucky whiskey and oysters in cream. And afterward, perhaps Eva Marie wasn't busy. Or—this was a special night—perhaps that flaming blonde from Paris with her Parisian tricks.

He heard McClanahan clucking to the horses as if he'd sensed the general's mood, and laughed out loud. Oh, those Spaniards had been eager, they'd hung on his words. For years he had been keeping the Spanish on edge with tales of planned American aggression. The officials in Washington always wondering why the Spanish were so hostile, why they took American political rhetoric as prelude to attack when no attack preparations were made. And the officials in Havana confident that only their hiring of General Wilkinson kept the Americans off their shores. God, it was rich, rich!

And the best joke of all was that while keeping them alarmed with imaginary American intentions, he'd said nothing of his own, the dreams that filled his mind these days and that needed the Spanish as friends now and in due time would make them enemies—when it was too late to damage the master planner. Then the twelve thousand in gold that so pleased him now would be a mere handful to be cast to the nearest beggar. And in the silence of midnight the sun was shining anew, for just as he had told the Spaniards, Mexico was the pot of gold at the end of the rainbow—and Aaron Burr was ruined and desperate.

Again he murmured, rolling the words in his mouth like fine brandy, "I own the son of a bitch."

THIRTEEN

Washington, November 1804

Aaron seemed to have disappeared. Dolley read the papers carefully, including several from Richmond and Baltimore, and though there were rumors aplenty, none asserted more than questions—had he been sighted here, had he been sighted there? The only thing clear was that he had fled Philadelphia under cover of an alias, wanted in New York and New Jersey, running ahead of extradition papers. It hurt her, somehow, this image of Aaron slipping through the night, hat brim pulled low, answering to some pseudonym. He had done a terrible thing, but it had been a duel, after all, and no one called duels murder. When gentlemen met on the Bladensburg Road outside Washington people might profess shock but they rarely condemned.

Had Jimmy heard anything? She asked so often that he shook his head irritably as if he suspected her feelings went further than friendship. They didn't, of course, she had thought that through quite carefully, but she saw that her questions exacerbated his own worries and she stopped asking. Aaron had fled south or west—he was popular in both regions—and sooner or later he would surface and then they would have to deal with him.

What she couldn't express to Jimmy was her real fear, that Aaron would dog him into a duel as he had Alex. She could see that wolfish warrior quality in Aaron, see him pressing Alex to conclusion, and she could see Jimmy unprepared. Jimmy would fight if he had to but he never would be prepared, never comfortable with pistol in hand and the force of settling things sharpening his eye and aim.

"He's gone south, I suppose," Jimmy said one evening and she knew he meant Aaron. "His daughter's in South Carolina, isn't she? What do you think he's doing? It's this silence I don't like. I'd prefer to have him in the open, see what he's about."

Yes, Jimmy was worried and so was Tom. Perhaps Aaron was ruined as everyone said, but perhaps he wasn't, too. Suddenly the obvious struck her.

"He'll be back here," she said. "He's still vice president." Jimmy said a New Jersey warrant would not have force here. Voting was under way now in the presidential election, each state choosing its own balloting date from September to December, every indication being that Tom would win, but until the inauguration in March, Aaron would be vice president. Aaron was not on the ballot, a move she knew he would take as insult added to injury.

"His pride won't let him hide," she said. "I'll bet he'll appear when the Congress opens. Sit on the dais and gavel them to order."

"That would be a day to remember," Jimmy said.

Mr. R. King ran south by lurching stage over roads that wound through dense woods. The ruts were deep, now hardened to the consistency of stone, the coach wheels thundering against them to hurl passengers about like dice in a cup. Nothing could be worse or more exhausting—until the rain started. It beat on the roof and hunted out the cracks and passengers twisted and turned, avoiding drips of cold water that seemed to aim at one's collar. The traveler had a cotton duster with strands woven so tight by the new mechanical looms in New England as to be semiwaterproof, but of course he used it to cover the only woman passenger. Then, just as nothing could possibly be worse the roadway turned to soup and the stage sank toward its hubs, the horses straining slower, until it was everyone out, women to huddle under umbrellas in the rain, men to wade in up to their knees and throw their shoulders against the wheels as the coach strained out to drier land. Mr. R. King took his turn without complaint but by the time he reached his daughter's plantation he was on the edge of pneumonia and felt the trip akin to being broken on the wheel.

He pushed on as hard as he could. On a moonlit night the stage might press on to the next station, going slowly against ruts and potholes invisible in the dark, to arrive at a log hut in the woods that combined tavern and stage station. Arriving, he stumbled from the stage for a supper of beans and salt pork washed down with a cup of whiskey, and slept on the puncheon floor thankful it wasn't just dirt. He laid his head on his boots to prevent their theft and wrapped himself in the blanket he carried in a tight roll lashed to his grip. There, amidst the cries and grunts of dreaming men he dreamed himself. He was on the heights of Quebec once again storming toward victory, and the great Montgomery fell with a loud cry. Then Montgomery's heavy body, inert, across his shoulders, he staggering toward the ladders they had scaled, finding his own legs buckling—God, the general was heavy!—and then dropping him and awakening with a cry, face wet with tears. Dreamed of Alex, his slender, handsome face drained of venom and then dissolving in a cloud of gunsmoke, a noise to awaken the dead. The dream slipping into the root of it all, the infamous tie, a voice like that of God judging him but he can't quite hear the words and he believes or at least hopes it will be favorable but before he can straighten the tangle of the words he starts awake and listens to the sighs and groans of the poor mortals around him, and swallows hard to avoid weeping in self-pity. . . .

No one recognized him. No one questioned his pseudonym. In Washington and New York his face was known, but nowhere else. Probably fifty, maybe a hundred, portraits had been taken, he sitting patiently as painters of varying skills labored, but how many people had seen them? The woodcuts and gross drawings in the papers made nothing recognizable. The vice president, the duel, the death of the great Mr. H was often discussed as the hours of stage transit crept by. Mr. R. King listened dispassionately and commented no more than an occasional murmur. He booked himself through Pittsburgh and Wheeling out in the western edge of Virginia and on south, far wide of Washington, and only then did sentiment shift to favor the beleaguered vice president who had disappeared so mysteriously.

Oaks, the handsome plantation of which marriage to Joseph Alston of the South Carolina Alstons had made Theodosia the mistress, struck the exhausted traveler as little short of heaven. He slept ten hours and awakened to find his clothes washed and dried and his daughter burning with fury at the willingness of the world to condemn a man who took honor seriously and enforced respect for his name! Indeed, she supplied the fury he felt so that he could revel in it while presenting himself as accepting fate, gravely acknowledging the perfidy of man, but always in the calm manner that suggested a man of great stature.

She staged a dinner and ball, and guests came from as far as Charleston. They clustered around Burr, listening gravely to his wisdom and betraying no disapproval. Theodosia was delighted. But gradually the questions grew more pointed. What were Hamilton's insults, how did it feel that day, what did he think when he saw Hamilton fall, how did it feel to kill the man whose design saved the national economy? A woman, near spitting—was he *proud* of himself?

Abruptly he realized that he was a mere object of curiosity, the man who killed Hamilton, what was he like? An object to be stared at, a dancing bear with a chain around its neck. Burr retreated to his room. He felt himself sinking again toward despair and suddenly the future loomed as impenetrable and mysterious. What would he do with himself? He wasn't finished yet—thus the pseudonym, R. King—but now that elegant defiance of a great man challenging the world had a hollow ring. Sometimes, thinking of it all, he began to sweat and he knew it wasn't from South Carolina heat.

More and more he thought of the West. Pittsburgh and Wheeling were its entrepôts, on the great westward flowing avenue, the Ohio River, and he had liked what he'd seen as he passed through. There was a rough, direct, openhanded—and opened-minded—attitude in which he saw he could prosper. Jim Wilkinson made the West seem the place of the future and perhaps it was. But how to approach it . . .

Then the letter arrived, New Orleans to New York to South Carolina. There was no signature and the seal was unmarked wax, but he recognized Wilkinsons's hand. It urged him to depart immediately for Washington where the writer would meet him. A careful study of the situation had convinced the writer that no legal entanglements would arise there. Indeed, the writer's information was that the late furor in New York had subsided quite remarkably. The meeting proposed between the writer and the vice president might well be the most important move of either man's life; let nothing keep you from being there.

Throughout the letter, which was written in direct terms with few of the usual embellishments of courtesy, there was a distinct tone of command. It didn't occur to the vice president that once he might have resented such a tone; now, scarcely noticing, he responded warmly to a strong voice. He would leave in the morning.

Ambassador and Mrs. August Merry, Britain's new representative in the United States, had an instant collision with the new democracy as practiced by Mr. Jefferson. This went right to the heart of democratic realities, Madison felt. Every man with equal voice, equal vote—and here came Mr. Merry, who regarded such ideas as heresy. The Briton had been awaited with anticipation but proved to be pompous, humorless, quarrelsome, and in thrall to his wife. Toujours Gai, indeed.

But what really unhinged things was the president's pell-mell practice at state dinners. No more seating by rank, no more gentlemen assigned to dinner partners. No, when dinner was announced everyone was to escort to table the woman closest to him, and as for seating, first come, first served. Laggards sat at the foot of the table—and Mr. Merry, unprepared since Thornton had gone off to England without explaining the custom, wound up with Mrs. Merry at the bottom of the table—the place of lowest rank for the ambassador who considered himself the ranking figure in the diplomatic community by the strength of his nation. Madison could see that both were enraged, and since Tom was very sensitive to individuals and their emotions, of course he could see it too. It struck Madison between soup and meat that Thornton had not told his replacement of this custom in retaliation for some sort of slight. Merry gave offense on every side by his obvious sense of superiority.

Yet by every account it was Mrs. Merry's rage that soon had the two nations at diplomatic swords' points, the Merrys' refusing social invitations from Democrats while lavishing attention to Federalists. The ambassador, who aside from pique demonstrated a certain competence despite his dull manner, might have been willing to declare a truce but his wife never. Madison wrote frequent dispatches to Monroe in London explaining each new twist lest Merry use it to assert American attacks on Britain. "I blush at having to put so much trash on paper," he told Monroe.

All their enemies perceived—and enjoyed—what they saw as the administration's disarray. Jaycee Barlow returned from the Hill in a state of obvious agitation. When Madison asked, he said he had stopped in the rotunda for a hot cruller and noticed Mr. Pickering talking to young Mr. Adams. Jaycee said he immediately turned his back as he stepped closer to eavesdrop.

"Well, sir, that scoundrel Mr. Pickering, and I don't care if he was secretary of state, his views are downright pernicious, yes, sir. Well, anyway, he's ranting away and what he says goes this way. Maybe not in exact words, you know, but he says, 'Think about it.' To Adams, you see. 'Think about it. For the first time ever Britain honors us with a full ranked ambassador. Sends a fine man, outstanding, brilliant, reasoned, just. Anthony Merry, cream of the diplomatic corps! And with a fine lady, handsome and cultured and rich. Damned rich. You should see her diamonds! An ornament to our fair city, if one can choke down laughter for such a term for this crossroads. And this puerile president insults both of them with such force as to make an international incident! What do you think of that?'

"Well, sir, Adams, he don't seem to think a lot about it. He talked like he'd been an ambassador himself."

"He was. Ten years in Europe, under his father."

Barlow nodded. "That would explain it. He talked a lot but seemed to be saying that the reason for diplomatic customs was that everyone would know where they stood, how to act, what to expect and what to perform, thus avoiding diplomatic fo—fo—"

"Faux pas."

"That's it, yes, sir. Anyway, Mr. Pickering said that he was taking every opportunity to tell Mr. Merry that he was right in all particulars and the Democrats were barbarians."

He thanked Jaycee. He wasn't sure he'd have eavesdropped himself but he was glad Jaycee had done so. Still, that was just Federalist talk that was not to be dismissed entirely but was somewhat discountable. But criticism was boiling. Madison was allowed no doubt of that. Two days later he was strolling down a Capitol corridor when John Randolph came bounding out of an office with those damned dogs.

The gaunt chairman reared back in mock astonishment. "Mr. Madison! Lowering yourself to go among the plebeians who merely make up the heart and guts and core of your party, which simple truth you and your high and mighty leader fail to understand. But now you've gone too far—"

"Sir?"

"This insult to Britain's ambassador, what is its purpose, sir?" The dogs draped themselves on the floor.

Madison stared at him. "My word, you who are always prating on the idea that we are too little democratic, too close to Federalists, you question the democratic principle of pell-mell, of first come, first served?"

"Don't try to fob me off, sir," Randolph shouted, voice going shrill. His dogs leaped up and glared at Madison. "This clearly is a plot. Insult Merry, he will report the abuse he receives, and in London they'll play tit for tat against Mr. Monroe. You are setting that fine man up for failure, we can see that, you will throw rocks in his path wherever you can, don't think we don't understand that."

"Oh, John," Madison said, and walked off, as the chairman shouted behind him, "We are watching, sir. We have our eye on you, we know your plans. Beware, sir . . ."

Madison returned to his office and spent an hour composing a message to Mr. Merry explaining that the president had no authority to discipline the mayor of Philadelphia whatever he said, and anyway, Mr. Merry should read newspapers with caution.

On the way home he paused at the mansion to find the president glowering over the report of a congressman who'd come for tea and related what Mrs. Merry was said to have said about Virginia manners in a gathering of Federalist wives. The president snapped that he could tell that woman with her vulgar diamonds a proper thing or two but it would be beneath his dignity, at which Madison said yes, wouldn't it, at which the president gave him a sharp look, and on that note he walked home.

There, in slippers and loose clothes, a cup of warm and mildly alcoholic punch in hand, he described these vexatious encounters to Dolley only to have her exclaim that it was all perfectly ridiculous.

"Exactly," he said. "People can be quite unbelievable."

"I meant the president," she said. "This pell-mell business. Really, Jimmy, I know the point of it, but what trouble it causes and all for what really is just a metaphor. Tom should find some other way."

But he stiffened at that and she broke off. He simply would not tolerate criticism of the president. It was too dangerous—once you let it start where would it end? Her remark rankled through the evening but was it really true? Obviously the new democracy was vulnerable in a dangerous world, the suction of a vast war dragging them toward the vortex, the Royal Navy abusing them, their own radicals undermining, their minister in London more fretful every day, Federalists constantly on the attach, this obscene talk of splitting the nation, New Orleans throbbing with discontent—given all this, could a metaphor that made the point of what really mattered about democracy be such a bad idea?

What did the new democracy really mean, after all? The Federalists had started bending the Constitution toward those they considered the best people, meaning the wise and the good, by whom they inevitably meant those properly rewarded with material goods by a beneficial God for their wisdom and goodness. Those times were past now and Madison intended to keep it that way.

Surely the only democracy in the world was a lonely beacon of hope. The French effort had destroyed itself. America stood as the solitary ideal, threatened on every side. If they made many false moves their own people would lose faith and turn back toward what the world had always been, the common man in thrall to those with the energy or intellect or opportunity or heritage to seize control. If Americans ever decided their safety depended on such a turn, they would make it. That was what freedom meant, after all. So, was a metaphor that reminded everyone of these principles so unfortunate?

Late that night, Dolley in her nightgown, covers drawn to her chin against cool night air coming through a window opened a sliver, and he standing by the bed in his nightshirt, his legs getting cold, about to sneeze, he reminded her of these things, which she knew as well as he did. Then, satisfied, he slid into bed beside her and was asleep as his eyes closed.

James Monroe was a big man, a stalwart Virginian, master of extensive lands, which he, like his friend Jefferson, farmed with scientific intensity. He was at home on horseback, handy with a bird gun, and sometimes it seemed a little odd that he had made his mark not in private but in public life, as diplomat representing his country in Europe and as governor of Virginia. He had fought in the Revolution, doing better than well, he had to admit that, though of course it was the sort of thing you left to others to say. Leading troops into a hail of gunfire taught you the value of seriousness, and Mr. Monroe was a serious man. He was minister to France during the thunder of the Revolution there, and by God, that taught you some things too, and gave you reason to be serious. Came home and ran the state of Virginia with backbiting scoundrels in the wings who didn't have to face the fire but were free with their criticisms. Back to France to secure the Louisiana Purchase with Mr. Livingston nattering on that that magnificent bargain resulted from his two years of effort, Monroe a man of too much dignity to respond to such carping but owing it to his own image of himself to let it be known quietly that it was the weight of his name that swung the deal. And now here he was in London, ambassador to Britain, replacing the old Federalist, Rufus King, who had stayed on for Jefferson's first term, and here was little James Madison yapping after him like a terrier. Monroe long had known that Madison was a bit of a noodle and good old Tom could have been doing something else when he named him secretary of state. So here was Madison displaying his ignorance in a series of instructions that ran against the grain of all reality.

Madison had never been abroad, that was the trouble, and Tom hadn't been abroad for a decade now, so naturally they were behind on the trends and thrusts of Europe on which Mr. Monroe was fully up-to-date. These instructions, for example. On a Sunday afternoon at the residence he sat in his deep chair tapping them with a long index figure and explaining to Elizabeth that they were idiotic. Seemed to say that impressment was everything when in fact impressment seemed a small matter these days compared with issues of trade and this abominable Rule of 1756 and this *Essex* foolishness under which the British Navy was seizing American ships right and left.

"But James," his wife said, "impressment does anger a lot of people. Cousin Harry told me he's lost twenty men off his ships in the last few years. So maybe at home it's bigger—"

"Your cousin Harry . . ." Monroe let his contempt for the said Harry seep through his tone. She flushed but didn't respond. "No, trade issues must be where we stand or fall. I'll just have to educate Mr. Madison."

"Oh, James, you always think you're right and you think everyone should see things as you see them."

"Well," he snapped, irritation growing, "I usually am, too."

"I think Mr. Randolph's letters upset you. That business where they want you to fail."

"Hah! Randolph is a very good friend, I've known him for years, brilliant man, you know. But I don't take everything he says as right. He can be extreme. But there's usually a grain of truth—well, this situation with Madison will bear watching, that's all. I'll be the first to notice if he really is undermining me. He's terribly hungry to succeed Tom, everyone knows that."

"I think you see yourself as a more likely figure to succeed Tom."

He stared at her. "I seek nothing, Elizabeth. But you know I always am ready to serve my country."

Four days before Congress reconvened Aaron Burr arrived in Washington. He went to Mrs. Simpson's boardinghouse and found to his pleasure that his old suite was vacant. He took it immediately—a suite fitted his view of himself—and queried the War Department to learn that General Wilkinson was expected to arrive at any moment. He left a message and then stayed quietly in his quarters, reading and thinking, taking a daily constitutional walk where he was not likely to be seen.

★ ★ ★ ★ ★

FOURTEEN

Washington, December 1804

The second session of the Eighth Congress was coming to order. Dolley Madison was in the Ladies' Gallery suspended above the hubbub on the Senate floor. Attendance at the Congress for great debates or on ceremonial days had become favored entertainment in this village capital that offered little frivolity. Hannah Gallatin had accompanied Dolley and Dorcas Dearborn sat nearby. Maggie Smith and Danny Mobry, one behind the other, were whispering and laughing. A year had passed since the transfer of New Orleans but Danny still got a hollow look around the eyes when she talked of the furious discontent of the people in New Orleans. Far from learning to like their new country, they seemed ever more bitter and extreme. Would they ever settle into being Americans?

She looked around the small Senate chamber where all was bustle and excitement. With the admission of Ohio, there were now thirty-four senators, each with desk and chair, and now they milled about shaking hands and slapping backs. Clerks clutching papers tugged at their sleeves. She saw Giles of Virginia, majority leader and an old friend; he caught her eye and bowed and she threw him a kiss.

Senators were taking their seats. Plumer of New Hampshire was standing by the president's chair, gavel in hand, ready to call them to order. Then came a sudden stir at the door and heads turned. A stricken silence fell across the chamber.

Aaron Burr came striding in. Aaron Burr! It was just as she had predicted and yet it did startle her. She saw him now through the eyes of others—Burr fresh from the slaughter of Alexander Hamilton on the sands of Wee-hawken. A man still under indictment who was, as she had reminded Jimmy, still vice president. Returns of the election of 1804 showed Tom reelected almost by accla-mation, with George Clinton of New York replacing Aaron, the danger of another disastrous tie having been eliminated by the Twelfth Amendment, thank God. Inau-guration was months away.

She watched him walk to the podium, his carriage easy, a faint smile on his handsome face. At the chair he bowed, said something with a smile, and extended his hand. Plumer gave him the gavel and stepped away as Aaron seated himself.

There was stony silence. Dolley's emotions remained in tumult, horror at the needless death of a great man pitted against a nagging sense that to call a fatal duel murder was selective and unfair. The reports from New York of Aaron pushing Alex to the wall gave him a cold-blooded sound, but she couldn't forget that he had been a real friend to her. Even now, watching him gaze about benignly, she could feel the graceful manner that made his company so pleasant. Aaron would always be Aaron and probably Jimmy was right to distrust him, but . . .

He rapped the gavel, two cracks that might have been pistol shots for their effect.

"The Senate will come to order. Mr. Majority Leader, you may present the first order of business."

Still that rigid, stunned silence held.

Then, from directly below her, a hoarse whisper that certainly carried across the whole chamber. "My God! I never thought I'd see the day when an indicted murderer would wield the gavel in the United States Senate."

She thought Aaron's eyes flickered at that, but his face remained relaxed, his hands at rest on the table before him.

Senator Giles stood. "Mr. President," he said, "on the first order of business . . ."

High on the dais, Burr saw Dolley flinch at that ugly slur. He had staged the scene carefully, sure that it would confound them, confident that none would have the nerve to challenge him directly. Yet even an anonymous sneer was enough to cast his mood down, transition in a second from triumph that was none too real to desperation that was all too real.

Not that he felt any sense of error. He was sure the public outrage was politically orchestrated, he supposed by the Virginia cabal. Burr had given Jefferson the election and thus was he repaid. His spirits sank steadily. He felt himself grand on the outside but empty within, jack-o'-lantern's bright glow naught but a mere candle stub. His eyes moistened and he blinked quickly. His hand tightened on the gavel till pain shot up his arm.

The danger now surpassed all that had gone before, for now he would have neither income nor prospects when his term ended. A simple law practice could never support the Aaron Burr of today. He had become a man of power and he knew that to step back would shatter his already precarious sense of himself. And even more immediate, debt hung over him like an avalanche ready to

give way. Those convivial men who'd been eager to lend
him money, how many times had he made them grovel a
bit? Any of them could throw him into bankruptcy and
consign him to debtor's prison, the only escape a pau-
per's grave.

He must *do* something. Strike some wild and awful
blow to change everything. The West glowed in his
mind . . . but the question was whether General Wilkinson was more than a talker.

Dolley had started to dress for the big congressional reception at Stelle's Hotel when Jimmy arrived. Dressing
was an art form that she didn't approach casually. The
colors, the combinations, the decision for or against lace
or the sash or the emerald necklace, the attention to her
hair, the balance of blush to her cheeks were all important. So she was preoccupied when he came into the bedroom. He peeled out of his coat, eased off the buckled
shoes, and sat down with a thump and a sigh. He looked
awful.

Dolley felt life would be dreary indeed if balls and parties were banned, but she didn't say so since Jimmy hated
them. She'd been coaching him for years but he still froze
and mumbled. She sent downstairs for tea and sandwiches of slivered Virginia ham and he brightened and
told her his troubles. They proved to be about as she'd expected, Aaron almost certainly up to something, Mr.
Yrujo of Spain suggesting that New Orleans faced immi-
nent attack, Ambassador Merry huffing and puffing. . . .

As if to make up for this gloom, the reception was
splendid, Champagne well iced, dainty tidbits, and savory morsels warm and tasty, graceful music, and much
happy laughter. The women's gowns were fine, gauzy,
rich in color, low in front for those who had anything to
show. Many women wore gold-threaded braid in their

hair. Several women had copied her way with a turban of matching silk; she saw it was becoming the rage. The diplomatic corps was here in force, bedecked with medals and sashes and swords of office. She saw Captain Decatur of the navy elegant and intense in gold-flashed blue. Even the president had made an effort with snowy hose and crisp cravat setting off good black broadcloth. Jimmy was quite presentable—she had forced him to break out a new pair of white silk hose and his newest buckled shoes.

She saw Aaron across the room. He started toward her. She looked away but in a moment he was bowing to her. Would she join him in the quadrille? She shook her head.

"I saw you at the Senate. You came to see me." She frowned. He leaned closer. "Are you my enemy, then?"

"No—but you should know better than to suggest we dance."

He smiled. "So long as we're friends, dear heart."

In a moment she saw him talking to Danny Mobry. He had that gentle smile and Danny was looking at him with an eagerness that Dolley recognized. He said something and Danny laughed out loud, a musical sound across the room, and shot something back that caused him to throw up his hands, laughing, not a care in the world. They chatted for twenty minutes, now serious, now light-hearted, and when they separated he bowed and brushed his lips against Danny's hand, and Dolley had the momentary impression that Danny had shivered. Couldn't tell from across the room, of course; maybe it was just that she knew Aaron. She remembered warning Danny at the big open house, but Aaron's charm was proof against warnings.

An hour later Danny approached with three rather odd-looking men. She presented them, French names Dolley didn't quite catch, and said they were delegates from the people of New Orleans. Oh, yes, the protest delegation sent to express New Orleanian anger.

"No one will talk to them," Danny said, voice nearly a wail. "They asked to meet you. Maybe if you—"

"No," Dolley said. She smiled at the men but said to Danny in a low voice, "This is totally inappropriate."

"Please, Dolley. Just listen a moment. This is important. The discontent in New Orleans is much more serious than anyone here seems to recognize. Mr. Madison, the president, anyone."

Dolley turned to the three men. "Good evening, gentlemen," she said in passable French, "I hope your visit is pleasant and your mission successful." Expressions blank with disappointment, the men bowed and turned away.

Danny's face was white and so, Dolley supposed, was her own. She took Danny's arm. "Don't you *ever* place me in the position of interfering in national policy *or* in Jimmy's work."

Angry blotches appeared on Danny's cheeks. Dolley pulled her closer. "*You* tell me. All unofficial, nothing reported, no involvement, and I'll speak to Jimmy, informally, at home. Now quick—tell me the gist of what they would have said."

"That New Orleans is in danger of revolt. That the governor you sent is an ass and infuriates people without reason. That the refusal of immediate citizenship is an affront, that the people expected to be a state and are refused, that they know the slogans of '76 as well as we do, 'No taxation without representation,' but they and only they are denied the vote. Dolley, something had better be done to make sense of this."

Dolley kissed her cheek. "Well said, dear. I'll talk to Jimmy. My guess is that it won't do any good because larger issues are afoot, but I promise I'll try."

Danny sighed, anger gone. "Thank you, Dolley. I just

don't want to see New Orleans in flames." She laughed then, a lightning shift of mood. "Here's something that doesn't interfere with Jimmy. That Mr. Burr—he really is rather something, rather, rather—"

"Special?"

"Exactly."

"He'll take you to bed quick as a wink, you give him a chance."

"Somehow, that's not a surprise."

Dolley laughed. "I told you, dear."

Danny had an impudent, dashing look. "Could that be some of the appeal?"

More seriously, Dolley said, "Don't give him your heart, sweetie. The rest of you, that's another matter. But he'll break your heart."

Madison was always pleased when Danny Mobry came to see him. She was very pretty and she often laughed. Sometimes he wondered if she laughed at his ironic observations because he expected it, but no, that denigrated them both. He decided he could be a witty fellow when stimulated by a pretty woman's smile. Danny's laugh had a bell-like ring. Yes, he was always glad to see her.

But this morning she wasn't laughing. He'd seen her the night before at the congressional reception that Dolley had insisted was a duty for them to attend. She'd seemed happy enough then, talking to Aaron, a special luminosity in her face. Now she settled herself before his desk. She wore a pale green gown that fit her form to the hips and then flared out, a froth of lace at the throat. Unsmiling, she said, "I have a serious problem on which I'll seek your help, but first let me offer information you may find of some value."

It seemed she was just in from New Orleans, and she poured out a litany of concern that on the one hand went straight to her business and on the other straight to his own business. She thought New Orleans was on the edge of revolt. The solid old names familiar from her girlhood were in a continuing state of shock and outrage. Her uncle, Daniel Clark, was scarcely coherent. She recalled how on Madison's instructions she had bludgeoned Mr. Clark into going to Paris to warn the money men he knew that Napoleon on the Mississippi would be a disaster. Madison nodded, remembering well the gentleman's icy eyes and manner. There was a hardness in this Daniel Clark that Madison had met with hardness of his own; the New Orleanian had sailed off to France because he'd been made to see that his future would be most difficult if he didn't. Oh, yes, Mr. Clark would be the man to stage a revolt if he saw advantage.

Madison didn't say so, but this word that her uncle was up in arms had more meaning than the barrage of complaints about the governor. Poor Mr. Claiborne seemed to please no one in any way whatsoever. It was enough to make you sympathize with the man, even though it was clear he had not been a wise choice. But it was much too late to change now. Soon enough proper government would come to New Orleans with full representation in the Congress, but these things took time. Another few years and the new territory would be part of the American system. Meanwhile he must simply pray that incoherence would stop short of revolt.

He cross-examined her and eventually was satisfied that while the ground might be ripe for revolt nothing had been prepared and she knew of nothing actually under way. She said the French and Spanish officials remaining there kept the people stirred up and should be ejected, but he saw that that would appear an act of weakness. Apparently she was in business with Ed Livingston; he was a man who had the capacity to lead something if he chose, but seemed utterly benign. Well, things clearly were tense there but there was nothing more he could do about it now. When she seemed to run down he thanked her gravely for her information, stressing its value and his concern. She seemed mollified. And he asked her about the problem she had mentioned.

A haggard look crossed her pretty face. Well, she said, yes, thank you, it was after they had cleared the Florida Straits and set a northbound course for New York . . .

Carlito had run downriver from New Orleans riding current and a following wind, light as a feather and swift as a bird, slicing through loops and bends and turns with sails slatted this way and that. Leaning on the taffrail, Danny had watched the banks slide by and she'd felt as happy as her ship was light and graceful, though now, talking to Mr. Madison, she left that part out. But she had done what she could.

Her business seemed as soundly set as a volatile situation would allow, her new partnership with the ebullient New Yorker offering real promise. She would report the turmoil in New Orleans when she reached Washington, but it hadn't exploded yet.

What really mattered, though certainly not to be discussed with Mr. Madison, was that her love affair wasn't over after all. So, running swiftly down the river and away from New Orleans and love, she had had a warm glow that she had cherished even as she suspected it was not entirely wise. The same hard issues separating her from Henri still stood between them; set aside now by agreement, they would not lie dormant forever.

The note had come the afternoon before: "Chérie: I can't bear for you to go with pain still between us. I will come at five; I beg you to receive me. Henri."

Everything was wrong with such a meeting and she had no doubt that pain would only grow, but she sharpened her quill and opened her ink bottle and sent a quick note pleading a sudden illness to Monsieur Lafollet at whose home she had been invited to dine. She waited in her room and presently she heard his quick step on the stairs, his signal rap on the door, two taps and another that she sometimes heard in her dreams, and she opened it with a joyous smile she couldn't subdue, mistake though it might be.

He had a basket over his left arm and with his right he caught her hand and brought it to his lips. He set the basket on a table on her balcony and unfolded the napkin to show a fine loaf of bread, cheese, fruit, two bottles of wine, crystal glasses.

Opening the wine, he said with quiet intensity, "I so feared your answer would be your absence. Coming up the stairs my heart was in my mouth. Thank you . . ."

She didn't answer and he laid out fine china plates and sliced bread with a long knife and laid slices of different cheeses on the plates and all the while she watched his hands, virile and strong, hair curling off the backs of his fingers, and she felt the old physical attraction growing. They ate and drank the wine and opened the second bottle and it grew dark outside and the air turned cool. They went inside and closed the doors to the balcony and sat in the dark and talked. An oil lamp on the street cast dim light into the room and she could see his face and the intensity of his gaze.

The talk was easy and liquid, of the old days, their shared childhood, his lovelorn hungering for her in those days when she scarcely noticed him and then was swept away when the American vessel came up her bayou. All the people they had known, all the gossip dredged from memory, much laughter over things they had not understood as children but did now. Henri could make her laugh, and that—and his physical presence—had been what had drawn her from the start. At the same time she

238 ★ DAVID NEVIN

felt the talk of old New Orleans and plantation life and the people of childhood drawing her back to her roots and it struck her that this she could ill afford. But she did nothing to block the pull.

"Oh, Danny," he said abruptly straightening in his chair, "I don't want matters of state to come between us, to shatter what we are and what we can be. You have become an American and I swear to you I accept this, and I am French to my very bones and I beg you to accept me as I am. Of course we will disagree on some things, we don't have to see everything alike to love each other, and oh, Danny, my beautiful darling, I do love you!"

And at that moment, she loved him. She supposed. It was too complicated for nearly midnight and wine fumes heavy in her head, and she was lonely and he was a powerful man, masculine as a bull, and she said, "Kiss me, Henri." Dawn was breaking as he left.

So, more or less, they were together again. Now, sitting in Mr. Madison's office all proper if not austere, it was odd remembering that glow. Brown pelicans riding the same wind had sailed alongside calling so gaily that it was like shouts of Bon voyage! from passersby. When they were far down the Delta the channel had straightened and then the banks had broken into separate clumps of tree-studded land that soon were clearly islands washed by the beginning of swells. The swells became real and definite and they passed the last island and felt the snap of sea wind as they set a southeasterly course for the Straits of Florida and the great turn to the north into the stormy Atlantic.

There they plunged from fair weather to foul, a more than brisk southerly wind driving *Carlito* crashing along. On the horizon to port they could glimpse the swampy brush of Florida beyond long white beaches; opposite, off to starboard but out of sight, the Bahamas. Mac trimmed sail but *Carlito* still went crashing along on a thirty-knot following wind. They were ahead of schedule; Mr. Livingston's cotton would be ashore in New York with days to spare and each day meant a bonus. For all her worry, the new ship had proved itself and she had no doubt cargoes would be awaiting the sister ships when they were ready.

"Yo, Cap'n," the lookout bawled down from far up the mainmast, "sail off the starboard quarter. Topgallants set and coming on hard."

Danny knew enough about ships to know that topgallants in semigale conditions were dangerous. Mac, who wouldn't dream of using all his canvas in this wind, swung up into the rigging and fixed a long glass to his eye. His agility surprised Danny. When he dropped onto the deck his expression was grim. "British, I expect," he said. "Frigate, probably thirty-two guns. Coming dead-on. She means to have us, all right."

"Can we outrun her?" Danny asked.

"We'll try, but they're fast, you know—don't have to carry aught but guns and men, so they can build for speed."

He shifted course a few points to port, take them closer to the Carolina shore, but scarcely had the men scrambled aloft and set the sails before the lookout had spotted a new vessel ahead and a bit to port, also coming on strong. Soon it revealed itself as a second frigate.

"A team," Mac said almost to himself. "Two warships, there's no eluding them."

"Do we have Britons aboard?"

Mac shrugged. "Sailors come and go, you know, ma'am. Long as they're on the ship, that's home. Then they leave and someone else takes their place. I don't ask much about their shore homes; half of 'em are running from something anyway, broken heart or an angry father or from the law. Don't pay to ask." He watched the men reef the sails until they were wallowing along at a crawl, awaiting the British vessels.

Danny stood at her usual spot by the taffrail watching the wake bubble up green and creamy and subside back into the blue sea. Mac had told her they were at a good hundred fathoms here. She liked the sea, if not with Carl's passion, and she thought how precious the ship against the ocean's vastness, not just that it preserved life but that it was an artifact of man and that you were part of it and it was part of you when all around you was the wilderness of the sea.

Now, extending the long glass that Carl always had carried, she could see the big frigate coming on from the right. The ship was lunging, bow crashing into waves and disappearing, then rising with tons of green water pouring from her scuppers, and there was a quality of deadly urgency about it and of unshakable power, and she felt a stirring in her guts and lowered the glass with her breath gone short.

The second ship had sheared off when it was clear that its prey—the thought gave her a new shiver for prey meant her ship and herself—was no longer fleeing. Steadily, plunging wildly, all the canvas she could carry crowding overhead, the first ship bore toward them on a collision course. It was huge, it dwarfed *Carlito,* not so much in length as in depth, weight, size, power, mast height. Now she could see men clearly with her naked eye, in the rigging and on the bow. Closer, closer, it towered over them, it was ready to run them down, break them in pieces and never pause—and then she heard the shrill of bo'sun pipes and men scrambled about taking in sail and the frigate spun about and came to, rocking in the swells.

Danny could read the name on a plate at the bow, *Leopard,* HMS *Leopard,* and knew the name would be

on a big plate across her stern as well. *Carlito* slacked
too and the ships lay in stays side by side on the rolling
ocean, the frigate towering over the little merchantman.
An ugly yellow band ran around her gray hull between
the upper and lower gunports. The ports were open, the
guns run out and ready, the tompions that protected the
muzzles from salt water pulled to leave black holes that
looked murderous; Mac said those on the main deck or
gun deck, the lower row, were long sixteens, hurling a
ball of that weight a mile or two, while those above, on
the spar deck, were short-range carronades, big-mouthed
and stubby, able to deliver a crushing thirty-two-pound
ball.

Leopard was cleared for action and as if she could see
them Danny could imagine gunners with matches glowing in their hands behind those open ports, those gaping
muzzles. Fear rose in her throat like bile, sank to her
belly and her bowels, left her momentarily weak, and she
put a hand on the rail as she braced herself to stand with
feet planted and head up as she watched. She saw Captain Mac giving the big ship a malevolent stare quite unlike him. Silence settled over *Carlito*.

A cutter with a crew of oarsmen and a coxswain was
lowered from the frigate, settling neatly into a swell. A
voice distorted by a megaphone boomed across the water: "Stand by to be boarded!" A dozen marines with
bayonets affixed to muskets slid down a rope ladder and
the cutter came across the interval between the two ships
with sparkling oars. A seaman in the bow was ready with
grappling hooks but Captain Mac had a rope ladder un-
rolled and ready and a line dangling from an extended
spar that the sailor with the grappling hook attached to a
bow cleat. The two vessels rocked side by side, the massive frigate towering overhead, the boat a sliver between
them.

The first marine came over the rail and whirled about

with musket leveled. He wore corporal's stripes and he
was a towhead, tall and rawboned with a scar on his
cheek and a nasty grin, and it was the grin that reached
Danny. Suddenly she was so damned mad at this insolent, grinning invasion of her ship, her home at this moment, that she forgot all about fear and wanted to *smite*
the oaf—and then the others came up and formed an
armed half-circle, making way for an elderly ensign with
a weathered face, He wore a mean, disappointed look,
officer held to a youngster's rank, passed over year after
year. He looked around belligerently, and growled,
"What cargo, Captain?"

"Cotton, out of New Orleans for New York City."

The graying ensign appeared to have a permanent
sneer. "Huh," he said, "probably a goddamned lie. More
likely out of Martinique or some goddamned Frenchie
hole. Where's your manifest? It don't tally, I'll put a
prize crew aboard and sail her up to London town and
sell her and her cargo for the good of the mother nation."
He studied the several sheets a long time. Then, looking
more irritated, he dropped them at his feet so that Mac
had to kneel to gather them, and growled, "Now muster
your crew and be quick about it!"

Danny watched the men line up. She knew only a few
of them personally. It didn't pay for a woman traveling
alone at sea to give any cause for talk; she stayed close to
Mrs. Mac, who traveled with her husband but wouldn't
think of appearing at a time like this. Danny knew the
chief mate and the bo'sun, ranking officers under Captain Mac. The mate was as old as Mac and had sailed as
skipper but he'd told her the pressure of decision got him
in the belly till he spit up blood and he figured mate
would do just fine. John Tolliver, the bo'sun, was a
broad-shouldered, red-faced man with a commanding
presence; he'd sailed for her for two years now. The only
other man she knew by name was Robbie Jones, who'd

been a seven-year-old cabin boy on the ship that Carl had sailed into their bayou and sailed away with her as prize. That was sixteen years ago and Robbie had grown into a powerful man with heavy chest and huge arms.

The officer walked along the line, studying each man. "You," he said suddenly to one, "what's your name?"

Danny couldn't distinguish the name but the sound of old England was clear in the man's voice.

"Where you from?"

"Baltimore."

The officer knocked him down with a hard open-handed slap. "Don't lie to me, goddamn you! You're British."

The man crawled to his knees. "Immigrant, sir. Come here eight years ago. American citizen, all proper."

"As I thought, a damned deserter."

"No, sir, I never been in the Royal Navy—"

"Once a Briton, always a Briton. You owe your mother country, my friend, you can't give up your allegiance." He laughed, a shrill bark. "Your country needs you. And even if it don't need you, it wants you." To the marines he said, "Take him," and the corporal seized the wretch's arm.

So far as Danny knew Britain was the only country that held that a native son was a subject forever and that whatever country he might adopt or might adopt him didn't matter—if Britain could set hands on him, he was her meat. She looked at the huge frigate looming over them, at the gaping holes of the muzzles of guns run out for action. But her fear was gone now, replaced by fury at her abject helplessness.

The officer moved along the row of men. "Sorry-looking bastards," he said, and spat on Captain Mac's deck. He glanced at the bo'sun. "How'd you pick such a scurvy crew?" Without awaiting an answer he rapped a slender man in the chest. "Got the consumption, sonny?

We'll leave you—man-of-war discipline would finish you in a week. You gotta be a *man* to make a Royal Navy tar." He whirled on the bo'sun. "Ain't that right, Boats?"

She saw Tolliver hesitate, not sure how to answer. "But you're a hearty damned specimen," the ensign said, and then, slapping his own forehead, added with a smirk, "Why, 'pon my word, now I remember the Captain reminded me we're in dire need of a bo'sun. You just come along, young feller, we've got the berth ready for you."

"But goddamn it," Tolliver yelled, "I ain't British. Never was. My pa was born in America, for Christ's sake, and so was his pa."

"Then they were goddamned rebels," the lieutenant said. He gestured and the corporal stepped forward, the musket at port arms. Quick as a snake he smashed the butt upward into Tolliver's chin and Boats fell like a stone.

Captain Mac stepped forward. "Sir," he cried, "I protest this brutality against unarmed men. I protest your seizing men who clearly are not British. I protest—"

"Shut your goddamned face or you'll get the same." Mac stared at him, mouth working, but said no more.

"Get him in the boat," the officer said of Boats, and continued his slow inspection tour. He paused at Robbie Jones. "Well, well," he said softly. He put his hand on Robbie's heavy biceps and there was something in his face that made Danny wonder about him. "You'll do, sonny," he said. "You look British to me." His hand was still on Robbie's arm. The corporal was grinning. The officer jerked his head: take him.

"No!" Danny cried. It was quite involuntary, she hadn't meant to speak, but taking Robbie, whom she'd known since he was seven, was just too much. "This man is not British. I've known him since he was a child, he's sailed with us, he's—"

The officer wheeled. "And who might you be? Captain's doxy, I wouldn't doubt."

"I am the owner of this vessel!" She was beside herself with fury. "Your government is forever saying it seeks only its own deserters and here you are playing the pirate! That man is not British, he's not a deserter, he has been in my employ for nineteen years and you can't—"

"Shut your trap, madam," he said. "I can and I will, and you and the whole American nation can go to hell."

"And you, sir," she said distinctly, "are scum."

He stared at her, then turned abruptly to the corporal, his thin face fiery. "Get the three in the boat. We won't spend the whole goddamned day here!"

"Aye, aye, sir." To Jones the corporal said, "You can crawl down that ladder or I'll crack your head and throw you over."

"I'll go," Robbie said. He glanced at her. "Thank you, Miss Danny."

The officer was the last over the side. Only his head was in view when he paused. Looking directly at her, he said, "Much obliged, Madam Ship-owner," and disappeared with a burst of laughter. The cutter cast off and rowed swiftly to the frigate, one man unconscious on the floorboards, two sitting upright with a guard to each side.

The boat shipped oars alongside the frigate and the men ran up the ladder. Robbie Jones, his hand on the ladder, turned and waved. The marine beside him backhanded him in the mouth just as she waved in return and she was sure he hadn't seen her. Then the cutter was hoisted aboard and without sign or signal the arrogant big ship turned and its sails took the wind and it flew off to the northeast, its wake a long straight arrow.

Captain Mac sighed. "Well, boys," he said to the men who still stood on deck staring at the departing warship, "we'll get 'em back someday but it'll take years, always

does, and maybe they'll be alive when the day comes
and maybe they won't. It's a rotten show and Miz Mobry
was dead-on—they're scum." He shook his head. "All
right—let's crack on sail and take her on home."

Madison gazed at the distraught woman. The image of
the young man she had known since boyhood turning to
wave as he was carried off to a desperate new life was
compelling. But so was another image strong in his
mind. . . .

A British frigate had seized a merchant vessel in New
York Harbor not long before. It impressed half the merchantman's crew. Ambassador Merry had agreed to return the men only because the case was truly egregious.
Impressment right in our harbor! But Merry said it all
was the fault of the Americans. They let their ships lure
British sailors to desert when they should be mounting
patrols to capture deserters and return them to the Royal
Navy. The secretary told the ambassador he could wait
forever and not see that.

The British captain had been ordered home, apparently in disgrace; now Madison had learned that far from
punishment, he had been rewarded with a bigger command—a ship of the line, seventy-four guns. That told
you all you needed to know about Mrs. Mobry's chances
of getting her men back anytime soon when they'd been
taken on the high seas.

Danny left Mr. Madison's office in dark mood. She
could sympathize with his bitter dilemmas, but this was
her ship, her men. It was time to call on that wounded
British officer who haunted her dock. He came almost
daily with book and cane to sit on a bollard and gaze

hungrily at the harbor with its ships and activity. Obviously he loved the sea.

His name was Bigbee, she recalled; as first lieutenant on convalescent leave from HMS *Scorpion* he must have connections. Perhaps he could wangle release for Robbie, at least, pull strings. New Orleans had taught her there usually was a way if you knew the right people.

The officer's limp seemed no better. Splinters had riddled his leg. She could see that when a cannonball struck a ship wood splinters became a cloud of missiles deadly as a hail of daggers. For every sailorman killed by a cannonball many more died from flying splinters. So he had explained casually in one of several brief chats since that first encounter, he on his bollard with a cane hooked over his arm and Thucydides on the Peloponnesian Wars in hand if rarely opened. He was not a handsome man with his big teeth and prominent mouth but his smile was infectious and he bore pain with courage.

But she wanted Clinch Johnson with her when she approached the officer. Clinch was such an odd fellow. Stuffed into a linen suit in summer or winter, coat always too tight and often soiled, unruly yellow hair standing in every direction when he took off his hat, he made her think of an owl, usually silent and motionless and yet very aware. His appearance seemed foolish but she knew that men on the waterfront respected him and she did too, if it was hard to take him fully seriously. His import-export business seemed to prosper though he rarely mentioned it. For that matter he rarely mentioned anything. He gave her a bit of business now and then but what really mattered was that he never pried but was always willing to listen. She needed to talk out her own thinking, and his occasional comments were valuable.

Month by month she grew more open with him, always waiting for him to step over the line and destroy everything by instructing her. He seemed to have business everywhere and it had become habit to end the day at her pier. She usually had a pot of coffee warming then, made from beans he had imported, which he said sold well in New York City, for what reasons she had no idea. Sometimes she was surprised by how much she found herself telling him as she talked her day over with him. Of course, she didn't tell him everything. He heard nothing of Henri Broussard. Nor of the physical longing that kept her awake at night. Now she wanted him along when she spoke to Lieutenant Terence Bigbee of HMS *Scorpion*.

A week later she heard slow steps on the stairs leading to her office in the loft on her pier. A step, a pause, a step, a longer pause. They were between ships and none of her men were about. She listened to the steps. An eighteen-inch oaken marlinespike lay on her desk. Long ago Carl had loaded the fat end with a lead slug. She held it in her right hand, feeling its heft. Step, pause, step, silence— she snatched open the door, the marlinespike cocked. Lieutenant Bigbee stood several steps down, face white as paper.

His voice was as pale as his face. "Did I alarm you? I'm sorry. I have answers to your questions." He was panting.

Yet she really didn't know him. No one was near. She wished Clinch would come; she'd have felt better. More proper, too.

The officer glanced at the marlinespike. "May I come up?"

She opened the door wide and he made the last few steps. She saw pain in his eyes. "May I sit down?" he asked.

At that moment she decided clearly that she liked him. It was a new thought that surprised her. He was a man of courage and of dignity, not a bad combination. She got him seated and offered him a cup of Clinch's coffee, which he took with gratitude. She put the marlinespike on her desk, near at hand.

"*Leopard* just anchored in Hampton Roads off Norfolk," he said. "I asked a friend in our naval office there to look into it." He unfolded a letter. "This is his answer. Pennywort, now, Peter Pennywort, turns out he was a bona fide deserter. An ensign on *Leopard* recognized him the moment he came aboard, deserted from HMS *Perry* two years ago."

Pennywort, the name she hadn't known at the time. First man taken that awful day.

"He'll be returned to *Perry*. Probably draw fifty lashes."

"He said he was an American citizen," Danny said. "If he was, even if a new citizen, that should mean something."

Bigbee shook his head. "Not for a prime deserter. Your navy wouldn't countenance that and neither will ours. No, he's back where he belongs. But the other two, Tolliver, the bo'sun, and the young fellow, Jones, I think—"

"Robbie Jones."

"Yes. Well, he and Tolliver, everyone agrees they are clearly Americans and shouldn't have been taken."

"Well, thank God! They've been released, then?"

The officer's face reddened. "No, ma'am, not till they're replaced. They're needed—*Leopard* will have to find someone to take their place before they can be released."

She stared at him. "That is obscene," she said.

He cleared his throat. "Yes, ma'am, I supposed you wouldn't find that attractive."

"I find it maddening. It doesn't make sense. What—"

"Well, you understand the whole reason the Royal Navy looks for men is because the ships are shorthanded. So if it takes a wrong man it's willing to restore him but since the ship always comes first, they'll want a replacement before they willingly turn him loose."

"Good God. So that's why it takes three or four years or more to get a man released when everyone knows he's been illegally taken in an open act of piracy."

He winced at that, but said, "Sometimes it does, yes, ma'am, not always."

"Often enough. How perfectly rotten, forcing Robbie Jones to serve indefinitely until they—the powers that be—decide in their majesty and their wisdom—and who's deciding, some officer with his own ax to grind, who cares nothing for human decency—"

She went on in this vein for some time. When at last she ran down, he said, "Yes, ma'am, but there's another side too."

"What, pray tell?"

She let him talk, his voice modest and quiet in the still of the office in the empty warehouse but threaded nonetheless with a vibrancy that spoke of strength. She heard a passion for his homeland that made her think of her own feelings for New Orleans now transferred to the new nation. He said Britain was under desperate threat from a mad tyrant who had bamboozled the French and was determined to conquer the world. Napoleon Bonaparte had the military genius to sweep all of Europe and on to the steppes of Russia. In due time the Orient and the Americas would be within his reach as he poured the world's treasure into France. The Americas too? Oh, yes, as one country and another fell, the world would be his. America too.

Only the British Isles and their doughty people stood between the French tyrant and this apocalyptic vision— and the Royal Navy, which was their personification as well as their protection. All their hopes rested on the navy as did their commerce, dependent as it was on ships exporting manufactured goods and importing raw materials. Yes, the French had a navy, but it didn't compare, and Lieutenant Bigbee believed that the great Admiral Nelson soon would seek it out and destroy it.

Royal Navy ships in turn depended on their crews. Had Danny ever been aboard a man-of-war? A magnificent sight, especially under sail. Seventy-four guns, with a crew to manage each. Thousands of square yards of canvas bent to spars and masts, men balanced on spars aloft and handling sail, mast whipping as the ship plunges, enemy shot crashing through rigging and tumbling men to the deck below, the ship twisting and turning and coming about in mad pursuit of advantage, every turn meaning take in and let out and reset sail, guns roaring, clouds of smoke, the enemy coming about and you see his guns lined on you and then the broadside's vast billow of smoke and in another second massive balls will batter the rigging and small shot fired with cannon force will slice among men who can only hold on and hope while splinters fly like poison darts—

"Well, you can see that you'll be losing some men, and those who survive sooner or later will start thinking on running away, and when you add desertion to losses you can have a crippled ship, and then how people feel and whether they are Americans and whether its fair really doesn't matter very much. The nation depends on your ship and the others, and your duty is not to be fair but to have your ship ready to fight."

She started to protest and he raised a hand. "Miz Mobry, any nation will do what it must to survive."

There was a silence. "You're saying," she said slowly, "that A, if his survival is at stake, may destroy B. You're saying that the little United States is B and powerful Great Britain is A. So the end justifies the means."

He had the grace to color at that. "We search for our own deserters, ma'am. They are all over American ships. Our officers walk your docks and literally see their own

men on your merchant ships. Sometimes the men see
their old officers watching and make an obscene gesture.
It's maddening."

"But two of the three from *Carlito* were Americans
and you just told me you'll keep them for years."

He sighed. "I won't argue that it's fair, only that it's
necessary. We fight a deadly war."

She left the marlinespike on the desk and gave him her
hand. "Thank you, Lieutenant. Thank you very much."

He held her hand a moment. "If I've done you a service, perhaps you'll grant me a boon—you might call me
Terry."

A little too forward, yes, and it struck her again, and
again it surprised her, that she liked him.

"All right," she said, ". . . Terry."

And back in the shadow of the Capitol Aaron Burr had
Mrs. Simpson, mistress of his boarding house, hard at
work on what would be the most important dinner of his
life. He kept it simple, plain food excellently prepared,
nothing elaborate, no sign that he attached any special
importance to this dinner among many. But he found a
superb wine and a twenty-five-year-old cognac. The dinner would be in his suite where none could overhear and
great issues could be decided.

FIFTEEN

Washington, early 1805

"Aaron," Jim Wilkinson said, "you should go west. See for yourself. They'll receive you with open arms—indeed, my friend, they'll love you—you're their kind of man."

Burr settled back with a small smile. He had begun to wonder if he would have to raise the subject himself. They were having that supper he'd planned so carefully. A fire glowed in the suite's sitting room. Mrs. Simpson had spread a cloth of white linen and brought out her finest dishes and silver. But the fare, as he'd decreed, was plain, direct, soldierlike, cold beef with fresh bread and butter with the last hothouse tomatoes. He had set the wine aside; they would wash down this repast with tankards of porter, the cognac to follow. Wilkinson was dressed in a plain black suit with black hose instead of his usual gaudy uniform. Always cautious, he obviously hoped to slip in and out of the disgraced vice president's quarters unnoticed. From someone else that would have been insulting, but Burr understood the general. He was the way he was, plumper still after the cuisine of New

Orleans, veins breaking in his cheeks, his small blue eyes unchanged in their knowing shrewdness.

Wilkinson waved a fork for emphasis. "Their kind of man," he said, "strong, direct, to traduce you is to pay the penalty, and yet wise, skilled, experienced in the ways of the world and the command realities of nations—a man, in short, whom they can trust, turn to, *cling to*! Go, and you'll find all I tell you is true, you'll be thrilled by your reception. It's a garden of opportunity, too. Why, you could start a whole new career there. Any western state would send you to the Senate in a flash. Senator Burr of Kentucky! How does that sound, eh? You could put some sticks in their spokes then, I'll warrant."

Burr stared at him. The room suddenly felt chill. "I've been the senator from New York. I've been—am—vice president of the United States. Senator from Kentucky— that does not have very strong appeal, Jim."

From Wilkinson's grin Burr saw he'd just been tested. "There's more, of course," Wilkinson said, "for a man of courage. A man of vision with the daring to carry it out." His voice fell to a dramatic whisper. "Mexico lies just beyond the horizon. A veritable treasure house. A golden apple awaiting the man with the stature to pluck it."

Now, that was more like it. "Mexico, eh?"

"Understand, Aaron, the Spanish empire is dying. Dying with its hands full of gold. That popinjay Yrujo—the ambassador, you know him?—yes, all his talk about Spanish honor and power is mere cloak for a man who sits with a deuce in the hole. Why do I say that empire is dying? Because it's rotten at its heart, its time has passed, revolution stalks its edges and leaves it embattled and inert. That's why Mexico is so vulnerable. The people there will separate on their own in a few more years. A hundred men could land at Vera Cruz, march into the Valley of Mexico in twenty days, and hammer open the vaults. I know about this. I've had reconnaissance in detail under the guise of commercial traveling. Reports on the defenses of every town, every pass as the road leads into the mountains—and there are no defenses. It's pitiful, it demonstrates the inherent collapse of the Spanish empire that awaits only the trigger. So who shall pull that trigger? Ah, that is the question."

"A hundred men, you say?"

"A hundred, five hundred. Tell me, Aaron, have you heard of the Mexican Association of New Orleans? No? I suppose not—secret society, more or less, been around a number of years and could hardly advertise itself with Spanish officials in charge. Now it's in full bloom, a good three hundred members, significant men in New Orleans, all dedicated to the idea of seizing Mexico."

"Of dreaming, you mean? Or of doing?"

"A brilliant question, Aaron! You see—*you* have the kind of trenchant mind that is crucial for such an enterprise. In answer, I suppose some of both, but there are strong men involved. New Orleans is different from anyplace you know. The pirate Jean Lafitte is an honored figure—the loot he takes from Spanish vessels feeds the economy of New Orleans. Such men won't hesitate over the niceties of international ownership."

"I talked to their commissioners," Burr said. "Apparently the town is bitterly dissatisfied with American rule."

"To say the least. On the knife edge of revolt right now."

"That's what they hinted."

"They're being polite. Look, these people didn't ask to be Americans and don't want to be. And the U.S. is treating them like so much dog manure. The governor, Claiborne—he's a fool. A donkey. A peanut. Rules them in English that they can't understand and refuses to learn their language. I don't have it either, no talent for languages, but I'm not ruling them. I believe your French is—"

"Adequate, certainly. I met these gentlemen at a reception and they poured their hearts out. Seemed thrilled to be talking to an official, even one in dubious odor. Everything you say was reflected. There was a fury in them and the more they talked the more I felt they were skirting the edge of revolt."

"You're quick, Aaron. You just got here and already you have the lay of the land. That's it, precisely. They are ripe for change and they don't much care what change. The Spanish weak, the French abandon them, the Americans buy them but treat them like dirt, refuse them citizenship, deny them the vote, impose leaders, give them no say—they're just waiting for a man of strength—"

"They said my old friend Ed Livingston actually drafted their petition."

"You know Ed? Splendid! He's made himself a strong figure in the Mexican Association. He's after a gorgeous Creole widow, she's teaching him the language, probably they've wed by now."

Burr was delighted. He'd served in the House with Livingston about the time Tennessee was coming in and afterward they'd both gotten to know the Tennessee delegate, Andrew Jackson, and what a character *he* was! Ed had been badly used in New York, the defalcation wasn't at all his fault, and Burr knew something about being badly used. Yes, indeed! And his heart went out to a good man and a friend who'd faced some of the same calumny. So Ed was a figure in this Mexican Association. . . . Immediately it took on stature in Burr's mind.

"You know," Wilkinson said, "that New Orleans is the choke point for the entire American West." He was slathering butter on bread and didn't look up, but Burr heard a subtle shift in his voice and realized he was moving to a new subject. "Everything, *everything*, depends on the river, and the river is easily plugged."

He took a huge bite of the bread and Burr saw butter

smeared on the side of his mouth. "I remember when I first went to Kentucky, right after the Revolution," he said, his tone reminiscent. "Even then it was stressed and strained. Still part of Virginia, you know, having to petition Richmond for everything. Well, a sizable movement for independence arose and you may be sure I was at its forefront. After statehood, it kept right on, what folks call the Kentucky Conspiracy. Well, hell's bells, I can tell you the conspiracy was real!"

He took a swallow of porter and belched. "And it's still there. 'Course, when I reentered the army I had to tone down my enthusiasms, but they haven't changed. Kentucky, the whole West, what's it doing tied to the moribund East? The East abuses us, takes advantage of us, takes our money with its manufactured goods and gives us damned little in return at outrageous prices. It overwhelms us in the Congress, the administration ladles out lip service on election day and forgets us for four years— God Almighty, why are we so anchored to the East?"

Burr's heart seemed to be thumping in his chest. "Are you saying . . ."

"Well, I don't know, I'm just a simple soldier, I'm not really saying anything. But I do know that a lot of men in the West are dissatisfied. I know that New Orleans is ready to turn and if it does it can control the West and those men would be doing a lot of thinking. From there—well, what do you think?"

"They say the West is the land of opportunity," Burr said softly.

Wilkinson pushed his plate aside. He sat lower in his chair, elbows on the table, hands holding his head. His voice was a whisper. "Do you know what the West lacks—what it *always* has lacked? A man of power. Of authority. Who can draw pictures for the ignorant masses, make them *see* what they're too dense to see on their own, who can show them the holy grail of their own desires buried in their hearts, a man who can raise his fist and make them leap to follow . . ."

A silence stretched. At last Burr sighed, and said, "And you're saying—"

"I'm not saying anything," Wilkinson said, rather sharply, Burr thought. They were coming to the crux. Soon he would discover whether the general was real or merely a talker.

"I'm a dreamer," Wilkinson said, "a spinner of air castles. I see great things—I see empire. Think of it, Aaron, stretching from the gold vaults of Mexico City to Cincinnati on the Ohio to the River Columbia on the Pacific, New Orleans its center, its controlling heart, its opening to the trade of Europe. It would take its place among great nations instantly, it would reduce the pitiful thirteen on the Atlantic seaboard to their actual impotence. That is empire, my friend; it lacks only an emperor."

"A role," Burr said, "in which you might see yourself."

"Ah, but I'm just a simple soldier."

Burr laughed outright.

Wilkinson smiled. "You think I'm falsely modest. Well, I have an eye for combinations and possibilities and I know men. I recognize hungry men. Perhaps I have a talent, such as it is, for drawing out, even for exploiting, their hungers. But leading a new nation, leading men to glory—that isn't my role."

Leading men to glory—Burr's dreams were summed in that phrase. In a flash he saw Wilkinson's purpose. The general would never have the rare power to rally men to storm the barricades. But Burr knew how to seize men's minds and hearts, make them hunger to be near the leader and earn his smiles, make them willing to follow him into the jaws of hell. Wilkinson was a schemer, not a leader, and he needed Burr out front. But then, for the moment at least, Burr needed him too. Instinct told him it was time to bring the general to heel.

Softly, Burr said, "Yet the greatest leader can't lead alone."

"Yes, he must have structure, support, weight."

"Weight, yes . . . military weight."

"Aye . . . military weight."

Burr stared at him. The room was silent. A horse's hoofs clattered on cobblestone outside. "You run the army," he said.

"I do indeed, and I keep it on tight rein. It does what I say, that and no more, no less. No one questions me."

"Three thousand men or more?" Burr said. "Concentrated in the West, I believe?"

"Yes, but now you must take care, sir!" Wilkinson slapped the table hard, rearing straight in his seat, a sudden glare showing the formidable man often disguised behind his easy exterior. "I am saying nothing at all. I am a patriot, sir! Perhaps more a patriot to my region than to my nation, but a patriot always. Now, faced with circumstances I can't predict, I suppose I'd have to decide what's best. . . ."

It was time. Burr leaped up, letting rage flash across his face. "No, by God!" He saw Wilkinson rear back startled and silenced. "You will not leave it up in the air. You sing your song but you fade away on the last verse. Now it's time to sing out loud and bright, or shut your mouth."

"Well, now," Wilkinson said, and Burr held up a hand.

"Listen to me, Jim. You want to seize the West and peel it off from the eastern states. You want to take Mexico, you say it's ready to swing. You say New Orleans is the natural capital of a new nation and the gold in the coffers of Mexico is ample to fund that new nation. You tell me—how did you put it?—'Mexico yearns to be taken as a woman yearns for a man.'"

"Hold on," Wilkinson said, a hand raised, whether in warning or resistance Burr had no idea.

"Be silent, sir," Burr snapped and watched the general

sag back in his chair. "You've had your say. Now it's time to hear me. And hear me well, for I won't say this again." He jabbed a finger almost against Wilkinson's nose, expecting the general to react with anger or at least offended dignity, but instead a calm watchfulness swept his fat face.

"Say on, Aaron," he said softly. "But keep your voice down. This is dangerous talk."

"We can do great things together, General. I can swing New Orleans behind me in a week's time—that was obvious from the way those delegates talked. Come and take charge, they were saying. They found the understanding in me they can't find elsewhere in America. *Simpatico,* they said. We can put that oaf Claiborne in a rowboat and float him out to sea. The men of Kentucky— why, I know them too, Brown and Smith and Adair, they all served in the Senate or on the bench, and believe me, I can make them listen. I can make them see how the East patronizes them, how little it gives them, how quick it will be to take from them—and then, I can make them see how *they* will profit in a new country that's under their control, not that of Virginia power grabbers.

"I can put together men and weapons. I can raise money in New York that you couldn't hope to do, gather weapons and supplies and fifteen hundred men. Please don't tell me a hundred men could take Mexico—that's ridiculous. Do me the credit to remember I have some military experience too. If you had spent more time in the field and less currying favor at headquarters, you wouldn't say such a thing."

He paused to see if Wilkinson would react, but the general simply watched him in silence.

"So," Burr said carefully, "we come to the question. Are you in this or are you not?"

"Meaning?"

"I mean, it takes an army to conquer Mexico! Not a

thousand ragtag youngsters out for adventure. The civilian army I can raise will be perfect to seize New Orleans but then we need a real army. The American army, your army, thrown against Spain."

Wilkinson stared at him, a tic quivering in his right cheek.

Burr took a long liberating draft of porter. He felt good, springy, in command. "I'll raise fifteen hundred men and we'll take New Orleans while your army stands by. We jail the officials, rally the people, seize the banks and the ships at the wharves. We load them with your troops and go conquer Mexico. We come back heavy with gold, declare New Orleans the new capital of a new nation that stretches from Ohio to Mexico City. Then Brown and Adair and all our friends along the river rise to say this is just what the region always has needed, and we shut the river to anyone and everyone who resists."

Wilkinson's eyes were bright and his mouth hung open slightly. "What about when the army realizes?"

"Well, hell, they're mostly westerners, aren't they? Why will they object? And if some do, fine, march 'em under guard to the Appalachians and tell 'em to keep on going."

A smile was growing on Wilkinson's face. "And if the navy objects?"

"How many capital ships does the navy have? Three? Four? Since the administration has gutted it to save money in the Democratic-Republican philosophy? A few frigates from the Royal Navy should settle that danger."

Wilkinson laughed out loud. "Call in the British, eh?"

"They'll be delighted to help. A new country allied with Canada that reduces the United States to a seaboard sliver? They'll be overjoyed."

There was a long silence. Burr sat down and put his elbows on the table. At last he said, "Fifteen hundred men, civilians all, they can't invade a nation and hold it. Need a real army for that. You have the army and you can control it long enough to take Mexico, and after that you can turn it loose. The question is whether you have the courage to use it. You've done a lot of talking, Jim; now tell me if you're real."

Wilkinson sat motionless, his hands flat on the table like paws. "A man could get his jaws slapped, questioning courage like that," he said.

Burr didn't let his gaze waver. Staring at Wilkinson, leaning into him, he said, "The man slaps my jaws will answer on the dueling field. And there I'll kill him."

Wilkinson looked aside. He licked his lips. Ignoring the challenge, he said, "This here is dangerous talk, taking over New Orleans and setting it free, using the army."

"It is." Burr smiled, feeling better and better. If the next two minutes went his way his future was unlimited, a flower opening to the light. If it went against him his ruin was compounded, for he had nothing else.

"It's treason," Wilkinson whispered.

"So it is," Burr said. "But put the army in and create empire and then it's not treason, it's a new country. Call it revolution."

"Get your neck stretched whatever you call it."

Burr laughed. "That's the truth, by God." Life on the razor's edge. He threw the dice. "So there you are. Count you in or count you out?"

For a long moment Wilkinson stared. "You surprise me, Aaron," he said at last. "You're tougher than I thought. We may get on well together."

Yet Burr saw something in Wilkinson's eyes and heard the same thing in his faint hesitation. The man was afraid.

Wilkinson's whisper fluttered the candle flame. "I'm in." His face was white, his jaw tight. "You handle the crowds. I'll deal with the army. And we'll build an empire."

He put out his hand and Burr took it.

All that winter, the year 1805 dawning crisp and cold, Burr worked on the West. He studied a stream of military reports that Wilkinson spirited from the War Department, sitting in his rooms with a long clay pipe gone cold in his hands, a candle guttering. He spread maps on a trestle table and weighted the corners with four pistols he'd purchased as part of a traveling outfit. He studied the rivers, the Ohio meandering from the Appalachians, the Tennessee and the Cumberland dipping into Tennessee and entering the Ohio together just short of the father of waters. He memorized both banks of the Mississippi, north to St. Louis and the Missouri's entry, south to Choctaw Bluffs, the city site-in-waiting ready to rise from campfire ashes at the western end of Tennessee, on to the mighty Arkansas boiling from the mountains, on to the swirling mouth of the Red staining the water for a hundred miles, on to Natchez and Fort Adams and the city on the crescent ringed by lakes and swamps.

Maps of the wild mangrove swamps of Florida that fed Ponce de Leon's dreams, maps that tracked the plains of Texas to the Rio Grande and on into the mountains of Mexico. Maps of the Red River winding through wild country where Spanish troops drifted, appearing and disappearing. All fanciful, full of guesswork and estimates and shaky lines to illustrate rumors of what might be there or more probably was not. Maps of the vast westward space of the purchase that the explorers were crossing now, big blanks with occasional squiggles marking rivers and mountains that might or might not be there or anywhere. Street maps of New Orleans on which he marked the Cabildo, the cathedral, the fortified places, the old powder magazine, the bridges, the levee, examining every spot vulnerable or optimal for attack or defense. Maps anchored to Vera Cruz, maps of the Valley of Mexico where the stunning City of Mexico lay like a golden prize. The copyist working at the trestle table reproducing these maps on parchment rolls put in ten hours a day while Burr was at the Senate.

Spain was making new threats. Spanish troops were massing to the east in Florida, to the west in Texas. New Orleans was alive with rumors, so said everyone.

"Give an ear to this," Wilkinson said over a Christmas turkey. He unfolded a letter. "From General Adair." Burr nodded. John Adair was *the* man to see in Kentucky. A U.S. senator who'd been elected from the Kentucky bench, he'd been everything. Everyone who looked at the frontier knew him. He shook the paper and cleared his throat. "Says, 'Kentuckians are full of enterprise and altho' not poor are as greedy after plunder as ever the old Romans were. Mexico glitters in our eyes—the word is all we wait for.' "

Wilkinson slapped his meaty hands together. "By God! What do you think of that? 'The word is all we wait for.' Just what I told you, eh?" He drained his glass and held it out for more. "Let Spain trigger off war and we can strip 'em bare." He gave Burr a meaningful look. "'Course, war with Spain, the U.S. government would welcome help from a party of bravos." He winked. "I can promise you that."

The future glowed like sunshine.

"Listen to this," Jimmy said. Dolley put down her embroidery frame. She saw he was reading that nasty Boston paper she'd learned to hate. Its very words struck her as so many violations. It was late, the streets outside silent. His reading candle and her candle threw flickering shadows around the third-floor sitting room adjoining their bedroom. It was a part of the day she liked, when they were alone and resting and soon would go to bed but now had blessed free time absent all demands.

" 'A democracy,' " he said, voice arch as he quoted, " 'A democracy is scarcely tolerable at any period of national history.' " He chuckled. She knew he felt no less strongly than she but showed it differently; he was calm while she was ready to fly up and denounce someone.

"Goes right on," he said. " 'Its omens'—that's democracy, understand—'its omens are always sinister. It is on trial and the issue will be civil war, desolation and anarchy. No wise man but discerns its imperfections, no good man but shudders at its miseries, no honest man but proclaims its fraud and no brave man but draws his sword against its force. A policy so radically contemptible and vicious is a memorable example of the villainy of some men and the folly of others. . . . ' "

"They're mad dogs, Jimmy," she cried. "They bay at the moon. They *want* failure."

He shrugged. "They want rule by the wise and the good—judges, preachers, the wealthy who must be wise else they wouldn't be wealthy—those who stand over the vulgar masses."

"It's dangerous, isn't it?" she said softly.

He nodded. "You know, I thought if we settled Louisiana we'd be in the clear, marching on to brilliant new day. But Governor Claiborne tells us New Orleans is full of treasonous talk, and Danny says the same, and there's precious little we can do about it anytime soon. Meanwhile the Spanish threaten, probably just talk but maybe not, and the Federalists are hitting harder than ever, calling us a mobocracy, saying the whole idea of liberty and equal rights is the mighty mischief."

He shook his head and drank the last of now cold tea. "It's narrow." His voice was a whisper. "So little margin for error. So many doubters, Federalists, secessionists in New England, radicals driving toward extremes, Spanish threatening, British squeezing, French attitude as hard on our commerce as the British. God, it is ironic, you know? Whole world denouncing democracy and in New Orleans people ready to revolt because we were afraid to give them democracy immediately. Maybe that was a mistake, I don't know. But this revolt talk in the West, I know I don't like that. Too far away and hard to handle. Wilkinson says he keeps his ears open, but—"

"Wilkinson," she said, frowning. She detested the man.

Jimmy shrugged. "He's all we've got."

And to that she had no answer.

Burr made himself a welcome visitor at the British embassy. Mr. Merry was a drudge but Elizabeth Merry had a certain charm, the more because she so offended official Washington. She was handsome, perhaps a bit on the stout side, but then a fleshy woman was not to be discounted. He made no move, of course, and he had a feeling she was disappointed. But they were allies, both shunned by Washington, and it was enough to compare notes on the gaucheries of the village capital.

The ambassador was terribly out of sorts over the Americans. Given that Britain was locked in a death struggle with a tyrant who intended to rule the world, the Americans should see that the Royal Navy could hardly allow its men to desert to American ships. Naturally British warships stopped vessels and took the pick of their crews. If an occasional American was taken it was what America should be volunteering anyway. Yet when a British warship took men in New York Harbor, that contemptible little Madison had acted most insultingly. Merry said he had countered by instinct—America should have discovered and returned the deserters, so the whole thing was America's fault! His eyes sparkled and he waved his cigar while his wife tittered dutifully. With another rumbling chuckle, Mr. Merry said he was thinking of demanding reparations. He was delighted to find a Democrat who understood reality.

After several such evenings, Mrs. Merry casting warm glances at Burr over stewed mutton, the American judged the time right to make his move. With a poor brandy in hand in the ambassador's study, he drew his chair close and whispered that he wanted Mr. Merry to know his plans. A greedy complicity shone in the Briton's eyes as Burr said in so many words that he intended to assume the leadership of revolt in New Orleans, make it an independent principality and revolutionize the entire American West. Everything beyond the Appalachians would become a new nation centering on New Orleans and then expanding westward into the Spanish gold regions. Fueled by that wealth, it would look to an alliance with Canada that would dominate North America.

He said exactly what he intended to say but hearing himself gave him a stunning sense of his own audacity. He had to struggle to keep a waver from his voice. Mr. Merry, however, was delighted. He said he would petition his government with high enthusiasm for what Burr said he would need: a hundred thousand dollars in operating cash and three Royal Navy frigates posted off the mouth of the Mississippi when the time came.

A look of contempt that Merry was too dull to suppress flashed over his face. Burr recognized it as reaction to a man who would betray his country. But walking away, he thought his plans were less betraying the old than inventing the new. In ridding the old country of an unruly tail that threatened to wag it, he would be doing it a favor. Could that be treason?

It was near sunset. Madison sat in the president's long office watching a single file of sheep moving up the south lawn toward the barn. "Burr has something on his mind," he said, "flirting with the British ambassador, gathering War Department maps of the West."

"Maps?" the president said.

"Had a professional copyist in his rooms, apparently."

The president's eyebrows raised. "Albert Gallatin said Burr was the great danger, and he might prove right yet."

"He'll bear watching," Madison said. Actually, he thought Tom's hatred of Burr excessive. Hate's effect on calm is itself dangerous. But he agreed that Burr was dangerous because he combined unusual ability with total self-focus. The man cared not a fig for the tenderness of the new democracy or the continental concept that Captain Lewis's expedition embodied. He thought only of himself. Now he was looking at the West, he a polished New Yorker who had never crossed the Appalachians.

Indeed, it would bear watching.

On the last day of the old Congress, the president and a new vice president awaiting inauguration, Burr rapped the gavel for the last time and granted himself the floor. He told startled senators that he rose to say farewell.

For a half hour he spoke on the glories of mankind and of the Senate, making them seem one and the same. Members listened in gripped silence, some touching handkerchiefs to their eyes. When he'd brought them to the heights, he closed with words cast so low they must strain to hear . . . farewell and Godspeed and may this great body's traditions go on forever, and so forth.

He walked out on rapt silence, no raw contumely this time. He had made them yield triumph, he of the golden tongue, and he could do the same for the West and in New Orleans.

He departed the next day. Now he must go west, see the region's scope, range, splendor. Sense its opportunity. Feel its anguish and unrest. Talk to the men who knew it best. No great enterprise should be undertaken on another's word; he must see for himself. Within the month he was on the Ohio floating toward the Mississippi.

SIXTEEN

Marietta, Ohio, spring 1805

Aaron Burr floated into Marietta on a spring day when snowmelt was raising the Ohio River and fishing birds were skimming the surface. He was starting a trial run that would take him clear to New Orleans to scout the ground and sound the people and decide for himself if General Wilkinson was talking sense.

Marietta proved to be a fine-looking little town and somehow this reassured him. But his lips tightened at that—he didn't need reassuring. Really. But he did have a lot riding on this—he stopped himself, blanking off the thought. This was the wrong time for that. No, the point was that Colonel Burr was an intensely urban man and as such was already sick of what he'd seen of wilderness, so that an urban scene was a pleasure. That's all. He brushed aside an errant thought that might have been a warning: for a man who intended to rule the West he didn't seem to have much pioneer instinct.

But never mind that—now the great adventure was beginning. It could yield him wealth and power beyond imagination or it could put him in a hangman's noose.

But then, he'd always been willing to dare, and to seek the golden chalice is to dare hugely. Now he dreamed a great dream and of course it carried commensurate risk. But he wasn't a fool—first he must see that it was real and not a Wilkinson fantasy. And so he traveled to explore for himself. If it were fantasy, the first signals should be evident here in Ohio.

A wharf ran along the riverbank. He saw a rat peering at him from its understructure. Across a dirt street facing the wharf were frame buildings with false fronts and up the hill a grid of streets with log homes. A handsome brick structure of two stories a bit up the hill must be the Marietta Inn. Wilkinson had assured him it was quite a decent place.

When his hired crew threw out lines fore and aft, he tossed a copper to a boy lounging on a bollard. "Run tell Mayor Johnson that Colonel Burr has arrived."

Marietta was a good three hundred miles down the Ohio from Pittsburgh where he'd taken delivery of his keelboat from a man named Hawkins, who was pleasant enough except for endless denunciations of liquor as the devil's tool. Said he had made the keelboat that young Meriwether Lewis and his friend Clark were taking up the Missouri right about now, and wasn't that a fantastic adventure? But—a private thought—no more so than the adventure on which Colonel Burr embarked.

An elegant boat was essential, for he must make a powerful impression. It was sixty feet by fourteen. A cabin with real glass windows ran its length. Atop the cabin was a catwalk where he could pace as they rode the current while miles of riverbank slid past. At first he had seen handsome farms reaching to the water, each with its wharf, but gradually the interludes of forest grew longer, the cleared farms rarer, the log huts meaner, the little towns farther apart and dismayingly rude. He supposed this was the frontier West.

A tall, heavily built man fifty or so with long gray hair and a bushy gray mustache came striding across the wharf to welcome Burr to the new state of Ohio. He proved to be the mayor, Rank Johnson. Behind him Burr saw three old friends, all powerful figures in the West and, oddly, each named John. They were longtime associates of Wilkinson who had said he would alert them to Burr's coming.

John Adair of Kentucky and John Smith of Ohio were sitting U.S. senators; John Brown had just stepped down from Kentucky's other senate seat. As a senator from New York Burr had helped the Kentucky men through many a parliamentary snarl. When Ohio won statehood in 1802 and sent Smith to Washington, Burr as president of the U.S. Senate had made it a point to guide him through the Senate's arcane rules, spoken and unspoken. Burr liked men of the West for their open manner but he also had sensed their coming importance and as an investment had cultivated them and helped ease their legislative burdens. Wilkinson said Burr's name was well known and highly respected west of the Appalachians. If he could trust anyone he could trust these three. They had stood with him against the administration when he was being abused and had done so publicly. Sympathy behind the hand isn't worth much but in the open it counts for a lot.

Furthermore, they had come hundreds of miles to be here when forty miles was a good day on a horse, eighty in a coach. Now, on a wharf in Marietta where he had come to start putting western men to the test, the three senators apparently offered respect and affection, their very presence an endorsement of mutual plans. He drew each into an embrace. It was a good start.

Mayor Johnson had organized a celebration and by midafternoon the crowd in the square was dense. A brass band played, militiamen marched in close order drill with guidons flying, a cannon saluted the guest and three damsels in flowing white delivered patriotic effusions. The mayor introduced the three senators, and Senator Smith, Ohio's own, introduced the guest. Smith lavished praise on the vice president as a man of honor, intellect, wisdom, rich experience and broad understanding. Above all, Aaron Burr was a friend of the West, a man who recognized equally the inherent virtue of the western American and the shabby treatment dealt him by the East.

It was late afternoon when Burr rose to speak, by now well warmed with praise. The sun was breaking on the false-front buildings, so half the square was in shadow. Men, women, children, and dogs gathered in audience with a holiday air. He started with his voice cast low so they must strain to hear, then let his enthusiasm for the West swell, voice rising until it soared. He'd heard the American West was the garden spot of the world and here he was in Marietta to swear that all the reports were understatements. How dismal was the cloudy East compared to Marietta in the sun! How could folks back East fail to understand or like or trust the blooming West? He had heard, they all had heard, the hard talk in the East—cut those worthless western folks loose, let 'em go, what good is the West to us? Well, Aaron Burr was here to tell them the West was the future, the hope, the glory of the American continent!

Burr had been making political speeches since he'd rallied troops as a stripling lieutenant in the Revolution and he knew how to hold an audience. You must reach beyond their minds to their hearts, you must strike a vision and then lift them and make them part of it, make them bigger, better, kinder, more noble than they knew they were, show them their best and let them know you understand even better than they how exemplary they are. And then remind them of their grievances, make them realize that you not only understand, you feel their anguish, for after all, even given their glories, they are victims too, and you are on their side. Then, very subtly, nothing at all specific, he set about conveying the sense that he was thinking in terms of doing something about it.

And they loved him! It was beyond his wildest expectations. It was what Wilkinson had promised but Burr couldn't have imagined the impact, the swelling in his heart, the sheer animal joy of their love. Women were laughing and crying and men were cheering and waving their hats and wiping their eyes. So you handle the crowd and sweep them along, you take their hands, you lead them toward a golden future and you have them laughing and crying and cheering all at once and then you bring it down to close, low, serious, from your heart, and end it while they still hunger for more.

Subtly, gracefully, his words actually chosen with great care, he let them know that this was important, that it was a start, that the best lay ahead, that he would be among them and beside them, that together he and they would be part of a future that shone like sunrise. He set the idea, passing on when he knew it was firm. Nothing definite, no one could say what it meant in so many words, but he saw the comprehension on their faces, saw them nod, yes, and then a growing eagerness, yes, they had heard him.

In the moment of rapt silence that followed he plunged into the crowd, using both hands to grasp the hands reaching for him with such eager yearning. A young woman in a blue bonnet thrust a baby into his arms. He smiled and held it high and kissed its cheek and the little thing had the good grace to smile instead of cry, and the crowd howled its pleasure.

And it warmed something in him that had been chilled, seemed to flow into if not fill a place that had been empty. He felt a momentary shiver of alarm at having such need that yearned to be filled, but he thrust it aside and raised his arms again to a new and thrilling cheer.

"Mr. Vice President, welcome as you are, I guess it ain't entirely clear why you're in Marietta, you don't mind my saying so." Alexander Henderson had a mud-spattered boot crossed on a knee. It seemed he was a militia captain. A hank of black hair fell across his forehead; he said he came from Upstate New York. His actual tone was polite enough but there was a tightness about his eyes that Burr didn't like, the suggestion of challenge in his manner.

Still, this wasn't the place to react. "Good question," Burr said. He looked around. The dinner with a dozen select Marietta men was in Rank Johnson's home, and they were down to brandy and cigars. Burr rolled his cigar in his fingers, looking judiciously at the coal.

"Well, I can only say so much, and I'll have to count on your discretion." He paused, looking around the room, letting that set in. "But you know the Spanish are talking war. You know West Florida certainly was part of the purchase, bought and paid for, and that probably includes the Florida peninsula and Texas as well."

"That's an article of faith hereabouts," someone said.

"Now, the Spanish empire is moribund." He saw some didn't know the word and added easily that it was collapsing of its own rot. "Meanwhile, its arrogant officers are thwarting honest American aspirations." He said the East wasn't concerned but *he* cared for the West. As long as West Florida was in Spanish hands, the people of Marietta were in jeopardy.

"There's a strong feeling that something should be done about that." He watched comprehension flash on faces at different rates and let the silence grow, waiting.

"I'm meeting General Wilkinson downriver. Of course, the army, its hands are more or less tied. But I think there are ways to have West Florida at the least." He sighed and shook his head and drew on the cigar. "Now, I think I've said quite enough. . . ."

"Mr. Vice President," Henderson said, "you go against the Spanish and you have my support. For a minute there I feared you had something more in mind, like the old days—well, I reckon I'm a pretty good patriot. But the Spanish, they're bastards. Last run I made to New Orleans, you know how you have to go right past Baton Rouge, and that's the west end of West Florida, right up against the river? The Spanish soldiers, they run out their guns ready to blow me to pieces, me with naught but a load of tobacco in a flatboat. Honest Americans shouldn't have to put up with such disrespect on our own river. Taking Florida? Count on me!"

There was a loud murmur of approval. The dinner broke up soon after. As Burr was leaving, the mayor caught his arm.

"Mr. Vice President."

"Oh, Rank—do call me Aaron," Burr said.

"Thank you, Aaron." He hesitated and swallowed. "Well, this afternoon and again this evening, I had a feeling there might be a little more to this than even you've hinted." Burr stared at him, waiting. "I just want to say, if that time comes I'd be honored were you to call on me. . . ."

"I won't forget that, Rank," Burr said, putting a quiver of sincerity into his voice.

When Burr and the three senators returned to the Marietta Inn he suggested a pipe and a nightcap. It was time to get down to real business, and he saw from their expressions that they understood him. He had the Inn's only two-room suite; the fact that Marietta even had a suite marked it as an up-and-coming town likely to star in the future. Most inns slept two or three to a bed with overflow on the floor.

They gathered around a table in shirtsleeves, cravats pulled loose. The room had a worn carpet under the table, a mirror in a plain frame, a bad painting of a man in buckskin watching the sun setting behind improbable mountains. A sperm oil lamp hanging from the ceiling cast a harsh light and an empty oaken bookcase had a forlorn look for lack of books.

Jack Adair put a square bottle on the table with a clatter. "Kentucky sour mash," he said. "Best whiskey ever made." He slapped the table for emphasis as if daring argument. He was a smallish man, sixty or so, gray hair and heavy eyebrows over oddly guileless blue eyes, his mouth tightened into a grim expression quite at odds with his usual good humor. Brown, who had just given up Kentucky's other senate seat, was a seemingly mild and gentle man, a bit older than Jack Adair. He and Burr had worked together in the old days in the Senate; his flowing hair had gone white now, but he still looked able to ride a hundred miles in any weather and function when he got there. The Ohio senator, Smith, coal black hair and heavy beard framing dark brown eyes, was younger. He had a rough-handed manner. Burr liked him; Smith had brooked no nonsense in ramming Ohio into statehood three years before and had carried the same manner to the Senate; he'd been downright refreshing. Trust might be too strong a word, but Burr had known these men long enough and had close enough dealings so that he was comfortable, if still wary.

He took a good sip from his glass, planning that as his last. He already was tired; this was no time to let liquor dull him further. But he smiled at the taste: by God, it *was* good whiskey. He raised a glass to Jack in tribute.

Adair extracted a worn corncob from an inside pocket. Burr had ordered clay pipes and soon the room was dense with smoke. He waited to see how things would unfold.

"That was a hell of speech," Adair said at last. You could sense his vigor in the way he talked. "Had 'em eating out of your hand. Struck just the right note."

"Oh?" Burr said, still waiting.

Looking discomfited as if having opened the subject he knew he had to say more, Adair said, "Told 'em something was up but didn't tell 'em what."

Brown, voice a rumble, said around his glass, "But that question from Henderson, so direct. I didn't like that. He's a troublemaker, you know, but you handled him just right."

"I told him what Jack just summed up: that something's up but I'm not saying what, at least not to the crowd."

Adair glanced at Brown. "That's it," he said, and clamped his pipe in his mouth as if to stop himself from saying more.

So now it was time to rein them in and find out where he stood—on the road to glory or on the edge of a cliff? "Now, gentlemen, I want to know just what you think that something is."

He watched their faces close. At last Adair said, "Better not to talk in so many words. We all know—"

"No, we don't," Burr said. "I know what Wilkinson has told me. He's told me that you support him. That the plan is mature, makes sense, will work. Good. But I want to hear from you that we're all talking of the same thing."

Again a long silence. Burr was beginning to wonder if there really was nothing here but wild imaginings and Wilkinson's dreams. If he'd come on a wild goose chase he must know right now, before he got in any deeper. The image of the hangman's noose, hemp raw and rough, was in his mind. But the alternative, debtor's prison, was there too. This needed to work.

The silence held. Then Jack Adair pushed back his chair. He went softly to the door and jerked it open. No one was there. He looked up and down the hall, then closed the door and hung a coat over the knob. "Well, boys," he said as he resumed his seat, "we're counting on Aaron for a lot. We can't do it ourselves, not without a leader, and he's our leader."

Brown's voice was low. It carried a phlegmy rattle. "Well, I ain't sure where to start. But we're already in this too deep to get out so I figure you can count on us. But personally, it would help me to hear just how you see this thing laying out. How it'll all work."

Wanted him out front. But that was fair enough, too.

"Here's the skeleton," Burr said slowly, and then let his voice take on a rhythm and a depth designed to carry them in his train. "I raise money in New York and bring down a small army, a thousand men armed and supplied. New Orleans treats us as liberators when we arrive. Governor Claiborne goes in a cell. Wilkinson has incited a Spanish attack in Texas and is moving to meet it. He calls a truce and comes to New Orleans, ostensibly to deal with us. He sets up martial law. Seizes banks and ships. There are several millions of dollars in the banks there, incidentally—might as well put it to use."

All three men laughed at that. "We sail across the Gulf," Burr went on, "seize Mexico and make it our own. Then back to New Orleans to declare Louisiana an independent nation with gold mines in Mexico its treasury. We urge soldiers to switch to the new country but those who want to go we turn loose with a handful of gold but no weapon. And we tell westerners that they are part of a new country in which they are paramount instead of adjunct, a country that honors what they are. Those not interested are free to move unmolested back to the mother country, the United States, in the same way loyalists moved back to Canada a quarter century ago. And we announce that the river is closed to all who have not adopted the new nation, open to those who have. Leading men—you three and all your associates—throw yourselves into a roaring campaign to accept this new largesse from a new independent nation that is all their own."

"Hear! Hear!" Smith banged on the table. "By God, if that don't say it perfect!" He reached for his glass.

"Sounds good, doesn't it?" Burr said. He smiled. "That's because I made it sound easy. But I don't think it'll be easy."

They watched him, not answering.

"So," he said, "let's take it element by element. First off, assume for the moment that I can get a thousand men down the river and into New Orleans. How will New Orleans respond?"

"Throw flowers under your feet," Adair said. He laughed a little too loudly and Brown looked alarmed.

"So I hear," Burr said. "New Orleans sent a delegation to Washington to protest the denial of democracy— they'd never had it, you see, sneered and laughed, but now they want it. Power of democracy, you think, or the perverseness of human nature?"

Brown smiled. His eyes had a weary look. "Both, I expect. Democracy's easy enough to honor long as you don't go any further than talk. I expect that covers New Orleans folk."

"This delegation, it got the cold shoulder from officialdom. Madison and his crowd of Virginians. But I spoke to them at length. In French, of course, which that idiotic governor, the fatuous Mr. Claiborne, refuses to learn. And they seemed delighted. Now, they insisted they were loyal but said the United States was rapidly alienating them. I suggested I might look in someday and they were beside themselves. You could *own* New Orleans, I remember one of them saying. They seem to be waiting for liberators; do you think that's true?"

"Of course," Adair said. He laughed. "Anyone who ain't representing the American government gets a king's welcome. Crown you in laurel."

"And follow us to war?"

"Aaron, they're angry. Looking for someone to fight, actually. They just haven't been focused yet."

"Now," Burr said, "Wilkinson implied he can put the U.S. Army behind this transaction. Can he?"

It was Smith who took this one. "Can he? Yes, indeed. He's very autocratic, even his assistants know little of what he's doing. Arrogant devil, really. He snaps orders for others to obey and he doesn't entertain questions. Doesn't have a deputy or even a close assistant because that would shift a little power from him. He holds it all in his fat hands. Means he can come and go as he pleases, no one the wiser. Now, assume Spain is attacking, he can shift to meet it and then invading Mexico becomes defensive."

"Spain attacking—that's a big assumption."

"But Jim can arrange it." He was laughing, but sobered under Burr's stare. "You gotta see, Aaron, he handles the Spanish like a sheep dog handling sheep. Funny thing is, apparently they pay him well for keeping them perpetually in a fearful lather that the United States intends to eat them up. He'll handle the Spanish, tell them the U.S. is mobilizing to attack, advise them to get their troops into Florida and Texas. They'll send battalions from Cuba and before you know it we'll have whatever kind of war Wilkinson wants to have."

"And the army will go along?"

"Same situation, really," the Ohio senator said. "The army's loyal, start with that. I know a lot of officers and there's hardly a bad apple among them. But Jim takes no one into his confidence; it's like he's always ready for some illicit move. Probably his nature but the end result is that if your people seized banks and ships Jim would have those men aboard and Mexico-bound before you could shake a stick."

"But the U.S. Navy might give some trouble," Brown said. "Wilkinson doesn't control them."

"No," Burr said, "but a couple of Royal Navy frigates lying off the mouth of the river will settle that."

They looked at him with sparkling eyes. "My," Adair said, "you've already arranged that, have you? Excellent!"

"Had a long talk," Burr said. "They seemed to like the idea of a western coup just fine. I think the ships will be there." His voice shifted. "But go back to the army. What happens when they discover this is more coup than war with Mexico?"

"Why wouldn't they sign on?" the Ohio senator said. "But the deed will be done and the war won, so devil take 'em, they want to go back to the States, give 'em a bonus in gold and send them on their way."

That was a crucial point but Burr thought they probably were right. Soldiers were mostly westerners and after years on frontier posts Burr had an idea they'd be glad to stay in the West with a share of the gold flowing from Mexico.

But would Mexico be so easy to take?

For a moment Adair's expression reminded Burr of a man betting on a cockfight. "Easy enough to take with a couple thousand well-armed soldiers plus your little army? I think so. Last time I was in New Orleans I went over this with Daniel Clark—you know Daniel?"

They had met; Clark was a big figure in New Orleans.

"Well," Adair said, "he's gone deep into Mexico, so he tells me, and it's defenseless. Like you said at dinner, the

Spanish empire is dying. Handful of soldiers and they spend most of their time terrorizing the people. Spain rarely pays them, you see, they have to grind their living out of the people. So there's plenty of resentment, you can be sure. Revolution is right about ready to start."

"Ready to blow," Smith said. He emptied his glass, belched, and reached for the bottle. "Will one of these days soon, sooner still with help. They'll line the streets in welcome."

"Somehow I doubt it'll be so easy," Burr said.

"Nothing's ever as easy as it looks." Adair shrugged. "Still, Mexico is ready to throw the Spanish out, their army is weak, everything I've heard has to make me confident."

Burr rubbed his hands together. He wasn't here to quarrel. "So let's say we have Mexico. We have the gold. New Orleans is ours and ready for a new government. What about the West? If we do all of the above but don't have the West the United States can rally a new army and clean us out. We'd find our British support backing away, too. On the other hand, if we do have the West I believe the U.S. will be too weak to come after us—and they'll be so busy fighting off secession by New England and New York they'll have no stomach for a second front. But will we have the West? That's your area, gentlemen."

Another long silence. Then Adair pushed back his chair, put a boot on his knee, and took a long drink of whiskey. "Take a while to explain it," he said. "So, how much do you know about what they used to call the Spanish Conspiracy? Sometimes the Kentucky Conspiracy?"

"I've heard of it. Not much more."

"Well, it goes way back. *Way* back. I came out to this country around seventeen and seventy, not so long after old Boone opened the way. We was the west end of Virginia in those days. So the war started and the British put the Indians on us and you think we got any help from the

East? Hell, no. George Rogers Clark, he was pretty much a youngster himself, but he put together a force and we went after 'em. You've heard of the Hair Buyer? British officer paying in gold plus powder and lead for American settler scalps—women, children, anyone would do. Haven't heard? Well, don't matter; I can tell you those were rough days and we were on our own. Now, I understand they were busy back East, too, but point is, it didn't give us a feeling we owed folks there much of anything."

He talked in a low, steady voice, the other two nodding and murmuring "Amen" from time to time, and Burr could see a separate culture taking hold. New York also had frontier in the west end of the state, around Niagara Falls. But he had been out to the village of Buffalo, and raw as things were there, the people never felt they weren't New Yorkers. Had plenty of demands for their senator, too. But this was different.

Meanwhile the Spanish were picking and prodding and giving them all manner of hell. Cash money was short on the frontier, always was, and what little produce they could raise and sell for cash had to go through New Orleans to reach the very Virginia that controlled their destiny from afar. The Spanish did as they pleased, slapped on what the Kentuckians considered a murderous export tax and shut down the river whenever they took a mind to make things hard on the Americans, and you couldn't get Richmond even to listen. Hell, it was a month's ride to Richmond and another month back, and nobody there gave a popcorn fart for the West anyway. They proved it in the Gardoqui matter.

Gardoqui . . . Burr had heard plenty about that but he sat quietly and let Adair run through their indignation again. What it amounted to, the Spanish minister, anchored in western lore as the slippery, slimy, madly scheming Señor Gardoqui, proposed a rich trade deal that would have fattened eastern merchants in return for acquiescing to Spain's closing the Mississippi to American traffic for a full twenty-five years!

"Well," Adair said, relishing the tale all over again, "in the pissant Continental Congress of those days, squabbling like dogs over a bone—that was before the Constitution, mind—and every state considering itself a separate power, it took the vote of nine of the thirteen states to pass anything and *seven* of the nine it would have taken to strike the deal voted in favor."

Adair slapped the table for emphasis. "Seven! You understand, it would have destroyed us. Seven eastern states were willing to do that. Told us just exactly where we stood once and for all, and don't think a single soul in the West has forgotten that."

"Amen," Smith and Brown said together. "And you know what they had in mind, the Spanish, in making that offer," Adair said. "If they could have closed the river they'd have had their hands on our throats and could've squeezed us to death. That was their plan. See, they always wanted to take over the West. Wanted to push their empire up the Mississippi Valley clear to Canada. They'd have had everything that mattered on the continent then, excluding the seaboard east of the Appalachians and the far north. And they'd have had us, and that's what they wanted."

"They was sniffing around, you know," Smith said. He had a way of smoothing down his black beard as if it bothered him somehow and yet was an object of pride. "I was a tyke in those days but I well remember my pa talking about it. Said the Spanish agents were always around, trying to get us to swing to them, cut off the U.S. and become part of the Spanish empire. Promised us everything, wouldn't have to be Spanish, wouldn't have to be Catholic, they'd waive that for us, free trade with the whole world—"

"And people out here were listening?" Burr asked.

"Enough," Adair said. "Enough so it was serious."

"So why didn't it happen?"

"Because about that time Virginia and the Carolinas decided to turn loose their western lands and that opened the way to statehood and that became the big cry."

"So why is it different now?" Burr asked softly.

Smith answered just as softly, something in his voice saying that he said what he said as the sitting senator from the state of Ohio and knew just how deadly his words were. "Because we ain't talking going over to Spain now. We're talking a new country. Fueled with Spanish gold, all right, but gold we take after we throw them out. Gold from Mexico."

Burr looked at Adair. "Why now? Why not last year or five years ago or the moment the purchase was announced?"

Brown's voice went softer still. "Because a revolution needs a leader and we didn't have one."

There! That said it. Talking treason. Talking a hempen noose if things went wrong. Burr decided he could use a drink after all. He spilled some of Jack Adair's sour mash into his glass. The square bottle, deep green, was half-empty now. Brown said, "Now, the three of us at this table, we carry a good bit of weight, and we can bring along a lot of the potent men when the time comes. Men who swing a lot of influence—financial, by reputation, by experience. You set up as you've discussed tonight and you'll find plenty of support among powerful men. We'll see to that."

"Well," Burr said at last, "we have a convincing case. We can set up a new nation to dominate the middle of North America. Leave the Spanish on the West, the United States on the East, long live the new nation of Louisiana in the center."

They stared at him, not quite certain of his mood.

"That means you like it?" Brown said. Burr heard a

quiver in his voice. Adair frowned. Smith paused as if frozen, his hand motionless on his black beard.

"I do like it," Burr said, and watched smiles ease their expressions. "But we have saved the hardest part for last."

Adair reared back in his chair. "Bringing over the West, you mean? But I think that can be done, it'll just take—"

"No, I mean getting a thousand heavily armed men down the river without drawing attention."

"Oh." Adair laid his arms on the table. "Oh."

Burr had their full attention now. He talked quickly, voice hushed and urgent. He thought it out as he went but knew he sounded like a practiced analyst. It was late and he was as tired as were they, but he knew exhaustion and the silence of deep night added intensity.

"Start with the idea that it's not possible to move so many men in secret. Then move on to what will we do about it?"

The building creaked suddenly and he paused, listening for footsteps outside the door. Nothing. He added two sticks to the fire. The oil lamp flickered and he extinguished it and lighted two candles in the blaze as the new sticks took fire.

First, make no mistake, that corps of a thousand men recruited from New York to Louisville was *the* crucial element. Nothing worked without them. Yet they were the most vulnerable element of the scheme at the start. Why were they so important? Because no matter his skill, a leader who has no weight behind him has no power either. Success depended on putting his own little army down the river. It was the trigger.

New Orleans wouldn't rise by itself; after eighteen months it still just grumbled. Nor could Wilkinson stage a rising by himself; he wasn't trusted in New Orleans. Nor could he invade Mexico alone. He would need extraordinary circumstances to launch such an attack without raising his officers' suspicion. But New Orleans would rise with the right leader. Next, see a private army backed by New Orlean's best and headed by the former vice president and see that he could have carried secret orders from Washington. For Wilkinson's officers that would remove the taint of illegality no matter how illegal it might appear to the world.

"But if my little army were stopped en route," Burr said, "the whole project could collapse." He had their attention, all right. Drop the idea, he told them, of keeping the movement secret. No matter how inconspicuously they travel, people will notice and wonder. Hence you must have a story to explain them. He paused, cleared his throat and threw out his idea. Back East, he said, you hear tall tales from the West of vast land tracts. If he had such a tract in the wilderness, his men could be settlers going to carve out frontier farms. Workable?

"Better than workable," Adair said. "Damned good. And I have your man. Name of Jacques Boudreau, in New Orleans. I'll write him to watch for you. He's got a million-odd acres he can't wait to get rid of."

"A *million* acres?"

More or less, Adair said, part of an old Spanish grant once issued to the Baron de Bastrop. Burr recognized that name; the baron had made himself an important if doubtful figure on the American frontier. The whole shebang could be had for fifty thousand dollars.

Burr's eyebrows rose at that. Adair added that the fellow probably would take a couple thousand dollars down.

"Two thousand? And when he wants the other forty-eight?"

"By then you don't need the land no more so you tell him you'll sue for the return of your two thousand."

"Really? On what basis?"

"Faulty title."

Burr almost choked. "Faulty title!"

"Look, Aaron, you haven't seen the real wilderness yet. Way up the Red it's Indian country. You have to fight to hold it, and anyway, there's no such thing as real surveying, it's just a loose grant, permission from a king sitting in Spain with his thumb up his bum saying certainly, Bastrop, go grab a million acres up the Red and make 'em your empire and don't bother me no more! Any civilized country, they'd arrest Boudreau for fraud, but it seems like anything goes in New Orleans."

Burr was instantly wary. "Royal grants are the basis for a lot of American land law. Is it different out here?"

"Of course, settled land, trace title back owner by owner to the grant, that's solid. But a million acres casually granted in a wilderness you can't visit without an army?"

"So you're saying for a small sum now I can buy a place that provides a destination as long as I need it. . . ."

Yet he was uneasy. He saw he didn't quite believe it all and what was making him uneasy was the understanding that no one else would believe it either. Not unless they absolutely wanted to believe. And then he saw that that was the key.

He laid out the idea. Settlement up the Red River would be the primary story, take it or leave it. But the secondary story would be the one with the appeal——the wink and the nod and the idea that ain't it just awful that the perfidious Spanish won't grant Florida and Texas as part of the purchase, and isn't it time something was done about it? Now, of course, doing something about it would be illegal on its face, so they couldn't actually say that. And people would accept the settler cover story as a cover story but one they could claim to believe.

"You see," he said, "any official, sheriff or mayor or district attorney or judge or governor told in so many words that we intend to snatch territory from Spain, let alone our more extensive dreams, he'll start thinking about hauling us before a grand jury. Failure to do so could make him an accessory, so to speak. Ergo, the land story must be sufficiently believable so that an official can say with a straight face that he didn't question it. So—give them a workable excuse and a laudable sub rosa goal and they'll have the bands out to drum us along. But we'll be walking on the knife edge."

"Well," Brown said, "you've made the case." He spoke with such sudden authority and strength that Burr saw he was the real leader of the three and that his gentle manner covered a tough-minded man anything but past his prime. The other two were silent.

"In fact," Brown said, "a damned good case. That getting the men downriver could be a problem, yes, a good point. But we can help you with that, pass the word to ask you few questions because you represent what the West has been waiting for. So now, of course, go on to New Orleans. We'll give you a list of men there worth sounding out. Acquire that land with its temporary title and talk up your settlement plans. Don't worry about sounding naive—admit you're new to the West but you're not new to enterprise, and you intend to make a fortune. Talk it up good. Westerners love to talk about land. Everyone has a few sections tucked away somewhere that are probably worthless unless something happens. Now, we can help with that, too. Talk up the land, see your plans as reasonable, influence newspaper editors, let folks know we're behind you—counts for a lot out here, more than in the East, I think."

"And afterwards?" Burr's voice was soft.

"Are we confident of our own people?" Brown said. He coughed. "Will they listen to us? The answer to both is yes. You take New Orleans and put the army in and seize Mexico and come back with that gold and declare a new country, folks hereabouts won't give you any trouble. We'll see to that."

Another silence. Brown cleared his throat and brushed back his heavy gray hair. "Look at it this way, Aaron. Ain't none of us going to live forever. Jack and me, we're at an age where we won't have many more chances to do something big, something different, and make us a fortune to boot. Smitty, he's younger, but how many chances does a man get?"

He looked directly at Burr. "And it appears you're the cat who's already used eight of his lives. . . ."

Well, by God, that was true, a bit too true. That image of debtor's prison flashed behind his eyes. Maybe it would be worse than a hempen noose after all . . . if things went wrong. "So, gentlemen," he said, looking at each separately, "you agree, all of you?"

He put his hand flat on the table. Three hands placed on his. "We're with you, Aaron. Count on it."

★ ★ ★ ★ ★

SEVENTEEN

On the Ohio River, summer 1805

When his keelboat cast off from the Marietta wharf Burr was feeling good. The talk with the three senators had gone well, pretty much confirming what Wilkinson had told him, easing his intrinsic doubts and giving rein to hopes and desires. God, he could see it now! And yet he realized that what he saw was less a matter of power and wealth than of confounding his enemies.

There were miles to go and many to see, but already he was catching the sense of the western man. Perhaps an open willingness was the right word, willingness to take things into his own hands, take chances offered. It didn't mean the senators or western men in general weren't patriots or didn't love their country, but if they struck a new country from the old, then the new would be the object of their patriotism, wouldn't it? The senators were serious men. Each had achieved power and reputation, which he certainly wouldn't risk on a fool's errand. But Burr also could see that the whole thing hadn't been much more than a dream until he came along, for none had the skills he possessed to move people from dream to action.

They had paved the way for him. Let him float on to Mayville, an important river shipping point, and thence to Cincinnati, now growing into a potent little town. Senator Smith would have important men at both places waiting to meet the vice president, men who with little actually said would understand that great things were afoot.

"They won't want to know just now," he said. "Not until things are ready. They'll just want to know that when whatever is to happen comes to pass, the door will be open to them. Just as you suggested in Marietta; this is a talent of yours, Aaron. Keep that tenor all the way to New Orleans but make yourself felt en route, make them understand that you and your plans are critical to this whole region and specifically to their own future even if no one is quite sure what that means."

From Cincinnati go on to Louisville; Jack Adair would have a welcoming committee. Moor the boat there, get a good horse, and cut across Kentucky to Frankfort where Brown lived. He would stage a huge reception for the vice president. Ride on to Lexington, then turn south to Nashville; prepare to be feted. He could see it unfolding, appearing in his elegant boat or on a handsome deep-chested horse with chased saddle and bridle, talking of the problems the East imposed on the West, the perfidy of New Englanders, the arrogance of the Spanish, the criminality of Spanish unwillingness to surrender Florida and Texas, both of which were so clearly part of the purchase. After a few days in Nashville take a boat down the Cumberland to Fort Massac, the old fur trader station, now an army post on the Ohio just above its meeting with the Mississippi. Wilkinson expected to be there.

Then, with an odd grin, Jack Adair had said, "One more thing. A little way downriver you'll come on an island and there you'll see the damnedest sight, a mansion to rival the best of New York and Philadelphia, or of London and Paris for all I know. Better than anything in the West, certainly. A fellow named Blennerhassett built it, some kind of a lord from Europe someplace, money coming out of his ears. Now, he'll like you, he's your kind—elegant, you know—and he's got twenty to thirty acres there. You'll need a staging station, you start bringing stuff downriver, place where there won't be folks poking around wondering what's in them boxes."

Again, that odd grin. "You'll like Mr. Blennerhassett."

For a hundred miles along the river Burr had been hearing tales of Harman Blennerhassett's house on Belpre Island, each description more extravagant than the last, but none had prepared him for what he saw. The house, huge and glistening white, was . . . well, magnificent was too pale a word. The keelboat ground against the wharf and steadied and he stared in awe.

For hundreds of miles he'd passed houses of logs, some with windows and some without, a few with glass. In town he'd seen an occasional frame house with upright plank walls, the seams covered with lathing, here and there a commercial building of brick. Now he gazed at a mansion. It was huge, a splendid house of twelve or fifteen or twenty rooms, depending on who was talking, from which two columned piazzas curved out on each side to fine outbuildings. A hundred twenty feet wide all told, so everyone said. Burr had been in many fine homes, including several of his own, but what flashed in his mind was calling on General Washington years ago. This home deep in the American wilderness rivaled the general's Mount Vernon.

The place literally shouted money.

He saw the owner hurrying down the graveled walk to greet him, a tall, graying man who walked with an odd lumbering awkwardness that Burr saw immediately was echoed in his hesitant speech and his tendency to confuse words in his odd lilting accent. Up and down the river Harman Blennerhassett was a puzzle. Wealthy, well educated and well read, a talented violinist, an amateur scientist of some skill, possessor of a handsome library, he seemed to have every kind of sense but common sense. Burr had the feeling men hereabouts found him more impressive than likable. All this made Burr agree readily that he must pay this man a visit.

Blennerhassett seemed to be expecting him. There was an undercurrent of excitement in the awkward man that at first Burr took as the pleasures of having a famous man in his home. Gradually, however, Burr concluded there was more to it than that. Naturally he marveled at the house, which was not difficult to do. Blennerhassett drank in every word, clearly hungering for approval. Burr insisted on seeing its rooms and outbuildings, and in truth it was magnificent. But what was its purpose? Surely there was nothing like it this side of the Appalachians and little to rival it on the other side of the mountains. Perhaps it was just a monument to its owner's wealth, but Burr shuddered to think of the cost of transporting its rich materials. He recognized immediately its Italian Palladian style and listened with real pleasure to the construction details, all oak and poplar, barrels of white paint and shipments of glass and marble brought downriver from Pittsburgh during the four years of construction and then the search for adequate furnishings—but come, he must meet Mrs. Blennerhassett.

Inside, across black-and-white marble laid in checkerboard fashion, past a gorgeous marble fireplace at one side, a curved staircase he recognized as finely done on the other, came a tall and rather stately woman whom he saw immediately was as beautiful as her house. Deep blue eyes, a well-formed if long nose sloping outward, creamy complexion, smooth brown hair in waves, in her early thirties as her husband was in his early forties, she was splendid. As he gave his deepest bow to her gracious curtsy, he knew this was a woman who could interest him.

But they talked for two hours, sat down to a well-turned dinner, and talked on into the night, and by then he knew that while she had responded to him, as women usually did, she was deeply in love with her husband and protective of him as well. Which was fine—Burr enjoyed the company of women, the way they thought and the way they talked, and he liked Margaret Blennerhassett. After a while, however, he saw that she was afraid of him. Interesting . . .

He drew out their story quickly enough. They were from Ireland. Blennerhassett had been a nobleman of some sort, master of what he called Castle Conway in County Kerry that had some four thousand acres farmed by tenants. He was the youngest of three brothers, no one had expected him to inherit, but both the brothers had met untimely ends and only he was left. From his frown and the worried note that crept into his voice Burr could see that his inheritance had been an intolerable burden that he couldn't wait to shed. So they had sold everything for a fortune, come to America, and plunged into the wilderness.

Yes, Burr could see it clearly. In some hungry part of his soul the man had tried to re-create here what he'd given up there. Something odd about that, too, something hidden in them both that centered on the decision to leave. Blennerhassett had been in political trouble, but it was more than that. Some personal thing, Burr thought.

As they became better friends, as the candles burned low into the night, Burr revealed a few of his own plans, responding in part to his host's rapture at having the vice president of the United States under his roof. Of course he was careful, hints and ellipses and certain things he couldn't say and possibilities he mustn't mention, Blennerhassett nodding eagerly. Florida as a goal, and Texas, and gradually, never fully said, Mexico's gold seen as a factor.

What that would mean, joined to New Orleans and all the West, became a live and vivid thing, perhaps the more real for its very hidden quality. There was western dissatisfaction with the East, which Blennerhassett echoed emphatically, and great changes that might come about and it was Burr's host who saw as if the idea had just come to him that the western empire deserved to stand among nations on its own.

Burr allowed himself to suggest that his host would be surprised at how many substantial men in the West had had just that thought. Blennerhassett's long, skinny frame was doubled on itself, folded deep into a sofa and at this he leaned forward with elbows on his knees, both hands clasping his head and whispered, "I could be of assistance there, you know. I understand Europe and I have resources."

His eyes were shining. There was a long silence. Then Burr said, "It will take resources. And if it happens— *when* it happens, perhaps I should say—you are an unbelievably prescient man to grasp this so quickly—foreign expertise will be essential. Every nation must have a foreign minister. . . ."

Instantly Burr knew he had gone too far. He felt suddenly dizzy, caught in a whirlpool. It was the man's damned adulation, folded on himself like a stork, eyes shining, hunger and need radiating, prepared to see his visitor as God's messenger for whom Mr. Blennerhassett had waited forever. But what did his own hunger say of Burr after years of abuse and battering? He remembered fleeing under an alias—R. King, that was as sad as it was brave. God! Maybe they needed each other equally.

But the effect on Blennerhassett was magical. He sighed, a deep gush of air. "Foreign minister. Oh, Colonel Burr, that would mean *everything* to me. And we have resources, we can help, we *want* to help." He glanced at his wife. "Oh, Margaret, isn't it *wonderful*?"

At which the beautiful Margaret stood and said she was going to bed. Of course Burr said he'd stayed too long and must return to his vessel, sure that Blennerhassett would insist on pouring more port and talking longer of glorious prospects. Reluctantly allowing his glass to be filled again and then again, Burr listened, saying little now, letting his host spin his own air castles. He wondered if Margaret were outside the door listening to them; he was beginning to see why she feared Mr. Burr.

Margaret Blennerhassett hadn't needed to listen. She already knew as she went up the graceful staircase that had cost them a small fortune, along with the silver door-knobs and the French clocks and the crystal mirrors and the paintings and the fine furniture from Paris, money that might as well have been tossed in the river, already knew they were in trouble with this silver-tongued man appearing from nowhere to seduce her husband.

He was a handsome man, this Mr. Burr, deeply appealing, and she'd quite understood the look he'd given her. But they said the devil could assume many visages, and Aaron Burr's face might be one of them. Poor, sweet, kindly, decent, bumbling Harman had leaped willingly into the trap that Mr. Burr probably hadn't even intended to set; indeed in his usual impetuous way, Harman had created the trap, persuaded Burr to agree, and leaped in to close the barred gate on himself . . . and on her.

Sometimes she wondered why his fecklessness hadn't chilled her heart, but it hadn't. She loved him now fully as much as she had at the start, and she'd burned for him then. Since she was a child, really, it had been Harman who had understood her, been interested in her, cared about her and for her, taken her riding, told her stories, invented fantasies so lovely that she laughed and cried at once. Sweet Harman . . . of course the inheritance of Castle Conway with all its responsibility had nearly killed him. It had broken her heart to watch him grow haggard, the laughter and joy of life gone, his eyes dull and haunted. And her mother, more and more worried, watching them ever more closely, remonstrating that she was a woman now, she was grown, she must begin thinking.

Well, she had become a woman by then, twenty-two years old and filled with the hungers that she supposed filled all women, and her hungers centered on Harman Blennerhassett. She loved him, she wanted him, and she knew now that he had wanted her for years, always keeping it hidden lest it destroy them. Her mother was Harman's sister. Harman was her uncle. Incest was in the whispers, the guarded looks from behind fans. Incest and disgrace . . .

So they had married amidst blazing family outrage and Harman had sold Castle Conway and they had come to America with their fortune and no one—*no one*—must know their terrible secret. Children came whom they had greeted with a mix of joy and terror, but all three were sound and bright, thank God in heaven. They had set out for the West, Harman in search of the Eden in the wilderness that Rousseau postulated. She now knew that Rousseau was all imagination. Harman talked of the ideal Democrat, the American common man, but she had come to understand that he liked commoners only in the abstract and that in truth he hungered for what had been.

Which explained this magnificent house that had eaten the bulk of their fortune and that she already could see was not sustainable. Harman had bought a share of a mercantile firm in Marietta that he hoped would yield revenue, but so far it had produced little indeed. And yet there was nothing she could say, nothing at all, the darling man surged on mad tides of enthusiasm that carried him from high to high. Now even he could see a dark end and she knew he was badly frightened, as frightened beneath the surface as when he'd known that the weight of Castle Conway must surely crush him.

And Mr. Burr had appeared from nowhere, full of plans and dreams. Would he be their rescuer or their destroyer? She'd seen Harman in his characteristic pose of hope, his long body folded into the sofa like a pocket knife, his eyes glistening with new enthusiasm, making up the dream as he went along, Mr. Burr feeding him the lines. She wondered if Mr. Burr even knew how he fed a fool's folly, but then she realized that of course he did, he was a very skilled old hand.

For Harman was a fool, her darling husband whose sweet, kind decency and raptly devoted love made up for his flaws. Perhaps his flaws would destroy them both but she would always love him. And she would never be able to still his enthusiasms, she knew that now and accepted it.

She was lying under a sheet when she heard Burr leave, and then Harman came and sat on the edge of the bed. "Oh, Margaret," he said softly, "I'm so happy. Isn't it wonderful!"

She put her hand to his cheek. "I hope so, darling," she said. "I hope so." His breathing quickened at her touch. He always wanted her when his enthusiasms were running high, and suddenly she wanted him, needed him to hold her, and she pulled him down on top of her.

When Burr left the amazing house he walked a bit to clear the port fumes. The night was very silent and then noises began to penetrate—the whistle of a night bird, a distant howl, hound or even wolf for all he knew, a yipping from another quarter that was too high and thin for a dog, probably coyotes. How painfully far all this was from the warm and good-natured streets of New York, where men jostled and laughed and fought and maneuvered for position, where a man knew his ground. But he was here, on his way, great dreams unfolding, and he told himself it was merely the quiet of the night, its foreign sounds, the gurgle of the river curling itself around his keelboat whispering of power far beyond that of paltry humans that explained the thread of alarm laced through exaltation.

Harman Blennerhassett was dangerous, but then everything about this venture was dangerous. He knew he'd gone too far with Blennerhassett, and saw it as a weakness in himself. That *adulation*—he smiled again, thinking of how good he'd felt as the man gazed at him with shining eyes. This rich nobleman who had come from abroad with a fortune, who could buy and sell Burr but was ready to weep at a kind word from the great man. And that was the point, wasn't it? Colonel Burr *was* a great man on a fabulous mission of daring magnitude that few men could even imagine. But he remembered the warning bells, the man was too grateful, and Burr had gone too far and told him too much. Colonel Burr was showing hunger himself, more than he had understood. Have to watch that. But he smiled again—God, that raw adulation *had* made him feel good. Filled a hungry place, an empty place—empty and cold.

Still, Harman Blennerhassett was a useful find. Strange fellow, granted, somewhat a fish out of water. It was quite clear why people smiled when they mentioned him. But Burr had felt an instant sympathy for the man, too, laughed at for creating beauty. He remembered Sim McAlester sneering because Burr had helped a few artists and writers create beauty and thus had put part of himself in their work, so he liked to think. Clearly Blennerhassett had tried to create here some of what he had left behind, and what was wrong with that? Apparently he had the resources to support it, for he had even pledged to support Burr's enterprise.

The island would be a perfect rendezvous for men and weapons, just as the senators had observed. Yes, Harman was strange, but so were many foreigners, and so fervently had he pledged himself to the cause, so obediently had he received orders to say nothing and wait, so willingly had he issued a draft on a Louisville bank, that Burr had to feel the Irishman was his most fortunate find so far. And the most dangerous.

He boarded his boat and went to his cabin, but he lay awake for a long time listening to that distant howling, that powerful gurgle around the hull, the boat rocking and bumping the wharf. He was far, far from home.

Eighteen

Washington, summer 1805

The way it started, he came into the bedroom and saw her sitting on the side of the bed with a leg cocked up. She was in her chemise, petticoat up around her waist, cambric drawers dropped on the floor, peering intently at her knee.

"What's the matter?"

Dolley flipped the petticoat down as if she'd been caught at something. "A bump just above my knee. It's beginning to hurt."

Madison felt a little tug of fear. Life was so fragile, so precious. Illness came out of the swamps or the low places or the night air or maybe just pure malignant chance, and swept people away.

"Let me see," he said.

"Really, Jimmy!" She pulled the skirt firmly over both knees.

"Now, now, I've seen your thigh before."

"Yes . . . but under different circumstances. Just looking, that's not the same."

"Dolley . . ."

She inched the skirt above her knee, then pinned it tightly around the leg. The milky flesh of her thigh was an angry red around a mottled spot about four inches above her knee that looked yellow in the center as if it already was making pus.

He touched the leg; it felt feverish. She winced.

"Hurts?"

She nodded.

"How long has this been—"

"A week or so. Puss scratched me and maybe it was there, I'm not sure. She was snatching for a ball of yarn."

"Oh, Dolley . . ."

"I'm not sure. It was a while ago and maybe it wasn't even that leg, I don't know." She looked up at him. "She didn't mean to do it, Puss."

"I'm going to send for Dr. Bullus," he said.

"Please, Jimmy, that's not necessary."

"But it's getting worse, isn't it?"

She nodded and again he felt that wash of fear. So many illnesses started as slight and then turned deadly.

In a small voice she said, "He'll want to look at it."

"Yes," he said gently. She hated the invasion of privacy in a doctor looking at her body. "For a moment. Just at your leg."

She nodded. "I suppose I must."

Jimmy returned at noon with Bullus. The doctor, solid and heavy, his beard tawny, face reddened as if permanently chapped by years at sea, bounded heartily into the room. He might have been in the dispensary of USS *Constitution*.

"Well, well, Miss Dolley," he boomed, "what have we here? Cat scratch, eh? They're devils, those kitties, eh? Let's have a look at the offending region."

She could hear him roaring cheerfully to some poor

devil of a sailor whose leg had been shattered by splinters and shell, even as he honed his saw and decided how far up he had to cut. She slid the robe off her knee, and said, "You won't need to see anything else. . . ."

He glanced at her quickly and then with gentleness that surprised her said, "No, madam, nothing else. I take it this is the only spot? No others here or there? That would be important, you see."

"No, just this one place."

"Good." Before she could object he put both hands around her leg just above the knee. His hands were warm. He pulled the skin this way and that, looking thoughtful. She tried to keep from crying out.

"I'm sorry," he said. "Hurts, eh?"

"Yes." Through gritted teeth. "Like the devil."

He touched the yellowish center and she yelped. "I don't like that puckering," she heard him mutter to himself, and immediately her own fear doubled. "Well, I'll give you some lotion. Rub it in three times daily. Really rub, now. It'll hurt, but you can bear it. Inside of a week, it should be much, much better."

"But what is it? Why did it—"

"A boil. Bad one, deep in the flesh. Why? God only knows. Night air, maybe, but I see 'em at sea plenty often and the air is pure as wine out there. Anyway, it'll cure right quickly with this lotion. I'll be back tomorrow." He started to slap her leg in dismissal and stopped himself.

Jimmy saw him to the door. She sniffed the lotion. It smelled appropriately vile; perhaps it would work. When Jimmy came back she started to ask what he thought but she saw the fear in his face and stopped herself.

"This lotion he gave me, I think it's good," she said, and forced a large smile.

But the doctor's lotions didn't work. Bullus came back every day and usually he had something new to try.

He opened the boil with a shiny scalpel that he wiped on his sleeve and drained the pus. It felt better for half a day, then worse. He sweated when he was there and after a bit she realized he was no longer looking directly at her, meeting her eye. Seemed not to see her above the waist, and left as soon as he could. Not a good sign, not at all.

They were taking tea with the president in the family sitting room and Dolley had grown tired of the conversation. Her leg hurt and she was thinking it was a mistake to have come. Gown and petticoat seemed to press against the bandage and she shifted uneasily to escape the weight of the cloth.

The day was cool for summer, the bull's-eye window turned open. Sparrows chattered on the outside sill and she watched how self-importantly they strutted. The president was rambling on about some remarkable agricultural advance from the south of France and Jimmy was asking questions, two farmers nattering away. Glancing at her, Tom switched to discussing a new play said to be taking the Paris boards by storm, and she saw he was being courteous. But she hadn't read the play and didn't know if she would, and anyway, her leg hurt. She lifted the cloth of her gown, trying to shift her weight, thinking she'd rather be home in her chemise lying down with the leg elevated. It was beginning to throb.

Abruptly the president said, "You were limping when you came in, Dolley." It was almost an accusation and for a giddy moment she started to deny it. Then she explained, with as little reference to her extremities as possible.

"Boil, eh?" he said, and she heard honest concern in his voice. "They can be serious sometimes. How long—"

"Three weeks now, and getting worse."

He glanced at Jimmy. "You have someone seeing it?"

"Dr. Bullus," Dolley said.

"Oh, Bullus—a good fellow, of course, and useful sometimes, but he's a ship's surgeon, oriented to gunshot wounds. Always got the saw handy."

A wave of fear struck her at this and her jaw sagged. He stood and covered the room in a couple of quick strides. He bent over her and cupped her chin in his hand.

"You're pale," he said.

"I don't feel well."

"I'm sure," he said. "A festering boil, it pours poison into your system."

Blood poisoning . . . she'd heard of it all her life. Her breath came more quickly.

He straightened and stared down at her, rusty hair graying now, face deeply lined in this past year of loss, his cambric shirt with bunched sleeves holed from pipe ashes, but with that immense authority he could summon when he chose.

"Jimmy," he said, "for God's sake, take her to Philadelphia. See Benjamin Rush—no, wait, get Physick. Philip Physick—they say he works magic with internal medicine. Rush is superb but, well, he's set in his ways. Physick, now, he's the one to see. I'll give you a letter—I know him well—tell him to spare no effort."

"But Philadelphia?" she said, voice faltering. Riding in a coach for days, every jolt a stab of pain?

"It's the only thing," he said. Then, standing over them with his face taking on an oddly crumpled look, he said, more to Jimmy than to her, "Please, don't risk it. These things sweep people away. Don't put yourself in the way of such pain." Suddenly his eyes filled and he raised a hand toward them, and said in a muffled whisper, "It hurts too much."

She gazed up at him, alarmed, and then his face seemed to disintegrate and tears ran and he walked out of the room. But at the door he turned, and muttered, "Believe me, it hurts too much," and then he was gone.

She realized he was talking about his daughter Polly and knew from that how real was his fear for her, which increased her own alarm. She remembered the day when migraine had felled him during a troubled cabinet meeting, as Jimmy had described it, and she had been sure that worry over Polly had been the underlying factor. Polly had been ill then, fading away in her second labor after the first had brought her so near death. She was twenty-six, slender, sweet, musically gifted, much like her mother, who had died when Polly was but a child. And sure enough, she had drifted away and broken her father's heart; perhaps her husband's too, but it was Tom's grief that Dolley understood, for he seemed frozen. Apparently it was much as he had grieved over his own wife when she too drifted away, beyond all his desperate efforts to hold her. Then too it seemed he had sealed himself, kept grief private.

After Polly's death Dolley and Jimmy had said the appropriate things and he had made the appropriate answers, thanking them gravely for trying to console that for which there was no consolation, and beyond that maintaining his lonely silence. Now, seeing him break that bulwark against feelings that he kept hidden to keep in control, she understood how warm he was in friendship—and she saw that he looked toward an end for her no different from Polly's end and this was terrifying.

"Maybe we better go to Philadelphia," she said to Jimmy, her voice a pale whisper in the quiet room.

Dr. Physick was a youngish man wearing a sharply pointed beard and dressed in a fashionable suit of light tan whipcord. He wore boots instead of slippers, doubtless needed for racing from patient to patient in muddy

Philadelphia. He radiated confidence, having been trained relatively recently at Edinburgh, which was more or less the center of the world in medicine. So it was said generally; so especially she wanted to believe. To her surprise he insisted on washing his hands before examining her, said the men at Ediburgh believed it a wise precaution that made sense though there was no real proof that it improved anything. But that showed Dolley the advantage of an advanced practitioner; Dr. Bullus certainly had never had such an idea.

He was precise in manner and speech, a little impatient as befit a man much sought after, but with an undercurrent of warmth as befit a man into whose hands you put your life. She decided immediately that she could trust him. She also decided that it was too late in the day to be squeamish about her extremities. For illnesses that could lie ahead she might well have to show a doctor a good deal more of herself than a knee. But she folded the sheet carefully not too far above what she had come to think of as the wound. His touch was light and gentle as he felt all around the eruption which now was open and draining.

"Well," he said with a smile, "we'll fix that right up. Few weeks and you'll be ready to dance the minuet."

She sighed with relief. All the way here, riding in a litter lashed in their lurching coach, reading the alarm in Jimmy's ashen face as she tried to reassure him, each lurch a new and separate pain, the image of the surgeon's bone saw had hovered on the edges of her mind and it had taken all her strength to keep it on the edges. The knife cutting down and around and the flaps of skin left to cover the stump and then the saw and the awful rasping roar and the screams that would be bursting from her own throat against her best efforts, body lunging as heavy men held her to the table. A good surgeon could take off a leg in under ten minutes—speed was the whole

essence of a good surgeon—but that ten minutes was a
lifetime of agony. Amputation was common in war on
land or on sea, gunfire making the awful wound, gangrene soon setting in, poison pouring into the system,
fever mounting, the patient swept away on a tide of pus.
Removing the limb and stopping the poison flow was the
only way to save the patient. And what was a bad boil but
a massive generator of poison, analogous to and finally
the equal of the gangrene that infested a terrible wound,
human tissue damaged beyond repair, putrefaction setting in, suppurating poisons? The solution was the same,
chop off the source of the poison and throw it away. And
then pray that the body possessed the inherent strength
to recover from the massive insult.

But about half the patients still died. The soldier's
body was shocked by the wound, soiled by the poison,
stunned by the violence of amputation—this before the
pus began to flow. At first the arrival of pus was deemed
to be good; laudable pus it was called, and doctors welcomed its onset as a sign of healthy healing. But all too
often the pus didn't ease back and stop; it became a
fountain gushing from the stump and fever soared beyond measuring and crisis came and before morning the
patient was gone.

But suppose she did survive it, she was strong, the best
medical men would fight to save her life. What then?
Life on crutches? In a wheelchair? Staggering and stumbling on a wooden leg? What would Jimmy say, he who
so prized her beauty. She chided herself, that was awful,
no one was more constant and faithful than he, and he
loved her, the whole of her. The thought shamed her but
still it crept in. Would it be the same, anchored to a
wheelchair or crutches, she who loved to dance? Would
there be life after amputation? She wasn't sure.

But now she was here in handsome rooms on Sansom
Street in cosmopolitan Philadelphia, which she loved,

with this extraordinary doctor who'd trained in the center of the medical world and was up on the very latest, and he was saying that it would be all right, she would walk again, dance again. Her spirits soared. Dr. Physick came every day. He prescribed baths, washes, soaks, salts. He brought a new lotion to rub on almost daily. He opened the boil again, carefully washing his scalpel when he washed his hands, cutting deeper than she'd thought possible, she biting a knotted handkerchief and willing herself not to cry out. He bandaged it tightly and then changed his mind and decided it should air. He rigged a tent; she must lie on a pallet on the floor with her elevated leg in the tent while a pot bubbled over a charcoal brazier set to the side and noxious fumes attacked the leg to draw out the poison. It didn't really seem to get a lot better but Dr. Physick never lost his cheerful manner.

It was on the basis of that good cheer that she invited all her old friends to call. She'd grown up in Philadelphia, married and lost her husband and baby to yellow fever, married again and lived here four years at the end of General Washington's second administration—oh, she had countless friends. To think, twelve years had passed since the yellow fever epidemic that she and her little boy, Payne, had survived; now Payne was fourteen, his voice ready to change, and she would admit to herself but to no one else that yes, he was a bit fractious. He had been sent to live on her sister's plantation while Mummy was ill. She wrote him and told him not to worry, though she knew perfectly well that he wasn't at all worried.

So it was that she was in high good humor when her old friend Edith Cunningham came to Sansom Street to call. It had been years but they'd been close once and they chattered away, catching up with old friends and recent gossip. Then, startling her, Edith said, "Have you heard about Colonel Burr? You used to know him, didn't you?"

Edith's eyes sparkled, a little guilt failing to mask a lot of pride, and she added, "I had—oh, what you might call an interlude with him." She smiled, the dimple deepening and slightly incongruous in what now was quite a mature face. "That was long before I met Mr. Cunningham, of course."

"He took you to bed, I suppose?"

"Dolley! How you talk!"

Dolley smiled.

"Well," Edith said, "he was persuasive. And handsome. And charming. I'll bet he charmed you, too."

"Not to that extent."

"Now, Dolley, don't be a prude."

"So what has Aaron done now?"

"Well! That's the question, isn't it?" She took a newspaper from her knitting satchel and snapped it open. Dolley saw that it was the well-regarded *United States Gazette* of Philadelphia. Edith handed it over, tapping a significant headline. Under "Queries," the editor had written: "How long will it be before we shall hear of *Col. Burr* being at the head of a *revolution* party on the western waters?" How soon, it demanded, would the western states heed a call from Burr to form a separate government and seize public lands in the West to make bounties to lure easterners? How soon would the forts and magazines and military cantonments of New Orleans and along the Mississippi be seized and turned to the rebel's aim of conquering Mexico and its riches with the aid of the Royal Navy?

The stark violence of these questions in cold type on already yellowing paper seemed the greater for having emerged from the idle talk of sophisticated women chuckling over *amour*. Suddenly she was very tired of Edith Cunningham. She remarked casually that Aaron was always stirring speculation, doubtless there was nothing to it. She allowed her eyelids to droop and did nothing to stifle a yawn. Soon Edith saw that she was worn out by pain and the wound's poisons. Edith departed amidst displays of mutual affection that neither really meant and Dolley was left alone to ponder the meaning of Aaron's latest . . . was peccadillo too strong a word? Or too mild?

"Queries" . . . meaning that the editor has no real information at all. Editors today didn't hesitate to print the vilest rumors. Look at things casually written about Anna and her, all those insinuations that so small a man as Madison could hardly satisfy a woman of her power, even the casual assertion that her husband rented her body for political favors and so forth and so on, all too vile even to summon to memory!

Yet papers rarely invented from whole cloth. They printed things that were being said. The slurs on her always quoted some vague person, an informed friend, a knowledgeable figure, a woman in the know who was not to be named. And somehow, this query—a form of rumor—had a ring of truth.

For after all, what would Aaron do now, his whole life blighted? He was a man of power and immense ability who had let greed and rage overtake reality, let alone wisdom. Challenging Tom over an electoral accident, banking all on a chancy election in New York, and then killing Alex were all the acts of a man wildly out of control. Yes, Jimmy and Tom had been too hard on him, and yes, a duel was not an assassination, but none of that mattered. He had challenged the very fundament of democratic society when he tried to steal a fairly fought election and he had shot down a national ornament. You pay a great price for great transgressions.

And yet, the core of sympathy in her heart held fast. It wasn't just that Aaron had been good to her when she needed help, though simple gratitude had its place, too. But more than that, it was recognition of great abilities

compared to faults that everyone shared, though Aaron
had let his desperate hungers get out of hand. But really,
what was Aaron to do? Return to Congress from some
weak western state? What a fall that would be! Go make
a fortune in business? That wasn't Aaron's way. She'd
heard stories of towering debt that were frightening even
if exaggerated. That wasn't the way of a man who knew
business. So what would he do? Try to create an empire
to surpass all that had gone before?

Maybe . . .

Her eyes filled. She was ill and her leg was throbbing
and Dr. Physick's nostrums really weren't working and it
still wasn't clear that she could escape the surgeon's saw
and keep her leg and her life. . . . She just didn't want to
think about it. She held a handkerchief to her eyes and
sleep crept upon her.

Madison returned to their chambers to find Dolley
asleep, her cheeks stained with tears. A copy of the
Gazette lay faceup on the floor. Had she been crying over
Burr? The thought gave an ugly turn to a day already
gone ugly. He knew as well as Dolley that newspapers
were rarely exactly correct, but he sensed some underlying reality in the *Gazette*'s questions. It galled him. Here
he was fighting to preserve the tender plant of democracy against all sorts of odds. There was John Randolph
agitating for extremes, New Orleans threatening revolt,
Monroe making no progress in London, the ill-named
Mr. Merry playing the insolent child, Britain squeezing
our shipping and stealing our men—and now Aaron Burr
up to something devious in the West. Any of these could
rip the tender plant from the ground.

He was still eyeing Dolley darkly when she awakened
and poured out the story, Edith Cunningham talking

about Aaron, and her leg had started to hurt, and all at once she'd seen that the great Dr. Physick didn't know any more than Dr. Bullus. She burst into new tears at the specter of the surgeon's saw, and he sat by the side of the bed holding her and stroking her hair while his own back muscles screamed in protest.

That was the last time she cried. Now she faced a grim future with a stony face; he comforted her with his presence when he sensed words would break her own resolve. She did all that Peter Physick recommended. She rubbed in all the lotions he offered, gritting her teeth against pain. She bit her knotted handkerchief when he cut down almost to the bone with his washed scalpel. She forced herself to walk, hobbling on a cane, and when her husband suggested crutches she shook her head with real anger flaring in her eyes and he said no more about crutches.

She'd been feverish for weeks. Now it seemed to mount. Her skin was hot to the touch and she breathed in little gasps. Peter Physick took Madison aside to say they would have to consider amputation before long. Try harder, he told the doctor. He put a pallet on the floor over her protests, fearful he would turn against her in his sleep and cause her new agony. Physick said they were coming toward crisis. Said holding off much longer would be risky and foolish.

Then one night her strangled cry brought him from sound sleep. He was up and on his feet before he knew what had awakened him and then he heard her low voice. "Jimmy, I'm all wet."

Her gown was drenched. He saw that her fever had broken. Her skin was cool to the touch. He stripped off her gown, ignoring her murmured protests, wrapped her in a dry sheet and moved her to the sofa. She fell instantly into deep and peaceful sleep and he sat by the sofa for the rest of the night. There was no more sweat and her skin remained cool. She smiled in her sleep when he touched forefingers to her forehead.

"We've turned the corner," Dr. Physick said the next day. He was exultant. "What I've been waiting for. We've defeated the fever, defeated the poison."

Thank heaven!

★　　　★　　　★　　　★　　　★

NINETEEN

New Orleans, summer 1805

Danny Mobry reached New Orleans three days before Burr's vessel appeared. Word had come down the river ahead of him and the town was agog. The vice president of the United States! Now maybe they could get some action on their petition, become a state, get rid of the idiotic governor Washington had imposed on them. Or maybe—there were rumors—Mr. Burr would have something even more interesting to say.

To her surprise, he arrived in a handsome military barge crewed by soldiers under a sergeant who laid the vessel smartly alongside the landing float, oars rising in perfect synchrony. Mr. Burr stood in the cockpit with his big hat raised, looking a prince in polished boots and breeches and an embroidered shirt of white linen with bunched sleeves that showed he understood the climate and adapted to it, a natural New Orleanian. The military escort gave him an official air that surprised her; she couldn't imagine that was Mr. Madison's intent.

She watched from the levee as Governor Claiborne offered an awkward welcome. Mr. Burr answered gracefully, first in English and then in French that was more than adequate, given the language distress now so fierce in New Orleans. A loud cheer arose at his first words in French. The governor stood beside him like a fish out of water. Burr singled out Daniel Clark in the welcoming delegation, wrung his hand and turned to Ed Livingston with emotional exuberance. She watched her uncle and her business partner from a distance.

Henri Broussard, studiously not meeting her eye, was in the second tier. Mr. Clark took Mr. Burr's arm and said something when they came to Henri that led Mr. Burr to seize Henri's hand with gusto, Henri smiling in that eager way that somehow reminded her of a dog panting in enthusiasm.

When Burr reached her place well down the reception line he remembered her instantly. "Madame Mobry," he cried. "You told me you were often in New Orleans but I didn't suppose I'd be so fortunate as to time my visit with yours."

He was immensely attractive, not just because he was handsome but because there was a warmth and a power in him, a wonderful gracious ease that made you want to be in his company, as if all manner of exciting things might happen there, made you want to make him smile, made you glow when you succeeded.

As Burr let the feckless governor lead him away for an official meeting, having made ostentatious arrangements with Clark and several of the French leaders to meet later at Clark's home, Henri caught her eye. Obviously feeling his importance magnified by Burr's attention, he wore an expression that mixed pride with arrogance. He came directly to her and bowed.

"There, madam," he said, "you see a man with fine French sensibilities. A man who will be important to New Orleans. He told me he wishes to sit down with me no later than tomorrow."

"Oh, Henri," she said. He had been her lover and he knew almost nothing of the world.

"Good day, madam."

He walked away, back stiff, a boy in a pet. And to think, she had throbbed with sensual hunger for him all the way to New Orleans. When *Carlito* tied up along the levee she had sent word and late that afternoon he had appeared, bronzed from the sun, strong, virile. They had gone to dinner, walking slowly through the heat that still clung to dusk, and immediately she had sensed his tension. At dinner she found herself trying to make conversation, asking about the sugar crop, about old friends, about the plantation, about his children. Exasperated— she should struggle for what was only courteous?—she had cried, "Whatever is the matter with you?"

It had been a dam breaking, a torrent of rage. The Americans, how vulgar, grasping, devious, mean-spirited they were. He went on at some length, his anger mounting steadily. He told her of the street fighting between French and Americans, the crude way the new-comers had taken over commerce, the way the rotten governor catered to their every demand.

"Ignores the French," he cried, "when it is *our* city!"

"He doesn't speak French," she said mildly.

"Another mark against him!"

God, she was weary of this. She put her hand on his. "Henri, I know how you feel. Please. Let's set politics aside." She knew her eyes conveyed the thought of pleasures to come.

But it didn't work this time. He glared at her. "I hold it against you, all of it."

"Me? Because I married—"

"Because you arranged it."

"What? That makes no sense at all."

"Oh, yes, Mr. Clark told me all about it."

"What? You're talking riddles."

"That *you* talked him into going to Paris and then Marseilles."

She gazed at him, disbelieving. Mr. Madison had indeed asked Mr. Clark to go to France and explain to the men he dealt with as a merchant that their losses would be horrendous if New Orleans became a cockpit of war, as it certainly would have done had Napoleon carried out his aim of reclaiming Louisiana from the Spanish and creating a French empire. It was one of a hundred avenues the administration had taken to dissuade the French dictator that he must come to grief in Louisiana.

At last she said, "I carried a letter from the secretary of state that spoke for the president of the United States."

"Yes, and you hammered the point, and in a moment of weakness he surrendered, which he now regrets beyond measure, and this is the result! If you hadn't persuaded him none of this would have happened."

"What wouldn't have happened?"

"The sale of Louisiana, what else? Napoleon yielding to the money men Mr. Clark went to see in France. And without that we would be French today, honored by the great Napoleon, once again part of the great nation, the Spanish yoke hurled off."

"Henri, that's ridiculous! Mr. Clark helped, but—"

"Oh, no, he swung it all. He told me so himself, he talked to the men who talked to the men who had the ear of the great leader himself. Now that the Americans betrayed him—"

"Betrayed?"

"Promised him the governorship and instead foisted this oaf Claiborne off on us."

"He wasn't promised—"

"Of course he was. Promised in so many words."

"Do you know that? Did he tell you what they said?"

He looked discomfited. "No, but he said he told them and, well, who else was fit? And if he'd been in charge, perhaps it all could have worked. Oh, he sees the mistake he made, letting you press him. And that damned Zulie, too, caught up in your rhetoric. He told me all about it."

The plate of shrimp and clams and blackened redfish, candied yams, and okra in a garlicky tomato sauce, scarcely touched, was growing cold. Now it seemed repellent. The wine seemed to curdle on her tongue and she longed for a glass of cold water. She felt nauseous as she tried to explain that Clark's trip to France, though doubtless helpful in the Louisiana Purchase, was only that, helpful, not crucial, to a campaign of a great many legs. Yes, she knew her uncle had conceived this gubernatorial hope, but it never had been real. He knew nothing of democracy and its ways, nothing of American attitudes and customs—

"That's enough!" he snapped, voice low and tense. She stared at him. "You are a damned fool, Danny. You know nothing of which you speak—a woman too big for her breeches. You stride about in a man's world, making money and shouting orders—why don't you act like a woman, for God's sake!"

She stood so suddenly her chair was knocked backward. She was choking with rage. "Sir, you will take me to my *pension* this instant!"

They walked in silence, heels scuffing on stone walks. At the *pension* he said in a slightly more conciliatory tone, "Danny, I love you. I won't apologize, I said what needed to be said." She stiffened but he went on heedlessly. "But you know the real trouble? Again and again I've told you—I want a wife, a woman of my own, to order my house, raise my children. Not for the bed—women's bodies are easily arranged. No, I want a woman's heart given freely and truly—and your heart is wrapped in stone. You think like a man, act like a man, posture—"

She had an overpowering impulse to slap him down

into the gutter. Instead, in a voice like stones grinding, she said, "Go, Henri, go." He bowed, turned, walked steadily away—and so it ended. This time she knew it was final.

She wasn't really angry; rather, the feeling had died. Without respect and love the physical appeal collapsed, and it was hard to respect a man of such stunning insularity as to attribute the Louisiana Purchase to her rhetoric, nor to love a man who had spoken with such inherent contempt. Of course, the whole city reflected Henri's insularity with its conviction that it was the center of the world. Her own sense of unrest seemed to match the city's throbbing discontent. The mood of New Orleans seemed dark, on edge and yet vulnerable, as if it sensed dangers ahead.

She heard much loose and ugly talk from people who should know better. Threats and defiance. Talk of petitioning France or Spain for troops. Talk of hanging Claiborne and taking their city back. Wilkinson's troops would be no problem, a single French cavalier was worth a dozen of the American rabble. Wilkinson as the ultimate traitor, betraying New Orleans and its people after the Spanish had paid him so long. That was certain? Of course, everyone knew it.

They swept Burr to their hearts. His French improved day by day. He cared for them. He saw the virtue and the valor of their unique culture. He sympathized. After that formal arrival, he cut Claiborne dead. He allied himself with Mr. Clark and Mr. Livingston, the governor's fiercest enemies. Everyone understood he'd been abused in Washington, which immediately endeared him, since they took abuse of people of quality as an American trademark.

And then his manner, suave and elegant—ah, kissing the fingertips, he might as well have been born and bred a New Orleanian himself! Watching him in society, Danny saw an intensity; he wanted something. But she also saw that to an uncommon degree, he was a man who needed to be loved. Ardent listeners warmed him and loosened his tongue and fed his hunger to be seen as important.

Well, why not? He'd been brutally treated at home. Brought it on himself, as don't we all. She remembered the constitutional crisis when he tried to unhorse the president, remembered carrying a warning of civil war to the Federalists, and Carl dying in the moments the House rejected the pretender. Killing Hamilton had torn away the last cover of gentility, but in New Orleans he was a hero. She sensed a change in him, too; she thought he'd survived on iron pride in Washington but now he seemed to glow with confidence.

His very presence was like a promise and everyone appeared to take it so. He was there to see to them, to open the way, to rescue them, to give them their rightful place in the universe. Everyone said he had come to meet and test them and to begin laying the foundation now of magnificent plans for the future which would put New Orleans in control of its own destiny—and give it the importance in the world that was its natural right.

A deep pessimism overtook her, quite unlike her nature, which she regarded as sunny and equable. But New Orleans was so far from the rest of the nation, its ways so different, that she feared two parts so disparate could never meld. Even under the Spanish there had been a tendency toward independence if not revolution and that surely was growing under a hapless governor and a nation that refused the new territory its democratic rights. Were there active plots? She thought so but had no proof.

She was "the American" and no plots against America were shared with her. But every instinct told her they were there.

Aaron Burr was delighted. He was getting a royal welcome in a city that swept him to its heart and clearly hungered for his leadership. Everywhere he went he was the center of attention, heads turning, smiles blooming, hats doffed, women looking in open admiration. There was something expectant in the air, a sense of ripening, great things lying ahead, no one actually speaking the forbidden but everyone seeming to know. His old friend Ed Livingston—New Yorkers arm-in-arm—and his new friend Daniel Clark both considered themselves the governor's worst enemies and Burr was happy to adopt their enmity. Doubtless Claiborne hated him but New Orleanians considered his sneers and snubs a rollicking comeuppance for the man who refused to learn the noble language.

Yet his exciting success here was just a continuation of his success across the whole West. He had pushed downstream from Harman Blennerhassett's island with crowds strewing figurative rose petals in his path. Down the Ohio he'd gone, deep into Kentucky, past Cincinnati, on to Louisville, overland on horseback to Frankfort and Lexington, on to Nashville and back to the Ohio, everywhere finding joyous crowds waiting to welcome the distinguished visitor. They listened raptly as he dropped skillful little hints of great things to unfold in due time, such as adding Florida and Texas to the purchase. At every stop Adair or Smith or Brown was on hand to introduce him privately to a few good men of power and authority who would be ready at some unspoken moment in the future. They loved him—a man of national power who understood them and looked to their future, all endorsed by their own familiar leaders. As he traveled they turned out in droves to interrupt his powerful speeches with cheers, as his rhetoric glowed hotter and grander, eloquence piled on eloquence, shouts of *Yes!* as at a revival meeting.

General Wilkinson had been awaiting him at Fort Massac, the old fur trade post taken over by the military on the Ohio just short of the Mississippi. The general seemed delighted to see him. He insisted that Burr shift to a military barge with armed soldiers in escort. The barge was less comfortable but would give a nice official character to his arrival. As it turned out, New Orleans, canny and devious after forty years of living under Spain, read the message clearly.

Wilkinson said every report he'd received was glowing with no word of suspicion. That was the acid test for Burr, who had deep respect for Wilkinson's duplicity and cunning. If he said all was well, it was. But caution was important, for they walked a narrow path. Wilkinson agreed instantly with the point Burr had made to the three senators—the opening move, getting his army downstream at the start, was the greatest danger. Once they reached New Orleans they'd be much too far along to be stopped.

But could Spain really be manipulated into war? Everything depended on speed once Burr arrived with his little army and seized the city. Momentum would be the crucial ingredient, everything off and running before people had much time to stop and consider. So war was essential to support collecting the little American army from all its diverse posts across the western wilderness, and moving it south certainly would attract attention. Wilkinson smiled. "Leave that to me," he said.

Burr let his genial manner fade. "That's not good enough," he said. "I need to know."

Wilkinson's voice hardened. "You'll know what I

choose to tell you." Then, as if relenting, he said, "Look, if the Spanish authorities learn from someone they trust and who is in a perfect position to know that the United States intends to take Florida and Texas forthwith, they will move defensive troops into place. Now, there is no difference in appearance between defensive and offensive troops. Their movement will constitute a threat; as commanding general I will move troops to counter such threats, with or without orders. And that will be that."

"And you can see to it that Spanish authorities so learn?"

"Trust me, my friend."

With Burr's arrival it seemed to Danny that the loose talk she heard around New Orleans grew looser and more dangerous. As if the dashing official so clearly in sympathy with New Orleans and its people, so clearly out of sympathy with the rude Americans, a man so gracefully *French* in manner and outlook, had given hope that had been lacking before. How many people had told her New Orleans was ready to ignite if the right leader appeared. Perhaps the right leader was here. . . .

Or perhaps she was becoming more alarmed and hence more aware, though the talk did seem newly pointed. She had to know—her whole business future rested on New Orleans sugar and the trade that the southernmost American port, comparing with New York and Baltimore in activity, might reasonably produce. She asked questions, feigning more knowledge than she had. She sent out the New Orleans men from *Carlito*'s crew to scout. She visited cousins and looked up old friends. Daily it became more clear that her uncle and Ed Livingston were in it up to their ears. They were principals in the Mexican Association, which aimed at liberating Mexico and seizing its gold. Liberating? That certainly meant conquering. She had the odd sense that it had been a dream that allowed men to play at heroics without much risk—and then Mr. Burr arrived to blow life into it.

Loose talk flowed. Seize New Orleans, eject Mr. Claiborne, strip the city's banks for expedition expenses, commandeer ships to haul an invasion force to Vera Cruz, the Royal Navy to stand offshore and prevent American interference. Then, powered by captured gold, they seal the Mississippi, the West swings to join them and voilà! a new nation stretching from the Valley of Mexico to the high Ohio, New Orleans its capital, Burr its ruler. It all seemed so . . . doubtful . . . until the last ingredient fell into place. General Wilkinson would turn his coat and swing the American army behind the new empire. By the time his men learned what really was afoot the thing would be settled and secure.

Danny was appalled, not the least because shipping would probably die in the consequent turmoil, and without shipping she would be ruined. The general shipping world still refused to deal with a woman as a business equal. She decided it was past time to see her partner. She hadn't exactly avoided Livingston, but he had married the Creole widow and they were so obviously in love that they made Danny's loneliness unbearable. When she told Ed her concern his smile vanished and she saw that behind his smooth geniality he was smart and tough.

"You've jumped to wrong conclusions," he said.

"Really? Tell me, Ed. I have a right to know."

"I suppose so," he said slowly. He looked at Louise. "All right, yes, we do aim at Mexico, but that's all. Mexico's been on the edge of revolution for years. Anyone can see the Spanish empire is dying, Central America and South America can't be held for long. Yet there's fabulous wealth—"

She cut him off. What about taking New Orleans,

stripping its banks, seizing ships, Wilkinson the turncoat, dreams of a new empire, splitting the American nation—

He raised a hand, laughing. "Hold on, hold on! My God, this is being done *for* the United States. Aaron wouldn't be party to treason, nor would I. I've known him for years, far better than you do. We were New York congressmen together and I dealt with him often as mayor of New York City. He's not a traitor."

"He told you he acted for government?"

"Hinted. One can't say too much."

"He's unpopular with the government, you know."

Livingston shrugged. "That's mostly cover. He's close to Secretary Dearborn, and Dearborn is close to Wilkinson. They want this done, else I wouldn't be involved."

Louise looked baffled and uneasy. Danny gazed at Ed. He was hungry and wanted to believe. She remembered that his trouble in New York had left a mountain of debt he insisted on repaying. Still, it was hard to imagine that a man whose brother had swung the triumph of the Louisiana Purchase would take part in its subversion. But somehow she wasn't reassured.

"See Daniel Clark," Wilkinson had said just before Burr departed Fort Massac in the barge. "He proves the simple truth that unfounded discontent is the most potent discontent of all—it severs one from reality and then can flourish endlessly. In matters of the world he's an ignoramus; in matters of New Orleans no one is more sophisticated or skilled."

Which was exactly how Burr found the merchant prince. His view of his city was razor edged; his belief that he should have been named governor was fantastic. He said he'd been promised the post, but perhaps by the janitor; Burr couldn't imagine Mr. Madison making such an offer. But no need to disabuse the gentleman of his

fiery notions. Burr said Clark's story quite fitted the duplicity so common in Washington today, and watched the
other glow with satisfaction. He had an idea that Clark's
expectations mirrored those of New Orleans in general.

They talked carefully around the edges of things until
Burr was sure that Clark had a good sense for those realities that didn't go to his own hopes. Neither really mentioned conspiracy, but it seemed that Wilkinson had said
that Burr had an interestingly entrepreneurial mind and
had myriad plans. Clark didn't ask for details, not yet,
which entirely fitted Burr's sense of how things should
be done.

He had dined the night before with Ed Livingston and
the beautiful Creole widow from Haiti whom he'd married. He had drawn out Ed and in the end had decided not
to mention the deeper aspects of his own plans. Ed had
great ideas for New Orleans as the southernmost American port. A streak of patriotism ran strong in Ed, always
had, and after all, it was his brother who had brought
Louisiana into the Union. Extracting it from the Union
might not appeal immediately to the little brother.

When he asked Clark's opinion of Livingston, the
merchant said, "Well, like so many Americans, you as
the exception proving the rule, there's an infantile quality about him. Perhaps innocence is the right word. A
faith in good to prevail that is quite unwarranted by experience. Not your average conspirator, certainly. That
said, he's intelligent and strong, and all told, a good man.
He's Governor Claiborne's enemy, and the idea of seizing Mexico thrills him—he can solve his financial problems in a swoop. But he doesn't really see the logical
consequences of where all this must take us."

Burr liked that. Doesn't see where things must go: that
was Ed all right. "If we gather a few choice spirits to discuss the future it might be as well not to include him."

"Probably wise."

Clark had an expectant look, waiting to hear more, and Burr saw that he knew a good deal more of the plans than he admitted. Anyway, sooner or later you have to set caution aside. At last, tone light and speculative, ready to dance back at the first hint of sharp reaction, Burr said, "As an academic exercise, so to speak, just for the sake of argument, if new Orleans were offered new options, how would it react?

"Options?"

"Perhaps to go a new course. Not Spanish or French but not American, either."

Clark stared at him, waiting.

"But suppose it found itself the capital of a great new empire, one that it commanded. What then?"

Clark smiled, the slyness in his eyes now open. He made a curious bowing gesture, sweeping broadly with his hand, giving Burr the city.

"New Orleans wouldn't rally to repel such an idea?"

"It would fashion laurel wreaths for the liberator."

"And the militia?"

Clark laughed out loud. "They would cheer him on."

Now they were at the core. "This gathering of choice spirits that we mentioned, how would they react?"

"Not one would stand against so interesting an idea."

"And since we have no idea if such a move might come, their discretion could be assured?"

His laugh was as harsh as a hawk's cry. "Given a hangman's noose for early disclosure, I think you could count on their silence. You'd like me to assemble such a group?"

"All solid, in your view?"

"The ones I'll assemble, yes. One though, I'll leave to you, a young man named Henri Broussard. Hotheaded, still well short of wisdom, but he has a definite power, and his hatred of the Americans is profound. Distant relative of mine. Suggest that French culture surpasses all

and you'll have him; suggest that things could change
and he'll jump into your lap."

Burr remembered Clark introducing Broussard the
day he arrived, a tall, rangy fellow, youth's brightness
still about him though he was in his early thirties, gave
you the impression he'd be good in a fight but would be
better taking orders than giving them.

"Commands a militia brigade, one of four here," Clark
said. "Are they any good? I don't know. They wear brilliant uniforms, have regular parades, and talk quite fero-
ciously but they're shy of experience. Social elite, really.
Still, they're armed, and if some other force were to lead
the way they'd be strong support."

Yes, one way or another, Mr. Clark most certainly had
heard from General Wilkinson.

He sent this Captain Broussard a note suggesting dinner this afternoon. Walking slowly to his hotel, holding
his shirt away from his chest to give himself air, a big
planter's hat shielding him from the sun, he encountered
Señor Juan Ventura Morales, the Spanish *intendente* who
had run New Orleans until it passed to France and from
France to the United States. That Morales was still here
agitating against Governor Claiborne and the U.S. Burr
took as sure indication that Washington knew little of
this distant bastion. Morales was a smallish man, very
neat, hair tied in a queue behind his head, his hands
puffy and well manicured. He was full of effusive charm.
Would Mr. Burr permit him to perform introductions to a
Spanish rum of quite unbelievable quality? Mr. Burr
would indeed; they walked a block to the river and sat in
the deep shade of a wide-spreading oak before an establishment that leaped to serve them. Of course the meeting was anything but accidental.

A breeze came off the river and with it a slightly
brackish odor that someone had told Burr was alligator
musk. Imagine, alligators . . . The rum was just as superb

as the Spaniard had said; Burr sipped with quiet pleasure as he listened. It seemed that Spain had learned the U.S. intended shortly to seize Florida and Texas under the spurious claim they were part of the purchase, which itself Spain disputed. With a second glass of rum in hand Burr expressed mild doubts. Could he be sure?

"Ah, señor, America's openly rapacious manner makes it near certainty alone, but we also have information directly from a most highly placed source. You understand I can say no more, but you should warn your countrymen, even now the captain general in Havana is moving troops forward, to Pensacola and to Texas."

In a reflective tone, Burr observed that perhaps the purchase itself was unfortunate; in other hands Louisiana would provide buffer between the U.S. and Spanish holdings.

Morales had the look of a man who bites into a chocolate and finds rum in its center. "Exactly, sir," he cried, "your prescience is startling." Then, as if seizing opportunity, he added, "They say New Orleans may not remain American—the whole West might break off. Spain would look on that with great favor."

Perhaps not after we seize Mexico, but Burr didn't voice this thought. They parted with mutual felicitations.

Over dinner that afternoon, when Henri Broussard had had several glasses of wine, Burr brought the conversation around to New Orleans and found the young man bristling and eager. Too eager, perhaps, sort of an anxiety to be included, fear he'd be left behind, a worrisome uncertainty. Still, for Burr's purposes, that might be just right. The willingness to follow orders can be more important than initiative sometimes.

Speaking hypothetically, one military man to another, how would the militia react to a separation force?

"Colonel Burr," Broussard said, "for twenty months

we have lived under the incompetence and rudeness and abuse of an idiotic administration that gives its people no say in their own affairs. This is democracy as it has been presented to us by the fountainhead of all democracy. Since the late afternoon of the day Mr. Claiborne took control we have lived on the edge of revolt. Nothing has quite triggered it, no single individual has emerged who could give it form and substance. If, as you put it, a separation force were to appear New Orleans would dance in the streets! And the militia would dance too."

When Burr returned late to his hotel, picking his way through dark streets, he found the door closed but not locked. A single candle lantern on the front desk cast dim light. He touched the dirk strapped to his forearm as he glanced about, but the room was empty, the clerk asleep somewhere. Then a small man in muddy boots, his britches looking as if he'd slept in them, emerged from an alcove and called Burr's name.

"Boudreau, Jacques Boudreau," the fellow whispered.

Ah . . . Boudreau of the Bastrop land grant. He let the little man lead him to a table in the corner, still whispering though there was no one to hear. "John Adair, he wrote me I should see you," he mumbled.

Burr waited, thinking of the conversation with Adair back in Marietta and the idea of land that would provide convenient excuse for taking young settlers downriver. The Bastrop grant in the wilderness up the Red River made a perfect destination.

It was just as Adair had predicted. The little man was anxious to sell and accepted various qualifications that by themselves would be enough to break the contract. Still, there would be something nicely ironic about refusing to pay the balance on the grounds of faulty title: he and little Mr. Boudreau, each trying to cheat the other. Burr gave him a draft drawn on Harman Blennerhassett.

Now he was more or less the owner of a four-hundred-thousand-acre destination.

Clark's meeting came the next day, ten men listening as the merchant laid out the realities in fluent French. They all understood American abuse, he said, but now a different kind of American has entered our midst, a man who knows our language, our customs, our culture, and yet has achieved brilliantly in the American society. He may well be, Clark added, an answer to prayers. Burr loosed a stream of golden oratory that he had to admit to himself was superb. He lauded all things French from the beautiful language to the extraordinary theater to the splendid music to the genius of the great Napoleon. Yet the reality was that they had passed from the French orbit and it was too late to return. They must face the truth: in the end they could preserve the glories of what they were only by gaining control of their own destiny. He held his voice low in the quiet room, letting passion creep into the vibrations in his throat, painting brilliant pictures in carefully chosen phrases. He could feel their reactions as he described the sheer nobility they brought to the American continent—and their vigor when he hinted at better days to follow.

Now it was all hypothetical, but suppose they were given a chance to act? He laid out a shortened version of his questions and watched comprehension fill their faces, heard their murmurs of approval. He had the sense they'd awaited him since the day they learned that Napoleon had sold them. They shook his hand afterward, faces full of emotion, several saying they would light candles and call on the saints to bless him. They had been awaiting rescue, one whispered, drawing him into a strong embrace. So they answered his question: they were with him.

Enthusiastic New Orleanians, leading men in Kentucky, Wilkinson and the army, everything set and ready—the way was unfolding before him like a road paved with gold. The time for action had come. He would leave within a week.

Danny would sail soon with nothing resolved. *Carlito* was nearly loaded. Her uncle was giving a reception to honor some Napoleonic excess—he said the Frenchmen loved that—and she went early to visit Zulie. Henri arrived as a guest. He nodded but didn't approach her.

When Burr appeared he worked his way around the room and when he came to her they fell into easy conversation that seemed anything but conspiratorial. Someone drew him away, he giving her an apologetic smile, and she went to the punch bowl. It was Champagne based and strong and she felt she needed it. She was refilling her glass when she heard Burr and her uncle behind her. Mr. Clark had been drinking; his voice was high. She tilted the ladle, pouring slowly, listening, and heard Clark say, "I'd as lief hang Claiborne when we take over. He's arrogant and not worth saving."

Take over . . . then it was true!

She heard Burr laugh, and then say, voice cast so low she strained to hear, "No need—once we've created a new nation we'll send him on his way. He's a very small potato . . ."

She found Zulie entertaining a cluster of women. She drew the majestic Frenchwoman aside and sketched what she had learned, doubts now made solid by Mr. Clark's overheard words. "It's worse than I thought," she whispered. "Zulie, you must get him to listen—"

But Zulie's manner changed. Her mouth drew down and her eyes were cold. Suddenly Danny was aware of her diamonds, her hair piled atop her head and wrapped in gold braid, her gown the latest from Paris. "It is not the place of women to interfere," she said. "I wouldn't dream of it."

"Zulie, listen to me, please. They're talking treason. They think they can get away with it, these New Orleans folk do, but Mr. Clark should know better."

Zulie shook her head. "No."

"Don't you understand? Treason is a hanging offense!"

Real anger swept the older woman's expression. "I've told you before, you've become too much the American. No one will come here and hang people. New Orleans is a law unto itself. It would never permit hanging."

Danny stared in consternation. Zulie's expression remained cold and implacable. Some chasm of unbearable insularity had opened and Danny was on the other side and there was no crossing. As with Henri. She glanced across the room. Henri was at the door, shaking Clark's hand, leaving. He didn't look at her.

She went swiftly to Clark, said she must talk to him, and drew him into his little study off the large room. He listened with darkening face.

"Zulie told you you're too American," he said, "and by God, you are. How dare you come here and question me! But since you have, I will tell you that I owe the United States nothing. Nothing! When they sent that oaf Claiborne, when they denied me my just due, they lost any claim to my allegiance."

He began to pace and she watched him in dismay. "New Orleans is not destined to be American. It doesn't fit, doesn't belong. It's a great center in its own right and Mr. Burr will make it a capital of an empire. He and that fat piece of *merde*, Wilkinson. And then they think they'll rule and maybe they will for a while, but not forever. Wilkinson will eat Burr, Burr is a baby, nothing more, and then someone will put a knife in Wilkinson and let the pus run out and then we will see who controls the empire. We will see."

In horror she snatched open the door and fled into the main room. Most of the guests were gone. Then it struck her that it was late and she was alone and far from her *pension* and the streets were dark. As if he'd been waiting, Mr. Burr stepped from the shadows and bowed, and said it would honor him to be permitted to escort her. It surprised her that he knew where she lodged.

She took his arm and they walked in silence, her mind in turmoil. The only light was an occasional oil lamp hung from a pole and the faint glow from windows they passed. Twice she stumbled on broken sidewalk; she clung harder to his arm. This was just what she had feared. She remembered trying to warn Dolley, trying to get Mr. Madison to see the peril, and she remembered their cold faces as they closed their ears. Now that the peril was so clear it seemed to her they had rebuffed her in wanton anger. Friends slapping her face. Were they even friends? Did people of power even have friends? Carl was dead and the shipping world refused to deal with her and she had broken with Henri and she had scarcely a friend in the world. She felt unbearably lonely. Would she try again to warn the Madisons? Face another slap in the face from Dolley? She didn't know.

She clung harder to his arm, tears in her eyes, her spirits sunk to the bottom of the sea, and then with a low chuckle Mr. Burr offered a small witticism. It wasn't all that funny but it came to her as rescue, it spoke of easy pleasure and good humor and lightheartedness, and it peeled away gloom. She said something in return, her mood lifting, and they strolled along, chuckling and chatting, growing at ease with each other. She could hardly imagine him the mad conspirator—or she didn't want to, which might be the same thing.

Abruptly he turned to her, put a hand over hers resting

on his arm, and said in a different voice, "You are a beautiful woman. It's an honor to walk with you." She was startled and yet she felt a sort of jolt deep within her.

At the house she asked him to see her to her room lest she encounter a surprise in the halls. When she opened the door with the big key it swung inward with a loud creaking, like an empty house full of haunts. Tonight it had an unbearably lonely sound. Perhaps it was everything, Henri and the chasm that had opened between her, and Zulie and her uncle's rage, and the way Dolley had rebuffed her warnings.

Or perhaps it was that electric jolt, she had to admit that, but the truth was that she didn't want to be alone. She drew him inside and threw the bolt with a startling sound of finality and stood with her back against the door, wordless.

Burr awakened in his own quarters with early shafts of sun in his eyes and thought immediately of Danny Mobry. She was powerful, as powerful a woman as he was a man—and she was wealthy to boot. These were the two ingredients essential to his feeling any real interest; here the signs were all positive. He washed, shaved carefully, dressed his hair, donned fresh linen and a sponged suit, took a swift cup of the wonderful coffee that swept all cobwebs from the mind, and hurried to her.

Gone, the establishment's host told him. Awakened the house before dawn to settle her account, his porter dragged from his bed to haul her trunk and find a hack. Where had she gone? The man shrugged. His eyes were rheumy, he'd seen all there was to see in the world. "Back to her ship, she said." He put slight emphasis on the last word.

Burr went to the waterfront but hesitated when he reached the levee and saw *Carlito*'s masts. This might not be so easy, barging aboard, asking for her. After all, her swift departure had to mean something. So he waited, expecting to see her at Clark's, and on the second morning found *Carlito* gone. Sailed for the States before dawn, so said a wharf rat.

Still, nothing could disturb his sunny mood. New Orleans was his, a bloodless conquest, his future as brilliant as the rising sun. He left three days later, bound north for another visit with Wilkinson and then on to New York to line up hard cash investors in his bright future. It would be a year before he could return but he had no doubt the city would be awaiting him with open arms. His reception here had swept away his last doubts. All that Wilkinson had said had proved true; Aaron Burr was on a trajectory for the stars.

TWENTY

Washington, early fall 1805

Dolley met Mr. Latrobe at the north entrance of the mansion and they sat on a marble bench just inside as he showed her drawings of chairs with a pronounced Greek motif that a Baltimore cabinetmaker had designed. Perfect for a redecorated mansion.

"If and when," she said.

"But if I may say so, madam, I think more when than if." She laughed and he slid effortlessly into a discussion of the virtues of the painted finish and she followed eagerly. Then, casually, he asked if she'd heard that Mr. Burr had turned up in New Orleans. Her head whipped around and she stared at him; was even her architect, this artist with whom she spun air castles of design for the future, glorying in their problems with Aaron?

He saw immediately that he'd stepped on sensitive ground even if he wasn't sure what made it sensitive. Quickly he said that he had been in New Orleans in the past to design a water system using pipe bored out of cypress logs. Nothing had come of it, though he still had hopes, but his point now was that he'd been impressed with both workmanship and fine woods fetched from Central America. Since New Orleans now was American, perhaps they could call on its skills. . . .

Dolley relaxed, thinking as he nattered on that if Danny's fears were at all right they might be hearing of New Orleans for a great deal more than good furniture. Indeed, Aaron had bobbed up in New Orleans to add to all their other troubles with the new province and its feckless governor. Still, once he started west, of course he'd go to New Orleans, a bee drawn to nectar. Danny hinted at rebellion in the air, with Aaron perhaps involved, but with nothing you could pin down. With Aaron there rarely was. And conspiracy talk had been old in New Orleans long before the current imbroglio.

But just the same, she hadn't forgotten those questions in the Philadelphia paper—nor had Jimmy, even if he didn't say much about it.

Danny had new worries. She had returned a month ago to find one of her ships had gone missing. *La Belle Juliette* had cleared New Orleans a week before *Carlito* departed but had never reached Boston. Danny's key customer, the rum distiller there, was clamoring for sugar. There had been no reports of violent weather, but after a month passed it was clear that there was real trouble—pirates or Spanish corsairs or an unsuspected reef or runaway slaves attacking before the ship even cleared the Delta. Each day Danny talked to her old friend Clinch Johnson. His queries sent up and down the coast yielded nothing. He appeared most afternoons about four and she found herself waiting for his heavy, even tread on the loft stairs. They drank coffee and he told her things would work out. God, she hoped so. She showed Clinch no tears but sometimes she knew her eyes were red. Captain and crew of the missing ship were her men, part of her company family. Were they all murdered, the ship swept away? And it would be a tremendous economic blow—loss of ship and cargo, insurance covering but a fraction. Day by day she waited.

Then, making it all worse somehow, she couldn't shake free of her discomfort over Aaron Burr. An hour after he left her room she'd awakened at the bottom of a well. The very sight of the room distressed her and she was gone within the hour over the landlord's grumbles. She was a free-spirited woman who operated in a man's business, but she wasn't casual in matters of love. She still ached for Carl and she had at least imagined herself in love with Henri. She had turned to Aaron abruptly when she felt desperately lonely, but she also knew she'd been drawn to him from the start. Well, it had simply happened . . . yet the uneasiness persisted.

And then, what of Burr's secret plans? She tried to tell Dolley but faltered when Dolley seemed to have no interest. And anyway, did she really know that Burr planned treasonous crime? An overheard comment, Henri's hopes, her uncle perhaps toying with her, this was hardly evidence. What could she report? Suspicions at best. And she had, after all, drawn him into her room. But did silence betray her country?

So she was pondering questions without answers when she heard Clinch's steady tread on her stairs. He came in, his linen trousers dusty and stained as if he'd been crawling in a ship's hold. He always reminded her of a sausage in that bulging coat, but his blue eyes were sharp and alert and kind.

"Miz Danny," he cried, "the question is answered but it's a bad answer. *Juliette*'s crew is here."

"The crew? They brought the ship—"

"No, ma'am—here, let Captain Oglecliff tell you."

And there was Oglecliff sidling into her room, tall, cadaverous, heavy brown hair falling to his shoulders, his boots worn and his coat dirty. "It warn't my fault, Miz Mobry. I done my best, truly I did."

"I'm sure you did, Captain. Now, tell me."

"The British, ma'am, they took the ship." He stood there rolling his master's hat in both hands. There was sweat on his face. "We was just swung north, don't you see, cleared the Florida Straits and took a long fetch up along them key islands down on the end of Florida. I hove to and let some of the boys go ashore, clamming, you see, to have a change of diet, and this here frigate flying the Union Jack come on us there."

"Another press-gang," she said. "Wanted your men."

"No, ma'am. Well, in the end they did take half a dozen of the boys, but what they wanted, they wanted ship and cargo. I showed 'em the manifest but this lieutenant, he said it was forged, said I was a goddamned liar, begging your pardon, ma'am, said we was hauling from the French sugar islands. He flang the manifest papers overboard and I told him he was a goddamned pirate and one of his flunky soldiers give me a musket butt in the back of the head and I don't remember too much after that."

"But the men are all right, either impressed but alive or returned with you?"

"Yes, ma'am, all hands accounted for."

"Well, thank God for that. But the ship?"

"They said it was confiscated for hauling contraband, read me a whole list citing this and that and I told 'em that was all lies and they told me to shut m'gob and a prize crew went aboard *Juliette* and said they'd sail her to London town where the sugar ought to fetch a pretty price. I tell you, ma'am, I like to bust but there wasn't nothing I could do."

The crew had been held until the frigate put into Norfolk for water and victuals, and then they were turned loose. Her ship seized! Cargo and vessel, taken as if by so many pirates under the color of self-generated, self-serving law. She was so angry she could scarcely see.

Dolley saw at a glance that her husband was upset when he came home at dusk. What's the matter? Nothing. Nothing at all. Giving her a sharp look.

She got him to doff coat and cravat in favor of a dressing gown and to trade his buckled shoes for slippers, he with lips pursed at this wifely thoughtfulness. She called down to the kitchen and Sukey appeared with a supper of cold beef and the last of the season's tomatoes and fresh bread and butter from a little dairy farm on N Street and a tankard of ale from a brewery across the river, and he began to brighten.

"Danny Mobry came to see me," he said, glancing sideways at her. "A new disaster." It seemed that in addition to losing her ship she would be responsible for the cargo too. "I wish she would sell out," he said.

That offended something deep in Dolley. "Why? She's very brave. It's her company. Why should she have to sell?"

Rather more sharply than she liked, he said, "Now, don't get your defenses up! She's a woman alone in a difficult business and things are getting steadily worse. She's already been press-ganged at sea, now ship and cargo are gone, who can she turn to?"

Simmering a little, she listened to him sketch out what had happened. "Piracy on the high seas if her story's right as she told it," he said.

She bristled again. "Why shouldn't it be right? Would she lie? You know her better than that."

"I know how people react under pressure. She might have detoured to Guadeloupe for a cargo. And not be quite straight about it when she's caught. She wouldn't be the first—"

"Jimmy! Why in the world are you carrying on so?"

He glared at her. "Because the British are seizing our ships right and left and it's so hard talking to these poor devils who've lost half their fortune when their ship's seized, and there's nothing I can do about it! And let me tell you, Dolley, it's a devil of a lot harder still when it's a woman whom you know and like and want to help, so don't—"

"I'm sorry, Jimmy." She had underestimated him again. She knew how grim it was, why argue? The British had reinstituted what they arrogantly called the Rule of 1756—the year *they* had made the rule!—to block U.S. ships from carrying produce from French colonies to France. Ships that violated were seized, condemned, and sold, vessel and cargo, in London.

He finished the meat and pulled the honey pot close. She knew that things grew steadily more dangerous. Napoleon was driving hard to bring all Europe under his control, leaving the British standing alone. Meanwhile a small book called *War in Disguise* had swept London with the argument that American trading vessels were waging war against Britain by destroying its trade. Americans, it argued, should be forced to become an adjunct source for the British war machine, like it or not. Then a new rule growing from the seizure of the American brig *Essex* wiped away another privilege of international trade for American vessels. Britain, in short, intended to abuse American shipping as it chose and let them whistle in the wind.

Stabbing his knife into the honey pot again, he snapped, "Rule of 1756! Huh!" Obviously he spoke more to the British than to her. "A confounded illegality on its face! Goes back to the Seven Years' War and it was just as illegal then." He glared at her, counting points on his fingers, jabbing an index finger as he proved its illegality point by point. He banged his fist on the table, rattling the lid of the honey jar. "It rests on force, nothing more, and depending on force contradicts law!"

Candle flames fluttered from his vehemence. "My," she said softly, "I see I should have been doing something else when I created the Rule of 1756."

"Eh? What?" He stared at her. "Oh—I've been declaiming again." He managed a smile. "Sorry. It does get under my skin." He twirled the honey pot lid in his fingers.

Presently she took his hand in hers and held it. He sighed and she could see him relaxing. His voice a whisper, he said, "I don't think the new democracy we've fought for could survive war with Britain. Not now, it's too new, too tender. Canada would be our only target and there's no challenging the Royal Navy. It would put us right back in Federalist hands. Courting the British, favoring the wealthy, perpetuate the wellborn, hereditary nobility around the corner—and then we can kiss democracy good-bye because it soon would be gone."

She listened quietly, his hand in hers. Britain was so arbitrary, but it was desperately pressed on the Continent, and she observed quietly that if Napoleon prevailed it would be a dangerous world.

"Good God, yes," he said. "But that doesn't mean—" She was smiling and he broke off. "All right, all right, you know. And what can we do but walk that narrow path between humiliation on the one hand and triggering war on the other? We just have to have a diplomatic solution. Jim Monroe's in London—at the least he must settle impressment. It's obscene, stealing our men, for them but for what it says about us, too. God, I hope Tom's faith in Jim is justified."

"Probably he'll do well," she said as they went up to the bedroom, but her thought was that if he did he'd be a national hero and a leading figure for president in 1808. The idea that Monroe with his bland, remote ways might euchre Jimmy out of the office that was rightfully his gave her such an acid stomach that she lay on the bed emitting gentle belches. But Jimmy was deep in a book by then and didn't notice.

The trouble was, Dolley saw Mr. Latrobe as she was walking to the President's House, and as usual, they fell into conversation about the deplorable state of the mansion. He told her the Baltimore cabinetmaker with the Greek key-motif chairs would make a break-even price for the honor of having his work in the President's House. "Oh, Mrs. Madison," he cried, enthusiasm contagious, "you must persuade him to go ahead. It simply must be done!"

The president had asked her in to discuss a dinner with an American if not rural flavor he wanted to give a number of congressmen. But unfortunately, the image of those chairs held in her mind and when the dinner was settled she told him of Mr. Latrobe's find. Then, knowing she was going too far but feeling pressed by his irritated expression, and rebellious as well, she blurted, "Mr. President, really, it's just a crime to let the inside of this magnificent building be so shabby. It's so beautiful architecturally, it glows white so brilliantly since you had it painted, but the inside—why, it's like a beautiful woman without strength or morals, dark inside to bright outside."

He stared at her. "I'm managing my home as a trollop, you're saying?"

"No—" Her hand went to her mouth.

"I'm living as a trollop lives?"

But that made her angry, he was laying it on, throwing the weight of his office at her, and she snapped, "You know perfectly well what I meant."

"You exceed yourself when you badger me, madam."

"I'm not badgering you." She was torn between rage and what she recognized to her dismay as fear, of his power if not of him. "I'm expressing a personal opinion, which I believe is my right. You don't object to my opinions when they're in your service."

His face was white. "You're hardly indentured. You may withdraw at will."

"Oh, my God," she said, "Is that what you really want?"

"No, of course not, you brought it up—" He stood abruptly to stare from his window. Feeling half-sick she asked if he wanted her to go. He shook his head. "Please don't."

When he turned the anger was gone. He took his seat by his worktable on which his agricultural journals were laid out. A letter from the American Philosophical Society lay atop a pile of correspondence. He settled back in his chair, resting his chin on tented hands. She stared back.

"These are difficult times," he said at last. "You hear it from Jimmy, so you know. The British are just impossible. Mr. Merry is no help at all—in bed with the Federalists. Mr. Monroe in London says he has to tug at their coattails even to get their attention. He doesn't even comment on his orders to put the impressment issue ahead of everything. Across the Channel, Napoleon is striding around the Continent in seven-league boots. On our own continent your friend Aaron Burr might just be thinking about doing the same thing."

She started to protest and thought better of it. Aaron was her friend. He also was up to something, she thought. But it had been a mere rhetorical thrust, for Mr. Jefferson went on without a break, "In the Congress John Randolph seems to be building a radical rebellion within our own party. And here we are trying to hold to the middle, trying to keep that of the Federalists that's useful like the bank, trying not to discharge government workers only because they first worked for the other party. But we're cutting taxes, cutting army and navy, paying down the debt—it just isn't the time for me to spend public money decorating my house, this being, after all, where I live. You should understand that, Dolley."

"Believe me, I won't raise the issue again." She couldn't keep the chill from her voice.

"Oh, Dolley." He stood, towering over her, then sat on the edge of his table and took her hand. "Now, now," he said, "raise it as you like. Don't be angry. I just can't have my two favorite women outside my own family angry at me at one time. So tell me you won't be."

She had to laugh and her irritation fled. He was as hard-pressed as Jimmy, and he had restored things between them graciously.

"Abigail Adams is, in fact, angry at me," he said, "and it seems there is nothing I can do to turn that around." He returned to his chair, sighing. "She's a hornet protecting John, you know. But once we were wonderful friends, and I miss that. When we were both in Paris we saw each other nearly every day, I dined with them constantly, and when Maria came to join me—she was six then, I suppose, quite a lost little girl after her mother passed—I was away on some mission, not knowing exactly when she would arrive, you see, and Abigail took her in and it was as if Maria had found a new mother. It was difficult prying her loose and I think Abigail took it as hard as Maria did."

His voice had a faraway, ruminative sound, and Dolley didn't interrupt him. "Those were happy days, in Paris. John and I were both representing the United States, he accredited to Britain but things were too hostile then to reside there, while I dealt with France. We talked constantly, traveled together, celebrated Christmas together—they eased the pain of—of—" He hesitated, then said softly, "Mrs. Jefferson's death."

He looked from the window, his expression immobile and contained, then said, "Politics swept us apart, granted. But it was never personal. I was vice president when John was president and we got along well enough. But it all changed when I was elected and he was defeated, and they've been hostile ever since. So you can imagine my joy when Abigail wrote a wonderfully warm letter when I lost Maria, full of memories of a child we both loved. And I answered, so happy that perhaps we could put old hard feeling behind us, and I said, which is true, really, that I'd never had a single quarrel with John except his naming the midnight judges."

On his last day in office the bitter Mr. Adams had named scores of judges, all arch-Federalists, obviously hoping to ensure a Federalist judiciary.

"Well, she answered with an enraged diatribe accusing me of the foulest betrayal, a snake in friend's clothing, evil at the core and so forth and so on. So there it stands." He smiled at her. "So you can see why my other favorite friend mustn't be put out with me too."

"I think we have fair understanding, Mr. President," Dolley said. Poor Tom: beyond his family and a few friends like the Madisons and, she supposed, the Monroes, he was alone.

Senator John Quincy Adams, Federalist of Massachusetts, sat on a stone bench in the rotunda marking up a bill and eating a sweet roll and cup of tea purchased from one of a dozen food vendors. He tried to ignore a straw-haired boy about eight who was holding out his cap in preemptory demand while making his little yellow dog sit up and roll over and walk on his forelegs. Adams finally tossed the boy a copper and gestured him off to plague any of the forty or fifty other men eating, drinking, talking, laughing. He penciled carefully on the bill's margins, artfully improving it, knowing that no one would pay his effort the slightest mind. Neither Federalists nor Democrats were keen on Mr. Adams, each party having found that it could not count on his vote. Mr. Adams hewed his own course, and if it was lonely at times, it suited him. So he told himself.

He was thinking he might have spoken to the boy, asked his name, the dog's name, how long it took to teach the trick, he could be a regular chatterbox. Yes, and what good would that do? Then with distinct displeasure he saw his fellow Massachusetts senator, the Honorable Mr. Pickering, hurrying across the floor toward him. Mr. Pickering carried a glass of ale and two sausages folded into buns.

"Damned cute, that little dog. Where'd the boy learn him that trick? I saw you talking to him."

Adams stared at him.

Pickering laughed. "Ah, Johnny, me boy, don't play the superior with me." He knew Pickering used the nickname to irritate him. "For we are about to win and your friends the Democrats are about to lose. I happen to know that the new Louisiana province of which they're so proud is about to blow up in their faces. And Brother Burr, that exemplary Democrat, is about to shove a fire cracker up their behind and touch his cigar to the fuse. Oh, yes, Burr is not a man to trifle with. Imagine, trouble in New Orleans, which is such a worthless weight, a leaden tail on the national dog sure to weigh it down. So, Johnny, tell me, isn't it rich irony that buying Louisiana and sinking Brother Burr, for which the country today salutes the Democrats, shall in the end be their downfall?

"So, yes, sir, your friends will be hurled out on their bums come the next election, you wait and see. And we'll be back in. Not that it'll do you much good, fine-feathered traitor to the party that you are, no, sir."

"My," Adams said, "you do seem sure of yourself."

"Can't miss! Absolutely can't miss! If not over Louisiana, then over this British thing, you see. We ought to be supporting Britain against that scamp Napoleon, should be giving that noble nation all our weight, and instead we're fighting them."

"We are?"

"Certainly. Trying to steal their trade—read *War in Disguise*, that'll tell you the whole thing, us trying to take advantage of them when they're at war with a tyrant. But it turns out that's the key to the whole thing. The administration, they've got Monroe over in London and they want him to get them a treaty where they won't impress sailors?"

"True."

"Well, they ain't going to get a treaty, you know it and I know it, and they would too if they weren't blind. But what they're doing, they want him to demand and then when he can't get it they can brand him a failure. That's the whole idea—and you know why? Because they know Monroe could beat little Jimmy Madison in a fair election and they want him to fail in London so they can darken his name here. And look—"

He pointed across the rotunda and there came John Randolph of Virginia with his three hounds at his heels, his whip curled in his hand, looking unbearably elegant in black with snowy hose and freshly brushed slippers with buckles that gleamed, men clearing a path for him and his dogs, he nodding this side and that, royalty on parade. "Randolph knows," Pickering said. "Sees the plot against Monroe and is making sure Monroe sees it. Getting him set to come back and run after the treaty fails, see, make everyone see that it's all that fatuous Mr. Jefferson's fault. They'll call him a failure and he'll make it blow up in their faces like backflash on a musket, and they'll be fighting like dogs. Split the vote, you see, 'tween Monroe and Madison, and you'll see, we'll come sliding right back in and restore some sense to the country."

He waved and Randolph turned abruptly toward them. "I've been working with him. He does hate little Mr. Madison, you know. And when it comes to hating, no one tops John Randolph."

The foppish man was half-hidden in a fashionable wig, emaciated face skull-like, his handsome hounds prancing behind him. Adams knew he was even more a power in the House for his scathing tongue, than for his position as chairman of Ways and Means. "Mr. Pickering," the gentleman from Virginia cried, "my favorite secretary of state! Far superior were you in all your apostasy and failures of philosophy and intellect to the present hermaphrodite occupant of the office, the foul Mr. Madison, who tries to serve both parties and succeeds with neither! The same hungry Mr. Madison whom the noble Mr. Monroe will sweep away like miller's chaff. The same evil Mr. Madison who has corrupted the easily corrupted Mr. Jefferson, I might add, and bent that foolish man to his own ignoble hungers for office—why, I find it alarming for the state of mankind that there are among us even in high places those who would sacrifice all honor and decency and truth for more political gain. Disgusting, sir!

"But we shall sweep all that aside." He gave a low, evil chuckle and pointed his stick at Pickering. "And when the people have rallied to us, never fear, we will still need you to cry and whimper and blather at the outside and remind our people the evil fate that awaits slack spirits, the ever-present Federalists ready to sell us to the British while they hunt for a king of their own!"

Pickering laughed. "Prate on, my friend, for soon

you'll see the truth ascendant and then don't come weeping to me."

"Weeping to you? That would be a day to confound the gods." The congressman snapped his fingers at the dogs and they moved off in grand procession.

"Ah, God," Pickering said, "I love that man. He's such an ass. He'll walk us right back into office." He finished his sausage, wiped his mouth on the paper wrapped around it, hurled the wadded paper toward a basket, and shrugged when he missed. "And then, my boy," he added, "you'll want to look right sharp to see if you can find a place in a party that ain't got a dime's worth of use for you." He laughed. "Not a dime's worth." And he strode off.

Adams's taste for arcane legislative exercises was gone. A newsboy passed with copies of the *National Intelligencer* clutched under his arm. "Tension in New Orleans," he cried with a hopeful look at Adams. "Mr. Burr said to be making plans for the Mississippi Valley but who knows what they are?" Adams took a copy, thrust the penciled bill into his case, and said to the boy with the dog, "What's his name and how'd you train him to do all those tricks?" The boy glowed with pleasure and pride. Spot was the dog's name, though Adams saw no spot in evidence, and the young master explained the training with joyous enthusiasm.

Adams gave him a silver piece and went down marble steps feeling better somehow. Soon he was striding along the gravel walk that Jefferson recently had ordered built beside Pennsylvania Avenue. A chilly wind was at his back, damp and penetrating. Clouds sagged and presently it began to rain. He liked walking in the rain, drops pattering on the sheltering umbrella, but today he was without an umbrella and was about to get damned wet and probably catch the ague and miss the next dozen sessions and any chance of passing his bill on—

A carriage drew alongside and Mrs. Madison lowered a window. "Get in, Mr. Adams—you'll catch a dreadful chill." He bounded in, pleasure evident in his thanks, and took the forward seat facing her. She was in a blue gown with a white lace bodice and a shawl of pale gray thrown over her shoulders against the chill, and she smiled and he thought the smile made her beautiful, and all at once the vile things the newspapers supported by the Federalists and those for the radical Democrats were saying about her flashed into his mind, instantly shaming him. As if she had read his expression—God, she couldn't have, surely not, and he felt himself turning crimson—she settled back in her seat looking contemplative. There was a moment of small talk, the president was planning a dinner, she was on some errand to facilitate it, and then in a firmer tone, as if she'd made up her mind on something, she said, "You know, the president is very fond of your family. Of you, your mother, your father."

He looked at her. Where in the world was this going?

"I don't think I'm talking out of turn, or maybe I am," she went on. "But there's so much unhappiness in the world . . . he was just thrilled when your mother wrote him about Maria."

Relieved, he said, "Yes, Maria, I remember her so well in Paris, just a little girl then, you know. She was frightened, her *maman* had just died, and she cried a lot and it kind of broke your heart. I was a lot older, and we became great friends. Poor thing. Mama loved her, of course she wrote—fearing, she said to me, that she might be misunderstood. And I suppose she was."

Rather carefully, Adams thought, Mrs. Madison said, "I think he felt that by citing only one thing that had disturbed him he was showing how much he wanted the old friendship to continue."

Equally carefully, seeing now that this was important, Adams said, "Perhaps. I saw his letter and thought it not bad. But she is very sensitive. My father is a great man, I don't think there's any doubt about that, and she felt the people turned on him after a lifetime in their service, repudiated him, hurled him into the gutter. She felt that Mr. Jefferson betrayed their old friendship. So I suppose even a single criticism grated against a spot that hasn't in the least healed. Perhaps it never will."

"And you, sir? Do you concur?"

He hesitated. This was a strange conversation and he wasn't sure of his ground. At last he said, "Not entirely. But I honor my mother and father, I won't speak against them."

"Certainly not, sir. Nothing critical of them is intended. But perhaps for you to know that he meant well in answering that letter as he did and now is hurt by the results could lead toward eventual rapprochement."

Eventual . . . Yes, perhaps. They rode in silence. She meant well, and on balance, he thought so did her husband and Mr. Jefferson. He didn't share his parents' hurt and anger though he understood it, and he certainly didn't share Pickering's rage. In fact, it seemed to him that the administration was following a balanced course, rather carefully nuanced. He wasn't sure that a return to what the Federalist party had become over his father's objections would be desirable, while Randolph's mad partisanship would shatter the country within a year if his views gained power. And here was this well-meaning woman going out of her way—and running some risks— to ease the pain that lay against his family and, he supposed, against Jefferson as well.

He sat straighter, making up his mind. "Mrs. Madison, I thank you for what you said. In the same spirit, I think I should tell you something to pass on to Mr. Madison. There is a well-advanced plan on the Hill to put Mr. Monroe into the presidency."

He hesitated. He was crossing party lines to warn the

opposition and he could hear Pickering denouncing him for a traitor. Certainly he would never speak so directly to Mr. Madison himself, but a warning to the sympathetic Mrs. Madison seemed less an apostasy. He plunged ahead.

"I understand the administration is pressing Mr. Monroe to demand a treaty with Britain that I personally and many others as well doubt is possible. Randolph, Chairman Randolph, you know his manner, of course—"

She rolled her eyes. "Oh, God—I do indeed."

"Well, he is busily persuading Monroe that the demands from here are part of a plot to force him into something that must fail in order to destroy his reputation and deny him a chance at the presidency. This to favor Mr. Madison, to eliminate a rival. I have it on good—on very good—authority that Randolph and his acolytes believe that once Monroe sees this as truth he will make furious remonstrance that will demonstrate his commanding presence and put Mr. Madison in the villain's role. I beg you to take this as accurate."

He saw deep sadness in her face. "I'm sure it is."

Then, surprising himself, he added, "The Federalists think they'll be swept back into office when Mr. Madison and Mr. Monroe split the Democratic vote. Federalists would be better than Monroe and Randolph, but perhaps not a lot better. Mayhap you'll find this worth mentioning. . . ."

"Believe me, I will," she said. As he would pass along to his embattled family in Braintree the idea that the president sought rapprochement; it might take years but he thought it would come. Of course he would never be seduced into joining the party that had defeated his father, but he had to admit it was the only line of thought that made much sense in today's turbulent world.

———

In St. Louis, with the wind coming cool out of the north and the fur trade bateaux setting out for the winter's trapping, Brigadier (God, how he hated that insulting denial of rank!) General James Wilkinson drafted a half dozen notes, each with the single word "Come," and no signature. He had considered carefully and decided he was well satisfied with Aaron's progress. Brown reported that things had gone well, Jack Adair was ebullient, and a note from Clark in New Orleans suggested that the angry Frenchmen there had been bowled over by Aaron's charm and polish—and his plans. All these letters, of course, were circumspect and oblique but the general could read them clearly enough. So now it was time.

He folded each note, melted the wax stick in candle flame, left the smooth seal unmarked, block-printed *Bone Hand* on the front, and called in Sergeant McClanahan. McClanahan had recovered from the beating he had taken in New Orleans and offered doglike devotion to the general, who had kept him on despite the grunts of pain that he couldn't suppress for months. He would deliver the messages to a half dozen taverns and presently Bone Hand would appear—his hand a burnt claw in which bones were clearly evident, the result of torture by Sioux up the Missouri from whom he had managed to escape before the final coup de grâce. Late each afternoon Wilkinson would ride by himself along the river trail, waiting. Eventually a dark and silent figure on a ragtag horse would fall in beside him, a ruined hat drooping around a ravaged face. The general would hand over a letter and a sack of gold coins, give brief instructions, and turn his horse back while Bone Hand rode on, their meeting apparently a matter of chance. Bone Hand would see the letter to Governor Folch in Pensacola and Folch would put it on a swift ship to the captain-general of the Spanish army at Havana. Since it reported, on the authority of the commanding general, that the United States intended to seize Texas with the aim of diverting the Spanish from the ultimate goal, West Florida, it would stir swift action. The place to stop the whole movement, the letter advised, was along the Sabine, the river separating the newly designated Orleans Territory from Spanish Texas. Prepare to strike hard there to stop the perfidy before it begins.

Six days later Bone Hand appeared on a lonely stretch of the river trail. The general passed on a letter and bag. The whole transaction took under a minute.

Madison listened in silence while his wife unfolded her encounter with young Adams. They had just come home from Dr. Thornton's house, where three tables of whist had been followed by an elaborate cold supper well oiled with a good Spanish wine. A successful evening, for he'd been in an open mood and had told stories that had them roaring so hard the sperm oil lamps shook. For a few friends, at least, such an evening belied his reputation as a social stick, and he was glowing. He wished Dolley would comment on how good he'd been but couldn't bring himself to ask her. So he hung up his black suit and donned his dressing gown and poured a late cognac for them both as she talked.

Well, the situation was tightening. The British were more aggressive even as American outrage over impressment soared. Yet nothing in Monroe's dispatches suggested that he considered impressment crucial, let alone felt much could be done about it. Randolph's activity on behalf of Monroe was more and more overt. Madison prided himself on a modest view of himself, but he certainly didn't think Monroe would be better than he as president. Doubtless someone would be better but he couldn't imagine who that person might be. And then, Monroe would listen to Randolph, another mark against him.

Randolph had been attacking from within since Tom was elected, labeling Madison the evil genius seducing the poor president into fatal error, and now the radical press was yelping the same tune like so many coyotes on the prowl. Abused Dolley, too, in terms too vile to believe they came from civilized men. No one could deny the waspish brilliance in Randolph but it was deeply corrupted by his venom and flamboyant hatreds and scabrous, flaying rhetoric that men more and more were coming to fear.

Madison sat with the cognac warming his belly, watching Dolley brush out her hair, a hundred strokes on this side, a hundred on that, and then again. She had rubbed some cream containing God only knew what into her cheeks and forehead, which she said aimed to preserve beauty. She worked at her looks as he worked at the State Department—seriously. He remembered how startled he'd been years before when she told him she used rouge and ointments. It was when he was trying to work up his nerve to propose marriage and he'd been pointing out their age differences to his own disadvantage, she so young and fresh and glowing, the color in her cheeks like a sunrise, and she had said yes, it is a work of art, isn't it, or something like that, and he'd been dumbfounded. She'd laughed and said it never hurt to improve on a good thing, and at once her beauty as barrier fell away, and maybe it was then he asked and she accepted. . . .

He sighed. It was a good marriage; he was a profoundly happy man. Here were the British harassing us, Randolph undermining, Monroe maneuvering, Burr up to God knew what, all of them with the secretary of state in their sights, and here was the secretary mooning after his wife!

"Trouble in the West, too, I gather," he said.

"Danny came to see you?" She was rubbing in the cream, wiping it off as she did so.

"I asked her if she'd seen Aaron in New Orleans—the papers are full of questions, you know, all centering around that trip of his—and I was so surprised. She turned forty colors of red. Acted as if I'd accused her—"

"She slept with him," Dolley said.

"What? Why do you say—"

"And it's been bothering her ever since and you uncorked—"

"How do you know?"

"Aaron can be very persuasive."

He looked at her, not answering. Suddenly she went sharp red. "Well, he didn't persuade me!"

He smiled. "Good," he said.

He poured another inch in each glass. "She told a story uncomfortably close to what the papers are hinting. Rumor, conjecture, overheard bits and pieces—she thinks Aaron wants to steal the West, New Orleans at least and maybe everything, split it off into something new. Invade Mexico, steal its gold, create a new nation, and farewell the new democracy."

"Good God," Dolley said softly. He nodded and she added, "But Jimmy, stealing the West, it sounds too much doesn't it?"

"Well, you know him—what do you think?"

"Would he, you mean, as opposed to could he?"

"Nicely put."

Hesitation, then a half-smile. "Probably, if he thought he could get away with it. I hate to say that. . . ." She had moved to the chaise and she straightened. "What will you do?"

He shrugged. "Nothing now. If I did anything, said anything, it would slide out of sight in his instant denials."

"I suppose . . . Aaron must be frantic for there to be even a hint of such a thing." Sadly, her gaze into the distance profoundly irritating her husband, she added, "Poor devil . . ."

Something in her pensive expression infuriated him and all at once everything seemed to pile on him, the day, the pressure, the British, Burr, New Orleans's never-ending whine, whether Wilkinson really could be a traitor, everything. "Yes," he snapped, "he tried to steal the election from Tom, leaving democracy in shreds, he killed Alex, and now maybe the poor fellow wants to split the nation in two, steal the West, finish democracy in one clean shot. I'll say it's a pity!"

She set the glass down with a click. "You know very well what I meant! He's his own worst enemy."

He felt a yawn coming on and yielded to it, his mood softening, not wanting to quarrel. "I know," he said, "a man of promise who defeats himself at every turn. But you are much too lenient in your views of Aaron Burr."

She bristled, but this was a subject he did not want to pursue, now or later, and he stood abruptly, loosing another yawn, and said, "Lord, I'm tired. Let's go to bed."

But sleep held off and after a while, listening to her gentle breathing, he slid out of bed to sit by a window. The sky had cleared and a half-moon gleamed through bare branches outside. He pondered what Aaron Burr might do, and the more he pondered the more uneasy he became. Yes, New Orleans was volatile and perhaps Governor Claiborne was a mistake. But what was Aaron thinking? He was highly intelligent and had an instinct for power and its uses. Of course he had dug the pits into which he'd fallen—didn't we all?—but he was not a man easily defeated. So what would he do now, tottering on the edge of ruin? Why had he gone west? Political office, senator from Kentucky? Not likely. Land speculation was a leading industry on the frontier but it took years to develop and Aaron would need something in a hurry.

Well, suppose Danny were right. Some insane scheme to steal the West, take New Orleans, seal the river, invade Mexico. It sounded incredible. Or did it? Suppose you raised money and arms in New York and headed down-river with small groups of men, maybe recruiting as you went. In New Orleans, from what everyone said, you'd find men willing for any desperate adventure and not constrained by any love of the new country.

But that didn't work well either. What the devil did Aaron think the army would be doing while he stole half a continent? An image of General Wilkinson flashed into Madison's mind, face round and puffy, stuffed into those ridiculous uniforms he designed, fawning to his betters, sly as a fox approaching a henhouse. What about those insistent rumors that he took gold from the Spanish? Every effort to catch him had failed, so maybe he was innocent. Maybe.

Still, Burr was no fool. It denied reason to suppose he would try to lead a rebellion of New Orleans men whom he scarcely knew. Yet Danny's account had disturbed Madison more than he liked. Yes, it was overheard remarks, some boasting, and that scamp of an uncle of hers might have been playing with her, but Madison had heard the ring of truth.

Still, there had to be more to it, and maybe there was. Maybe Aaron had some weapon they hadn't considered, some way to counteract the army. Or neutralize it. Or . . . use . . . it.

Oh, my God . . .

He sat rigid in his chair by the window. Suppose that in fact Wilkinson was a traitor, as so many people suspected. Suppose he were to declare a conspiracy in New

Orleans, which he must put down with troops and thus engage the army. Suppose he could trigger a Spanish mobilization that then would make it seem natural to use the army to attack Mexico, supported by Aaron's young adventurers. Suppose Aaron knew exactly what he was doing because he knew he was supported. He and Wilkinson were famously close. They had gathered maps of the West, which you would need in order to take bodies of men into the wilderness. Burr had been flirting with the hostile Mr. Merry, who would be valuable to a conspiracy. And Burr was touring the West and visiting New Orleans for no earthly reason. Strong hints with nothing proven.

For it did make sense. If Wilkinson turned the army to the conspiracy there would be nothing to stop it. The army's officers and men were loyal, they never would agree to a coup, but soldiers are trained to obey and especially if a war with Spain were concocted, a coup could be complete and beyond their recall before they understood what had happened. And then it would be too late.

He had the breathtaking sense of a man who learns suddenly that he is bankrupt, that all his anchors and guarantees and assurances and promises have been swept away or never were, that he is naked to his enemies. The army was the bulwark, the peacekeeper, the protector, the law. Conspiracy, coup, stealing the West, shattering the nation's hopes, destroying the young democracy, all were possible and even likely if you postulated General Wilkinson turning his coat and standing as traitor.

The moon had slipped out of sight, the dark was intense, and suddenly he was cold, whether physically or mentally he didn't know. He slipped into bed and lay there shivering with his eyes wide open.

Now if this scenario was anything, if it even existed, it

was still just an idea, a dream, at most a plan. Try to attack it now and it would go underground in a cloud of denials, and there continue to grow. They would have to wait and see, knowing that if it did exist, to wait too long would also be fatal.

Dawn was cracking before he slept.

★ ★ ★ ★ ★

TWENTY-ONE

New York City, spring 1806

It was late on a March day when the *Mary Kramer* out of
Baltimore eased against Hanneman's wharf and the lines
flew out. Aaron Burr stood at the rail, drinking the sights
and sounds and odors of old New York, Peck's Slip
where so many votes rode on a tide of beer, Tammany a
little way up still smarting, he didn't doubt, from a clean
victory stolen away by Mr. Hamilton. Alex should have
let well enough alone. Burr sighed. The New York indictment—inciting a duel or some such—had been quashed
and his friends were working to wipe away the murder
charge in Jersey. So for the moment no one hungered for
his arrest.

On the other hand, no need to advertise his presence.
He flipped a coin to the mob of boys on the dock and
sent the one who caught it to Peter Van Ness and Matt
Davis with a note. They appeared within the hour, still
the unlikeliest pair, Matt big and rather raw, Peter slender and polished, an accountant at heart. Right behind
them came Sammy Swartwout, his old friend John
Swartwout's little brother who'd been so much a part of

Burr's political legerdemain. Now Sammy had grown from eager boy to stalwart young man without losing that enthusiasm that seemed to find good—and opportunity—wherever he looked. Handshakes became embraces as Burr felt a rush of emotion for a city that had been his. But he dismissed it: his future was in the West.

At Indian Duke's for a late supper he ordered Champagne. It was that kind of night. They listened eagerly as he laid out the immense success of his western exploration, New Orleans in his hand, Tennessee and Kentucky enthusiastic, Wilkinson cautious but solid, his new friend whose island in the Ohio would make a perfect rendezvous point.

He didn't mention the long, steady look that Margaret Blennerhassett had given him when he paused to anchor that relationship, and he certainly didn't mention Danny Mobry. God, *she* was a woman to stir a man to his core. It still bothered him that she'd hurried away. He had routed himself through Washington and had sent a note but it appeared that again she was away somewhere; someone named Johnson had answered for her.

But he had really stopped there to see Ambassador Merry, who was enthusiastic but was not yet authorized to advance him real money. No response on his request for frigates standing off the mouth of the Mississippi but it was perfectly obvious that Britain would never pass up the opportunity to regain a dominant position on the North American continent. He remembered Merry observing in his dull way that doubtless Burr would go ahead on his own. But men at this level did not talk carelessly. What had Merry really meant? Then it all came clear—the British wouldn't commit until something real happened. When Burr had New Orleans in his hand and Mexico's gold in his sights, he'd find Royal Navy frigates standing offshore with their guns run out. What he was offering was just too good to pass up.

He had made another visit, too, that he now regretted. He had called on Mr. Jefferson at the President's House and been received with a grave courtesy that now made him writhe. It had been a profound mistake, a moment of weakness.

Mr. Jefferson had said in passing there would be no war with Spain; the U.S. had decided not to press its claim on Mobile Bay and nothing else was at contention. That did amuse Burr; it simply meant that General Wilkinson's machinations had not yet taken effect. He would soldier on, as he always had done. And he'd been successful, too, in a life that had brought him honors galore and a plan that would put him on a level with Napoleon Bonaparte!

Look how well he'd survived the blow of his parents dying when he was only six, plague him as the pain of that loss might. But even as a child he had been a man. He would never forget the surge of confidence and, yes, pride, he'd felt at the age of ten prowling the New York waterfront and talking himself into a berth as cabin boy on a brig bound for Liverpool. Never mind that his stiff-necked uncle had snatched him off before they sailed, he still liked to review those accomplishments of his boy-self, the man prefigured. Rammed his way right into the college at Princeton that his father had started . . . oh, yes, he took care of himself, liked himself, admired himself. He was happy, that's why women warmed to him. He made them feel good, and more, he generated that little frisson that was full of promise of something more, something mysterious and perhaps thrilling.

Thus the sun was shining—New Orleans set, things solid from Pittsburgh to the Gulf, everyone on board, no one told more than he needed to know. His three friends, devoted acolytes, really, put down their dinner with scarcely a word, listening entranced. When a waiter cleared their plates they switched to grog and sat

hunched forward, grasping pewter tankards, voices cast
low, intensely aware when others came near.

First, the money, real money. Raising it was Burr's
role and he felt a nervous quiver in his stomach. Still, he
knew where to find it and how to pry it loose; it would be
all right. Then supplies in volume, barrels of beef and
pork and flour, weapons, ammunition, boatloads packed
in solid vessels, canvas covers lashed tight against prying
eyes.

"All that gear, how many men do you plan on,
Aaron?" Matt Davis whispered, his glance around a bit
too furtive.

"Say a thousand."

"Jesus Christ!" Matt cried and several men looked
around.

"Shut up, Matt," Burr said, voice tight. "How did you
think we were going to take over Louisiana and invade
Mexico—with a little campfire group?"

"But where we going to get 'em?"

"Recruit them—give them a shot at the greatest adventure of their lives." He needed a recruiter, someone
who wouldn't ask a lot of questions, who could talk to
men and make them see the glory lying ahead, then handle them once they signed on and get them down the
river in small groups to avoid attention. He had plenty
for the three of them to do here; he needed someone who
could go all the way to Mexico City.

"Comfort Tyler," Peter and Matt said together.

Burr smiled. "Just whom I had in mind."

"How much money we talking about, Aaron?"

Burr studied the two. William Smith and Samuel Ogden, factors, shippers, entrepreneurs, finaglers, arrangers,
political dabblers, moneymen. Smith was tall, cadaverous, pale, a scrim of beard dark on sunken cheeks. His

partner was a near opposite, broad, fleshy but strong bodied, hair gone gray. Ogden looked like a bulldog suspecting that you had designs on his bone. They were veterans in international intrigue. He knew they'd put money behind Miranda in Venezuela and the talk was they'd supported Nolan's plans for his filibuster in Texas before the Spanish snuffed him out.

He was in their new office on Wall Street, one of the buildings just gone up, five full stories with a hand-powered elevator, a tower that gave them a panoramic view of the harbor, everything from the East River around to the Hudson, watching ships come and go hauling their money in one form or another. The building was a block or so from his old office and walking here he'd had a fit of nostalgia. Life was simpler in the old days, he a king of politics, a lawyer of superb skills, a man about town. Until it was all swept away—but forget that. The wheel turns, life changes, the wise man changes with it—and what magnificent prospects he had now!

He elaborated on these in detail, the wonderful vastness of the West with its countless square miles of rich virgin land untouched by ax or saw. He went on to New Orleans throbbing with fury and discontent, swept them into visions of the streams of gold pouring from the mountains of Mexico. He waxed downright lyrical, surprised even himself, as he sang of the power New Orleans's position, at the mouth of the river that drained the continent, gave it in determining the future of the West.

And he considered Ogden's question. A clerk's wage might be three hundred dollars a year and found.

"A hundred thousand dollars," he said, and smiled.

"Jesus! That's ridiculous," Ogden snapped.

Burr stood immediately. He slapped his gloves into his left hand and took up his hat. "Thank you, gentlemen. I won't trouble you further—"

"Wait now, Aaron, for Christ's sake, don't be so

damned quick, flying off the handle like that. I mean, we ain't—" Ogden's mouth worked, ready to drop the bone. "But it's a hellacious lot of money."

Burr smiled. "Please," he said, "don't strain my patience." Of course they couldn't handle it alone, but he knew they would factor most of it off to wealthier men; that's what made his offer so sweet. And they were good front men—they took risks and danced with the law. He threw the gloves in his hat, dropped it on Ogden's desk, and said, "I may need a hundred more when the first is done. So stop bucking and snorting and form a syndicate. But I'll be gone—I want you as my contact men."

A syndicate, sell thousand-dollar shares, maybe a few five-hundred shares. He could see it growing in their minds.

"All that gold, it's real, eh?" Ogden said. Sweat stood on his pendulous face.

"The Spanish have financed three hundred years of empire on that gold, there and South America and the Philippines."

"So why will they give it up now?"

"They won't give it—I'll take it. Look, that whole region is on the edge of revolution, Spanish empire fading away. We march into Mexico City, the people will welcome us."

"So what kind of return can we promise?"

"Hundred to one. Thousand to one. Who knows? For a thousand-dollar share you can be part of *the* great adventure of modern times. Gold to make Croesus pant with envy."

"That's all well and good," Smith said, dark jaw thrust out, "but this taking New Orleans, you think that'll work?"

Burr laid out the rage that seemed to affect the whole city, the downright hatred for the new masters imposed without a word of warning, denying them all rights. . . .

"But the army," Ogden said, "won't the army—"

"I don't think the army will trouble us."

"But why the hell not?"

Burr smiled. He sat there smiling into silence that stretched and strained toward a breaking point.

"You're saying . . ." Ogden breathed.

"I'm not saying."

Smith cleared his throat. "I always said Wilkinson is a damned slippery customer."

"I can tell you I trust Jim Wilkinson explicitly," Burr said. He waited, letting his meaning blossom in their minds. They were coming along, he could see it in their faces.

"But Aaron," Smith said, "can you just go downriver with a bunch of armed men—I mean, won't it be conspicuous?"

"Going down," Burr said, "traveling in small groups, they'll just be settlers. There's always a stream of settlers heading west, they'll fit right in."

He set out his plan. His vast tract up the Red River a couple hundred miles north of New Orleans would be the perfect cover. They talked for an hour, feeling things out, tasting possibilities.

He saw Ogden's furtive glance at Smith, the trace of a smile. "I suppose we can try to sell it," Ogden said.

"Try?" Burr started to rise. "Perhaps I've misjudged. I thought I was dealing with men who knew politics and find myself among *naïfs*."

"I don't care for such talk," Smith snapped.

"Oh, don't you?" Burr's voice rose, anger carefully sifted in. "Well, listen whether you like it or not. I'll be seeing Woody Woodson on this too, and don't tell me you weren't part of his group and didn't know exactly what he was doing and saying and what he wanted from me and why he wanted it. *You* came to me when I ran for governor, represented New York Federalists whom you know damned well includes ninety-five percent of the moneymen in this city, you threw Federalist weight behind me, and but for——"

"Yes, Alex running a whole campaign against you. I didn't hold with you killing him, but he didn't have any call——"

Burr waved his hand. "Water under the bridge. Point is, why were you supporting me?"

"Why, because, because——"

"Say it, goddamn you!"

Ogden's voice was a whisper. "Some of 'em—wasn't me, understand, some of 'em was looking to split——"

"Secede, you mean. Secession. Use the word. Split off New England and take New York with it. Wrap up the North in a tight little country, manufacturing, world trade, strong shipping, tuck yourself under Britain's wing. Senator Pickering and Senator Plumer, the New Hampshire twins, Roger Griswold of Connecticut and his fellow hurler of penny rockets from the nutmeg state, that great Federalist master of bombast, Senator Hillhouse——"

"Jesus, Aaron," Ogden said with a nervous glance at the door, "it don't pay to throw names around——"

"That's why they supported me then, it's why they'll support me now."

"'Cause you can split off the West?"

"Like halving an apple. Then I don't suppose you and Senator P would find it so hard to cut your half again, eh?"

Ogden and Smith looked at each other and their smiles grew and Ogden stood to shake Burr's hand. They talked arrangements, drafts and bills and structure and money handling, but there was no more resistance. Finally Burr shook hands again and went walking down Wall Street— away from his old office, no reason to stir up memories—feeling good. The lure of profits ran hot and heavy in Federalists but there was no lure like power. The Louisiana Purchase had terrified them, they saw vast new territory coming in, all Democratic, saw their last power base in New England and New York certain to erode, leaving them with nothing. But a new country, New England and New York combined, small, compact, rich, would restore that unparalleled elixir, power. It was men who would profit from that happy state who would clamor to join the syndicate.

Comfort Tyler was a big rawboned man from up on the Mohawk with black hair that fell over one eye, looked as if he had some Indian in him, a hearty fellow with an air of confident command that was belied by the tendency of his glance to slide aside when faced with any pressure not physical. He would make a fine foreman, you could trust him to take orders and carry them out, he could make lesser men leap to obey him, and he was loyal. He'd been a man of some consequence at home until he made the only business decision of his life, which almost immediately bankrupted him. Burr, who'd known him in the New York Assembly, saved him from debtor's prison, which was no more than he'd done for various writers and artists, the difference being that Comfort remembered and they didn't.

Of course Comfort was thrilled to be included in the great adventure, more because it testified to Burr's faith in him than for the gain he might himself expect. All the way to New Orleans, and on to the Valley of Mexico! Who could have imagined it back on the Mohawk, who could have dreamed that knowing Aaron Burr in the assembly would lead to such splendor? Certainly he could recruit for it.

Burr gave careful instructions. First off, everything must be quiet—*very* quiet. Undue attention so early could be . . . ah, damaging. In fact, it could put the gallows in their faces, but there was no point in alarming Comfort. Keep it quiet and indirect. He was recruiting for the Bastrop lands a skip and a jump up the Red River from the Mississippi, every man to get a rifle and tools and a hundred fifty acres guaranteed, twenty-dollar gold piece on signing up. But that was just the rendezvous, the starting place. Here Comfort's voice would drop, he'd order another round and wait till the bartender moved away, and then he'd hint more than he could really tell, but listen to me now. . . .

Sure, the Bastrop lands were just the preamble to the real thing, letting them in on the secret so slowly they couldn't say how much they'd been told and how much they'd read into hints that just the same made it clear that this was an adventure that would flat knock the socks off the folks back home, walking palm-lined streets with pockets full of gold and on each arm a gorgeous señorita with breasts like musk melons, see what cousin Johnny thought about that when he heard!

Comfort Tyler was just the man to put that across. Burr listened to him a couple of times, sitting anonymously down the bar, Comfort with his big paw curled around a whiskey glass, his conspiratorial voice drawing them deeper into mystery and adventure. He was good, better than Burr with young men of no particular culture or attainment.

Next, the equipment—rifles and pistols, powder and lead, molds to cast balls, knives, pots and pans, blankets, haversacks, canvas shirts and denim britches. Comfort must start lining up gunsmiths, look for up to a dozen pieces from each. It was an unusual gunsmith who turned out more than sixty to a hundred pieces a year so he must work way up the Hudson and the Mohawk, one little shop after another. Burr would put forty thousand dollars to his order and he could pay as he went along.

Tears welled in Comfort's eyes.

"What?" Burr said.

"That much? You'd trust me so?" He wiped his eyes. His voice was thick. "God, Mr. Burr, I won't never let you down. Trusting me like that, it means so much."

Woody Woodson sought Burr out. Sent a note—could they dine in a private room at the Rusty Nail? Burr had been waiting for this.

"Why didn't you come to me first?" Woody asked the moment a waiter had set a plate of turtle soup before them with a tankard of porter and cleared the room. "I thought we were friends—"

"I wanted you to hear about it, Woody—think about it and work out the knots. I knew you'd want to do that before we talked, you're too smart to be precipitous."

That was good. By implication Smith and Ogden were not so smart, so capable. Yes, Woody agreed that he was a very solid man. Burr watched him adopt a sage expression. "Well," he said, "tell me about it," and then listened with shining eyes. Licking his lips and ignoring the food, he forgot the sage look and lapsed back into himself. "What do you want, Aaron?" he whispered at last; Burr judged him hooked and ready.

"Smith and Ogden are good men but they run with a different crowd. I want you to gather your people together for an opportunity that—"

"How much, Aaron?"

"A hundred thousand."

"Dollars?"

"Dollars."

Woody smiled. "I like a man who thinks big," he said. "We can do a lot of business together, my friend."

Simmons McAlester hailed him on Broadway. Burr turned and watched him approach with that rolling stride he affected as a ship owner, though he never went to sea. Sim seized his hand and then enveloped him in a hug that Burr found immensely distasteful. It set the drape of his coat askew and twisted his cravat. He put himself aright with an irritated shrug.

"Aaron, what a great friend you are," Sim said. "Sam Ogden said you absolutely insisted I be included in the syndicate. I asked him, you see—he's used to dealing with much bigger men than me, I can tell you that, and he said it was all your doing. I take that right warmly, my friend—thank you!"

"Why, Sim—that's what friends are for."

Great enterprises are not put together in a week or a month. Spring stretched into summer, summer toward fall. Burr had comfortable rooms on Broadway not far from the battery. Mr. Astor, the vulgar huckster who had bought Richmond Hill, was already erecting small houses on small lots and doubtless making another fortune to go with his fur millions. New York was changing, growing steadily up the island. Why, the gap between old New York and the village of Greenwich narrowed every day and soon they would be one. He sought out few of his old friends, but when he saw men on the street they treated him with the respect a man involved in important if mysterious affairs merited. He dined in fine restaurants with small groups of men assembled by Smith and Ogden or by Woody, whom he admired more day by day for his fluidity of manner. He gave each set of dinner guests the cover story of the Bastrop lands, and the volatility of the West, the tenuousness of the Spanish connection, the plain fact that Texas and Florida were wide open, the molten stream of gold flowing from Mexico's mountains. He gave them Spain in thrall to Napoleon, ever weaker, its empire collapsing, rich pickings for men with nerve and skill.

He signed no contracts, made no guarantees, offered no assurances or promises. He was going to do great things and they knew him as a man of action, of grace, of character, familiar with power and skilled in the main chance. This was bigger than anything he had ever done; did they want to step aboard?

Sign up, sign on, anchor yourself to a glowing future!

"Well, I may put up the money but I don't know as I want my name connected." This from a rawboned specimen who'd been a hide merchant and now owned taverns and was no better than he need be.

"Save your name, sir!" Burr said. "Woody, strike Mr. Pettibone's name from the list."

"Well, wait—"

"No, I don't want those with doubts. Doubts undermine a great enterprise. Now, I am a private person and have neither reason to nor intention of making public the names of those who join me in a golden venture. No need to, you see. Perhaps it's not too blunt to say that comparing the names of Pettibone and Burr, the latter hardly needs the former to establish position!"

A burst of laughter settled that. Of course he must have the names and details on everyone who joined him: how else could he distribute the spoils?

General Presley Neville gave Burr a dinner in a handsome house on Fulton Street. Colonel Thomas Butler, still on active duty with the army, showed up with his son, Tom Jr. Pres's son, Morgan Neville, joined them. The dinner was good, the wine poured liberally, and Burr waxed eloquent. He knew that Butler hated Wilkinson, so he made little of that connection. The older men, at least, were ardent Federalists who considered the West seriously destabilizing to the country, but he still was careful to skirt direct discussion of separation. There are things that don't disturb if they are well presented but that can't just be slapped down on the table. So he stressed seizing Mexico and its wealth and punishing Spain. Perhaps the idea of separation was implicit, but he didn't say so.

A few days later Burr found the two young men waiting at his hotel. He led them into the taproom for brandy and a cigar. Morgan Neville presented a letter from his father saying that Morgan and Tom Jr. thought they would never see another such chance for adventure and were eager to join the expedition.

"What can we do to help, sir?" Tom Jr. asked. Bright as a button, all right. Burr told them to gather another half dozen choice spirits such as themselves and lay hands on a boat in Pittsburgh. Morgan said his father would have a handsome keelboat made for them. With Burr's permission, they would send the order to the Pittsburgh builder without delay. Burr smiled and drew on his cigar; things were going well indeed.

That summer of 1806 young men all along the Mohawk Valley were bestirring themselves, rolling blanket and clothes in a pack and heading south. Boys were always going West—everyone knew that's where adventure and opportunity lay—but this year some were heading down the Allegheny to pick up the Ohio beyond the mountains and continue down to a particular island where Comfort Tyler would be awaiting them.

The news came like a confirmation, even a benediction. It proved Burr's case. War with Spain was becoming certain, not because the U.S. coveted Florida and Texas but because Spain was pushing from the West. Apparently the Mobile Act so alarmed them or the purchase so angered them that they wanted to fight. Such careless and indeed pointless folly surprised everyone. Only Burr stood reassured, recognizing the fine hand of General Wilkinson at work.

The U.S. said Louisiana's western border was the Rio Grande, meaning Texas was included, but it didn't press the issue. It seemed willing to accept the Sabine River out in the swamps of west Louisiana as de facto border. But a new Spanish army in Texas already had crossed the Sabine and pushed into central Louisiana. Orders went to Wilkinson to push them back over the Sabine and keep them there. Hence war; there's no other way to push armies.

And the world would look indulgently on an adventure against Mexico, and the United States would applaud anything that helped. Everyone would cheer Burr on. He glowed with optimism.

"Colonel Burr," Sammy Swartwout said, nearly beside himself with enthusiasm, "this here is Dr. Bollman, him who risked his life at Olmutz trying to save Lafayette."

The gentleman, midsized, fifty or so, a fine curling mustache turning a bit gray, clicked his heels and bowed. "Justus Erich Bollman, medical doctor, at your service, Colonel Burr. May I say that meeting you is an honor—"

"Medical doctor and adventurer," Sammy said. "We had dinner, he's been telling me, he—"

Smiling at his young friend's enthusiasm, a man of the world seeing in Burr another man of the world, Bollman held up a hand to stop Sammy's gush. Burr saw that the doctor was confident that his name was known, as indeed it was. The great Lafayette had been caught in the grip of the French Revolution when it turned on the nobility, though he had supported its original democratic aims. Only General Washington's intercession had saved him from the guillotine. He was imprisoned at Olmutz in Austria, where Bollman took it upon himself to organize a rescue that inexplicably went wrong at the last moment. This made him a wanted man in France and a hero everywhere else.

A German national, his English was good, his French flawless. That and his long residence in France meant he would fit readily in New Orleans. That he was a skilled medical doctor recommended him to a great adventure involving troops, as Burr now saw his young men. That he was as much soldier of fortune as doctor recommended him further. Altogether, he was a find. In the end, Burr commissioned him and sent him by sea to New Orleans with orders to dig in, acquaint himself, connect with the right people, and stand by.

The spirit of adventure seized Samuel Ogden, who told Burr he wanted to join the action and felt entitled. William Smith said his old friend Sam was mad as a hatter. But justice was justice; Ogden had earned the right, and Burr dispatched him to New Orleans with Dr. Bollman, figuring his talents would be useful there and his flabby physique would not be a detriment. When he finished explaining the nature of life in an open boat on a boiling river far beyond the nearest town and tavern, Ogden was more than happy to take ship for a civilized city.

Burr sent John Wilkins in Pittsburgh an order for twenty thousand pounds of flour and five thousand pounds of pork to be consigned to D. W. Eliot of Natchez and held there. He enclosed a draft on Sam Ogden. Another draft on Ogden settled the balance of the five-thousand-dollar initial payment on the Bastrop lands. A draft on Blennerhassett paid for an order of open boats to be built in Pittsburgh and held ready for the troops.

He wanted Sammy in New Orleans with Bollman but first Sammy must go downriver in advance with a letter for Wilkinson wrapped in oilskin, sealed with wax, and sewed into the inner lining of his coat. The air of mystery thrilled Sammy and he set out in high good humor. Burr spent a long time on that letter. He reported high success on all counts. Recruiting was going well, young men eager to participate with their persons, older men with their money. Gunsmiths were turning out weapons with unusual bayonet mounts added to rifles that more commonly were used for game. Powder in lead casks and bar lead for balls were in good supply. Boats were being prepared up and down the river. His troops were ready to move and soon he would start his own trek downriver.

Meanwhile, he wasn't hearing much from Wilkinson and time was growing short. He sought an immediate piece of advice: should he seize the Spanish garrison at Baton Rouge above New Orleans before he went on to seize the prize city or should he bypass the Spanish? More important, when he reached New Orleans how soon could he expect to hear from Wilkinson and the army?

It really was a demand letter, he realized as he reviewed it. It was saying plainly that it was too late to stop now, the whole affair was moving, and he wanted to hear from Wilkinson.

And then a letter came from the errant general. It was much too soon to be in answer to his missive and he tore it open eagerly. It proved to be in cipher, which would take a night's work to translate, but he saw immediately that across the bottom Wilkinson had scrawled in plain English, "I am ready!" and that was what Burr really needed to know.

★　　★　　★　　★　　★

TWENTY-TWO

Day by day it became more evident to Madison that Aaron Burr was up to something. But what that something might be was much less clear. Wildly contradictory reports arrived in fragments, hints, oddities, a loose word here or there. Someone named Comfort Tyler was recruiting men up the Mohawk and hinting at conquering Mexico and filling their pockets with gold. This from a major landowner in the Mohawk country who was himself a powerful Federalist. A gunsmith was too busy to make a fowling piece; so was the next and the next. Why so busy? None would say. Mystery and suspense were in the air.

All of it circulated around Burr. To Madison he seemed a man in anguish, ruined by his own hand, digging toward some ultimate disgrace. Yet he was a man of talent, and underestimating him was a fool's game. So was too much thinking in terms of tragedy and sorrow— the man had been willing once to split the nation for his own narrow interests—why not again? To this day Federalists insisted that Burr's strike for self-glory showed that democracy must break into anarchy.

This was uniquely Madison's fight. His was the only cabinet office not bound to a specific area like war or treasury. Madison devoted most of more his time to domestic affairs. But more importantly, it was his connection with Aaron over so many years in so many ways that made it a personal matter. For a vivid moment he saw himself as gladiator in a cobbled courtyard, man to man, sword to sword. He smiled at the solipsism, but the image didn't really fade. As never before he stood alone for great national stakes. Not even Dolley, intertwined as she was with his conflicted feeling about Aaron Burr, could really help. He was alone.

Reports poured in. A couple of merchant-traders in New York City named Ogden and Smith were raising huge sums in Burr's name. For what? It seemed that he had extraordinary possibilities in the West but no one knew what they were. Hints, nudges, hesitations, sudden silence when certain men were encountered—something was up, all right. But what? A friend in Pittsburgh wrote that he was hearing rumors far beyond the usual. Light boats being built, groups of quiet young men passing through, surprise orders for expeditionlike supplies shipped downriver. Gideon Granger, postmaster general, had collected and correlated a good many of these stories; you couldn't doubt something serious was afoot.

The *Aurora* in Philadelphia published new questions and reports and guesses and hazards almost daily and newspapers around the country reprinted its material. Dr. Bollman, welcome for his attempted aid to Lafayette, had connected with Burr and was hinting of great events to come downriver. Suddenly he vanished, shipped for New Orleans, so it was said.

Rumors from the West piled high, all suspicious, none conclusive. Joseph Hamilton Daviess, United States Attorney for the Kentucky district, wrote: "We have traitors among us. A separation of the Union in favor of Spain is the object finally." The plot, he said, was to subvert the city of New Orleans and launch an attack on Mexico and alienate the western states into a new empire. Said he had many reports of widely spread conspiracy and was looking toward indictments.

But there was a story on Mr. Daviess. An ardent Federalist, he saw conspiracy wherever he looked. He was a brother-in-law of Chief Justice John Marshall, the most ardent of Federalist. Now, that wasn't exactly his fault but it did tell you where his political sympathies probably lay. After all, when Aaron was contesting for the presidency, when Federalists dreamed of naming a caretaker leader to keep the government from the Democrats, they had had John Marshall with his rough-hewn manner and his big square jaw in mind for the role. Not Daviess's fault, granted, but you did want to take him with a grain of salt.

Kentucky Democrats who were vastly in the majority, had expected the new administration to tie a can to Mr. Daviess's tail. But as Madison had not dropped his own chief clerk for errant political views, so too the otherwise honest and capable Mr. Daviess was left in place. But ever since, as their old friend Senator Brown complained, Daviess had been scratching around for reasons to put Democrats in jail.

His latest move sounded unfortunately like all the rest. "He says 'a massive conspiracy,' so ask him for names," Tom said. Sure enough, back came the list in record time of barely six weeks and who should be at its head but good old John Brown and John Smith, the senator from Ohio, and Jack Adair, the Kentucky cockerel. For good measure Daviess announced that Burr was involved and that it long had been known that Wilkinson was in the pay of Spain and was not to be trusted. Democrats all, the cream of the party in the West. That pretty well told you what value to put on Mr. Daviess.

But that drumbeat of reports continued. . . .

But could this Comfort Tyler really raise an army along the Mohawk? Could New York Federalists fund an army? Burr was an opportunist intoxicated with the moment but he was not a fool. He dreamed, but was not merely a dreamer. There had to be something more.

The blazing insight that that something involved Wilkinson and the army deepened steadily when no word came from the general on the far frontier. With the papers talking plot you'd think the general would hasten to report the talk and refute it or say he was investigating. But not a word. Each week of silence deepened further Madison's conviction that Wilkinson was involved.

Burr and Wilkinson were close. Probably they were much alike, oriented to the mysterious and elliptical, and to the main chance. Wilkinson had supplied Burr with War Department maps of the West but Burr was rumored to be involved in rampant western land speculation and the maps might be for no more than that. Except somehow that didn't sound right.

But how vulnerable was the military? That the army as a whole might condone treason was ludicrous; that its commander could do so was quite possible. Known already as dictatorial and secretive, operating on a volatile frontier two to three months away from the capital in communication time, yes, he could order an invasion of Mexico. Who would question him? Doubtless his officers were more loyal to their country than to him, but they'd have no basis to challenge orders that he said came from Washington. And obedience is necessarily ingrained in the military man.

And now, quite inexplicably unless there was something mysterious about that, too, Spanish troops were moving into Texas and apparently intended to cross the border into Orleans Territory that was marked by the Sabine River. At the last cabinet meeting they had agreed that Wilkinson would have to be told to advance and meet the enemy before long. And yet, it made no real sense. While we insisted that Florida and Texas were ours by the purchase, we had made it very clear we were willing to wait for the westward tide of American settlers to determine the final story. But now, if Spanish troops actually crossed the Sabine it would precipitate war for which there was no reason on either side. It was strange. There was so much about all this that was strange.

Madison as gladiator saving the nation with sword in hand was all very well, but in fact the situation was delicate. His gut said that something big and menacing was stirring on that far frontier, but what did he really know? The most immediate danger was that a public accusation of conspiracy would certainly drive whatever there was underground. If Burr were guilty, if Wilkinson were involved, a flood of denials and angry remonstrances would cover their hasty withdrawal into their holes. The administration would seem flighty and alarmist and perhaps vindictive, the conspirators would emerge as innocent victims, and the plot would fester in secret, merely delayed. No—they needed some proof to emerge, so they must wait.

Yet more and more he suspected the plot turned less on Burr than on Wilkinson. So who was this man who commanded the army on which the nation relied for its safety?

Jaycee Barlow, who had served under him and had fifteen years in the army, said Wilkinson was a political general and was hated by the rank and file. Political?

Madison walked across the grassy expanse before the President's House where the department mare cropped her neat circle, went into the little brick building housing the war and navy departments and put his head in Henry Dearborn's door. The secretary was eating a doughnut and he held up the plate in invitation. Madison couldn't resist. Dearborn called for more tea and considered the question.

Well, Wilkinson had served as a staff officer in the Revolution, which was pretty political. He'd married Ann Biddle of the Philadelphia Biddles, and of course they carried a lot of weight. It seemed his wife had loved him dearly—no one could see exactly why, but there you are—and he'd been faithful to her until her death not so long ago. It was somewhat in her memory that the Biddles put their weight behind him now.

But then, Henry said, the man had a talent for making friends in the right places. It was surprising how many senators and congressmen he could call by their first names. Dearborn added that he considered Wilkinson a friend.

"I know he grates on a lot of soldiers, but really, what you want in a peacetime commander is a good administrator." Having finished the doughnut he pushed the plate again toward his guest. Madison shook his head; his first two bites lay on his stomach like shot. Dearborn took another and sighed, exuding a contentment that Madison envied.

"Now, in war," he said, "you want a combat figure. Like Wayne, you know, old Mad Anthony, God, when he called the charge it seemed like he was charmed, run through lead storms. Takes guts, private soldier or general officer, you jump up there and the whole enemy line opens and you know damned well every piece is set on you, every ball is whistling at you." He sighed, shaking his head. "That's not Wilkinson's dish, granted, but we're not facing those times now."

You know . . . but of course, Madison didn't know. At this description, which so epitomized the war that Madison had not attended, he fell silent. Too sick, too delicate, he'd have held back the troops, not his fault, anyone could see that, but still, every time there was talk of war it flashed into his mind. And Dearborn went on, not even aware of Madison's momentary discomfort, or maybe too polite to comment.

"You remember when I took this post it was six months or so before I could clean things up in Boston and get down here," Dearborn said, "and during that time Wilkinson ran the department and did it well. Turned it over to me in apple-pie order. So, yes, the men dislike him and he has unpleasant idiosyncrasies—those damned uniforms he designs!—but overall—"

"I suppose you could order him to wear regular—"

An odd expression flashed over the other's face. "If I'm going to challenge Wilkinson it'll be over something that matters. He's mean as a snake when you cross him, Jimmy. Starts bleating that he's been accused of high crimes, demands a court-martial, rallies political weight, carries on like a madman. You tackle Wilkinson, you better be ready for a fight."

Back in the comfort of his own office, digesting what Henry had said even as his stomach refused to digest the doughnut, he called in Barlow. Why did the rank and file dislike Wilkinson? His new clerk hesitated, then said because the general was pompous, arrogant, cruel. He demanded instant obedience to arbitrary orders and made heavy use of the stocks. Sometimes he had men lined up waiting their turn at pain and humiliation. He was given to having men bucked and gagged.

At Madison's puzzled expression Barlow said in surprise, "You haven't heard of that?" which was enough to bring up the old sensitivity again. Perhaps his face reflected discomfort, for Barlow added hastily, "Sit a man on the ground, slip a pole under his knees, tie his arms together around his knees and under the pole and gag him so you don't have to listen to him cry. You'd be surprised by how quick he goes to moaning."

And, Barlow added, the general was a coward.

That was important, but when he probed the answer was disappointing. Had Barlow been in combat with Wilkinson? Just at Fallen Timbers, the battle in which General Wayne subdued the Indians in upper Indiana. Barlow had been a young aide to Wayne at the time and, yes, he'd have known if there real ground for cowardice charges. Still, in a hundred small ways Wilkinson exhibited the attitudes of a coward, Barlow said, and the view was widely held in the army.

And then there was the injustice toward General Wayne. Had Madison known the General? Not personally; everyone knew him by reputation, Mad Anthony Wayne whose wild saber charges frightened his own men, let alone the enemy. Dearborn's description flashed to mind. A soldier's soldier, Barlow said, rough handed when necessary but never arbitrary and never using his power to humiliate and hurt men in his command, let alone seem to enjoy it.

"Tell me about Wayne," Madison said.

"Well, St. Clair had lost a couple of all-out battles up in the Wabash country and the Indians—they had British backing, you know, paid them, armed them, bought the booty they took off the settlers they killed—the Indians were running wild. The army had been pushed back, this was in '92 or maybe '93 and the men were . . . well, it's not too much to say they were demoralized. Needed to be whipped back into shape—morale issue, you see, nothing wrong with the men or their equipment. So,

General St. Clair, they get rid of him and bring in Wayne to restore the men's faith in themselves and go recover lost ground.

"Naturally in such circumstances the troops had taken on bad habits, and their officers worse. Thing is, a man can't really take on a bad habit if his officer is up to snuff. So Wayne had plenty of rooting out to do, mostly officers and some sergeants, and of course he made plenty of enemies as he went along. Then Wilkinson turned up—wangled himself a colonelcy and was named second in command. Nobody asked Wayne, I can tell you—it was purely politics. Wilkinson wanted to destroy Wayne right from the start. Didn't know anything else, you see. Like a snake, you walk too close and he's going to strike, nothing against you, that's just the way he is. So he goes to work gathering in these malcontents and fashioning a case against Wayne. You know, dereliction of duty, abuse of troops—the idea was to depose Wayne in favor of Wilkinson. But then Wayne took ill and died—broke a lot of our hearts, I can tell you—he was just fifty-one—and then, God, you talk about irony, here comes Wilkinson, his deadliest enemy, stepping into his shoes."

Suddenly Barlow's face lit up. "Here's one for you. Meriwether Lewis, the same one who—"

"Of course, the expedition—"

"Well, he was a rough young fellow in those days—I haven't seen him in years—but anyway, he was drinking one night and got in a quarrel with another officer and slapped him around pretty hard. Everyone figured the other would challenge but instead he filed charges. Conduct unbecoming, et cetera, et cetera. So Wayne had to convene a court-martial, madder than a wet hen, not at Merry but at the other officer. Waste of time, he kept saying, why the hell didn't the man just challenge, settle it with pistols like a gentleman?

"So the court found Lewis not guilty and Wayne sent him off to a honey of an assignment, the rifle company, and that's where he met William Clark, who was commanding. But you can see that this other officer would have no great love for Wayne, and might welcome Wilkinson's plotting."

Well, Madison could see why real soldiers would hold a faux general in contempt, but that didn't prove much. Treacherous he certainly was, but treasonous as well? The evidence was inconclusive. He had been a trader before he returned to the army and had connected with the Spanish in New Orleans. He continued trading after reentering the army, which was legal enough. Nobody thought he was successful but he always had a supply of gold. Was he on the Spanish payroll? Everyone suspected, but Barlow added that he certainly didn't know.

Once a strong rumor arose that a keelboat bringing a few casks of sugar north for sale carried gold for Wilkinson. General Wayne sent a detail to search the keelboat. Barlow knew the officer heading the detail, who told him they had opened everything but the sugar casks and had found nothing. Later they heard the gold was hidden in the sugar casks. . . .

So Wilkinson was a nasty man. Beyond that, little was proven. But maybe it didn't really matter. Maybe when great issues were afloat you would never be sure and must take your position and strike your blow on instinct, and if you were wrong and failed, face that, too. There never would be easy answers.

"Johnny," Madison said to John Graham, "what do you make of all this? Daviess's report, this Comfort Tyler person on the Mohawk and then going downriver, all this talk about Burr with no one seeming to know anything real?"

He trusted Johnny Graham for his experience and good sense as well as his origins and frequent visits to the West. He came from Mayfield, Kentucky, on the Ohio River, and his parents were still there. He had returned from a tour in the U.S. embassy in Madrid looking younger than he probably was even then. He was Scotch-Irish in origin, or so Madison assumed from his looks; he had a shock of tawny hair and a high pink complexion so he always looked as if he'd been running somewhere, and often enough that was just what he had been doing, for he was energy personified.

Six years in Madison's office had matured him substantially; now that Mr. Wagner was talking of leaving, Madison had Johnny in mind for chief clerk. Marriage to a very pretty young woman named Faith Cunningham had steadied him, and the arrival of their first child had matured him further. The baby was a girl, who giggled and drooled through a huge smile when Madison picked her up, quite winning his heart. Now Faith was well along on their second child. The doctors thought it had come a little too soon after the first and it didn't seem so easy this time.

"I think there's something to all the talk," Johnny said.

"Think Daviess is right?"

"I don't know about that—I'd hate to think our strongest supporters in the West are conspirators." He paused, his features at rest, which increased his appearance of strength. "Still, I don't know."

"Wouldn't surprise you unduly?"

"Not unduly, no . . ." He smiled. "They're different folks out there, you know, different from Virginians. They were Virginians until a few years ago when the mother state turned loose her west end and Kentucky was born. But they always were different."

"That's why they left Virginia in the first place, eh?"

Johnny laughed. "That's about it."

Madison filled his clay pipe and passed the tobacco jar over to Johnny. He cocked back in his chair and put his feet on the corner of his desk, pulling up sagging hose as he did so. The pewter buckle on one shoe had torn loose the week before and he had refastened it with string. Now it was coming loose again.

"All right," Madison said. "Something is going on, we're agreed. Suppose Daviess is more or less right in outline—Burr puts together a little army and comes downriver. Plans to seize New Orleans, maybe go on to Mexico. Would westerners, those along the river, say, welcome him?"

"If he told them his real aim was Florida and Texas they'd crown him with roses. Anyway, the army would be ready to break up anything more, wouldn't it?"

"All this talk, but I've heard nothing from the army."

Comprehension flashed over Johnny's face. "My," he said softly. "If the army—well, it would have to be Wilkinson. The army would never turn."

"That's my assumption. So suppose Wilkinson—well, suppose the whole thing, Wilkinson turns, they seize New Orleans, they go on to Mexico, which—well, I don't know how easy—"

"Easy, if they get that far. Everyone in the West knows the Spanish empire is dying."

"Well, if all this happened, New Orleans in conspirator's hands, Mexico subdued and its gold mines pouring forth, they would have to have the West, wouldn't they, to make it all viable?"

Johnny nodded and Madison cast the dice. "Could they have it? Could the people there be turned?" There was a long silence. Please God, Madison thought, let him say no, not a chance, they're utterly loyal—

"Yes," Johnny said, "they could be turned, if it were handled right."

The words were such a blow that Madison knew his expression had betrayed his feelings.

Johnny gazed at him. "It's what we were saying," he said at last. "The people there are different. They've up-rooted themselves from settled lives in the East—maybe not prosperous or anything, but settled. So your west-erner, he's up and moved, looking for something—ad-venture, gold, thievery sometimes, but something. So the idea of change doesn't shock him. Now, he's as patriotic as the next fellow—Spain or Britain invade us and he'll pull down his rifle and march. The militia movement is still strong in the West, you know. I hear tell it's losing its strength here in the East but out there Indian fighting was only a few years ago and ain't really over yet."

"But this would be different," Madison said. "Not like an invasion. I mean, they'd be presented with a whole new situation. Do they accept it or do they rally them-selves up and fight it?"

"Yes, sir, that's it—the old anchors would be cut loose. They'd have prominent men behind them and it wouldn't be like foreigners taking over. It would be more like a political turn. And if they had the river where they could seal off shipping of western produce to the world that would be—well, you know, that really is what it boils down to. The river."

"That was my thinking." Madison's voice was steady now.

"Yes, sir," Johnny said, "give them the river, control of traffic, hands on the economic windpipe of the West, as-sume an army no longer a focused force, add to that a steady gold supply from conquering Mexico, which would mean no taxes, no custom duties, plenty of wealth for roads and such—"

"Western people wouldn't hold out, you think?"

"For an abstract ideal called the United States of

America? Maybe not. I don't know. If they're any age they've been through one revolution already, so another might not be so outlandish. Anyway, if they joined a new country they could argue it wasn't really revolution, couldn't they?"

Madison sighed. "You make a painfully coherent case. I think the danger is great and I may have to send you west."

"But—"

"I know, Faith's confinement is coming soon and I won't ask you to go if I can avoid it. If you must, I want Faith to come and stay at our house and let Dolley see to her. She'll be safer than in your hands."

"That's kind of you, Mr. Madison, but—"

"Of course, you want to be on hand. But this is important, Johnny. If what seems to be true is true, it's the most dangerous moment this nation has ever faced."

"I'll talk to Faith," Johnny said. "Just in case."

TWENTY-THREE

Westbound on the Ohio, fall 1806

This would solve all his problems and work his vengeance and prove what he hungered to prove once and for all, that Aron Burr was a king among men. And yet Burr had an odd, queasy feeling. It wasn't fear—he'd known fear on the heights of Quebec after Montgomery fell with big devils in red coats coming on the run with bayonets before them like spears. He'd felt his bowels turn to water and still he'd hoisted the big man's body onto his back and run until he dropped, redcoats so close you could smell their breath. You understand fear after that. No, this wasn't fear. Nor was it offended patriotism—he was beyond that. He had no country. That the country he was leaving would be destroyed by his success, split and broken and nevermore as its people knew it, really didn't matter. The country owed him repayment. You had to take what you wanted in this world; life would abuse you if you let it, and Aaron Burr was not a man to be abused. Alexander Hamilton should have understood that earlier.

He sighed. Even as he had put all this together over

spring and summer he'd been torn, anxious to be gone but reluctant to go. Well, maybe it was just that he was burning his bridges. Cutting off from all he had known and plunging toward a new life that would be utterly different. The past would be forgotten but the older a man gets the more he needs a past. Aaron Burr was fifty years old and fifty is a dangerous age when all is changing and nothing is holding. As on a ship in trouble, he was taking an ax to the anchor cable. The metaphor disturbed him but he shrugged again; it did apply.

So, at last, later than he really liked, the great adventure was starting. Soon the river threading west would be too low in summer dryness to travel, snowmelt far behind them, well levels dropping daily. Everything had taken longer—pledged money to come in, recruits to get their blankets together and kiss everybody good-bye and move, gunsmiths to finish their orders, barrels of salted meat and sacks of beans actually to be gathered and shipped. It hadn't really surprised him; he was sufficiently an old soldier to understand that taking a thousand men armed for war through settled country to the wilderness beyond would be no quick undertaking.

But now he must hurry, get on down the river while he could with days shortening and leaves ready to show color. He must anchor things at the island and get on to Kentucky and Tennessee to see the right people and pave the way, picking up more recruits with more supplies and the boats to carry them.

He found things moving well in Pittsburgh. Comfort Tyler's first recruits had passed through and more were coming; Comfort was shifting his operations to Ohio. John Wilkins was busy gathering two thousand barrels of flour and five hundred of pork. Delivery in Natchez or here? Half and half, Burr decided, and ordered boats with canvas covers to haul what he took here. He scouted gunsmiths and placed orders. Drafts on Sam Ogden. Sammy Swartwout had passed through on his way to Wilkinson with the cipher letter that should stir the general.

You had to hand it to old Jim. The papers were full of the inexplicable advance of Spanish troops into Texas, Wilkinson ordered to rally the army and meet the enemy in the Louisiana wilderness, all of this Jim's arranging in the first place. It was a marvel to Burr that the Spanish could put so much trust in a man who was betraying his own country—wouldn't he betray them as well? Still, he doubted Wilkinson was the first commander to inspire an attack so that he could march heroically to repel it. But he would like to hear from Jim a little more regularly— the "I am ready!" letter was months in the past now.

His old friend George Morgan invited him to his place near Pittsburgh and inadvertently showed him how vulnerable they were at the start. He'd known George for years—they'd been at school at Princeton together—and he knew George had heavy investments in western lands included in old Spanish grants that modern government disallowed unless they were very well established. Sort of like his own Bastrop lands, not likely to hold up when new land registrars arrived. A new, more lenient government might smile on such lands, but when Burr so hinted, old George stiffened and grew cold. Burr had been careless; now George felt endangered himself, as if listening compromised him.

Burr backed off but it did point up the cold fact: any sheriff or district attorney or judge or governor or even mayor could decide that treason was afoot in his jurisdiction and slap Burr and his men into a cell to await confirmation from Washington that this expedition really was secretly sanctioned by government, which would be the end of Burr. Later, of course, it would be different. Let them seize New Orleans and take Mexico and set up a new empire, then the George Morgans of the West would come right along. Give them a touch of the lash. . . but for now caution was the word as they slipped westward. He must convey his aims as patriotic without raising any impulse to look behind the surface story. It wouldn't be easy. Wilkinson's job wasn't easy either, first inspiring and then combatting the Spanish invasion, then timing a descent on New Orleans. But men who had as much at stake as he and Jim had together should be in frequent contact with each other. He had made that point force-fully in the cipher letter Sammy carried.

Would George write to the president? Well, Burr had spoken in generalities about urgent needs in the West, no more. But count on Madison to put the worst construc-tion on whatever was said. They knew by now that he was operating in the West; sooner or later they would have a man coming down the river after him. Time to be moving along . . .

As the keelboat bumped the long wharf Burr saw Har-man Blennerhassett's tall, stooped figure hurrying down the path from that incredible, ridiculous, sublime man-sion he had built in the wilderness for no earthly purpose but to destroy himself. He stumbled as he crossed the wharf, hand extended. Burr met him with a two-hand grasp, then threw an arm around his bony shoulders and held him hard, shaking him a little in his enthusiasm at this reunion. Harman would have wagged his tail if he'd had one. They walked around the island.

Early recruits were already here. They were grinding and sacking corn in the barn. Burr gave them a rousing little talk about what they could expect. Of course they understood there was only so much he could say, but the fact was that the Spanish were asking for trouble and Jim

Wilkinson was getting ready to give it to them, and wouldn't that spark an invasion that would take them right into the vaults of Spain?

He named the oldest a sergeant and put him in command. The tents he'd ordered had just arrived and he showed them how to shape the necessary poles, how to ditch a tent properly, the military importance of straight lines. They were among the first, he said, watching them glow with pride; they must prepare the ground for the hundreds more who were coming.

Harman sent for Dudley Woodbridge, the merchant in Marietta with whom he'd invested. When he called Margaret she appeared from an unexpected direction, moving so silently she startled them. Burr bowed; he saw in her face that she feared him. And yet, facing her level stare, he knew she wasn't at all intimidated. For some reason, Danny Mobry popped to mind. Something similar about them. Both drawn to him, too.

They had mint juleps and Harman listened eagerly as Burr laid out the opportunities before them. He spoke elliptically, cautiously, many things not needing to be said. And again the man's sheer devotion drew him in. Harman was like an adoring lapdog hanging on every word, nothing in the least critical. But the picture Burr drew was clear—of an Elysium lying ahead in which all problems would be solved and life would be secure and their authority would be unquestioned. They would be a new nobility; he noticed how Harman's eyes widened and glowed at that thought. Once again Burr found himself swelling in the face of totally uncritical approval, there having been so much of the opposite in recent years. The man seemed to look on his leader as much more than just that, as sort of a god, leader and savior combined. It was hypnotic, Burr found, that loving gaze raising his own enthusiasm and confidence, and quite intoxicating; with a quiver of alarm it occurred to him that it could become addictive. But he dismissed the thought, product of too much tension. Still, especially with someone like Harman, you had to be mindful of the dangers. Over and over he reminded the lumbering Irishman that these dreams were more vulnerable at this moment than they ever would be again. Now they must gather quietly and prepare for a future that ultimately would sweep all the West under their banner. Now caution was the word.

Margaret stood and walked out, which was just as well since her stare was becoming unnerving. Damned handsome women, though. An image of her without clothes crossed his mind and he had to drag his thoughts back to Harman. He sketched the Spanish situation, the Sabine River the nominal border between Texas and Louisiana, and they had plunged across it, Wilkinson going south to drive them back. That meant Washington would welcome their own strike against Mexico's gold. Meanwhile, New Orleans was ready. Any day now the people would seize the government, empty the banks and the customs house, take over the armories. The young men of the Mexican Association wanted Burr's leadership on the road to Spanish gold. With Mexico's gold in hand and the river closed, the West would swing. Had to. No choice. This was a certainty. If Washington objected— well, there wasn't a pass in the Appalachians that Burr couldn't defend with three hundred men and three field pieces. Not one. But any objection would be token; the forces that already wanted to shed the West were too powerful for the administration to resist for long. Behind all this, not quite said, *and we will have the army.*

Harman nodded, head bobbing on his long neck. "I'm ready, Aaron, I'm ready," he whispered. It gave Burr a faintly unpleasant reminder of Wilkinson's words, now in the ever more distant past. Over Harman's shoulder Burr saw a shadow. Margaret. This time she had been listening.

Woodbridge appeared just then. The merchant had supplied the tents and was eager for more business. Burr ordered a hundred barrels of pork; He would have plenty of hungry men who might well run ahead of supplies. Watching his new friend, Burr said Harman would meet all costs; he saw Harman's eager nod. Woodbridge owned a boatyard up the Muskingum River. Burr ordered fifteen shallow draft boats of the sort common on the Mohawk that could row upstream or down. Present a bill to Harman. The merchant took down the order and hurried off.

They talked into the night; Burr would be going downriver on the morrow. Harman said he was having a boat built to move his family in style; he said Margaret was already packing for the journey. Again she gave Burr that long, level look, this time with a faint smile shot with irony. An interesting woman.

The thing about Harman, Margaret saw now, was that at heart he still was an Irish lord. For all his distaste for the family title and estate, his impatience with its formalities and fear of its responsibilities, even his desperate turn to her despite scandal and outrage, beneath all he needed the trappings that had been his.

They had come to America full of fevered faith in the theory of democracy only to find that rubbing elbows with the common man didn't suit him at all. So he had tried to re-create his world with this beautiful castle in the wilderness that had drained so much of the wealth that the sale of the estate had given them.

Hence Harman's rapture when Mr. Burr proposed a new country in which he could be a lord again. And she—how did she really feel? Was Burr tempter or rescuer? They did need rescue. The money was running out. Crops on an island of twenty acres would never support such an establishment. Harman's investments had produced little. Rescuer or tempter? She suspected the latter, hoped for the former, and knew there was no turning back now.

So she was packing to leave the beautiful home that was their only anchor, millstone though it was. What else could they do but go? It was all or nothing, Harman investing money as well as his heart. And maybe Burr's plans would work—how could she know? They must float on their hopes, down the great rolling river to whatever lay at its end.

A week after Burr's departure Harman went to town for a couple of days. He returned with a copy of the *Ohio Gazette*, Marietta's weekly paper, and pointed to a column signed "Querist."

"You wrote it?" she asked with growing dread.

He nodded, beaming. "Read it. Rather good, I think. It's just the first of four."

Four! She swallowed, looking up at him. "The others are already written?"

"And in the editor's hands. He loves them. He said this is analysis of the highest order. You know I don't like to boast, but it was rather nice to hear that."

Harman the expert analyst of American affairs. It proved to be exactly what she had overheard Mr. Burr telling him, enlivened if that was the word by Harman's attempts at humor and sarcasm. In effect, it said that the commercial East controlled the government and manipulated its practices on public land sales, on exports and imports, on taxation, on trade regulations, all for the express purpose of exploiting the agricultural West. With the political control inherent in the East's numbers, the West soon would have no choice but to separate and establish itself as a nation outright with its own laws, commerce, and trade policies.

"Whole community's talking about it," Harman said.

"They love the ideas. Not just regular folks, leading men, too."

She felt a frisson of panic. "But—but, do you think Mr. Burr was ready for this to be talked about?"

He bristled. "Well, he warned me to be cautious and I was. Stated things quite generally, you'll see when you read it all." He knelt by her chair and put his hand to her chin and shook it gently. "Don't frown, Margaret. If these things are to happen, people must know about them."

"I expect so, but should you be the one—"

"Mr. Burr has given me the responsibility, don't you see? I suppose I'm his chief lieutenant—responsibility goes with position, you know that, same as at home. Mr. Burr wants me to take an active part—"

"What did you mean, leading men approve? You talked to someone?"

"I rode over to see Captain Henderson. His brother John went with me. I enlisted them both. You know, Alexander Henderson is important in this community. He can bring everyone in behind him if he wants to."

"How much did you tell him, Harman?"

"Not everything, certainly. West will separate from East, the army will seize Mexico, New Orleans will turn in new directions—"

"But isn't that just what Mr. Burr said not to do—put people in the position where their silence becomes complicity? An endorsement—or could seem so later?"

"Well, I swore them to secrecy. Walked outside in the pasture after dinner, you see, no chance of being overheard. They were excited—didn't seem alarmed at all. They seemed fascinated and asked a lot of questions. Of course, I didn't answer most of them, just looked wise. They'll be with us when the time comes."

"Really? They agreed?"

"Well, I told them I wanted them on it and they nodded, they didn't make any objection." She frowned, and he added, "Everything doesn't need to be said. Understandings just arise."

"Oh, do they?"

"Margaret, Margaret, this is going to save us. I *must* do all I can to advance it. What more can you want?"

That you talk to me first, she wanted to say, but didn't. All his Irish lord's pride would come up and he would stalk around for a day or two in silence before he found some excuse to come to her with a smile and patch matters up. And perhaps this was just the exposure Mr. Burr had wanted. Perhaps this was how conspiracy worked. But she doubted it.

Burr ran swiftly down the river, making as much as eight miles an hour when they didn't hang up on a shoal, tying the new keelboat to a tree at night and posting a rotating guard. Everything was going well, not a hitch in sight, but he was uneasy.

Comfort Tyler said recruiting was better in Ohio than in New York, western lads seemed eager for adventure. In Cincinnati Senator Smith greeted him with a loud cry and a bear hug. Smith had arranged a couple of dinners with prominent men to renew his acquaintance from the year before. They cheered when he spoke, dealing with the Florida and Texas issue, settling Spanish impertinence at last. There was Wilkinson marching on the Sabine to restore Louisiana Territory integrity, and we're not going to let it stop there!

On to Louisville where Jack Adair had a new hand for him. Jack would be leaving soon for Washington to take his seat in the Senate when it convened. The new man was named Davis Floyd, and within an hour he showed Burr he was just right for recruiting in Kentucky and Indiana Territory. Floyd was a top sergeant by nature who could reel men in and hold them together and didn't ask questions beyond immediate duty. He was big and slow talking, something in his eyes telling you he wasn't a man to trifle with. Burr thought his reassuring confidence grew from knowing better than to exceed his limits. Immediately Davis Floyd became a lead figure in the conspiracy for Kentucky and Indiana Territory.

But the uneasiness held. He had talked too much to Harman Blennerhassett. The further he got from that awestruck man the more he could see that while he had been seducing Harman, Harman had been seducing him, the difference being that Burr seducing Harman had been intentional. But this man was a fool and fools are dangerous. Yet Burr did have a soft spot for Harman, the man made him feel so good.

But there was a greater question than poor bumbling Harman, who probably would hold his tongue, especially with Margaret to remind him. She didn't need to be told; she had comprehension written all over her face. The greater question was Washington's response. Ever since he'd talked a little loosely to George Morgan he had been turning the equation around. George certainly had written the president by now, and indeed, there must be a stream of information about Burr across the president's desk.

This stream would go to the president but that wasn't the problem. The president would pass it all over to James Madison, and Madison was a dangerous man. He had a depth and range of mind that Burr considered no greater than his own but that surpassed that of anyone else he knew. Jimmy would call for his horse and ride up the trail along Rock Creek thinking as the horse's motion and the open air and the sight of birds on high opened his mind, and his thoughts would go very deep. On the way back he would stop for a breakfast at Absalom's, whose breakfasts at his place up the creek were famous as a stopping place for men who found a morning ride the perfect constitutional.

And Jimmy would order tea and biscuits and honey and sit there thinking and things would come clear. He would see what his old friend from New York aimed at. He would perceive that it could only work with Wilkinson in combine. But wait—Jimmy knew this already, didn't he? He also knew that to move before things were clear would give plotters time to run for cover. So Jimmy would hold back and that would give Burr the margin of time he needed. But soon, if not already, someone would be coming down the river in pursuit, someone intent on proving treason.

Little Jimmy Madison, whom he had taken around to Dolley so long ago was coming after him.

TWENTY-FOUR

Washington, fall 1806

"Jimmy," Dolley Madison said, "What do you think Aaron's up to in the West? Really up to?"

"I don't know!" he said. It had a petulant sound that he immediately regretted. He saw her lips tighten. But he was desperately tired. Late at night, she already in bed, he sat in the lounge chair in the bay window straining to read by a flickering candle. He adjusted his little round spectacles for the tenth time but nothing helped. He struggled to regain his place in the angry details of another British outrage sprawling over the pages in crabbed handwriting.

Well, it was as late for her as for him and they both knew better than to raise serious questions late at night, though they often did. He knew that Danny Mobry was just back from another run to New Orleans and he supposed she'd brought more news about the whole confounded mess and Dolley had been brooding. But now she glared and found just the right remark to bring his hackles straight up.

"Don't know or don't want to think about it?"

He was on his feet without realizing he'd moved; he

was enraged. "That's ridiculous!" he roared. He summoned his best secretary-of-state manner. "I happen to be quite occupied dealing with the British and their damned impressments, madam." Snatching our seamen right and left, sailing into our harbors as if they owned them.

Now she looked as angry as he felt. "Don't you 'madam' me, Jimmy Madison. All this impressment talk and no action, we're leaving the door wide open for James Monroe!"

Ah, there was her real interest! "For God's sake, Dolley—you think I should precipitate war with Britain to get ahead of Monroe?" She wanted him in the President's House more than he did, but even as the thought formed he knew it wasn't true.

"Don't put words in my mouth, James Madison. All I know is that he's in London right now sending encouraging reports, and if he can settle impressment he'll walk right over you—"

"If he can settle impressment without war, perhaps he'd deserve—"

"Deserve, my foot! He'd ruin things, you know that."

He did, as a matter of fact. He was calming. Monroe was a fine man. They had been friends—and rivals—all their lives. The only time he ever had opposition for his seat in Congress, Monroe was his opponent. Went to an outdoor speaking engagement in winter and on the way home Madison's nose froze and a piece of it fell off and he felt he'd been a bit funny looking ever since. Before too, to be honest about it, but worse after. Monroe had had a fine record in the Revolution, too, when Madison was too ill to fight, a point on which he reminded himself more than was healthy, even he admitted that. He didn't mention that old pain and regret—Dolley would be all over him. Monroe might make a fine president someday but now he was being pushed by the radical Democrats, and if he jumped over Madison he must dance to their tune. Madison simply knew that Americans would abandon the new democracy before they would accept the radical agenda.

"And don't tell me you don't know if you want it," she said.

"Well, I—at least, I don't hunger—"

"Jimmy, please! You do, too. I've seen you. Anyway, never mind Monroe. if Aaron Burr steals half the country neither one of you will be president. Isn't that true?"

"If he did, of course. But we don't know—"

"But the indications are there. You told me so yourself."

"All right, Dolley! Yes, straws in the wind—"

"Haystack in a tornado."

"Oh, what overstatement! Really!"

She grinned, anger easing because she'd scored a point. "Aaron is a devious man and I think he's dangerous. He has been badly hurt. I know he never dreamed the world would treat him so over the duel and he never understood it. He's had everything taken from him—"

"Entirely his own fault, I might add."

"Of course, but it's always our own flaws that hoist us, isn't it? He's extremely intelligent, I've heard him speak and he can have a whole hall weeping. Good Lord, I was outside the Senate chamber when he said good-bye and they came out in tears—"

"Oh!"

"Yes, they did! He can talk the birds from the trees, and I think he has no conscience, at least in the usual sense. I think he'll betray without even being aware he's betraying. Danny says he took over New Orleans, sort of a conqueror of the golden tongue. She says they're as rapt now as they were last year, waiting for him to come back, and he can have whatever he wants."

His anger was passing. Maybe she was right. Certainly more reports than she knew about had been coming in with ever greater impact. Tom was getting nervous about it, but then, Tom hated Burr with such a passion that it was hard for him to make a calm judgment. As for Madison, Burr dismayed him: what kind of man would shatter the glorious experiment for his own ends? Madison listened to his wife, too. Often she sensed more than he could see, and often she was right. They would have to deal with it before long.

For a Burr plot could destroy the nation, to say nothing of the new democracy. If he subverted the army, attacked Mexico, led New Orleans in revolt, the people would turn back to the old as the only form of government strong enough to deal with real trouble. And that would be catastrophic. Made his head ache to think of it, and damn it all, midnight was not the time to bring it up!

"Well," he said, hearing the residue of anger still in his voice, "I'll tell you, dealing with this, it's not nearly so easy as you seem to think. It's full of peril."

She grinned again. "Just what I've been saying."

"You have not! You've been saying—"

"Oh, Jimmy, come to bed! Dealing with problems, that's what you do. You just have to do it. And I think Aaron's a real problem. I know him—he's capable of most anything."

The secretary of war was angry, face red, breath short, fists clenched on the cabinet table. It struck Madison with surprise that Henry Dearborn was considerably more formidable than his usual demeanor suggested. He slapped the table so hard the cups rattled. "One moment, sir! Let me remind you that as we speak General Wilkinson is advancing to meet the enemy."

Yes, and that was part of the problem, too. Why were the Spanish attacking now since we'd made it clear we wouldn't seize West Florida or Mobile? Their troops had crossed the Sabine River from Texas and appeared ready to march to the Mississippi. Enough was enough. It was time for Wilkinson and the army to confront them. Of course it was obvious to Madison that war with Spain would be the perfect cover for an invasion of Mexico.

It was Madison's questioning Wilkinson's loyalty that had led to Dearborn's outburst.

"Gentlemen," the secretary said, "I've been to war. I've heard bullets fly. So have Wilkinson and Burr." Madison read the unspoken accusation; no one else in the room could make that claim. He suppressed the urge to apologize for ill health.

"Hardest part about it was knowing half the people were agin us. That winter at Valley Forge, how much worse it was knowing that so many didn't care. So I don't like to hear a man attacked at the moment he may be putting his life at risk—"

"That will do, Henry," the president said with a force he rarely displayed. He put his hand on an opened letter. "This from George Morgan in Pittsburgh must be tended to."

Madison had known Morgan most of his life. George wasn't a bad fellow after you discounted some frontier slipperiness. A month or so had passed after Aaron's visit before George decided to write; Madison surmised he had waited to see if any advantage might fall his way before reporting. It appeared that Burr had talked rather grandly over dinner, dropping hints of great plans that suggested a lot more than actually was said. But you couldn't read Morgan's letter without feeling pretty certain that Aaron was up to something.

The question was, what? And was it real or was it dreaming?

"Well," Madison said, "there's enough talk about Wilkinson to raise questions. But Henry, what makes me wonder is that we haven't heard from him."

"Well," Dearborn said, "an army in the field, he's busy!"

"He's both governor and general, eastern papers are full of innuendo and they're drawing on western papers, you'd think one or another aides would call this to his attention and then you'd think he'd be reporting the talk, saying it's not true or maybe that he's investigating. Something, anyway—not just silence."

Dearborn settled back in his chair, some of the fight going out of him. Madison caught the president's faint smile.

"So what can we do?" Albert Gallatin asked. The treasury secretary was often the practical one.

"Go down and get the bastard," Dearborn growled. "Burr. Drag him back in irons and let him answer. If he's guilty—"

"Problem with that, too," Madison said. "We're talking treason and treason's hard to prove." He liked the law; its order and logic suited his mind. He remembered how fiercely the debate on the Constitution revolved around this point that summer in Philadelphia. There was to be no careless charging of a capital offense. Only two things constituted treason: waging war on your country or adhering to its enemies and giving them aid and comfort. It had to be proved by an overt act to which there were two witnesses.

"Overt act, remember," Madison said. "Not just talk. Morgan's letter suggests treason contemplated, not done. We flush Burr now and he'll run for cover, claim nothing was done, say the government is attacking him, claim we're taking revenge for his challenging the president, present himself as a martyr, making himself a darling of the Federalists, while he draws attention away from a continuing plot. Let's go slowly."

He let that sink in. "Another thing. If Wilkinson is involved"—he held up a hand to stop Dearborn's outburst—"we might push him into the open. Against us, you see." He smiled. "If rebellion is afoot, our only instrument to break it would be the army. If it already had the army . . ."

The president cleared his throat. "All right. We have enough to proceed cautiously. Send a man down the river to begin alerting the West, but not with such hue and cry that we have Burr running for cover before he commits the overt act that will entitle us to hang him."

The bare word startled Madison and he saw that he hadn't looked fully himself. This was treason, and treason was a hanging offense. Certainly Dolley hadn't focused: the day Aaron Burr swung from the gallows would be a bad day for them all.

"Are we agreed, then?" Madison said. "I can send Johnny Graham to roll up his hopes behind him. Johnny will carry a private presidential message advising governors of potential treason, overt act required. He'll be looking for that act on which Mr. Burr can be arrested and he'll carry the authority to clap him in irons."

"Perfect," the president said. "Remember, gentlemen, Federalists to this day believe and preach that democracy must fail, implode or explode, turn into chaos and disaster. A knave seizing New Orleans, attacking Mexico, splitting the nation in parts would certainly seem to bear out their predictions, don't you think? So not only is the country at risk, so is the second revolution turning us toward a people's democracy. Make sure Johnny understands all this—it's a lot resting on that young man's shoulders."

"He has broad shoulders, Mr. President," Madison said.

Now Faith Graham was crying on Johnny's broad shoulder. They were lying down and he held her and wiped her tears with a cambric handkerchief and promised her that it would be all right. She could see his distress and she said so; she knew he didn't want to leave her alone. Still, she would be with Mrs. Madison; he supposed she could hardly be in a better place, doctor and midwife ready, the Madisons the kind of people who could produce in a finger snap anything needed that was within the power of man to deliver. It was what lay in God's hands that worried him.

★ ★ ★ ★ ★

TWENTY-FIVE

Westbound on the Ohio, late fall 1806

When Aaron Burr was ready to leave Andrew Jackson's comfortable home, a pair of old blockhouses that had seen real service in the not-so-long-ago days of Indian warfare, he was so delighted with the tenor of the Nashville visit that for a bare moment he let caution slip. It had been a splendid few days, men and women lining up to honor him, and he was profoundly grateful. He kissed Rachel Jackson's hand and turned to his host with eyes suddenly damp, and heard himself say, "Believe me, dear friend, there'll be an important place for you when we—" And stopped. For a split instant he hung in tongue-tied horror, and then continued smoothly, "when events unfold."

Riding down the long double row of poplars that marked the entrance to Jackson's home on the main pike east of Nashville, Burr shuddered at how close he had come to unhorsing himself. But no flicker of expression had betrayed any special interest on Jackson's part, and gradually Burr persuaded himself that he had done no damage. And it had been an extraordinary visit that had done him infinite good, for obviously all of Tennessee was behind him.

Jackson could do that for him because he was an extraordinary character. He was wild and rough but only a fool would fail to see the strength that glowed in him. Burr didn't doubt that someday he would be a man of real power, however the future unfolded. Already he had made himself the most significant man in west Tennessee. He probably wasn't much more than thirty but was major general commanding Tennessee militia and a sitting justice on the Tennessee supreme court, which really was the circuit court sitting en banc. Not bad for a raw young man.

He'd served a term or two as a Tennessee congressman. Burr, who had made it a point in those days to take likely newcomers under his wing, had appointed himself guide to see the fiery young man through congressional intricacies. He'd seen immediately that the younger man, stiffly prickly, seemed always on guard. Apparently some scandal far in the past had marred them, him and his now plump and fading but intensely kindly wife, Rachel. No one talked much about it because Jackson made such talk dangerous, but it seemed that they had married assuming she was divorced from a prior husband, found divorce had not yet been granted, and the community had condemned them as adulterers. Divorce was as notoriously difficult to get through the legislature as adultery was roundly condemned. Barbaric, in Burr's view, and cruelly seen as much worse on the woman's part than on the man's. Nevertheless, he gathered that gossip had rocked the whole state. Cautiously, though, because Jackson was ready with whip or pistol to punish anyone who spoke ill of Rachel, or if the speaker were a woman, her husband or brother.

He was tall and deceptively slender with that strength that marks certain strains of the Scotch and the Irish, and which Burr saw again and again in the Tennessee and Kentucky mountains. Jackson's hair, already graying despite his youth, stood up on his head like a fighting rooster's comb, and his volatile manner completed the illusion. When Burr tied Jefferson for the presidency, as Burr liked to put it, Jackson had trumpeted that Tennessee would fight Federalist usurpation but felt that Burr or Jefferson, both Democrats, would do equally well. Warmed Burr's heart.

Now he shared Randolph's view that Jefferson's democracy had abandoned purity in favor of partial Federalism. "We'd be a sight better off with you in the office," he said when Burr arrived. It was like a warm bath. Indeed, Jackson talked so fiercely of the democratic ideal that Burr decided it wasn't the time to discuss his plans in full. Let it seem that punishing Spanish effrontery in refusing to surrender Florida and Texas was the whole aim.

He had ridden over to Nashville after seeing John Brown and Jack Adair in Kentucky. Things were going beautifully, royal welcomes in Louisville and Frankfort, no signs of suspicion. Burr's confidence was rising as days passed without challenge. Still, he was more than ever mindful that Jimmy Madison's avenging man was somewhere behind him. This was no longer surmise; now he knew it by logic and by intuition.

In Nashville he found that the general had laid on a huge reception in the City Hotel, a vast log structure that was the pride of Nashville. It stood on the main square, across from the courthouse with its gallows and stocks awaiting malefactors, Judge Jackson being just the man to put them there.

At Louisville old Senator Brown had said that Jackson had had a fight with Governor Sevier of Tennessee employing knives, canes, pistols, and foaming invective. Scarcely had the image of violence faded but what he

had had a perfectly savage duel. He had done nothing
dishonorable in the context of the fight but it looked bad.
Mr. Burr of New York knew all about the way people
will turn an honest duel into murder.

"Your visit'll do him as much good as he'll do for
you," Brown had said, but the crowd Jackson turned out
to meet the vice president was impressive. Men in their
dressiest breeches and hose formed a line that snaked
around the room, their ladies beside them in gowns long
kept in storage. In his best uniform, Major General
Jackson walked Burr from one to the next, introducing
each, remembering every name, laying in each man's
background to suggest the vice president's response. He
was, in short, startlingly graceful. Burr felt he was at his
own best, bowing, now and then kissing a lady's hand,
summoning some pleasing memory to fit what Jackson
said of each man's background. Made it up as he went
along, of course, but he knew it sounded utterly sincere.

At the podium he kept his voice low, just talking to
friends, but clear to everyone. He told them how much
he cared for the West and how little his fellow easterners
understood this great region. To ringing cheers he said
the abuse given the West by a government captive of the
commercial East must end. He reminded them how the
Spanish stirred trouble, the evil dons blocking us in
Florida and denying us Texas, pushing us toward war. He
couldn't say too much just now but he could say changes
were coming that would delight Tennessee. . . .

Couldn't have been better. Burr wanted to recruit
seventy-five men from west Tennessee? Consider it
done. He ordered fifty barrels of pork and two hundred
of flour, and five boats to float men and supplies down
the Cumberland to its juncture with the Ohio. For payment he gave Jackson $3,500 in Kentucky banknotes,
courtesy, he didn't say, of Harman Blennerhassett.

So it was a smashing success. And then that slip as

he'd been ready to leave. So utterly careless. Or was it careless? Or rather, perhaps, the mark of his own integrity? Burr had always prided himself on his honesty. He found duplicity horrid. But he also knew that the first law of life said that sometimes expediency must rule. You must weigh issues, calculate significance. After all, he was engaged in an enterprise that would change the history of half the world. It was no less than a crusade; its needs must be paramount.

Some men clung to a nation that obviously cared little for them, but whether the common herd saw it or not, sensible men understood that separation of East and West was inevitable. Since Jackson had not yet grasped that underlying reality, Burr emphasized Spanish troops on American soil, five American settlers known to be held in Spanish dungeons, a rogue nation obviously spoiling for a fight. This wasn't so much duplicitous as telling them no more than they needed to know.

Still, he could ill afford speaking out of turn, walking the narrow edge as he did. Again, he'd been trapped in warm approval. But Andrew Jackson was no Irish lord yearning for a lost peerage. He was a man of power quite ready to destroy anyone who violated his integrity.

He kept a steady pace for Kentucky, telling himself it would be all right. The man's warm expression hadn't changed, it had been but a momentary slip, it would be all right. . . .

He was saddlesore after nearly a week on the road and in need of a bath and a good supper when he dismounted at Senator Brown's house in Frankfort. Good news awaited him. Comfort Tyler was recruiting in Ohio, as was Davis Floyd around Louisville and Elias Glover near Cincinnati. With the seventy-five recruits promised from Nashville, a small army was forming. Boats were being built at three places, each two or three hundred miles apart—on the Muskingum near Marietta, at Louisville and in Nashville. Bargeloads of beef and pork and flour in barrels, weapons, powder and lead . . .

Harman, beginning to sound as much the damned fool as Burr had feared, sent the first of his articles signed "Querist" and said he was enlisting prominent men, including a Captain Henderson, whom he described as a natural leader. Burr remembered Henderson's quasi-challenge on his first visit to Marietta. The article proved to be Burr's own argument for separation much too aggressively put. The image of Harman talking freely was disturbing; he dashed off a cautionary letter that should bridle him.

Burr found he was becoming well known as the man who would solve the Florida and Texas problem. Travelers turned out of their way to ride with him, innkeepers refused payment, plantation owners opened their homes. All understood the abuse the East worked on the West and cheered him on against the Spanish; most seemed ready for the great change. But still no word from Wilkinson. Well, maybe actions spoke louder than words. Jim had taken the field to drive the Spanish back into Texas, which fitted the larger plan perfectly. But Burr would like to have heard. He was ever more conscious of walking on a knife edge.

Senator Adair, who had taken Brown's seat when Brown stepped down, brought Harry Innis over to Brown's house for dinner. Innis was judge of the federal district court for Kentucky. Over cigars afterward, Brown said, "I hear Joe Daviess has been asking questions, Aaron. You know him?" Burr shook his head.

Adair laughed harshly. "United States district attorney for Kentucky and a damned-fool Federalist busybody who spends all his time trying to indict Democrats. Mania on the subject."

Judge Innis drew on his cigar and smiled.

"Proof of a weak administration," Brown said. "Jefferson should have cleaned out these Federalists wholesale right at the start. Madison still has that Wagner fellow—what an affront! And Daviess sees conspiracy everywhere. Dreams about it. Brother-in-law to John Marshall, you know."

"The chief justice?" Burr said. "Really?"

"Much too close. You know how Adams packed the court before he went out—well, John Marshall, he's determined to see Federalists rule no matter what. And his brother-in-law out here, he's doing his best—"

"Questions?" Burr said.

"Don't give it a thought," Brown said. "No one pays any attention to his Federalist ranting."

But Burr did give it a thought. It could mean delay, and he couldn't afford delay.

Margaret Blennerhassett was frightened. She was alone in the big house with the children, Harman having gone down the river on another of the endless tasks that occupied him since Mr. Burr's return earlier this year. His sense of importance seemed magnified. A letter came from Mr. Burr in Frankfort; she read it as cautionary, Harman as endorsement of his stewardship as foreign minister.

She was packing for the trip downriver, a leap into the unknown but escape from slowly unfolding disaster here.

The ground was crumbling under her feet. It was worse even than in Ireland when disgrace drove them out. But it seemed the opposite for Harman. She realized now he had been sinking into melancholy for years, but with the promise of a commanding role in a new nation, he had become again the carefree man he'd been in Ireland before the trouble started. The man with whom she'd fallen in love. And Burr? Guardian angel or Beelzebub? Come to rescue them or to destroy them? His plans sounded so . . . so extraordinary . . . and yet, wasn't this the most extraordinary of countries? Where all was possible and one could—

"Ma? You're crying. What's the matter?"

She swept the child into her arms, wiping· her wet cheeks. "Nothing, little cherub. Just thinking of your pa."

The bell at their shore landing began to clamor, loud and insistent. She leveled Harman's spyglass and saw a woman in a bonnet and faded blue gown. A buggy was behind her, the horse cropping grass around its bit. Sam crossed to fetch her and as the boat returned, Margaret was astounded to see that the woman was Mrs. Sonnfelt, from whose smokehouse she bought hams.

She shivered. She and Mrs. Sonnfelt weren't friends. They'd never spoken beyond the pleasantries incident to buying a ham. For that matter, Margaret had few friends, and not for lack of trying. She wanted to blend in but these people seemed to find insurmountable differences in the Blennerhassetts. She supposed there was no common ground be-tween them.

Mrs. Sonnfelt clambered from the boat as Margaret reached the landing. She was very nervous, glancing toward shore as if she feared being caught here. "Mrs. Bloomerhass," she said, "I figured you needed to know. The mens are having a meeting."

"Well, Mr. Blennerhasset is away—"

"Whole county meeting, all the mens."

"But—"

"Thing is, don't you see, meeting's about you."

"Me?" She felt a shaft of horror: had the reality of their marriage, uncle to niece, penetrated even here? But Mrs. Sonnfelt was shaking her head.

"Not you yourself, dear. The island. The things been

going on here. That thing in the paper, everyone says
your husband wrote it. This Mr. Burr. That's what it's
about."

At first, relief, then new concern. She touched the
woman's hand. "Thank you, Mrs. Sonnfelt. You're generous to come—"

"Wasn't nothing. You see, you ain't the only woman
hereabouts with a crazy husband." With which she
stepped back into the boat and Sam rowed her across.
She didn't look back or wave.

Margaret hurried to the north end of the island where
Peter Taylor was erecting a fish trap. Peter was their
foreman, a decent man who lived on the island with his
wife and children, a good worker but a man who held
himself apart. She'd known many like him in Ireland;
their own integrity depended on holding separate from
the gentry. That separateness blocked everything; she
could never tell what Peter was thinking. She told him
about the meeting and though his face didn't change,
she was sure he already knew about it. And had said
nothing. She asked him to attend and report what happened. Mr. Blennerhassett will want to know, she said
lamely.

He left and she found herself pacing restlessly around
the big house. This was trouble, she was sure. Why
would they meet; were they riffraff resenting wealth?
What about Captain Henderson? Harman intended to
make him an officer in Burr's crusade and said he was
eager to serve. Henderson would know what to do about
this, how to counsel her. Why, if the meeting were un-
friendly he would probably squelch it and see that she
and the children were protected. She would go to him—
but then she realized she didn't know where he lived.
And what would he think? Flighty woman alarmed by a
meeting? Would it suggest they had something to hide?
No . . . she would have to await Peter's return.

426 ★ DAVID NEVIN

She pondered the farm woman's manner. It wasn't respect or friendship that brought her. It was sympathy.

Margaret wasn't the only woman with a crazy husband.

Is that what people thought? She shook her head. The Blennerhassetts would never fit in here. . . .

It was dusk the next day before Peter Taylor returned. This time she could read his expression. He was frightened.

Yes, there'd been a meeting along about dusk, big bonfire, torches, flatbed wagon for a speaker's platform, two, three hundred men, orderly and steady. He cleared his throat.

"It was all about us, here on the island. Said this was the headquarters for rebellion, Mr. Burr and Mr. Blennerhassett planned to break up the country and steal this part for themselves. Said all that talk about Mexico was just to hide what they really was up to, getting a hold of New Orleans and that way they can control the river and make us all dance to their tune. They was talking fierce."

"What—what did they do?"

"Passed resolutions. That they were agin treason. That they were loyal. That this here island was the center of the plot. That the boats abuilding up on the Muskingum, they was for treason too. They formed up a special militia, they was to arm and protect the country."

"Do you mean they're coming . . . coming here?"

"Not now, anyway. I stayed in town the full day waiting to see what would happen and they went on about their business. Seems like they was putting themselves on notice."

That decided it. She couldn't wait longer. "Peter," she said, "do you know where Captain Henderson lives?" He nodded. She said, "We must go there first thing in the morning. Tell him about this . . ." Her voice died. He was gazing at her as if she'd lost her mind. "What?" she whispered.

"Why, Miz Blennerhassett, Cap'n Henderson, it was him as called the meeting. Him that give the information about the treason and all. Said Mr. Blennerhassett told him he wrote them articles. This is all Cap'n Henderson's doing."

Burr rode eastward to see Senator Smith at Cincinnati and found things going perfectly. He sent a note a hundred fifty miles upstream to Harman on his island telling him to gather things and come on. When he returned to Senator Brown's house, however, the senator met him with a worried frown.

"Joe Daviess," he said, "I told you he was a busybody son of a bitch. Now he's kicked over the milk pail."

Busybody he clearly was, mad Federalist in a sea of Democrats, but he swung a good-sized stick as district attorney. Brown gave him a stiff drink of corn liquor. Said he would need it.

Daviess had been snooping around Louisville where Davis Floyd was in charge. He'd seen supplies pouring in, cattle on the hoof, heavy flour barrels, salt pork in casks, all being stowed on big boats and covered with canvas, bound downstream. Everyone he met seemed to know what was going on.

"Which is?" Burr asked.

"That a thousand men are coming, aiming at Mexico and then the territories along the Mississippi, and maybe eventually everything west of the Appalachians."

Burr's mind was churning. Busybody son of a bitch was right! The image of putting a pistol to Daviess's ear passed through his mind. Pretty clearly, this was a smart lawyer. But then, so was Aaron Burr.

"That sounds about right," he said, voice nicely casual.

428 ★ DAVID NEVIN

Brown peered at him.

"Well, war's coming with Spain, we'll pitch in and who's to say we shouldn't go all the way to Mexico when we whip them on the Texas border? Territories on the Mississippi?" He shrugged. "New Orleans can't wait to go, it's none of our doing. With Mexico in our hands, New Orleans's shift is inevitable. But we're not separating them, we're *predicting* separation will happen in the future. Big difference. Western states? They'll see the wisdom of the split in a few years. That's all."

Brown grinned. "Predicting, eh? You know, Aaron, you'd make a smart lawyer if you weren't busy being a king!"

Burr smiled. "Isn't Davis Floyd a member of the Indiana Territorial Legislature? He'd better go tend to legislative business for a while—and I suppose I'll need a local attorney."

"Henry Clay's your man," Brown said immediately. "Young, smart as all get-out, he'll be going to the Senate soon, taking Adair's seat."

Clay proved to be a tall, gangly man who looked younger than his twenty-nine years. He had a dome of the sort required by a big brain and a wide, quirking mouth usually tilted into a smile. He had jousted more than once with Daviess and detested him.

Daviess filed an affidavit in Judge Innis's court accusing Burr of mounting a military expedition to the detriment of the United States and asked for an arrest warrant. Clay objected and Innis ruled there were no grounds for an inquiry before a trial. Daviess countered with a demand for a grand jury.

"Your Honor," Clay said, "it's unfair to hold my client to some nebulous date in the future."

"Agreed," Innis said. "Mr. District Attorney, assemble your witnesses for tomorrow morning." His hammering gavel cut off Daviess's protests that he couldn't be ready so soon. Spectators hissed Mr. Daviess at each objection; Judge Innis ruled that they must stop but with such a genial smile that they kept right on.

"They love you here, Mr. Burr," said Clay. "Anyone who'll go take Florida and Texas from the dons, they're for him!"

Harry Innis dined at Brown's house that night. "Can't speak out of court, you understand," he said, "but I wouldn't want you losing any sleep over this."

The grand jury was ready in the morning. Judge Innis winked when Burr appeared in court. Daviess said he couldn't assemble witnesses so rapidly. Could he have another day? Granted. On the next day Daviess had to admit that the only witness who counted, Davis Floyd, was off in Vincennes attending the Indiana Territorial Legislature. All other testimony would be hearsay.

A burly man in the front row stood up. "Joe," he bellowed at Daviess, "you're just a goddamned fool!" Laughter exploded as Judge Innis, smothering his own smile, rapped for order.

Burr laughed with the crowd, knowing he looked relaxed and confident. The people loved him, the judge was his friend, his attorney was the best. But Daviess moved for a new grand jury and Innis had no choice but to grant the motion. He gave Daviess twenty-one days to prepare. Into December.

It was a delay Burr couldn't afford. He was due in New Orleans in December. Briefly he debated running on downriver and letting Daviess go to hell. But then he would be a fugitive subject to immediate arrest, branded wherever he went. No, he'd have to let this play itself out. But the danger was growing, the time collapsing, the alarm beginning to spread. He could almost see the faceless man coming down the river after him. This miserable district attorney with his suspicions was costing him a month or more of dead time, time he didn't have. Things were cutting too close.

He awakened with a jolt. He'd been dreaming and sweating, nightshirt soaked. He wrapped a blanket around his shoulders and sat by the open window. The night was still; a dog barking in the distance sounded small and slight. Must be a mile away. A horse stamped in Judge Brown's barn, which Burr's room overlooked. He heard a low voice, stableman quieting the beast. In the dream Daviess had been huge and domineering and Judge Innis had glared at Burr and granted Daviess everything he wanted.

The strain of keeping utter calm, his manner genial and confident while men were trying to kill him, was beginning to tell on him. Reviewing his position with its power and rectitude was the only way he could calm himself after these disturbances in the night, which came more and more often. Was the whole thing humbug? The people were with him and against Daviess because they thought he intended to liberate Florida and Texas and had unspoken government support. Suppose he told them that Daviess was right, the plot as he described it was just what Burr intended?

But that was silly. He thumped his forehead with a fist. For God's sake, get it straight! Of course they would repudiate him now should he make such admission. This wasn't revolution and he wasn't trying to turn anyone now. Rather he intended to turn New Orleans, which couldn't wait to turn, and then to seize Mexico with its unfathomable gold. Then everything would be different. He would be coming to the West as conquering hero paving the way with gold, and he would have control of their future trade held tight in his hand. Squeeze it and they would suffer. Squeeze it tight and they would die.

Now his only aim was to get down the river with men and supplies to implement his plans. He was vulnerable now; later he would be too strong to touch and none would dare try. Now his popularity, based on a mistaken belief of the people, was essential to getting through at all. He must be too popular, and must seem to be carrying out foreign policy that everyone wanted too clearly to brook interference from partisan pygmies. Public opinion would ease him out of Daviess's clutches so long as he stayed calm and so plainly stood above it all.

All he needed—he found himself shaking a finger at himself in the darkness and laughed—was to get through this dangerous phase when any law officer could charge him with treason and send him east. But get through this and no one could stop him.

The dog had worn itself out barking and the night was silent. Stars glittering overhead cheered him. Suddenly he felt fine. The dream was a fool's dream. Yes, Madison's man was on his trail, and yes, he and Madison were titans clashing on a sparkling plain. But Madison had moved too late. The man on Burr's trail was still far off, so some intuition he trusted told him. And Burr was moving on. Satisfy this Daviess thing and be gone!

So whether the people would accept revolution now wasn't the point. When they found that the ox to be gored was their own he expected to find them lining up in droves. Not now, but when the time came. That was all that mattered.

Faint light cracked in the east; the barn took shape. He lay down still wrapped in the blanket and slept.

Johnny Graham made good but exhausting time in a day-and-night stage westward from Washington to Baltimore to Pittsburgh. At every stop he sent another letter to

Faith—be brave, be strong, he loved her. A day in Pittsburgh was all he needed to know the conspiracy was real and developed and under way. This brought him no special joy. He liked Burr. They'd had dealings at the State Department and though Burr knew he was in bad odor, he had never taken any venom out on Johnny. He'd been gracious, even lighthearted. There was an elegance about him, though apparently he could be slippery, too. And it had occurred to Johnny that there was something unknowable in him, surface glitter that defied penetration, suggesting inner depths that might be vast and capacious—or might be empty.

Pittsburgh made it clear that Blennerhassett's island really was the focus point, and Johnny hurried down the Ohio, travel by keelboat a vast relief from the jouncing stage. The baby would be coming any day now; each time he thought of Faith he said a prayer. The first storm of winter came howling in from the north while he was on the river, freezing wind producing watery eyes and aching cheekbones. Ice formed in the water butts and he retreated to the keelboat cabin to warm his hands at a stove. Sitting there a moment before making room for someone else, he found himself hoping he wouldn't find Burr at the island, for even with proof of his iniquity, taking the former vice president under arrest would be painful for them both. Or an angry crowd might decide to set Burr free if he were arrested, so wide was the enthusiasm for him as the man to rectify Spanish balkiness over Florida and Texas.

It seemed early for snow, but everyone in Marietta said look at that sky, we'll get it afore long. He found Burr activity everywhere, passing boats with recruits, more boats under construction, supplies purchased in bulk for cash. The next morning a tall, shambling man with a guileless and rather sweet expression stopped him on the street.

"I hear you're looking to join up with Mr. Burr's expedition," he said, a surprising Irish lilt in his voice. "I'm Harman Blennerhassett and I suppose I'm the man you should see, for he's on downriver and I'm in charge here." He wore a waistcoat of fantastic design.

"Well," Johnny said, "I've heard enough about it to get really interested."

"Excellent. I can sign you right on."

Graham saw immediately that there was an innocence in the Irishman, and he simply let him talk. He heard about men, boats, supplies, the Spanish and their recalcitrance, the significance of Mexico's gold, the Mexican Association of New Orleans that sought Mr. Burr as its leader and was dedicated to taking Mexico, hence, don't you see, its name. Blennerhassett proved to be one of those men who talked more as his listener talked less, and soon had convinced Graham that everything he'd heard about Burr was true. When Graham observed mildly that it was against law and custom to stage private filibuster raids from one nation to the possessions of another nation—that, indeed, wars had started for less— Blennerhassett assumed a wise expression and said that perhaps the raid would be staged from a newly independent nation. Graham took that to mean that Mexico was a secondary objective and New Orleans the primary. He said he must think it over, and Blennerhassett went off with a satisfied look, telling him not to delay in reporting to the island. Things would be moving soon.

Within twenty-four hours, Graham had confirmed the immediate—boats certainly were under construction up the Muskingum, boats with supplies under canvas were passing through, more supplies stacked on wharves awaiting loading in the Muskingum boats, closemouthed young men disappearing downriver.

Among the supplies coming from Pittsburgh: twelve hundred stands of arms complete with bayonets.

Twelve hundred. This was no small matter. He wondered if Faith would share his feeling of importance; perhaps nothing but the baby was really important to her.

He crossed the river to Parkersburg in Wood County, Virginia, which had legal jurisdiction over the island, and met with the committee formed to watch for illegal activity. A slender, punctilious man with pencil mustache and heavy black eyebrows who identified himself as Captain Henderson laid out almost everything that Graham had learned in the last day, confirming detail by detail. He said that Blennerhassett had sworn him to secrecy so he couldn't in conscience repeat what had been said but he did feel free to warn Graham that the administration should put troops into New Orleans by ship, independently of Wilkinson's force. Graham thought it a bit precious in such a situation to refuse to reveal what had been said, until he realized that Henderson had in fact revealed all that mattered. New Orleans. Then it was his turn to talk.

Late that day he took the stage for Chillicothe to see Governor Tiffin of Ohio, in whose jurisdiction Marietta and the Muskingum lay. The Wood County officers who had authority over the island were standing by.

Margaret Blennerhassett felt the cold seeping into her bones. Or was it into her spirits? It was cold in Ireland, too, but somehow not like this. Winter after winter this Ohio cold came sweeping in from the north to shock her; she never seemed prepared for the sudden icy wind whipping off the river. It was worse this time, or her spirits were lower, or both. It snowed sometime during the night and the children were tracking in mud.

She heard an odd noise. Her nerves were raw and she was attuned to the unusual. She went to the window and saw a commotion down by the water, saw Harman's tall form—thank God he was back—with Comfort Tyler beside him. Comfort was a bright fellow, solid and steady, and there was every reason to like him except that she didn't. Nevertheless, she urged Harman to listen to him because except for his doglike devotion to Mr. Burr, Comfort Tyler was a sensible man. She could never decide whether Burr was savior or destroyer but there was nothing doglike in her feelings. Apparently Mr. Burr had rescued Comfort from some disaster; he said he'd been down and out, which seemed unlikely to Margaret unless his problem was grog.

She knew why she disliked him: he made everything too real. He was a big, rangy fellow, almost as tall as Harman and much heavier, whose manner was authoritative and crisp; he knew what he was doing and why. As nothing had quite done before, his arrival with four boats and a milling crowd of young men who erected rows of tents and occupied themselves running ball had shown her more than she wanted to see. Rifle balls were for waging war, for killing people—that's what this was all about, war.

Hurrying down the path she saw that Dudley Woodbridge was pressing money into Harman's hand. She noticed because it was the first money they'd seen from Dudley since Harman invested in his business. "I don't want no more part of this," Dudley said as she came up. "This squares our debt, what you put in plus accrued profits. I figured I owed you a warning, too. They're coming. They're up on the Muskingum right now breaking up your boats. This side of the river, Wood County boys are getting ready, be here before long. All on account of *this*."

He handed Harman a flier from the Marietta paper. Harman held it upside down. She saw he was badly rattled and took it from him. She slipped an arm through his and held him until she felt his tension begin to subside. Then, still holding him, she read the paper that was quivering in her left hand. It was a proclamation from Governor Tiffin announcing that a treasonous plot was afoot to seize New Orleans, separate the West from the East, and launch an illegal attack on Mexico. It called on Ohio citizens to resist this enterprise with all means at their disposal and cause the arrest of the perpetrators.

It mentioned no names but she understood by instinct that that simply meant they knew the facts but were short of legal proof. Boats, supplies, weapons, men in passage told their own story. Perpetrators—they meant Mr. Burr and Comfort—and Harman too! Everyone knew their island was the center of it all. Everyone knew they planned to grab Florida and Texas. But now they were branded with the mark of treason and you didn't have to know much to know that treason led to the hangman's noose.

Melted snow seeped into her boots and a bunion began to ache. She drew her coat closer. "Mr. Woodbridge," she said, "can you be sure? Can they really take our boats?"

"Surely they can, Mrs. Blennerhassett," he said, his voice softening. She'd always known he liked her better than he did Harman. "It's all over Marietta—took the boats, took a hundred barrels of provisions already loaded, another hundred on the wharf. You see, the legislature, it passed a bill making this treason business a crime in Ohio, that's what they're acting under. Governor's militia, you see, full authority."

He looked at her. "Godspeed, madam," he said softly. He didn't shake hands with Harman but turned and hurried down the path and boarded his boat, the men on the oars casting off the painter. He didn't look back. Black clouds were rolling in and it was near dark; soon his boat disappeared.

She understood: the Wood County men would be coming soon and Mr. Woodbridge didn't want to be caught here. It struck her that the most surprising thing was that they hadn't come long ago. Harman had talked to Captain Henderson and Henderson had called the meeting that condemned them a month ago, and she'd known from that moment that their days on the island were numbered. But then nothing had happened. It was as if Henderson and his men were waiting for something to trigger their action, but she couldn't imagine what.

She heard the tremor in Harman's voice. "What should we do?" he whispered. Comfort Tyler smiled. His voice deepened and slowed. "Why, Harman, this is probably some big misunderstanding, but it won't pay us to wait around and argue it. We got four boats, that's plenty. We better run on downstream and tell Mr. Burr about this—he'll know what to do."

"Yes," Harman said, "but the boats they're building, we're supposed to bring them too."

"Harman," she said softly. A fine rain began to fall.

"Don't sound like there's much of 'em left," Comfort said. "Let's get on down the river—Mr. Burr'll have boats. We'll see—this here business won't amount to a hill of beans."

"Yes—yes, I think you're right. How soon can we leave?"

"You folks get your kit together. My boys'll strike camp, we'll be ready in an hour or two."

The rain grew heavier. It was very cold. She could feel it on her hair. Harman stared at Tyler. "Tonight?" he said. "You mean tonight?"

"Well, sir, it won't pay to wait around for these militia boys. I expect they'd be here now but for the weather."

She knew instantly that he was right. She put her hand in Harman's. To Mr. Tyler she said, "It'll take Mr. Blennerhassett a bit longer than that."

"Yes, ma'am," Tyler said, "but we aim to go tonight."

She shut her eyes. "So do we," she said.

"Oh, God," Harman said as she led him back to the house. It came out as a soft moan.

"It'll be all right," she said.

"For me, yes, I'm used to hardship. But darling, you and the children—"

"We're not going. Not now."

"What—what do you mean?"

"I can't gather everything I'll need for us and for the children—what, for a month, for six months? Can't do that in an evening, Harman. That's why you ordered a boat for me."

"Yes, but now—"

"No, you must go by yourself. I'll follow along soon. I'll make them release my boat."

"I can't have you here by yourself. If you won't go, I won't go."

Of course he would say that. Kindly, sweet, decent, responsible, a wonderful father, he was a good man, a darling man. He just wasn't decisive. And he deceived himself.

"You owe it to me to go," she said. "They won't do anything to me and the children, but you—they'll arrest you, God knows what will happen. I'll be lost if you're seized. You *must* go."

It was two in the morning before all was ready. The rain was driving hard. She had a canvas thrown over her shoulders, a bonnet on her head. Harman kissed her and she clung to him. "I love you," she murmured, and then she pulled free and turned him toward the boats. Holding a whale oil lantern high overhead she watched them cast off, oars taking the water. Harman was still looking back when the last boat vanished into the rolling gloom.

Rain slashed her face. She stood a long time looking into the mists where her husband had disappeared, and then she walked back to the house.

The next day the militia came, almost a hundred men. Captain Henderson bowed and told her she would be perfectly safe. The men camped on the island. That night they got drunk and she could hear laughter and shouts and glass breaking.

"Ma'am," Henderson said the next day, "I'm afraid the boys broke into one of your storerooms and found a supply of spirits."

"But you'll see that they don't come in the house? I'm alone with the children."

"Yes, ma'am!"

After three days they left. She sent a note to Mr. Woodbridge: couldn't he arrange the release of the boat made specially for her? His answer came the next day: it was under lock and key, officially impounded as evidence. It was very hard that night; she thought that she'd have broken down but for the children. She had never felt more alone, Harman a hundred miles or more away, she trapped in her magnificent house with no means of escape.

A keelboat stopped at the island; it looked sixty feet or so and had cabins with glass windows and chimneys. A number of young men stepped ashore to stretch their legs. Two hurried toward the house as she emerged to meet them.

"I'm Tom Butler Jr. from New York City," one said, "and this is Morgan Neville. Mr. Burr said to meet him here."

They were elegant, cultured, educated, very different from the men she usually saw. Even their clothes bespoke wealth. Her memory ticked over.

"Neville," she said. "I met a General Neville in Philadelphia. . . ."

"My father, ma'am."

Thank God! They were gentlemen.

She explained the situation, saw them exchange uneasy glances, and hastily added that it was all an obvious mistake that would be immediately corrected downriver. Did they carry weapons? Supplies in bulk?

"Only fowling pieces. And supplies to our own needs."

Then there would be no basis on which the authorities could challenge them. She made up her mind. It was imperative that they all go down and join Mr. Burr but she must impose on them for passage.

"'Twill be our honor, ma'am," young Neville said. "You shall have the main cabin and we'll bunk with the others."

They would leave the next day. That night she paced about the magnificent house that had been their glory and their ruin, going from room to room, engraving it all on memory, examining all that she was leaving behind, all the books and paintings and fine furniture and special wall paneling and sterling doorknobs—every heartbreaking thing. She had absolutely no idea if she would ever see it again.

The next morning the men loaded the essentials she felt she must take and she led the children aboard. They cast off not so long after dawn and she stood at the stern and watched her gleaming home grow smaller until a bend in the river hid it from view.

And so Margaret Blennerhassett began her second great journey into the unknown.

★　　★　　★　　★　　★

TWENTY-SIX

Washington, midfall, 1806

The letter from New Orleans lying on Madison's desk that morning was fat, the somewhat uncertain handwriting of Governor Claiborne looking even more agitated than usual. The letter poured out a litany of complaint—treasonous conduct everywhere, constant attacks on the governor, French, Spanish, and American at each other's throats, talk of seizing banks and ships and invading Mexico, all the heights of shocking illegality. All this uproar seemed to be based on the idea that Burr was coming to take over and seize their hands and lead them to the Promised Land, good times coming after the hated American administration.

Congress had granted Orleans Territory proper territorial status now and that had entitled it to one territorial delegate. The territory immediately elected Daniel Clark to fill that seat. This was done for no reason but to affront the governor further, since Mr. Clark was famous as Mr. Claiborne's most furious enemy. No other reason. Well, Madison thought, dropping the letter, perhaps one other—Daniel Clark probably was the most competent man there.

He remembered Danny's uncle very well, icy eyed and supercilious, among the least pleasant but for the moment most useful men Madison had ever known. So Mr. Clark was here. Or coming. Good . . . a plan was taking shape.

When *Carlito* nosed into the Mobry Shipping wharf in the Eastern Branch, Danny and Clinch Johnson were on hand as the lines flew over. Much of *Carlito*'s cargo belonged to Clinch.

"I brung Mr. Clark," Captain Mac said sotto voce. "He rode the owner's cabin."

She nodded; she'd been looking for Clark since he was named territorial delegate. What was the situation in New Orleans? Captain Mac cleared his throat. Constant talk of treason, he said, American days numbered, Burr coming down the river to rescue them, on and on.

"A revolution, I suppose you might say. Throw the governor in the river or hang him, one. Burr behind everything. Some folks say the army is involved, General Wilkinson and all, but no one knows. But constant whispers, seize banks and ships—"

"Seize shipping?"

"Yes, ma'am, that's what caught my eye."

She saw Clinch sit forward in his chair.

"What does Ed Livingston say?"

"He came down to the levee day we left. Charged me to tell you about all this. Said you'd understand why it wasn't wise to put it on paper. He don't like this talk. Raiding Mexico, that's one thing, subverting United States territory, that's another. He won't have any part of that—says he'll sacrifice his own interests and ours too if it comes to that before he'll go along with—well, he said treason."

He fixed her with a long look. "That's where we stand, too, ain't it, ma'am?"

"Of course." That he would wonder irritated her.

Clinch's mouth opened as if to speak and then closed. He sat back in his chair, looking satisfied. Mac said they should wait a bit before returning lest some fool seize the ship. She glanced at Clinch. His goods would be aboard. He nodded, those ridiculous tufts of hair standing on each side of his head. "Sounds all right to me," he said.

Just then her uncle appeared, dressed to perfection for New Orleans if not Washington, heavy on the velvet. He bowed to her curtsy and shook hands warmly with Clinch. They long had done business together; indeed, her uncle had brought Clinch to her in the first place when they were setting up a small wine import business from Portugal to Louisiana. She always found it strange that men didn't seem to regard Clinch as odd looking at all. They uniformly respected his business acumen. That his white linen suits winter or summer had a dusty, wrinkled look as if he slept in them, that they were too small and buttoned too tight and encased him like sausage skin, those tufts of yellow hair like horns . . . She'd asked an acquaintance about this once and he had grinned, and said, "Well, Clinch, he ain't no beauty, that's a fact." And he wasn't, but he was proving himself a good friend to her, and he never presumed on their friendship.

"Let's walk down the wharf," she said to Mr. Clark, and they strolled arm in arm to the end and stood leaning on a railing watching river traffic of which she never wearied.

"So," she said, "the new territorial delegate in all his finery. Now tell me true, Uncle, what are you doing here?"

"Came to be insulted, niece. For the very idea of a territory insults Louisiana. The Americans wanted us, now they don't want us—"

"What?"

"We should be a state. Territory demeans us. What, a single nonvoting delegate in the House, nothing in the Senate, which is where the real power lies—faugh! Disgusting."

"So why did you come?"

He gave her an odd, twisted smile. "Oh, I decided a trip would suit me."

"Suit you . . ."

"In view of everything, don't you see?"

"Everything that Captain Mac has been telling me about?"

He shrugged. She laid out Captain Mac's report.

"That's about it," he said with that faint smile that she took to mean that he wanted her to see that he knew much more than he would ever say. And probably he did, too. "The city's in a fury. It's getting worse and worse. Any day I expect a mob to carry Claiborne down to the river and heave him in. He's an oaf and a fool, not the slightest sensibility, raw American and glorying in it, clinging to every miserable American attitude, learning nothing of the rich culture—"

"Now, now, Uncle, he *is* American, after all. So is New Orleans, now."

"More's the pity. But yes, there's plenty of talk. It seems your friend Burr is cutting a wide swath."

"My friend? What do you mean?"

"Why, Zulie says you slept with him, says it was written all over your face the next day. That doesn't necessarily make you a friend, granted, but still—"

"That's enough of that, Uncle. We will drop that right now." She put iron in her voice and he chuckled.

"As you wish, my dear. But Burr, friend or no friend, is setting New Orleans on its ear and everyone is talking—"

"My memory is that you and he were quite cozy."

He laughed. "Hardly an appropriate term, my dear. I simply welcomed a distinguished visitor."

"Mr. Burr will be disappointed to find you gone."

"Perhaps, though I suspect he'd be looking forward even more to another session with you."

"Sir!"

"By session, Danny, of course I meant the chance to converse. Talk over novels you've read."

He grinned like a shark. It occurred to her that she detested him. But he did know everything about New Orleans, and New Orleans was crucial to her business. Whether Mobry Shipping would survive was still an open question, but without New Orleans it certainly would fail. Clinch was still the only figure in the shipping world willing to trust a woman in command of hard-living sailormen. And Mr. Clark was her cousin, uncle being a courtesy title, and in the end blood would hold them together even as its closeness irritated them.

So New Orleans was at once a lifeline and a chain around her neck. If this business of treason were to take hold, Mr. Burr seizing town and people, she would be finished.

Now, frowning, he said, "Cozy is as cozy does, Danny. And I found cozy wearing a little thin, what with all the talk. So why not honor my appointment as territorial delegate to which the people graciously elected me?"

"Probably wise," Danny said. "From what I heard, the two of you were in bed together."

"No, dear, the two of you were in bed."

She knew she'd gone scarlet. But then she laughed. God, she had impaled herself on that one!

"All the same," she said, still laughing, "I did hear you—"

"Ah, eavesdropping, were you, before you took him off for your own purposes? Well, dear niece, there were

no witnesses to that conversation unless you count yourself, whereas I have careful copies of many letters setting
out my distress, alarm, shock, and dismay to hear talk of
disloyalty to my new country."

He smiled and she saw he was genuinely amused. "I
am, after all, a territorial delegate. It's hard to get much
more important than that, eh?" And he laughed louder.

Danny was in Mr. Madison's office on his summons. He
had that austere, businesslike look that always intimidated her a little. He asked about New Orleans shipping.

"We're holding our ships for the nonce," she said.
She paused. She had been bringing bad news from New
Orleans for months if not years and no one paid attention. She lurched on. "There's so much talk—well, revolution, I suppose, talk of seizing banks and ships and
attacking Mexico and hanging Governor Claiborne,
though I can't believe they really would hang him, you
know, so you can't tell how much is talk and how
much—"

Which wasn't true, she thought. Mr. Clark had as
much as admitted that what she had overheard was real.
Cozy is as cozy does. But they had laughed so often—

"Oh, I think it's real," Mr. Madison said. She stared at
him. After all her warnings, now he believed? "That's
why I asked you to come by. I need to talk to Mr. Clark."
She reminded him of her uncle's official status.

"Territorial delegate," Mr. Madison said with a little
laugh. "An American official."

"So to speak," she said. "But I wouldn't assume from
that any friendly desire to cooperate on his part."

He laughed out loud. "Very good advice, I'm sure. I
remember the last time—he had to be shown rather
forcefully where his real interests lay."

She had in fact delivered her uncle just as Henri had

charged, and Mr. Madison had pressured him into becoming a voice in France for American interests. She remembered Mr. Clark telling her after the session that the little secretary was a lot tougher than he looked.

She had protested then and Mr. Clark had said quietly, "I see you don't know him." But of course she knew him, polite, gracious, gentle, a bit somber among crowds certainly a warm hearted man. And her uncle had said, "No, you see only the social side. The real man has metal." And he'd added, "That's why I'm going to France."

Well, she told Mr. Madison now, she supposed he also knew that as a result of that trip Mr. Clark had conceived the idea that the Louisiana Purchase was entirely his doing. And hence felt the governorship was his due?

Mr. Madison's eyebrows rose. "Governor? But he's not even an American. We'd have to have an American governor, you know."

"I know, yes. But he doesn't." She hesitated; were her loyalties to origins and blood or to the country she had chosen? At last, voice a whisper, "I have to say, this Burr matter, Burr conspiracy—I think my uncle is involved. You should know that."

He smiled again. "Thank you, Danny. I'm sure you're right. That's why I want to see him."

"Good," she said, surprised again, but her duty done. "As for a visit, he'll react much better to a direct summons from you."

"Summons . . . oh, my dear, that's too strong. I'll invite him to breakfast at Absalom's up Rock Creek. But you might tell him he'll hear from me."

Absalom's was at the peak of its normal clamor. Thirty or forty horses were tied outside, their riders scattered at tables, busty women with trays overhead threading expertly here and there, setting down dishes with a clamor.

Madison saw Clark come through the door and pause as he looked about, the very picture of superciliousness. He stood, energetically waving his guest over. Very American.

"Here, my dear fellow," he cried, pumping his guest's hand, "sit yourself down. I have ordered us a robust American breakfast, keyed to your arrival."

. Clark sniffed. "A mere croissant with tea will do very well for me, thank you."

"Oh, no, that won't get you started." In fact, Madison's usual fare when he stopped here on his morning ride was biscuits and honey with tea, but this wasn't a usual day. And here came Matilda to drop her big tray on the table and unload platters of hotcakes awash in butter, honey and syrup pitchers beside them, a rasher of bacon, a half dozen fried eggs, freshly fried ham curling and still smoking, chopped potatoes fried in bacon grease, a platter of biscuits, a pot of tea and a pot of coffee. He watched Clark stare at this munificence. "This is America?" the Louisianan said in a whisper.

"Designed," Madison said, "to delight or disgust." He saw Clark stiffen at the last word and added lightly, "And how does it strike you?"

A bubble of saliva appeared. The man's mouth was watering! It was a fine beginning. "Disgust—" He grinned, unable to go on. "Gross, perhaps, but it does look delicious," he said, and reached for the hotcakes as Madison poured tea.

As Madison had expected, numerous men stopped at their table and to all of them he introduced the new territorial delegate from Orleans Territory, which could be expected to emerge as a state shortly. Mr. Clark, he told them, was a good Democrat.

Between visitors, Clark said, "I should imagine I'm a natural Federalist."

"I wouldn't be surprised." He fixed Clark with a steady gaze. "But today you're a Democrat."

Clark chuckled. "What else do you want me to be today? There's some purpose to this breakfast beyond food, I take it."

"Why, yes, now that you mention it, there is something on my mind. I want you to write a letter."

Clark laughed out loud. "Really? Endorse you for some position? You seek a college presidency, perhaps? Or I should recommend you to my good friend Governor Claiborne for some post of importance in Louisiana? What shall it be, dear sir?"

"Ah," Madison said dryly, "would that I had your wit." He watched Clark color. "No, Mr. Clark, I want you to write a letter to General Wilkinson."

"But he's off in the wilds somewhere, facing down the Spanish, whom it wouldn't surprise me to learn he instigated himself. Hadn't thought of that, I'll bet."

"As a matter of fact, I had concluded that that is exactly how the Spanish were led to a pointless attack."

Clark's eyebrows rose. "You're more clever than I'd expected."

"But since you hadn't expected much, it's no great endorsement, I suppose?"

"Well, yes, I expect that's right."

"Good. We understand each other. No love lost on either side, individually or, I take it from your comment, nationally?"

"If the question is do I love the country that has taken over my land and all I own, the answer is no."

"Good again. Honesty over sentiment, I always say."

"What is this letter anyway?"

Madison smiled. "It goes to General Wilkinson."

"So you said." Caution slid over his face like a veil. "But I have nothing to do with Wilkinson."

"Really?"

Clark colored. "Well, I know him, of course. Everyone in the West does."

"Good. That's sufficient reason for you to write."

As if humoring him, Clark said, "And what am I supposed to write?"

Madison took a sheet from an inside pocket and unfolded it. "This," he said.

Clark took the sheet and read it. When he finished he lowered it and stared at Madison. Then he read it again. And shook his head. "I can't write such a letter. Why, it suggests I'm involved. Could almost be construed as confession. I sign this and—"

"I'll give you a second letter absolving you of any liability in this one."

"No, no," Clark said. "My God, what do you take me for? A fool of the first order? Why would I want to get involved?"

"Why, Mr. Clark, for your own benefit, of course."

"No benefit to me in this, certainly."

"Why, sir, you would render signal service to your country. There is great benefit in being recognized as a patriot."

"I am an Irishman, sir, not an American."

Madison laughed out loud. "Irishmen come here in great numbers. One of the great migrations, Scotch and Irish landing in Philadelphia and working their way west to the Appalachians and down the spine of the mountains to the Carolinas and over into Kentucky and Tennessee. General Jackson out in Tennessee, an Irishman of the first order, second or third generation. Oh, an Irishman is a welcome figure—"

Clark was frowning. "You jest with me, sir. I am a New Orleanian—"

"And New Orleans is American," Madison said, and then letting his voice harden, "and I promise you, sir, it will always be American. Always. Those who can't see beyond its levee may disagree, but they are wrong. As are you, Mr. Clark, in so many of your assumptions."

"I? Wrong?"

"Why, yes. In supposing, for example, that you have much choice in this matter."

Clark's face reddened and then paled. "I have ample choice. I won't write the goddamned letter! Why should I have truck with that oaf? He's nothing to me nor me to him." He stood, throwing his napkin down on his plate.

"Oh, do sit down, Mr. Clark," Madison said. "Immediately!"

Clark sank slowly into his chair. He gave Madison a murderous look. "Suppose you tell me exactly what's on your mind."

"I haven't been to New Orleans," Madison said, "but I'm told it's remarkable and that you are a leading merchant there. Now, sir, if I understand things correctly, there is not a lot of civilized society in that vicinity and so trade tends to be in goods shipped down the river and transferred to sea vessels. Isn't that so? And I'm told that no one factors more goods en route to the sea than do you. Is that about right?"

"I'm a successful merchant, granted."

"In export trade."

"Yes, damn it, in export trade. What is your point?"

"Now, sir, I'm told there is what you might call a wild element in New Orleans too. I'm told of a bay down on the coast, Barataria Bay, where pirate ships call regularly. That indeed this Barataria Bay is the headquarters of the Lafitte brothers, Jean and Louis, eh? That there may be twenty pirate vessels operating out of the bay on a regular basis."

Clark watched with a wary expression and made no attempt to interrupt. "Further," Madison said, "I'm told that New Orleans is so tolerant in its attitudes that it welcomes these pirates to its confines. That the Lafitte brothers and others walk the streets. That Jean Lafitte in particular is so suave and polished that he's accepted at the best tables in the city, welcomed, sir, for his elegance and his riches, gotten however questionably."

Clark laughed. "He only steals from the Spanish. They did Lafitte awful dirt and he's taking revenge. That's what you call piracy."

Madison laughed too. "That's what the world calls piracy, my dear Mr. Clark. Stopping ships at sea, taking their guns and goods and murdering their sailors and ravishing their women if any they find—that is piracy, sir. And do you know, New Orleans is the only American port where pirates are even tolerated, let alone welcomed to the best tables?"

As if seizing a small triumph, Clark said, "As we have been trying to say all along, New Orleans is unique."

"Well, the United States Customs Service will be there and the United States Navy. And I can tell you that they will take a close interest in whether vessels leaving New Orleans do so with pirate booty in their cargo. It might be necessary to stop each vessel as it prepares to depart and have it fully unloaded under a customs officer's eye. And then reloaded only when the customs officer is available to watch." Madison watched his breakfast guest go pale.

Then, blustering, Clark cried, "You'd go crazy, trying to handle all ships that way."

"Well," Madison said softly, "I don't suppose we'd handle *all* that way. I would think we'd choose the biggest shipper and make an example. The others would soon get the idea."

Clark stared at him. "American law would so allow?"

Madison shook his head. "Probably not," he said. "Probably you could file a lawsuit and after a few years you might win. And maybe you could hold out a few years and maybe you couldn't. And maybe I could find other ways to make my point after you won on that."

Clark stared at him and didn't answer.

Madison poured a cup of coffee, now cold, and made a face. "Isn't this a silly conversation?" he said. "Suppose you just write the letter."

There was a long, uncomfortable silence. Madison poured honey over another biscuit, quite sure he had won.

At last Clark said, "Actually, I wrote such a letter to Wilkinson last year. Told him his name was being bandied about and so was mine. I didn't like it—had business in Vera Cruz and here I was being publicly branded in a plot against Mexico. Could have put me in a pretty hobble."

"How did he respond?"

"Didn't, as I recall. And my Vera Cruz venture went well enough. But I didn't like it."

"And when Mr. Burr arrived?"

"Oh, Burr—he's a talker, you know, has a grand image of himself, sort of a king among princes. Loves the idea that he's in command of something. I began to see why you dropped him."

"We didn't, really."

"Yes, yes—I'd say you dropped him with a thud we could hear all the way to New Orleans." He waved a hand. "Water under the bridge. Point is, Burr isn't much. Wilkinson is the key to all this." He smiled, looking startlingly malevolent. "From what I hear, you understand— I know nothing firsthand."

"Oh, I'm sure. I wouldn't impugn you. But Wilkinson, now, he's been going to New Orleans for years?"

"Flirting with the Spanish, that's what."

"Exactly. So tell me about him."

"He's *merde*. You know the term?"

"Shit, I believe."

"Quite so. Wilkinson carries his own stink."

Madison nodded. All was working well.

"This letter," Clark said, "I'm to post it by mail?"

"Return it to me. I'll see to its transmission. And make it word for word except add the reminder that you so wrote him last year. I don't doubt he'll remember. Write enough drafts so that you achieve that spontaneous look. Have it to me tomorrow morning. And please—don't thank me for the breakfast. It was my great pleasure to entertain you."

TWENTY-SEVEN

Frankfort, Kentucky, fall 1806

In these months since Burr had left the East he'd labored to hold everything together, men and supplies gathering, his standing with the public higher than ever. Moving rapidly was the key, staying ahead of reaction. He'd had things rolling when this miserable pettifogging district attorney raised his damnable charges. Rotten little Federalist terrier nipping at the ankles of a giant! Yet if indicted Burr could be held indefinitely for trial and everything would collapse. That yearning to slip off in the night was stopped again by where that would leave him, a fugitive subject to arrest without question, flight standing as proof of guilt. So he must stay here and fight, as the man little Jimmy Madison certainly had on his trail must be advancing relentlessly. The benign view he'd held of Madison—titans clashing on a glowing field—gave way to bitter fury, that whey-faced little bastard who had managed to lord it over Aaron Burr for thirty years and now at it again, personification of importance while Burr ran for his life. And there was Harman Blennerhassett crashing around like a loose cannon four or five hundred river miles to the east. The administration man probably was there by now. Time was wasting!

His digestion boiled, every tremor made worse by the necessity to show utter confidence. But the situation still held on a morning in December when Judge Innis convened court on the second floor of the Kentucky statehouse in Frankfort. The air was raw and wet, another storm on the horizon, but the crowd milling in the street before the courthouse and pushing inside was in a holiday mood. Smiling and relaxed, Burr climbed the broad staircase, observing to someone that the building, three stories of gray limestone with carved banisters and luxurious curlicues, was as handsome as anything you'd find in the East. They loved such talk.

He was dressed in his best, a dark blue coat with sterling buttons, buff pantaloons thrust into Hessian boots, fine cambric stock around a high rolling collar and a white satin waistcoat. He lounged comfortably in a wooden armchair, making sure he appeared totally at ease as Judge Innis tried to gavel the noisy courtroom to order, oak rapping on oak with high authority. The crowd howled its approval of the man who aimed at Texas and Florida. Insults and ribald comments rained on Mr. Daviess. Slender and young, a lonely Federalist in a sea of Democrats, he winced and stared straight ahead.

Burr knew his own calm made him an even more formidable figure. He glanced about with a warm smile and a new cheer started. Mr. Daviess's jaw muscles bunched.

Judge Innis stood, hammered his gavel, and roared, "Now, that'll do, boys!" and seeing that this time he meant it, they subsided. Everything went Burr's way. Henry Clay objected to Mr. Daviess's every move, Judge Innis sustained every objection, the crowd cheered, the gavel hammered. Eventually the grand jury retired with the witnesses, whom Mr. Daviess believed would convict Burr of plotting treason. Davis Floyd, Senator

Brown, Senator Adair, and 'most everyone who'd offered the hand of friendship were haled into the room
and questioned.

Burr doubted their testimony could hurt him, since he
rarely spoke in specifics and knew the difference between inference and implication on the one hand and
statements that could return to haunt you on the other.
Davis Floyd could honestly say he'd heard a lot about
settling the Bastrop lands and lending Wilkinson's men a
hand in throwing Spain's troops back into Texas. Yes, the
fortunes of that war might carry them all the way to
Mexico and everyone knew there was gold in Mexico.
Yes, there was talk that New Orleans folk hated Americans, but everyone knew that. Anyway, you could hear
'most anything on the banks of the Ohio. Seemed that
everyone talked and no one knew, and him as did know
didn't talk, and that was the long and the short of it.

So the grand jury reported no proof of crime in Kentucky and pandemonium exploded all over. Harry Innis
let it run for a while and only stepped in to gavel calm
when a tall gangly fellow began to exhort the crowd to
throw Mr. Daviess into the courthouse outhouse. Burr
shook Daviess's hand and said Daviess was a fine public
servant doing his duty, whom he hoped was now convinced that his suspicions were unfounded. Daviess
looked as if he'd swallowed a green persimmon, but the
story of Burr's magnanimity swept Frankfort. Early the
next day he and Senator Adair were in the saddle for
Nashville. He'd slipped Daviess's net but things were
narrowing.

They crossed Kentucky and into Tennessee driving extra
horses, making time. Every few miles they changed
mounts. Nights passed in smoky taverns rolled in a blanket on the floor, dinner of pork and beans and whiskey

heavy on the gut. Adair was going on to New Orleans; a hundred miles past Nashville he would find parties making up for travel on the Natchez Trace to New Orleans—no one rode it alone. In New Orleans he would connect with Erich Bollman and Sammy Swartwout. Surely Sammy was there by now—plenty of time to deliver the cipher letter to Wilkinson and get on down the river. Burr still had heard nothing from Wilkinson and a steady anger was beginning to burn.

Near Nashville Adair veered off. "See you in New Orleans, my friend," he shouted. Burr went on to Jackson's home. The cold was damp and piercing and he was thoroughly chilled when he rode up the line of poplars to the two blockhouses. He'd sent word ahead to General Jackson so he assumed they'd be awaiting him, but the buildings looked deserted.

The door finally opened. A mountainous black woman looked him up and down. Suddenly uncomfortable, hearing an unwelcome touch of bluster in his voice, he said, "Aaron Burr to see General Jackson," though he recognized her and knew she recognized him. A bad beginning.

"General ain't here," the woman said. He couldn't remember her name. "Missus, she says you wait, she see you in a bit."

There was nothing to do but wait. He began to shiver and pacing didn't cure it. The door creaked when it opened and he turned eagerly.

"Good morning, Mrs. Jackson."

"Mr. Burr," she said. She didn't smile. "General Jackson will return tomorrow. You'll find lodging at Clover Bottom. He said to tell you he would see you there."

So something had gone wrong here, too. He waited, because he had no choice. It was late the next day, thirty-six hours wasted, before Jackson and Jack Coffee strode into the tavern grim as the weather outside. Burr felt a

shiver of fear that surprised and angered him. Coffee was
so huge that his glowering manner was threat by itself,
but it was Jackson who riveted his attention, radiating
force in the intensity of his stare, the way he jerked his
head: outside, right now, he had something to say.

Suddenly Burr was enraged. By *God*! he'd come a
long way in life and done many a thing to be intimidated
by a pair of Tennessee yokels, and he said as much when
they stepped into the cold.

"Including functioning as a goddamned merchant of
treason!" Jackson snapped.

Sometimes anger will fight off accusations all by itself, and Burr tried, but the implacable righteousness of
the Tennesseean beat him down. But what the hell was
he talking about?

The tall, stern general was nearly incoherent in his
rage, and Coffee, huge and implacable, stood silently,
arms folded, looking ready to strike at a moment's notice.
But it was the terrible force in Jackson that was frightening. Burr didn't alarm easily but now his mouth was dry
and he thrust his hands in his pockets lest they quiver.

As best he could piece it together from the general's
roaring, someone named Fort had been through, present-
ing himself as part of Burr's force. Jackson had made
him welcome but late at night, over wine and whiskey,
Fort had said something damned peculiar.

"What he said, he said, 'When we take New Orleans.'
So you see, right off, I thunk me of your little slip the day
you left here."

"I didn't—"

"Yes, you did. Plain as the leaves on a tree. I didn't
call you on it but I thought right smart on it afterward. It
was plain there was more to this than you was telling. I
told Fort I'd saberwhip him in my own living room, he
didn't 'fess up right this goddamned minute—"

"But Andrew," Burr squalled, "I've never heard of the

man, don't know him, who, name of Fort? It doesn't make sense."

"He didn't know you, either. Said he got it all from Sammy Swartwout. Said Sammy was delivering your letter to Wilkinson, proving him the traitor I've always known him to be, and going to New Orleans to await you there. You and Wilkinson to take over the city, seize banks, ships, invade Mexico—"

He broke off, stammering in rage. Burr instinctively lurched back to his old cover—he acted in secret for the president. Then he remembered an undated blank commission signed by Jefferson that Wilkinson had given him, one of a dozen given the army commander for such temporary appointments as might be needed. He ran inside and returned with his saddlebags.

"Look," he said, "if you doubt I have the president's confidence in this matter, look at the blank commission he pressed into my hands on the day I left Washington. 'Use it well, Aaron, and Godspeed,' he said. Those were his last words to me. I tell you, I had tears in my eyes. Now, sir, that is good enough for me and if it's not for you, so be it."

Jackson studied the paper, then folded his arms. "Maybe," he said. "Maybe." He turned toward his horse.

"Wait," Burr said. "I've got recruits here, you ordered boats for me—"

"I stopped the recruiting and canceled the orders." He fished in his pocket. "Here's seventeen hundred of your dollars not yet spent. Quicker you're out of Nashville, better it'll be."

They mounted, Coffee riding a huge brute of a beast, and were gone. Burr stood shivering, more from the encounter than from the weather. The trail was rolling up behind him. But it hadn't caught him yet.

———

Johnny Graham was acutely disappointed. He'd come overland at a hard pace and gone straight to the district attorney. Joe Daviess was sputtering, "I had him in my hand and couldn't tie him down. In my hand!"

But that was two weeks ago and now Burr was gone. Daviess told Graham he'd been in Louisville since the trial and had seen Davis Floyd loading boats with supplies, including weapons, right out in the open, blatant as a whore in church. And who was with him? Why, all manner of officialdom, all Democrats, mind you. That got Johnny's attention.

"Ain't a party matter, Mr. Daviess. Democratic administration is what's moving now to bring him to justice."

"Yes, yes, that's all very well, locking the barn after the horse is gone. But I've been warning for a year. Where the hell were you then? Eh?"

Graham stood suddenly. Daviess shrank back. His eyes fell. "Well," he said, "water under the bridge. But go talk to Adair and Brown, they were in it sure as Burr was."

Brown gave him dinner. "Senator Adair and I, we've known Aaron for years," Brown said. "Capital fellow. And believe me, the West is right behind the administration plan to settle Texas and Florida once and for all. High time, too. I understand it can't be spoken of directly, but when you see the president you tell him—"

Graham broke in to explain the situation.

Brown gazed at him, stunned. "You mean he *didn't* have government backing? But he's the vice president."

"Was."

Brown shrugged. "Well, Adair and I, we're both of us former senators. I don't suppose a man loses the authority of his office the moment he leaves it." He paused, cleared this throat, fixed Graham with a baleful stare. "Don't say a hell of a lot for the administration, it lets its vice president run around telling folks things and then won't support him."

He stood and pointed an accusing finger. "Let me tell you something, young feller. You better hie back to Washington and tell the president the West expects some action on completing the Louisiana Purchase. Florida, Texas, they're *ours*. . . ."

This went on for some time. Then Graham walked back to Daviess's office and showed him Governor Tiffin's proclamation. "I think we better get over to the statehouse and see if the governor won't issue an arrest order for Burr and his men."

A week later Graham was in Nashville. He met Jackson in the log courthouse on the main square.

"Goddamn it," Jackson roared on listening to Graham's report. "I *knew* something was wrong. But he had the president's signature—"

"The president issues blank temporary commissions with his signature. For use on small matters when far from authority. Wilkinson would have a supply."

"Wilkinson! That would explain it! And I'll warrant that son of a bitch is in it up to his hocks. I sent the president a letter soon as I talked to this Captain Fort, told him that something dangerous was afoot. I don't want any question *I* was supporting treason. . . ."

That was fine. It would clear Jackson but it didn't do anything for Graham's quest. Burr was miles ahead, moving on with less and less chance of stopping him. For this he had abandoned his wife in her confinement, just when she most needed him.

Without Jackson's help, Burr had purchased two small flatboats and enlisted a few recruits before he set out from Nashville to follow the Cumberland on its long curving path to the Ohio. Now they were near that juncture, moving swiftly with the current, the shore gliding by, startled deer pausing to stare, a bear drinking with threatening paw lifted. Massive trees floated with them, torn-out roots grotesque shapes; when they snagged the bottom whole massive trunks lifted and turned over in ponderous cartwheels and smashed down on the water as the men leaped to the long sweeps to lever the boats out of the way. They camped in a clearing each night and Burr took the long midnight watch.

He traveled in silence, mouth set in a hard line. Things were pressing him, pursuit coming on but still behind. He just didn't know how far. But things would still be all right if Comfort and Davis Floyd and the others were waiting at the mouth of the Cumberland ready to race on downstream. His gut ached. What would he do if they weren't there? Go on by himself? Find passage somehow? Or wait? What would it mean? Comfort would never disobey orders, so it would have to mean . . . He shook his head, suddenly furious with himself. Nothing will destroy a man more rapidly than panic, nor demean him more.

"Up yonder," one of the men said, pointing, "that there's the Ohier." Burr stood at the bow, staring ahead. After a while he could make out the separate shorelines and see the outline of the vast stream they were entering. A long, narrow sandbar island now heavily wooded had raised itself across from the mouth of the Cumberland. The boats bobbed and wobbled when they took the Ohio's stronger current and soon they were floating the length of the island. They passed two cabins with smoke curling from chimneys but aside from that, nothing.

Burr felt nauseated. Comfort and the others weren't here, hadn't made it, they'd been stopped, seized, that bastard Daviess had nailed them at Louisville, found some new trumped-up charge—it was too late, they had run too close to the line, he'd known it was imploding behind him, he'd sensed it and now—

One of the new men nudged him, pointing. "Up ahead—that our party?"

And by God, it was! Yes! He could see it now. They'd camped on the lower tip of the island. Seven or eight boats tied together in a long chain and allowed to stream in the current from a tree, meaning they were loaded, too heavy to pull ashore without breaking their backs. A lone figure standing on a log that lay half in the water clapped a long glass to his eye and then began to wave. Comfort—Burr was sure of it. The man turned and shouted something and men came pouring out of the woods, twenty, thirty, fifty—they kept coming, looked like a hundred or more, an army!

He could hardly breathe for joy, heart crashing around in his chest like a bull in a chute—it would be all right, his army had come through, he need only float down, join Wilkinson, go on to New Orleans, the plan was as solid as it ever had been. He was going to win; nothing could stop him now. Nothing!

When he stepped ashore he was perfectly calm. He grasped Comfort's eagerly proffered hand. "Oh, Mr. Burr, thank God! I was so afeared you'd get here before us and you'd think—"

Burr laughed. "Comfort, old friend, I knew you'd be here. If you weren't I'd just have waited a bit, that's all."

Harman Blennerhassett must have been prowling up the island for now he came trotting down the beach. He was limping; Comfort said he'd torn a muscle jumping into a boat. "Ol' Harman, he's a little bit fussed up," Comfort said. "He'll tell you about it."

Burr and his secretary for foreign affairs walked up the beach. Harman was trembling. Everything had exploded in their faces, he said, voice near tears. The governor's proclamation had denounced them, officers seized their boats, the militia boys were coming to arrest them when they fled in the night. He couldn't understand it. Captain Henderson, who'd proved such a disappointment, his meeting had been a month before and nothing had happened then. As to the meeting, it was obvious to Burr that Harman simply had talked too much. He had put Henderson in a position from which he must take action or be branded a conspirator. That's why the captain had waited that month—to see if any advantage would accrue to him before it was necessary to act to cover his own complicity. Burr found Harman's innocent assurance that he'd made no errors in dealing with the man almost unbearable. Harman said he had wanted to demand explanations but Margaret forbade it. Then he colored, stammered, and said he didn't take orders from his wife, but he'd seen how upset she was, so . . .

Burr understood the explosion. The administration man on his trail carried presidential authority, ample to turn out the locals and energize governor and legislature lest they themselves seem suspect. The storm was rolling up behind him, and probably Daviess was crowing. But only one thing mattered now: how far ahead was he? Harman said they had made good time, skirted Cincinnati in the dark and found Louisville quiet. Davis Floyd joined them there with his boats.

So everything was collapsing behind him just as he had feared, but it was still behind. He took Harman back and forth over times and concluded he had at least a week's lead, and a week was as good as a year. Pursuit couldn't travel any faster than he could, humping downriver with oars streaming. He'd still be a week ahead when he hit Natchez and linked with Wilkinson and pushed on to New Orleans, and by God, it all was going to work!

He felt like throwing his hat in the air and shouting, but of course he didn't. They were in the clear, he said, but Harman stood on one foot and then the other, jaw still quivering, looking upstream every minute or two.

"What's wrong with you?" Burr snapped. "Think your Captain Henderson'll show up with a flotilla?"

Harman gave him a hurt look. "Margaret and the children aren't with us. I left her on the island with the militia coming. She was supposed to get a boat and follow but she hasn't come and now she's alone on the river somewhere."

"Oh, my friend," Burr said, gentling his voice, "she'll be fine, never you fear. Western men are all gallant. They see a woman and children, they'll do anything to help them."

"We can't leave," Harman said.

"What's that?"

"We can't go any farther till she gets here. Poor thing, she'll be terrified."

Burr stared at him. Things sliced as close to the bone as they were and the fool wanted to wait for his wife?

"Probably she'll be here before it's time, Harman."

Blennerhassett caught the equivocation in his tone. "We will wait, Aaron, won't we?" His jaw was trembling again.

"Never you fear," Burr said. He pointed at a boat floating into view, far up the island. "Look—that's probably her now." And if it isn't, he thought, you can wait for her by yourself. Be foreign minister of this little principality. And Margaret would be president. He smiled to himself. She was already.

Trying not to sound as if there were any cause for alarm, Margaret Blennerhassett had been hurrying the young men along in their fancy keelboat. She was making them see the magnitude of the enterprise they'd joined, slowly shifting what had been a lark into an important mission on which no time could be lost. They caught the spirit of great events and bent to the oars; she persuaded them to slip by Cincinnati and again by Louisville in the dark of the night, stirred by their own daring, by mystery and intrigue, the adventure growing more profound.

She explained away the raid that sent her husband fleeing as the result of local misapprehensions. After all, her new young friends understood that the government could hardly acknowledge the intention of adding Florida and Texas by force. Unsophisticated men didn't understand international nuance but they would be cheering when it was all over.

Whenever they met local folk she asked the distance to the Cumberland, and the day came when someone said, oh, ten, fifteen miles. So it was that with the boat floating down the length of what looked like a big island, she saw figures up ahead. She started up, heart pounding, and then she recognized the tall, shambling, lopsided figure of her husband running and stumbling up the beach toward her. She shouted for the children, who scrambled forward. Harman threw his arms over his head, shouting her name, then plunged into the icy water to catch the boat's painter and pull it ashore, and she half stepped, half fell into his arms. Together they lifted the children ashore. She threw her arms around his waist and held him locked tight, her face pressed to his chest. Oh, thank God, thank God . . .

They walked down the beach, the children laughing and skipping ahead. The young men were greeting Mr. Burr and to Margaret's surprise, she found she was glad to see him. Puzzled, she realized it was simply that perhaps he knew what to do now. She certainly didn't and she knew Harman didn't.

When Mr. Burr came to her and took her hand in his, warm and assured, she saw he'd read her expression.

"You see," he said, "perhaps I'm not the devil you thought."

"Perhaps," she said. "We'll have to see, won't we?"

———

They broke camp in the icy dark and at first light were on the river. Burr took his place in Davis Floyd's Mohawk River boat. The oars dug deep and it hurtled downstream toward Fort Massac, the last outpost on the Ohio where he and Wilkinson had met the year before. Maybe word would await him there from Wilkinson. His anger at the other's silence was a steady drumbeat in his mind. Burr was the captain of this enterprise and it looked as if he would have to make that a bit more evident when he met the general again. Wilkinson had waited for years for a man with the force of character and the political capacity to make this work; Burr had that capacity and he intended to tighten the leash and bring the general to heel when they met. His silence was not only rude and demeaning, but was dangerous as well. They needed frequent consultation even when a week or two apart. That was the point made by the letter that Sammy had carried, and for a couple of months he had awaited Jim's answer. Yes, indeed, Jim would hear about this lapse when they next met.

The boats spread out. Burr posted lookouts who knew the river; he wanted warning when they neared the fort. He had kept Harman with him and ordered Margaret to remain in the comfort of Tom Butler's slower keelboat. He didn't want Harman talking to strangers and he didn't want to face Margaret's steady, wondering look so full of skepticism. Did he know what he was doing?

Well, did he? He probed Harman carefully on the failure at Marietta, satisfying himself that the sharp reaction had been as he'd seen from the start. Don't put anyone in the position of seeming to endorse an illegality, as Harman had done with Henderson. He remembered Henderson, militia captain, lean, hungry-looking man out for the main chance if Burr had ever met one. This was no ranking patriot. Andrew Jackson might be that naive, but not Henderson. He'd waited a month before he'd peached on Harman. Why the wait? To see if advantage might come his way. But then the administration man came through. Graham, Madison's prize clerk, just the man Burr should have figured would be sent. He remembered Graham as pleasant enough but also as fundamentally tough. So when Graham appeared with his ominous word, Henderson saw the handwriting on the wall and raced to betray Harman. About what you'd expect, when you made a popinjay a complicit confederate.

"That there's the Tennessee," Davis Floyd said, pointing, "Massac coming up right smart." The boats rocked in the vast tide of water flooding in from the left. They stopped a quarter mile short of the fort. He had to know if the administration man could have leapfrogged him. Seemed impossible, but if it had happened, armed troops might be awaiting him. So this was another break point. If Daviess had won an indictment and held him for trial it would have finished him; if arrest orders had reached the troops here it could all be over in a moment.

He and Davis and a couple of his best men went ashore and walked through the woods until from a leafy screen they could see the fort. It was as he remembered, a standard frontier fort a hundred yards back from the river, palisade of logs set deep in the ground standing fifteen feet, tops cut to sharp points. An old fur trade fort, built even before the military arrived, it had a weathered, well-established look. Buildings stood flush against the wall inside, their roofs a firing platform. A flag rolled fitfully on a tall peeled pole. The gates were open but could be easily closed and locked with a heavy bar; he saw a small door at the bottom where stragglers could be admitted if a sudden attack surprised a detail outside.

It looked quiet. Several soldiers were digging late potatoes in the garden and he saw others bringing in a small herd of cows from a pasture. A punishment squad spun to and fro in rapid close-order drill, haversacks probably filled with stone. If there was an alert it was well concealed. Should he risk stopping? Should he try to slip by in the night? They certainly had sentries and there was a moon tonight. Failing to stop would arouse automatic suspicion. He returned to the boats.

They landed just below the fort. The men swarmed ashore, eyeing the walls warily. Presently a half dozen horsemen loped toward them. It was ominous—four of the riders carried muskets out of the boot—but when they drew close Burr recognized Massac's commander, Captain Bissell, who raised a hand in friendly greeting. Burr liked the captain but knew he was tough and direct; if the administration man had reached here he would say so immediately. Burr held his breath.

"Permit me to offer you the comfort of my quarters, Mr. Burr," the captain said.

Thank God! He was on his way, last barrier surmounted and nothing ahead to stop him, future solid. They cast off at dawn and Bissell saluted men going to settle new lands on the Ouachita. The weather had eased and was near balmy. He heard laughter from the other boats before he started to pull ahead.

What could stop them now? Massac was the last possible barrier; Burr had outrun mishaps, the administration man left in destiny's dust. New Orleans awaited him with open arms. The doors of Mexico's gold vaults stood ajar. When Britain saw the lay of the land it would have no choice but to throw in because the prize was too valuable. When the United States Navy came, assuming the administration even bothered after it lost its army, it would find a Royal Navy squadron off the mouth of the river.

And the West? It would come along for the same reason that a bull follows when there's a ring in his nose. And since it really was dissatisfied with the East and obviously would prosper in a western empire, it would come to its senses soon enough.

The Ohio debouched into the muddy Mississippi, the boats lurching and spinning in the clash of currents before they straightened and started south to a future that glowed. He would pause at the settlements at New Madrid and again at the little military detachment at Choctaw Bluffs, but then it was on to Bayou Pierre just this side of Natchez where his old friend, Judge Bruin, awaited him. And there he surely would find word from Wilkinson. There really was just one question, which he had asked in the cipher letter—should he and the several hundred men who'd gone down the river ahead of him take Baton Rouge from its Spanish masters or bypass it on his way to his triumphal entry to New Orleans?

★　　★　　★　　★　　★

Twenty-eight

James Wilkinson, far up the Red River with fifteen hundred American troops, grew more desperate day by day. Spanish troops were posted but ten miles away, well this side of the Sabine, and General Herrera was pressing him as to what now? Herrera was friendly, he understood the relationship, but two ostensibly hostile armies poised within a few miles of each other could precipitate a war that no one really wanted.

Anyway, if war really were to erupt here how would he get New Orleans in control and set about the real prize, Mexico? But he couldn't just sit here twiddling his thumbs until—well, until what? Nothing is static, and above all, an army is a living, breathing organism, his army and General Herrera's alike. It was time for decisions and Wilkinson didn't like decisions.

Then there was the letter from Aaron delivered in easily cracked code by an arrogant young snot named Swartwout who seemed to feel he was a figure of importance. Said he was Burr's right-hand man and that he could promise Wilkinson that Burr would be mad as a hornet by now, so long had it been since the general had written the commander.

Burr, the commander?

That had grated pretty hard, as had the boy's attitude. Treated the general as an equal, and had a big mouth to boot. Talked about Mexico and gold until Wilkinson threatened to put him in irons. The next day Swartwout lit out for New Orleans, where he said Burr's men already were collecting.

But Aaron was the problem. He was saying, "Let's march!" Saying it in an unpleasantly aggressive way, too, as if he suspected the general of dragging his feet. As if Wilkinson needed guidance of any sort, military or otherwise. He thought the letter a disgrace. It spelled out everything, Burr to do this, Wilkinson to do that, step by step what he expected. He seemed to see himself the leader when Wilkinson knew he himself had only brought Burr in for his temporary usefulness. Protected only by flimsy code and sewn into a popinjay's coat, the letter had enough material to hang them both. What was Burr thinking?

The letter also swept them into the future. It said not only that Burr was ready to go but that he was going. It spelled out his plans, laid out the numbers of men and weapons he'd collected, given estimates of the dates when he would be here or there, accomplish this or that. It debated attacking or bypassing the Spanish garrison at Baton Rouge, western end of West Florida, before descending on New Orleans. Which broadcast that New Orleans was the goal—the damned fool!

As Wilkinson brought each new sentence out of cipher he felt a bit more sick. Burr must be on the Mississippi now, pressing ahead with weapons and men. And supplies. *Twelve hundred stands of rifles with bayonets!* Think of it!

Aaron's problem was that he thought he understood

the military but didn't, thought he understood the nature
of decision but didn't. He was precipitate! It was that enthusiasm of his that had inspired Wilkinson in the first
place. Of course they'd been dreaming for years, but
Burr was experienced—he should have understood the
difference between talking and doing!

But why all this caviling on his own part, Wilkinson
asked himself, stomach lurching. The plan was workable, the dream no less bright, with Burr bringing on a
private army that Wilkinson's regulars could merely support. Wilkinson could strike a truce with Herrera anytime, announce to his senior officers that he had orders to
invade Mexico, hurry to New Orleans to find Burr taking
control, tell his own men that catastrophic seizure of
New Orleans planned by Spanish and French forces
combined necessitated temporary military rule, get them
on ships, and march into Mexico where every indication
said the people as a whole would welcome them. Nothing to stop them.

But he hung here, knowing he had to do something
soon. He'd had a few reports. Burr was talking too much.
This miserable Daviess apparently had the whole story.
Aaron had escaped Daviess by the skin of his teeth, too,
meaning that a lot of people had the facts even if they
wouldn't admit it to a grand jury or couldn't prove it.
And that meant some of them knew Wilkinson's part,
too. A lot of people knew. He could feel it, his breath
gone short.

He stood abruptly and kicked his foot locker and
roared, "The whole goddamned world knows!" Then,
alarmed, he peered from his tent flap. Had he been overheard? But no one was near.

But wait, wait. Nothing had gone wrong. Everything
was there to be done, just as planned. Why was he caviling so? He remembered his pleasure in seducing the profoundly seducible Mr. Burr, playing him like a midsized

fish, imagining so fully the seizure of banks and vessels, the surprise on Mr. Claiborne's foolish face when he saw his general in a different kind of command, and then on to the riches in Mexico and leapfrog from that to empire, citizens cheering madly as leaders stacked doubloons freshly minted from raw gold. Think of it, tangible hard gold that a man could play with, stacking coins, spreading them and restacking them, fingers rubbing their satiny sheen, fingernail tracing the occasional mar in the die made in colonial Mexico . . .

Magnificent dream and yet practical, there to be done, waiting to explode across the earth. Wilkinson as Napoleon. Keep Burr so long as he could swing the crowds but eventually find charges to bring against him, let him languish in prison, look for the opportunity to take permanent care of him. Wilkinson as Napoleon. But his hands shook and he felt sick and Herrera was waiting and he didn't move. His officers were giving him hard looks, what was the plan, what next, what now? Soon there would be supply problems and discipline problems in a motionless army. But he didn't move.

Ten days passed. He had to move! Then another messenger arrived. Came quietly into the camp, asked for the general, reported to his tent, gave a sort-of salute that might or might not have been military, handed over a letter sealed in wax, and was gone.

Wilkinson recognized Daniel Clark's distinctive hand. His hands shook as he slipped a blade under the seals and unfolded the sheet. He read it rapidly. Then he read it slowly. Then he stepped from his tent and vomited into the dust.

That night he paced. He threw himself on his cot, rolled in a blanket, lay with his eyes open and sprang up to pace. It didn't occur to him that with the light of his oil lamp casting his shadow, this restless pacing was visible through the tent's translucent walls. At midnight he walked the guard perimeter. Then back to his tent. At dawn he sat at his camp desk and began to write, pen speeding across the paper. At eight he summoned his officers and told them to be prepared to march at noon. They were going to New Orleans. And he wanted a man on a fast horse to take this dispatch ahead.

TWENTY-NINE

Bayou Pierre, Mississippi Territory,
January 1807

Triumph was sweet as nectar. Burr was ecstatic. He was far down the Mississippi; just ahead lay Bayou Pierre, Natchez a bit beyond. Then Baton Rouge, which he would bypass in view of having had no answer to his cipher letter. And on to New Orleans itself, which Wilkinson presumably had in hand now, awaiting the ultimate leader. The administration man was left far behind along with the ugly questions, the fine distinctions, the duplicity so foreign to the leader's nature.

He was on Comfort Tyler's boat ahead of the others and had rid himself of Blennerhassett at last, sent him back to join his wife when another moment of his company would have been unbearable. A hundred men sailed in this small flotilla, and Comfort and Davis Floyd figured another five hundred had gone ahead and should be waiting at Bayou Pierre and Natchez. Maybe the alarm spreading along his trail had pinched off larger numbers behind but six hundred would be enough.

Bayou Pierre and his old friend Judge Bruin was the

immediate goal. Peter Bruin should have the latest word from Wilkinson. Perhaps the general's caution now was wise, but it didn't matter, they were ready for the dash to triumph. Anyway, Burr was the leader who must stand in front and swing the multitudes; he was the one who mattered. The cipher letter that Sammy Swartwout had carried had been a gentle prod. He had no doubt that word would be awaiting him at Judge Bruin's house.

Peter Bruin was a superior court judge who swung a big stick in Mississippi Territory. He was an old friend—they'd seen combat together in the Revolution—and was close to Wilkinson as well. Exemplary fellow, really, and sophisticated—not much surprised him. Burr had found that every man of scale on the frontier had a natural conspirator's eye. Apparently there were endless ways to profit out here for those with a canny view. Bruin was aptly named, with both the figure and the authority of a bear. He was a strong judge but not above a bit of profit, and last year after Burr's well-placed hints, he'd been thrilled to serve as a key figure in communications and contacts.

When the boat was near Bayou Pierre Burr dressed carefully and posted himself on the bow. They turned into the muddy stream and soon the town appeared, but to his surprise it looked deserted. At least a hundred of his men should be awaiting him; indeed, he'd expected some cheering. They must be bivouacked downstream.

The boat bumped the wharf with a noise that seemed loud in the silence. A yellow dog on the bank studied him, then sat down to scratch. Hardly what he'd expected. As he stepped onto the wharf a wizened man ducked from a store and went scuttling up the road. A lookout? With a leisurely stride, Burr followed toward Bruin's house. A woman burst from a cabin to call in children playing in front; she kept her eyes averted. Otherwise he saw no one.

At Bruin's house he was surprised to see the judge standing at his gate, obviously alerted. It was all very strange and Bruin did not have a welcoming expression but Burr fixed a smile and advanced with hand extended. But, shockingly, the other stepped back, out of reach, arms still folded, the gate locked.

He might have been on the bench passing sentence to the gallows. "What are you doing here?" he said, suppressed fury in his voice.

Burr felt disoriented, the ground shifting beneath his feet. "What?" he stammered. Then, feeling the loss of dignity, cried, "I sent word. Didn't you know I was coming?"

"I never thought you'd come after—"

Burr's stomach was boiling and his tongue stuck in a dry mouth but he managed a calm voice. "After what, Peter?"

Bruin clapped a hand to his forehead. "My God, Aaron, don't you know you've been exposed? Everybody knows what you're doing and I won't be associated with it. I had no part in it, I want no part in it—"

"Goddamn it, Peter, tell me exactly what you mean!"

Bruin's eyes were wild. "And don't give me that claptrap about your grant up the Ouachita. Every fool knows it's worthless, your title's no good. No, no, you planned to attack Spanish territory, you were going to separate the West from the nation, steal Louisiana—it's all over the country that's your plan. Blackens everyone who knows you. Well, let me tell you, I knew nothing—nothing! You never mentioned such to me!"

They'd speculated half the night on the value of Bruin's land grants if there were changes, but he let it pass. "Calm down, Peter," he said, carefully gentling his voice, "and tell me what you're talking about."

"I can't believe you don't know. About the proclamation? You don't know? The president of the United States.

Says an illegal combination is afoot in the West to attack Spanish territory. Says this is a criminal enterprise and calls on all citizens involved to withdraw instanter—"

It came with the suddenness of a punch to the belly and left him gasping. He couldn't understand it, the administration man was far behind him. Something was wrong here. Of course there were rumors, Burr had been fending them off for months, but rumors weren't proof, and he knew Jefferson wouldn't act without proof. If he made charges he couldn't prove Burr could make an absolute fool of him—

But meanwhile Bruin was taking it seriously, and almost automatically Burr said, "That's not my plan. They're talking about someone else. I'll wager it doesn't mention me by name, either, does it?" He could count on Jefferson's caution.

"No," Bruin said, "but the governor's proclamation leaves no doubt. Mississippi Territory. He's called out the militia and posted a warrant for your arrest."

"Peter, Peter, believe me, there's some terrible mistake. I'll have to see the governor, explain—"

Bruin, calmer now, laughed harshly and somehow that made everything he said worse. "I'll give it to you, Aaron, you've got the balls of a mountain bear. But there's no mistake. Wilkinson spelled it all out."

"Wilkinson?"

"Lots of people thought he was in it with you. Everyone suspected, you know, we just tried to believe better—"

No, no, some terrible confusion, Jim Wilkinson was his friend—his voice sounded a squawk in his own ears. "This must be rumor. I doubt Jim would do—"

"Doubt, do you? Why do you think he went to New Orleans? Jehoshaphat! He's arrested half the town. Says there are conspirators everywhere. He's got Adair and Bollman and Swartwout and two dozen others, everyone you talked to there. Shipping them to Washington under guard. He says Clark is involved, only Clark skipped out, went east pretending he's never heard of such a thing. Wilkinson says he just discovered that you were the center of it all. He's cleaning up the edges till he can get his hands on you, then he'll ship you to Washington for trial."

For a moment it were as if his hearing failed, Bruin's lips moving but no sound emerging, so loud was the shriek in his own brain: *It was Wilkinson's idea! He brought it to me, he showed me the way, he invented it, designed it, it was his dream that he sold to me!* He blinked, vision momentarily blurred, then regained control, managed to say, managed even a tone of bemused wonderment, "Ship me for trial? Trial for what?"

"Treason, for Christ's sake!" Bruin had an exasperated tone, felt he was being played with when in fact Burr was struggling to stay on his feet. "Trying to steal the country. He says you're the engineer of it all and he discovered it just in time and ran to New Orleans to pinch it off. He's been sweeping clean ever since, says the conspiracy is so widespread every other man is suspect." He stepped forward, fist cocked. "I don't intend to be suspect, understand? I didn't know a thing about it and if you say I did I'll brand you the miserable damned liar that you are. How dare you bring this on me!"

"Peter, this is rumor, gossip, some idle thought exaggerated into a—"

"Exaggerated? I'll show you—you wait right here. Don't come in—I don't want you in my house!" He ran onto the veranda and returned with a newspaper.

Natchez *Mississippi Messenger* dated January 6, four days ago. Burr read it with mounting horror, mouth dry, hands quivering. The president's proclamation set in large type. The governor's. The arrest order. Burr to be arrested on sight and shifted under guard to the capital of

Mississippi Territory, a hamlet near Natchez called
Washington. Seize Burr, take him under arms, bind him
like a felon, and bring him to authority! He felt a curious
sense of dignity stripped by the very words. It was awful.

Bruin struck the paper with a stiff index finger. "Look
down there at the bottom—some fool sent Wilkinson a
letter in cipher, tells the whole plot. Names you and
everything."

At sight of the letter such nausea swept him that he
feared he would vomit. But he swallowed down his bile
and read the cipher letter that Sammy Swartwout had delivered laying out what he intended and what he expected
from Wilkinson. He had referred to himself in the third
person for clarity and brevity, and he saw instantly as he
had not before that, made public, this would come back
to haunt him. Burr will be here, Burr will be there, Burr
will do this and that, Burr will have two thousand men—

But wait! The letter implicated Wilkinson as fully as it
did him! It was entirely clear what they had planned together. He had to read it twice to see that it wasn't the
original, so artfully had it been altered. Burr's statement
of his plans had been polished so that they became his
alone and Wilkinson's role had vanished. It no longer
was from Burr but had become an anonymous letter
from some patriot who had discovered Burr's plans and
was reporting them to the authorities.

An image of Wilkinson rose before his eyes, fat face
with the broken veins, the little blue eyes hungry and cal-
culating, the way they shifted and slid away, the elliptical
manner of speaking—my God, he'd been the model for
the style Burr had adopted, the old master who led him
on, showed him the way, painted the gold at the end of
the rainbow, sold him the plot—

Bruin was looking at him in a more kindly way.
"Comes as a shock, does it?" he said. "Well, Aaron, I'm
an officer of the court and sooner or later I'll have to re-

port your presence. But I remember dodging British lead with you and that counts for a lot and I ain't going to be too quick to write the governor. But I think you'd better hie yourself across the river out of Mississippi's jurisdiction while you figure out what to do next."

Burr walked back to the boat with bile rising in his throat, the fatal newspaper carefully out of sight under his coat. He swallowed and tried to keep from stumbling. He found Comfort standing on the wharf with a worried frown.

"Something's wrong, Mr. Burr," Comfort said. "Town looked deserted but it ain't. Folks are in their houses, we see 'em peeping at us, but they don't come out. Like they're scared. And where are our boys? They was to meet us here."

Voice as steady as ever, Burr said that plans had changed a little, the early arrivals had already gone downstream and they were to cross the river to a village with a small tavern. He didn't add that it was safely in Orleans Territory.

"You feeling all right, Mr. Burr? You look pale, like you seen a ghost or something."

"Touch of dysentery giving me a little gut pain," Burr said. "Malady of the old campaigner, you know, crops up now and again."

At the tiny settlement on the opposite bank he handed Comfort a roll of banknotes and told him treat the boys. Collect the other boats as they arrived and treat them all. He would walk a bit, see if he could settle the hurt in his belly.

The river had formed a sandy shore here and he walked steadily downstream, beyond sight of his men and into a blessed privacy where he didn't have to guard his expression, where he could face the reality of total disaster.

Yet his mind darted in mad circles from pain to pain,

pausing, tasting, rushing on, but always aware that the ultimate truth lay like a monster in icy depths far below: Aaron Burr was finished. Hopes, dreams, plans, gold like that of Midas, Napoleonic power to cast enemies into the dust, vast *showing* of all who had traduced him—once Wilkinson betrayed him, once the weight of the army was denied him it all was gone, over, done, finished forever.

So total was his defeat. But he must come to that in small steps, must circle at the edges for a while, come cautiously inward. Madness lay in plunging immediately to the center.

Nothing quite shocks and hurts as does betrayal, coming as it must from someone you have trusted. As did no one else in the world, not even his loving daughter, Theodosia, Wilkinson knew everything that Burr planned, everything of which he dreamed. He paced steadily along the vast muddy river boiling toward the sea, his mind darting about like a rat seeking a hole, looking for some explanation that didn't cry betrayal. But there was none.

The thought of Theodosia produced a new shudder. What horror the poor girl would feel; her love for him would be unshaken, indeed would grow stronger as his need increased, but pain would tear at her heart as she saw attacks from every side shatter all his bright promise. Surely this crushing of a young woman's hopes was the cruelest aspect of Wilkinson's betrayal.

And then his daughter's tear-streaked face was dashed from his mind by fresh fury. How could Wilkinson dare to treat him so when the whole idea had been his? His mind swept back across the years. Like a wolf tracking wounded prey, Wilkinson had kept after him, always there at the crucial moment to cheer him, raise his spirits, hint at great things in the offing. Even in the most tense days of the tie with Jefferson, Wilkinson had been there whispering in his ear of the golden West beckoning with the face of fortune. Let's talk of dreams and castles and golden vaults and empires and futures without limits, of vast open country boiling with unrest and hungering for leadership, of an American Napoleon creating a new nation. . . .

But consider. Burr knew nothing about the West. How could he plan to deliver it? Wilkinson was the westerner, the man who knew everyone and everything and could pave the way, the man who forged the dream and sold it whole. And yet the fat general had been cautious to a fault, voluble in his encouragement and flattery, loud in his claims for the West, ardent in his vision of political promise—but conveying every promise by hint and innuendo. The very sound of his own ideas seemed to frighten him—or was he covering his tracks even then? Or had he intended to betray from the start? The whole miserable charade nothing but an evil joke to destroy the only man who made the mistake of trusting him fully? Why, even Senator Smith in Cincinnati, despite years of friendship with Wilkinson, had taken Burr aside to warn him about the kind of man he dealt with. And he had ignored—worse than ignored, he hadn't even heard!

Yet always, everything had depended on Wilkinson delivering the army. Burr wasn't such a fool as to believe a private army alone could invade and subdue Mexico, seize New Orleans, keep it against the might of the United States. But with the U.S. Army on their side, with Britain certain to come in, anything and everything was possible. But Wilkinson had lost his nerve.

Burr came to a fallen tree with its crown drowning in the water, and sat down to restudy the paper Bruin had given him. His own letter, glaring, damning, Wilkinson's role excised. The general's feverish announcement, a vast international conspiracy involving thousands that this moment had come to his attention, every loyal citizen must stand to the defense of the country lest conspirators sweep it away, and so forth and so on.

Next to his letter was one from someone in New Orleans telling of Wilkinson's depredations there. Issued a battery of frantic announcements, established martial law, suspended habeas corpus while ignoring the judge's outrage, thirty or forty people arrested and shipped to Washington for trial, more arrests coming every day, no one dares open his mouth because to complain of high-handed treatment ipso facto makes the complainer part of the conspiracy and leads to immediate arrest. Wilkinson seemed out of his wits.

Then, suddenly, ice water dashed in his face, Burr recognized his own danger. Wilkinson had become his deadliest enemy. Burr was the one man who could destroy him, and while to do so he must also destroy himself, the general couldn't be sure he wouldn't do it. He must stay clear of Wilkinson; if he fell into the general's hands he had no doubt he would be murdered the same night.

For Wilkinson was a frightened man. The fog of fury and pain was rising from Burr's mind, leaving a welcome clarity. Everything said that fear ran the general. His frantic statement and release of the letter, the mad swath he was cutting through New Orleans, the plain fact that explained everything was that Wilkinson had lost his nerve. Faced with the reality of a vast conspiracy maturing after he himself had set it in motion, he had quailed and run for cover. In the end he was a small, frightened man, a natural coward.

And Aaron Burr was a ruined man. As his mind calmed, this was the thought he had kept hidden at the depths behind horror and outrage and fury and wonderment and contempt for the man who betrayed him—but none of that mattered, not really. What mattered was that he wouldn't recover from this. The moment he saw his own cipher letter in print he knew he was finished, that all his hopes and dreams and expectations were washed away. Now he must scramble for his life.

By morning he had decided on everything. The expedition was dead. He would send an emissary to Mississippi authorities: he would surrender if they guaranteed not to send him to Wilkinson but to try him in their jurisdiction where they alleged he had committed offenses. He'd beaten charges in Kentucky and thought he could beat them here. If they wouldn't agree to his terms they would have to come for him, and he wouldn't be easy.

Now he must speak to the men. Two of the boats hadn't arrived, so he waited. A light mist lay on the river. At about ten a small boat carrying a single figure poked out of the mist and made its way to shore with a steady stroke of oars. A solid-looking fellow about fifty in homespun and a hat that had seen much weather stepped ashore. Without a word he drew the boat well onto the beach. The boys watched in silence.

When he was satisfied, he said, "I'm looking for Aaron Burr."

"What can I do for you?" Burr said. He waved back his men who had gathered protectively.

"I'm Colonel Stolt Turner, Mississippi militia. I'm out of my jurisdiction, so I'm not here to give you any trouble. But thing is, I went to see Judge Bruin this morning, and he said I ought to come over and tell you what's on my mind."

"Appreciate it," Burr said. "Come—we'll walk a bit."

They started along the river where Burr had walked the day before, and presently Turner said, "You know how Wilkinson was up on the Red River a little while back, worrying over the Spanish pushing in from the Sabine? Well, I had half of my regiment there to back him up. Now, Mr. Burr, it could be that you like Wilkinson, or did, but I'll tell you flat out I hate the son of a bitch. Acts like he's God Almighty come down to earth. And if he ain't in Spain's pay, my name ain't Stolt Turner. Well, I'm in camp one day and here comes this young rooster talks funny, says his name is Swartwout, asks for directions to Wilkinson.

"Well, shee-it! but don't this young feller think he's somebody! Treats me like I'm his servant. Another minute of that and I might pull his nose for him, but I lead him to Wilkinson's tent and right away I see he treats ol' Wilkinson like an equal, and I see the general don't like that for sour apples. Now, as I turn away I see this young Swartwout hands him a letter that he real quick tucks into his coat."

Turner said all this looked right odd to him, and since he'd like nothing better than to get something on Wilkinson, he sat down under a tree nearby and kept an eye cocked. Pretty soon he saw Wilkinson's orderly lead Swartwout off to the mess tent. It was nearly dark by this time and the general had a big oil lantern in his tent and he went to walking up and down, the light throwing his shadow on the tent wall. Turner found this so interestingly curious that when it went full dark he positioned himself close to the tent.

"And he's walking, pacing, you see, muttering like he's in a temper, and all at once there's this big crash and I see he's kicked over the table, forgets his shadow makes him visible, don't you know, and he says plain as can be and mad as a hornet, he says, 'Goddamn it—the whole goddamned world has heard about it by now!' Then he goes to the flap of his tent and yells for his orderly and I figure I'd better make tracks. But you know, when I read the paper the other day and seen he was blaming you, saying he'd just discovered it, what he said that night, I thought he knew a hell of a lot more about it than he was letting on. And Judge Bruin, he figured you might like to know."

"I do, indeed. Colonel, would you appear—"

"Good God, no! Way things are?" He stared at Burr. "Lookee here—Bruin said you had good sense. You go to calling me, I'll forget what I told you, I'll say Wilkinson's a prince."

Burr wrung Turner's hand. "I understand," he said. "No calls. But thank you—this was valuable." Indeed it was, he thought, watching Turner's boat recede. It answered why Wilkinson lost his nerve. Sammy Swartwout was a cocky young fellow, a regular rooster just as Turner had said, but that wasn't it.

Rather it was that the cipher letter had made everything real for Wilkinson. It said action now. Said let's go. Said, so Burr could see now, *last chance to back out*. It peeled away dreams and rhetoric and boasting and all that talk in smoky taverns so far from the hard facts of conspiracy and treason. But the letter saying now is the time and all is ready and here we go and where are you had faced the general with a stark reality that he had never quite seen before.

For this was a great conspiracy and of course it was dangerous. Of course its perpetrators could finish with their heads in a noose. Wasn't that the nature of great dreams, of plans to seize an empire and reshape the entire face of the world and alter history for all time? What could it be but dangerous? What gain is there without risk? The eternal equation: expand gain while lowering risk. But of course risk is proportional to gain. Burr had always understood that they well could swing for it if this high flyer went wrong, and he was surprised to see that Wilkinson had never quite understood.

Or maybe he had just never looked because the sight was too dark and it interfered with the gentle pleasure of plotting over wine and a well-turned bird. But all that mattered was that Wilkinson was a coward. Risk becomes real and he forgets gain and dreams and instead runs with his tail tucked. He was a goddamned coward!

The plan was workable. They had ample forces. New Orleans right now throbbed with desire to shuck off the United States, seize Mexico, make itself financially and militarily secure, and stand on its own feet. Claiborne could easily be deposed; no one would fight for him. Burr had no doubt that British frigates from the West Indies station would arrive when needed. No, as he had seen all along, the tricky part was to get forces with weapons and money down the river undetected, in position to establish the coup. They had done that, the road was open—and Wilkinson's nerve went.

He was a coward and in the end he acted the coward.

The last boat arrived at noon. Harman Blennerhassett handed Margaret ashore, then swung the children down, then came limping toward Burr with that eagerness in his eyes. Not just now, Burr thought, God, not just now, he couldn't stand to hear Harman's whine, and he put up a rude hand, palm out, that stopped the shambling fool in his tracks. Over Harman's shoulder he saw Margaret watching him.

"I need to talk to everyone together, Harman," Burr said, trying for a gentler tone. "Then we'll see."

This wiped the look of hurt from Harman's face. He smiled. "Thank you, Aaron. Of course I'll wait."

Burr gathered the boys around and gave it to them plain. A plot had been hatched against them. Men who hated him and feared his followers had concocted lying charges that the governor of Mississippi Territory seemed to believe. The president had some concerns too, but that was just residue of the Mississippi claims. The result was that the authorities wanted to talk to Burr, and since he was the essence of law-abiding, of course he was going immediately to turn himself in.

"The charges, of rebellion and so forth, are all lies. Every one. I know and you know we never planned more than a private raid on Spanish possessions, and that was my doing, not yours. You aren't guilty of anything, not one damned thing, so hold your heads high. Remember that you set out on a noble venture, and even if here is where it ends, it'll be high adventure to tell your grandchildren.

"I'll go down to Natchez and see the governor and get this all straightened out. Be back in a couple of days and we'll get on with our plans. But if I'm not, if things go wrong, if they kill me on sight—and that could happen, too—well, I'm leaving a roll of banknotes with Comfort, and you boys sell the boats and the supplies and divide everything."

He pitched his voice lower and lower for drama to stir their emotions and then he added a careful little vibration of emotion of his own. "Now I want to walk among you and wish you Godspeed, want to shake every man's hand and say you've been noble comrades in an adventure that will go down through the ages."

More than one had a tear in his eye and several insisted they would wait for him, he had to come back. But Comfort Tyler folded his arms. "You lied to me, Aaron," Comfort said in a quiet voice. "And you made me lie to these men. You know, I seen it coming a long time now, just couldn't believe it, didn't want to believe it. But you lied to us."

"No, Comfort—"

"*Yes!* Goddamn it, don't lie to me now. You're running out on us way I should've guessed you would, and all I got to say is, you can go to hell!"

Burr tried to continue his farewell but now it was flat, the nobility and grandeur he'd vested in his words drained away.

Harman was standing back with Margaret and Burr came to him last. He took the man's hand but found it limp. Harman's lips were quivering. "What will we do now, Aaron?" he whispered. "What will we do now?"

But before Burr could answer, Margaret stepped before her husband, actually turned and pushed him backward and spun about to face Burr.

"Well, Mr. Burr," she said, "you've given me my answer at last."

"Answer to what?" he said, but the contempt that flashed in her eyes was beyond bearing.

He looked down because he couldn't look up, and so he only heard her answer in a whisper that floated on the wind, "It doesn't really matter now, does it?"

He felt like a whipped dog.

The trial came three weeks later in Mississippi Territory's tiny capital. It was held in a little log courthouse where men hung in the windows to hear the testimony and solicitous court clerks made sure the defendant had a comfortable chair. The proceeding went about as Burr expected since he'd committed no crime in Mississippi Territory. The jury foreman pronounced him not guilty—in Mississippi, anyway—and he walked out to accept the crowd's congratulations. Folks here were still enthusiastic, the residue of his Florida plans. Taking West Florida would give Mississippi Territory access to the sea through Mobile.

He'd spied Bob Ashley in the courtroom, needed a moment to place him, and now he was surprised to find Ashley cutting through the crowd and taking his arm.

They had met in New Orleans the year before; Ashley's pale blue eyes, cool and distant, to say nothing of the fighting dirk he carried strapped to his forearm, hilt plainly visible under his sleeve, immediately suggested that he was a dangerous man. A drooping brown mustache framed a cruel mouth. He was an adventurer; he'd been freebooting in Texas with Nolan when Spanish troops trapped them on the Brazos and killed Nolan and half the party. Ashley had cut his way out with that bloody dirk his only remaining weapon and walked three hundred miles to safety.

Now he had a grip on Burr's arm that was becoming unpleasant as he steered him away from the crowd. Then, master of the covert, he stepped Burr behind a tree and slipped him a letter. "From Ed Livingston in New Orleans. Says you'll know his hand."

The letter, unsigned but certainly in Ed's hand, said, "Your life's in danger. Follow Bob Ashley's lead. Trust him as you would me."

"So?" Burr said, extracting his arm from Ashley's grip and leaning against the tree.

"Wilkinson has sent a detail up to grab you. Six soldiers and Cap'n Hook. You know Hook? No? Slimy son of a bitch—does Wilkinson's dirty work and gets well paid for it. Governor here wouldn't turn you loose long as you faced trial; now you've beaten it, he will. Hook, he'll take you overland to New Orleans and first night out someone'll bust into camp yelling on how you cheated him and put a knife in your belly, rip you from balls to gullet and then escape, and believe me, Aaron, Wilkinson'll just regret the hell out of this accident."

"Um," Burr said. It had an unfortunate ring of truth. "What do you suggest?"

"Get out tonight. I got four horses—ride all night and all tomorrow, we can get well along."

"Going where?"

"Over to the Tombigbee. Folks there are ready to seize Mobile in a moment if you'll lead 'em."

In parallel with the Alabama, the Tombigbee River fed into Mobile Bay and made a perfect outlet for settlers' produce except that the Spanish held the bay. Tombigbee folk saw that as an absolute violation of their natural rights and of the purchase, and they figured Burr talked their language.

He wondered if Ashley was in fact Wilkinson's man, sent to get him alone and kill him. It could be. He looked at the letter again; yes, it certainly was Ed's writing. And Hook was what he'd expected. It would mean leaving his boys stranded, but what the hell. Comfort and Blennerhassett and Davis Floyd and a few others already had been arrested and shipped down the river and probably were on their way to Washington by now. Margaret's face flashed in his mind but he put it aside.

"When?" he said.

"Half hour before midnight. I'll have old clothes for you."

"I'll be ready."

It was brutal. Long before dawn it made Burr feel every minute of his fifty years. Also before dawn he knew the idea of leading Tombigbee settlers in an attack on Spanish Mobile or anything else was a chimera. It would never work. He didn't share this thought with Ashley: riding out of Wilkinson's grasp was what mattered now. He ignored his aching body.

At dawn Ashley cooked a rude meal over a small fire by a creek; they let the horses graze an hour and rode on. There was no talk; Ashley posted himself a hundred yards ahead to deflect questions from passersby. The day was chill and overcast, suiting Burr's mood. His mind circled obsessively back to the betrayal: the whole wonderful scheme had always been Wilkinson's idea. Again he worked through all their encounters as Wilkinson developed and expanded his case as Burr's affairs worsened. Talking and dreaming over bird and bottle, educating Burr on the West, the conspirator's view that imagined all the possibilities, the promise of revolt in New Orleans that his own trip had confirmed, the seductive whisper of gold there for the taking . . .

Yet there was more to it, wasn't there? Something had triggered betrayal. Just Sammy's callow manner? Just the insight that this was real? There had to be more. Something had triggered, someone had turned the key to Wilkinson's fears. Who? Madison? Yes, maybe Madison. How didn't matter; Madison's hand was involved.

It could have worked, too—but the coward had thrown it away. But then with a shaft of insight Burr saw a truth that he had overlooked from the beginning. He had put everything into this venture, life had dealt him cards that forced his hand, he must make this work or he would be destroyed. As he was now. But Wilkinson had put little at risk for he'd always had an alternative. With Burr in the lead, he could lie back and wait to reap the rewards of empire and gold—or he could turn on Burr, denounce conspiracy and become the hero who had saved the nation.

Wilkinson was well hated and his command was always at risk. But now the hero had made himself secure. Jefferson would never cashier him; indeed, Jefferson would laud him as the man who had saved them from Burr. They would try Burr for treason and Wilkinson would be the chief witness for the prosecution.

The sheer cynicism of the man from Monticello who presented himself as the acme of nobility was stunning when Burr considered the timing. The administration man—it proved to be Johnny Graham who'd finally caught up with him and whom Burr had always liked—had started long before Jefferson issued his proclamation. So why did Jefferson wait to denounce Burr? In a flash he saw the answer. They suspected that Wilkinson was involved and feared to drive him into Burr's arms. But when the general declared himself on their side, they would laud him to the skies and use him against Burr. This was cynicism on a grand scale.

Yet as he rode on, slept exhausted by a silent bayou, rode the next day toward the Alabama country with every muscle and joint aflame, the fury and horror and outrage that had assailed him passed on. Wilkinson was slime and in the end had acted as slime. Maybe Burr had always understood him but had refused to see it. Maybe the general's capacity to stir great dreams was all Burr had ever liked about him. Maybe Burr had been too ready to dream, too slow to probe and question. He remembered that Wilkinson had always kept the upper hand, always ready to withdraw the prize. The man had played him like a fish and he had allowed it. Because he had dreamed . . .

Suddenly he was crying. Tears streamed down his face. Thank God Ashley was riding ahead and he was alone. He couldn't seem to control himself; his nerves must be stretched much tighter than he had understood. He wiped his face and the tears increased, gushing from his eyes, a choking sob torn from his throat. He was dumbfounded—and then he realized he was assailed by grief. Grief for a magnificent dream, a dream that had been strangled at birth by cowardice and betrayal.

Gradually the tears dried. He wiped his face as new calm took hold. He felt that yielding to grief had cleansed him and now he could face the future. It was dark but not black. They would seize him soon but he would be out of Wilkinson's way. He would be sent to Washington and tried for treason but they would never convict him. Yes, they would bring Wilkinson against him but they would find they had a troubled witness.

There would be too many questions Wilkinson couldn't answer.

Burr saw that now he must take hold of what would be an unexpected new future. He must preserve his dignity, which was the first step in preserving his neck and then his liberty. Then he must find something to do with the rest of his life. But all would be different too. He had lived on a great scale but now all would be small, pedestrian, mundane.

Yet he couldn't complain. He had soared—because he had summoned courage and made the great gamble. Yes, he had trusted Wilkinson, but then, he never could have started it without Wilkinson. So Wilkinson lived true to his own nature and betrayed. But Burr had made the huge gamble. There is a splendor in trying to rule half a world, and failure in such undertaking is no disgrace. If Napoleon had been destroyed, if he yet came to failure, he would be no less great. Would the world soon forget Aaron Burr? He thought not. For generations to come, long after he withered to dust, his name would be on men's lips. That was no small thing.

★　　★　　★　　★　　★

THIRTY

Washington, early 1807

In some way that quite surprised Dolley Madison, Aaron's capture deep in the woods came as a blow. He had fled Natchez and surrendered to soldiers from Fort Stoddert, the American outpost nearest Mobile. But imagine Aaron Burr, so neat and fastidious and handsome, conveyed across the country in a closed carriage, escort of eight armed troopers, not allowed to talk to passersby, as if he might foment revolution in Carolina. Now he was under guard at Richmond, where the trial would be held.

He was finished, had been since he killed Alex, really, and certainly was now. And he deserved punishment, trying to steal the West and shatter the nation—but she didn't want him hanged. And especially not on the word of James Wilkinson. The general's letter had unlocked everything. It had come like a bombshell, dashed off at top speed, full of florid phrasing, underlining, exclamation points. He had just discovered a vast conspiracy in which countless people were involved and he was striking right and left to weed it out. Burr, the leader, master of western intrigue, would be arrested forthwith. It was this letter that allowed Tom to issue his national proclamation calling on all citizens to resist treason.

Wilkinson's letter included a copy in his own hand of a letter in cipher he said came anonymously but that made Burr's role entirely clear. Yet it was odd, seemed to have no real purpose, and then she realized that the role of the addressee had been omitted. Of course—because the addressee was Wilkinson himself! The general reported that he had struck a truce with the Spanish commander, neither one to attack, and with select troops would race to New Orleans to attack the conspiracy at its source.

Jimmy told her the news of Aaron's capture over dinner.

"Well," she said, "thank God he's out of Wilkinson's clutches." He didn't answer and she couldn't read his expression. "I mean, he probably wouldn't last long in that oaf's custody."

"Really," he said, "that goes much too far." He looked very tired and she knew she should let it go for now, but the national outcry lauding Wilkinson galled her. The general was raising the devil in New Orleans, with some forty men arrested and shipped to Richmond without regard to law. Adair, Swartwout, Bollman, Blennerhassett, Comfort Tyler, Davis Floyd, put in irons on ships and sent to Richmond, all by his report part of the vast conspiracy. For a man who said he had just discovered it, he seemed to know everything about it.

"I mean," she said, "he never would have sent that letter if you hadn't concocted something to frighten him."

He didn't like "concocted" with its suggestion of something underhanded, but in fact she thought the letter he had pressured Clark into sending was pretty sneaky. He had shown it to her the day after it was sent and this is what it said:

*My Dear Friend: I must warn you—everyone knows.
Everyone. Now your plans, your dreams, your hopes
are described as if every man, woman, and child has
looked into your heart. Countless people say they
have heard from you or from someone close to you or
from Mr. Burr that you plan the most horrendous of
high treason.*

*By every account Mr. Burr is seen as part of the
conspiracy but as the lesser figure—you are seen as
the planner, dreamer, instigator who has drawn Mr.
Burr to his doom. Thank God from the start I refused
all your blandishments to join mad adventures. You
will recall that I wrote you a year ago telling you that
talk had become very public and seemed focused on
you as chief instigator. Now it has reached crescendo
and I see little hope for your future. I have removed
myself to Washington mainly to stand aside from the
debris when your inevitable crash comes.*

*O, my friend, I see but one hope for you, though it
may be much too late. Perhaps if you are wise
enough to see the way, you can be the one man, ma-
ligned, attacked, lied about on every side, accused of
treason without parallel, who can yet save himself
and emerge as hero to enter the pantheon of great
Americans who in one way or another have saved
their country.*

*I think there is still time. I write this in hopes you
will seize your last chance.*

Farewell, my friend; I don't expect to see you again.

The letter was brilliant, no question about that—it
played on the weak man's weakness and broke the cabal
that intact was very powerful. She understood that.
Bonded, each with his skill, the general controlling the
army and Burr the politics, they might have been invinci-
ble, and that could have been fatal. Granted, all of it. But

somehow the idea of Aaron Burr hanged on the word of the man who probably lured him in the first place gave her an ache deep in her heart.

Oblivious to her feelings—or perhaps subtly instructing her that she was mistaken—Jimmy was talking about the evil that Aaron had tried to unleash. He was right, too. Aaron was ambitious to a fault, always reaching for the grand prize.

Jimmy said Aaron's attempt on Louisiana was the most serious threat the nation had faced since its birth, and she was sure he was right.

"But it doesn't seem right to have Wilkinson testify against Burr when you know they were in it together."

"Use one to catch the other."

"And let the other go free. Not just free but honored, the hero who saved his country."

"He did, though, in a sense."

"Because he's a coward and you scared him."

"Yes . . . It worked well, too."

She sighed, struggling for what concerned her. Then, "It seems dirty, somehow."

He frowned. "Why? Because we manipulated the manipulators? Broke a combination that could have destroyed us?"

"No, that part's fine. But to use the one you're sure is the guiltiest to convict the other—it has a bad odor. To me, at least."

"But you agree this was deadly dangerous."

"Of course."

"And should be punished. Shouldn't go untouched, no penalty, invitation to others to commit treason?"

"Then you're saying the end, saving democracy, justifies the means?"

"No, I'm—" Exasperation was hardening into anger. "I'm saying if I have two malefactors and can prove one guilty I should do it."

"Even on suspect testimony?"

"I don't know that the testimony as to Burr's role is suspect. That it doesn't include the second perpetrator's role doesn't invalidate it per se."

She started to protest more but thought better of it. Aaron would be tried and should be. She hoped it didn't come to hanging, but there was no doubt he was guilty, no matter how much General Wilkinson might gall her. And then Jimmy said, "Anyway, Burr probably won't be convicted."

That surprised her. She asked why and he pointed out that treason was notoriously hard to prove, and should be. He recalled the debates over that point at the Constitutional Convention. If treason is loosely defined many acts and even words could be construed as treason. So, he went on, it requires a specific act in a specific place before two witnesses.

"But the real reason for doubt—our chief justice intends to try the case personally, sitting as district judge in Richmond. You know how partisan a Federalist he is—and his party is treating this as all political. He won't give us any leeway, you may be sure."

John Marshall enraged the president always and Jimmy often, though in mild moments Jimmy said Marshall was on the way to being a great chief justice. He was defining areas of law in ways that in effect were completing the Constitution. She liked to see Jimmy as the father of that great document, but he told her they'd always known that its application would have to be fleshed out in practice. Marshall was brilliant and perhaps would live in history but he was a partisan mad dog and she could see why his decision to try Aaron himself disturbed Jimmy. That his brother-in-law was the same District Attorney Daviess who had done his best to stop Aaron en route was ample reason for him to appoint another judge, but he had already refused a motion.

Well, Dolley thought, the difference between her and her husband was that he thought in the factual terms of reality and law while she thought in terms of human beings and why they did the things they did. Some arguments are without answers and certainly without victories. They finished dinner and went up to the big bedroom on the third floor. Jimmy read for a while and eventually went to bed while she sat before her dresser mirror with a single candle and slowly rubbed unguent into her glowing complexion.

And she thought about her old friend who had done so many evil things but was not himself an evil man. She knew Jimmy would suggest that to do evil things is the mark of evil, and perhaps he'd be right, she didn't know, but maybe what really bothered her was a conviction that Wilkinson was evil but Aaron, despite his intelligence, was an innocent and a fool.

He put blinders on himself that blocked the vast reality of the world and limited his view to his own narrow self. Perhaps it was hunger more than ambition or greed that drove him. Parents snatched away when he was barely out of swaddling clothes, wife ten years his senior who'd been mother as well as wife, gone to disease. No one admitted a connection between early events and today and she supposed Jimmy would scoff, but she remembered the hurts of her own Quaker youth and knew, for example, that her love of bright clothes was as much defiance of things long ago as a taste for beauty, though she had that too.

Aaron wasn't evil; he dreamed, but they were magnificent dreams. He had lost hugely in his life; perhaps great dreams are necessary for great losses. There is a grandeur to such scale. He wouldn't hang, she didn't want him to hang, and she thought he would not be remembered as a traitor like Benedict Arnold but rather for the splendor of his dreams.

Jimmy had gone to bed, and at last, content in her view, she pinched out the candle and joined him.

Burr saw immediately that they would never convict him. Richmond Federalists welcomed him as a man prepared to defeat and embarrass the hated Democratic administration. Right here in Jefferson's Virginia Burr found plenty of men who couldn't wait to humiliate their putative leader.

John Marshall, chief justice role set aside and sitting as district judge, stood totally opposite to his Kentucky brother-in-law. Of course, Mr. Daviess had been after Burr when he was a real threat. Now captured and impotent, Burr became a new opportunity to attack Democrats. The court immediately released Burr to the custody of John Wickham, one of his lawyers who were provided without charge. The best people in Richmond came to visit and to dine at Wickham's table with the accused. On one evening rather startling even to Burr, the chief justice himself came to dinner. That occasioned some talking even among Federalists, the sitting judge dining with the accused, and Marshall didn't come back.

It was all handled quite nicely; Burr, himself a lawyer of towering skill, had to admire the finesse. A treasonous act must be witnessed by two persons. And such treasonous acts as Burr had committed had all taken place on the Ohio River. The witnesses necessary to prove them were six to eight weeks away. But citing the constitutional right to a swift trial, Marshall set the trial date for sooner than these witnesses possibly could arrive. Those arrested with Burr could not testify against him without testifying against themselves. That left only the fat general with his mutilated cipher letter. Let him show the original and destroy himself along with Burr—or claim he'd mislaid the original, which would reduce the evidentiary value of the copy to zero.

Yet Burr also could see that in his way Marshall was a noble figure. In a series of powerful decisions that attested to the man's mental capacity he had been at work defining constitutional law. Burr had read these decisions with intellectual joy and believed they would stand forever to define American law. Marshall's name doubtless would live in history, but now, in Richmond, he was showing that he didn't intend to give a Democratic administration any comfort.

Conviction seemed out of the question, but what then? What was left him? Burr could see occasionally and dimly that he had brought his woes onto himself. He rarely paused long on that thought but neither did he spend much time on hating Madison. Jimmy had won the great battle, for Burr had no doubt that Jimmy had managed Wilkinson's turn, and how didn't matter. But it was Wilkinson who was the coward and the betrayer. And he had to admit this, too: it was Burr himself who had not perceived the general's weakness until the end. Anyway, life went on; of what value was blame?

There was, though, the matter of debtor's prison that without the gold of Mexico's mines now had resumed its position over his head, hanging by a thread.

So it was no surprise when Simmons McAlester appeared in Richmond. Took one of his ships down from New York, first time he'd been to sea in years despite his brass-buttoned nautical coat and the rolling gait he affected, old sea dog taking his sea legs ashore for an unexpected turn.

He found Burr at lawyer Wickham's house. Burr suggested a turn in the garden. "But Aaron," Sim whispered as soon as they were alone, "what will happen now?"

"Oh, I'll be acquitted."

"Will you be testifying? About . . . about—you know?"

"It'll all work as I say, Sim. You have nothing to worry about. No one will be implicated."

A look combining relief with avarice flashed over Sim's face. "But what then? Do you have plans?"

"Worried about your money, Sim?" Burr asked.

"Well, God Almighty, do you even know how much it totals up to now?"

Burr inspected his fingernails. "Not really."

"Goddamn it, you'd better think about it. Just under twenty thousand dollars in gold, and I ain't your biggest debtor, not by a long shot. When you was vice president and going to be governor and going to rule the West and all that, the money didn't matter, you'd be good for it or you could pull strings that would repay me ten times over. That's how your other creditors felt, and I've talked to a lot of 'em, too. Investing in you was worthwhile. But you're like one of them bare-knuckle fighters, you pour money into him and next day he gets in the ring and gets himself beat to death and where the hell is your investment then? You ain't got no hopes after this, Aaron. Beat the charges and you're still dead. Nobody'll trust you with a dime. So that's the question; when are we going to see some of our money?"

"Speak for all the creditors, do you?"

"Enough of 'em, that's for sure."

"So don't worry so, Sim, really, old man. I'll be acquitted and at that point I'll have a thing of great value."

"This thing, I hope to hell it's saleable."

"Oh, it is. Once I'm acquitted I can't be tried again—can't try a man twice for the same crime, you know. So I'll be free to talk without penalty. And believe me, if anyone, you or anyone else, initiates an action against me for debt, I will publish it all. Names, amounts, promises made, offers tendered—everything. Everyone who stood to profit from my little adventure."

Sim had gone white. "But the money borrowed, that's separate, didn't have nothing to do—"

"Oh, it's all part and parcel, one big package. You were a leading part of the combine but there were others, too. Remind them of that. I have records of everything. Written proof. And I'll nail you all to the wall, you push me on the debt."

Sim was swallowing hard. "But Aaron, hell, you know we're your friends, we ain't talking about—"

"It wasn't just an attack on Mexico, you know, or on New Orleans. No, it was secession, split off New England and New York, that was the real aim and it makes everyone who put a copper into the plot guilty of treason—"

Sim's voice rose to a wail. "God Almighty, Aaron, I never—"

"Others did, and you were involved. Believe me, if anyone takes action against me, everyone will turn out to be guilty of everything. It may not put you in the stocks but it will sure knock your reputation in the head. Tell everyone, now, Sim."

"Aaron, I promise you, no one has such a thought."

"That's good to hear, Sim. We've been great friends over the years—let's do stay that way."

The trial of Aaron Burr exerted a fascination on Danny Mobry. This surprised her for she had not seen him since that night in New Orleans and had avoided his several attempts to call. Yet now she found in him a feckless quality that put a gloss of—well, not innocence, hardly innocence, but as it became ever more evident to everyone but Dolley and the administration that Wilkinson, now testifying as his chief acuser, was in fact the chief perpetrator, Burr seemed more than ever the snipe hunter left holding the sack.

"He was the puppet dancing across the stage," her uncle said with that superior smile, he having escaped prosecution by the skin of his teeth and now the soul of innocence, "and who do you suppose pulled the strings?" He alternatingly amused and infuriated her, but she thought the strings were quite evident.

She even spent a hard day on the stage to Richmond to go see for herself and managed to squeeze her way into the crowded courtroom. She saw Burr at the defense table elegant in a fine suit, his hair properly powdered, his figure erect and confident, his smile even to his adversaries benign and forgiving. Theodosia wore a huge smile but Danny saw that her eyes were red. At a recess Aaron hurried to take Danny's hand and raise it to his lips. "I dare not hope it is my poor travail that brings you here," he murmured, "but it raises my heart till it sings aloud."

Oh, Aaron! He did have a way about him. She wasn't sure quite how the heart sings, but it made a lovely picture, and for just an instant she wanted to kiss him and the force of that night came back fullfold. He saw her response and his hand drew her closer, too close, and she quickly extricated herself and backed away, at which he smiled with even greater satisfaction.

For two days she watched the presentation of testimony. He appeared to be conducting his own defense, at least he was frequently on his feet objecting to this or that, always with graceful allusions and warm respect for the court's dignity. Chief Justice Marshall looked in the mood to send someone to the gallows, preferably a member of the prosecution, whose lawyers he seemed to loathe.

She watched General Wilkinson on the stand bulging in the weird uniform he had designed himself, stumbling, painfully forgetful, amending what he said yesterday in light of what he meant today. To her he seemed to shriek his guilt, but she wasn't the judge. Everything seemed to turn around the cipher letter, which he said was in Burr's writing but which he had somehow mislaid. Since it defied imagination that Burr had written to Wilkinson to confess without involving Wilkinson it became clear that the general couldn't produce the letter nor the defendant describe it without mutual self-immolation.

She would leave at the end of the day; he saw her in the hall outside the courtroom and took her hand.

"They'll never convict me, dear one," he said.

"And then what?"

He struck a tragic pose, hand to his breast. "I shall go into exile; Europe shall be the home that here is denied me."

She was amused and yet touched and again she felt that powerful attraction to him and she stepped back and again he saw it and smiled. Exile . . . the poor devil.

"When you're ready," she said, voice huskier than she'd expected, "let me know. My ships run to Europe; I'll assure you the most comfortable passage."

He took her hand again, brought it to his lips, murmured, "You are as generous as you are beautiful," at which she fled the courthouse and caught the next stage.

For Jaycee Barlow the assignment seemed at once exciting and sad. Mr. Madison told him to go to Richmond to observe and report on the Burr trial and how it was being conducted. Barlow was a soldier, which meant he had plenty of ideas about the chief witness but little knowledge of law or courtroom procedure.

He did know he was involved with a hot potato. Mr. Madison had been in the president's office and had sent for papers that Barlow delivered; he'd arrived at the moment the president exploded in a way quite different from his usual relaxed manner. Immediately Barlow had seen that when crossed this was a formidable man, a point sometimes overlooked. At any rate he had just received a report from Richmond and was livid—Burr was slipping and sliding and pulling all sorts of legal maneuvers, seemed to be conducting his own defense, putting witness after witness to shame, none of them apparently able to touch a man who obviously was guilty. It was infuriating!

Quite surprised, Barlow saw that Mr. Jefferson hated Burr in a way that Mr. Madison didn't. He wanted the man guilty and condemned, and if they hanged him it would only be justice. Maybe it went back to Burr trying to steal the presidency from him, but after all, in the end that hadn't worked. You'd think the president would put it behind him. But then one day in another burst of rage Mr. Jefferson shouted that any man willing to destroy so noble an experiment as the second revolution embodied—the capacity to lead the whole world toward democracy!—should rot in hell. Barlow knew the president considered this second revolution idea—and truly it was a radical change from the days of Federalism—his special legacy. Perhaps hating the man who would destroy it out of his own cupidity was only natural.

As soon as Barlow reached Richmond he found that Wilkinson was creating a real stir. Everyone seemed to believe him the guilty one and Burr the dupe. Wherever Wilkinson went he was jeered. In a tavern one night the remarks hurled at Wilkinson as he tried to eat dinner were downright painful, even though Barlow couldn't stand the man. The talk was all over town that Sammy Swartwout, who was quite a brawny fellow, had shouldered Wilkinson off the sidewalk so that he fell prone in the mud in his fancy uniform. Swartwout stood on the sidewalk cursing him and offering a challenge while Wilkinson picked himself up, wiping mud from his face, then slowly walked away through the mud.

Andrew Jackson came to Richmond prepared to testify and was so choleric he frightened both sides, roaring and fulminating his assurance that Burr was guilty but that the real criminal of the enterprise was Wilkinson. He pushed Wilkinson around a taproom one night, literally thumping stiff fingers against the fat general's chest, walking him backward all over the room, begging him to challenge. Jackson was a major general commanding Tennessee militia and seemed to love the military, which Barlow could fully understand. Doubtless that added to his hatred for Wilkinson, since for a soldier the army commander was an immense disgrace. Jackson called Wilkinson a proven traitor and an arrant coward who would brook any insult rather than challenge. Which appeared to be true, for that matter.

On the stand, never mind the legal folderol, Barlow could see that Wilkinson was hopeless. He sat there sweating, his strange uniform askew, his saber laid half across his knees, stumbling, hesitating, contradicting himself. He seemed never sure quite where he was, what he was doing here, what he should be saying. That is your testimony today, General? It contradicts your testimony of yesterday. Ah, then I mispoke yesterday. Yes, confused, upset. Misspoke yesterday. An hour later he contradicted something of three days ago. Misspoke then, too. Made you sick to see that the simple truth was quite beyond him, and the reason for this was almost instantly clear. He was too deeply involved.

Take the cipher letter that stated so clearly that Burr was guilty of this and of that. How did Wilkinson receive it? To whom was it addressed? From the wording it clearly was not just a report from some interested citizen alerting the general. It was meant for someone. But whom? It seemed to assume the recipient would do something, involve himself in some way. Apparently something called the rules of evidence said that an original document always was the best evidence, a copy was largely to be discounted.

But the letter Wilkinson published was a copy. Well, yes, he said, stammering, but he had had to decode the cipher Burr used. So produce the original. He would love to do that, it would explain all, but it had been mislaid. Mislaid? This document central to the most dangerous conspiracy the nation had ever faced? Mislaid? Mr. Chief Justice Marshall glared at the general with a force that Barlow could feel in his own chest. Gripping both arms of the witness chair Wilkinson began to cry.

A pox on both their houses, Barlow thought. Burr certainly wrote the letter and can't produce his own copy because it would convict him. It obviously was addressed to Wilkinson; there was no other reason for it to be written, since, taken as doctored, it amounted to a confession. But the original was mislaid, doubtless in a fire, obviously because it would incriminate Wilkinson. The whole thing was downright disgusting.

When he felt he'd seen enough he caught a night stage to Washington, arriving exhausted at noon the next day. As ordered, he reported immediately to Madison.

"Sir," he said, "there's a miscarriage of justice going on in Richmond. Anyone can see that Wilkinson is guilty as hell but the prosecutors are using him as chief witness to convict Burr. I don't hold any brief for Burr but it don't seem fair. I figured you'd want to take a hand— seems like a rank injustice. Burr shouldn't get convicted on a lying mountebank's testimony. . . ."

His voice trailed off. Mr. Madison was gazing at him with cold, harsh expression, no give at all in his manner. "The general may have been involved in some way," he said, "but at the moment the point is to convict Burr."

Barlow was shocked. "Even with tainted evidence?" He saw anger flash over the secretary's face and realized that he had just more or less accused the man of dishonesty.

"I don't know that it's tainted and neither do you," he snapped.

"I know he's lying," Barlow said.

"But about what? His own role, yes. Burr's role, no, I don't think he's lying."

"Sir," Barlow said, "are you agreeing that he was involved and is trying to hang it all on Burr?"

"Yes. Burr is the important one."

"Because the president hates him, sir?"

"Captain Barlow, you are on the edge of impertinence. Just what do you mean, sir?"

"Well, seems to me Burr's not in position to do much harm but this will leave a piece of lying scum in command of our army. I'd think he was the important one."

Madison sighed. "I think we've talked enough. Write out your report for me."

"Yes, sir."

Barlow went off and was back in an hour.

"I believe I'll offer my resignation, acceptance at your convenience."

"What in God's name—why?" Mr. Madison cried.

"Well, sir, I reckon you'd tell me you and the president support this rotten creature in testimony that you know skirts the full truth even if it doesn't lie outright—and I believe it does—and I expect you'd tell me that's the nature of politics."

"I might," Madison said. "It's a matter of nuances of authority and responsibility. I say it's not the end justifying the means, but you may take it that way if you wish. I think it is keeping what is important in clear view. What matters is that the country was saved and Burr was the man who could destroy it. Not Wilkinson. You've just seen Wilkinson in action. Tell me you think he could undermine the nation. But Burr? Burr is a man of power, al-

ways has been. Look how he's conducting this trial. Butter wouldn't melt in his mouth."

"Maybe you're right, Mr. Madison," Barlow said
slowly. "I wouldn't know. Man lying under oath, swears
to tell truth, whole truth, all the truth, and then leaves out
his own role, sounds like lying to me. I tell you, sir,
you've been mighty kind to me and I appreciate your
giving me this education, but I've seen enough politics
now to see I'm not cut out for the life. I don't think I
want to run when old Mr. Cunliffe steps down. It ain't
the life for me."

Mr. Madison sighed. "I'm sorry to hear that, Jaycee.
Yes, there's an ambiguity in politics, always has been, always will, I don't doubt. If you have trouble with ambiguity, if you like things direct and clear-cut, perhaps
you're making the right move."

"I like things honest, sir."

Mr. Madison flushed. "That will do, sir," he said. And
then, "You may consider your resignation accepted as of
now." He took up papers from his desk, glanced up at
Barlow and said, "Good day, sir."

Barlow slowly cleared off his desk. He spoke to no
one. That last remark, he could have kept it to himself.
But it did sum up how he felt. He remember thrusting out
a foot to break up that press-gang. He just did it. Didn't
think it over, didn't question himself or consider consequences. Put his foot out and yelled for the youngster to
run.

That's what he had done today. Thrust his foot out.
Tripped himself, maybe, but goddamn it, the man had
guilt written all over him and they were using him to get
the other, and that raised the same feelings the press-
gang had raised. But maybe he'd come back someday
and thank Mr. Madison proper and apologize for that last
gibe. Or maybe he wouldn't.

Margaret Blennerhassett simply waited for Harman to come. She'd last seen him when he was seized before her and the children, manacled, and taken to New Orleans. From there, with Comfort Tyler and Davis Floyd and a few others, he was shipped to Richmond for trial. A stream of letters arrived to reassure her; he was imprisoned awaiting trial but wasn't uncomfortable. His comments on it all showed his intelligence—if only he could use that faculty in his own behalf! And in hers . . .

She was still in Natchez. Young Butler and Neville had given her their keelboat, an act of kindness that brought her to tears. She considered living on the boat, but Mrs. Mead said that would never do. Mrs. Mead was the wife of the acting governor who'd smashed Mr. Burr's plans, and she had appointed herself Margaret's protector, which Margaret sorely needed. Mrs. Mead arranged an even swap of the boat for a tiny house with garden and shed in back which included a cow.

A neighboring woman taught her to milk the cow without getting kicked and showed her the intricacies of making a garden yield food. She took in washing for boatmen and soon had income that allowed her to leave sealed the jewelry and silver she had hidden among the children's clothes in her big trunk. Mrs. Mead sent a gentleman who presented a shotgun with the barrel cropped short and showed her how to use it, admonishing her not to present it till she was prepared to fire. A new world of reality was opening for her, which gave her immense assurance for the future.

Would that she had learned such lessons long ago! Life in an Irish noble family surrounded by servants and tenants had prepared her for nothing but its continuance. And Harman insisting on replicating that life in the New

World, throwing away their resources until there was scarcely anything left. Of course Harman had fallen at Mr. Burr's feet—that machinating little man had seemed to offer him a way out.

She would have been willing to kill Mr. Burr the day he left them—fortunate for him she hadn't yet acquired a shotgun—but as the months wore on she saw the Blennerhassetts' situation ever more clearly as of their own making. Poor Harman with his dreams, and she with no way to counter them.

His long, insightful letters were as good as attending the trial. In the end he was found not guilty, along with Burr himself and Comfort and the others. Interesting, she thought, given that she knew they all were guilty, but maybe God had intervened on their behalf because aside from the law she could see now that they were all innocents. Even Aaron Burr.

Harman wrote that he was free to leave at last and that he was going to their island in the Ohio to salvage what he could. Of course there would be nothing realizable, but in her new course of thinking she made no protests. Let him go and see what he could find and when he finally reached here she would introduce him to reality. Meanwhile she had clothes to wash; her business was growing and she had a few coins set aside.

Late in the year he finally arrived, empty-handed, of course, creditors had claimed the island in full. The great house on which they had lavished a fortune was gone. Harman swept the children up in his arms and they all laughed and cried and she was full of joy on which no shadows were cast. For he had brought something else. As they talked it became evident to her that he had absorbed some of the hard lessons she had learned and had drawn some of the same conclusions. Harman was Harman—he would never be fully cured of dreaming, but he would dream within limits, limits she would set.

She folded herself into his arms. "Oh, darling," she whispered, "I'm so happy!"

A bit after the verdict of not guilty filled Washington papers Danny Mobry received a note signed Aaron. He was going into exile in Europe. Had her offer been serious?

She consulted Captain Mac. In the seven years since Carl's death, miserable and lonely years in fact, Mobry Shipping had prospered. Slowly and painfully she had proved herself to the shipping fraternity. She had seventeen vessels now and Captain Mac stayed ashore these days seeing to their scheduling, loading and unloading, and repair. Danny could see that he and Mrs. Mac were getting old.

Most of their ships were on the New Orleans run but Mac said *Clarissa Ann* would sail to New York, then to Halifax, back to New York and on to Liverpool. Aaron said that was splendid; he had business in New York and would be waiting when his vessel returned, and then off to merry England.

Clarissa Ann sailed in a week. Aaron boarded that morning at the Mobry wharf and she was there to welcome him. She showed him his handsome cabin well fitted for comfort. In a small book rack he spotted a copy of Plutarch's *Lives* and smiled.

"You honor me," he said. "I shan't be alone at sea."

He looked at her with such appeal, at once dashing and vulnerable, proud warrior brought to his knees but never humbled, that she felt stricken. She stepped close to him, put her arms around his neck, and kissed him. The kiss went on and on, deeper and stronger. She felt him harden against her. At last, gasping, she tore her mouth away.

He was breathing hard. "You're coming with me," he said, voice high with hope. "Oh, Danny, it will be wonderful!"

She stepped back, moving her shoulders to resettle her gown, and said, "No, Aaron. I am not coming with you. Bon voyage—may the future deal with you more kindly than has the past."

"Danny—" he said, but she stepped out of the cabin, firmly closed the door, and made for the gangway. On the dock she turned; lines were being cast off and she saw him at the taffrail. He gazed at her, not smiling, and then he bowed; she curtsied in response and turned and hurried along the wharf.

Clinch Johnson stepped from a shadow. Without a word he offered her his arm. She clung to him realizing with absolute amazement that she was delighted to see him, though she had seen him the day before and the day before that. It was the way she had been delighted to see Carl whenever he came home, for he was friend and lover and husband and partner and the guarantor of her happiness—and now he was dead. And Clinch Johnson in his quiet way, always there but rarely speaking, bits of advice coming as sage comments but never as suggestions, a friend on whom she counted ever more fully, always available but never making an advance, like a husband in all but . . .

She stopped him, turned, pressed her face against his shoulder. "Oh, Clinch . . ." Then, leaping from the cliff with an exultant inner shout, she whispered, "Take me home, Clinch. Make love to me."

At the big house Carl had built with its view of the Capitol she called Millie, a tiny black woman, freed slave, who was much more Danny's lifelong friend and mentor than housekeeper. Millie was always after her—said a woman without a man was just naturally incomplete and it was time she faced up to life, crying over Mr. Carl was fine but *years* had passed.

"Millie," she said, "Mr. Johnson is coming upstairs with me and I don't want one word from you!"

"Yes, *ma'am!*" Millie looked for a moment as if she would applaud, and then Danny took Clinch's hand and led him up to the bed she had shared with Carl. He was a big, vigorous man and he took her with an enthusiasm that left her gasping. Afterward, lying with a leg over his, hands caressing his face as she smoothed back those tufts of hair, she murmured, "Oh, my dear, what are we going to do?"

He kissed the palm of her hand. "Well, it happens I own the house next to mine."

"And?"

"I could sell it to you."

"My. Wouldn't that be obvious?"

"Not really. The back doors are close together and I put in a hedge that by now has grown so tall and full that no eyes can penetrate it."

"My," she said again. She slid closer to him and felt his reaction. "When did you buy this house?" It emerged as a whisper.

"Not long after I met you."

She was very close to him now. "And when did you put in the hedge?"

"Not long after that."

"Kiss me again," she said.

★　　★　　★　　★　　★

THIRTY-ONE

Washington, late summer 1807

So Aaron was gone in search of such advantage as he
might scrape together in Europe and Dolley was pleased
to be done with him. Of course she had followed the trial
as well as she could from a distance, and with decidedly
mixed feelings. It had been so political, so little interested in facts, so obsessed with scoring angry points, that
you could say it didn't mean much. But at another level
she saw it as full of meaning.

Aaron escaped punishment but he couldn't escape
his obvious guilt. The administration had plunged into
the politics, using the oafish Wilkinson as chief prosecution witness when it was obvious that he had been
participant if not leader. But no, not the leader, really.
Instigator, that was it. She didn't doubt it was Wilkinson's idea from the start but he was not the man to carry
it out.

She knew what wasn't known by more than a half
dozen people and would never be made public—that
Jimmy's letter had gone like a stiletto to Wilkinson's
core, which was a ball of cowardice. That Jimmy could

divine that with such clarity was another signal of his brilliance. Probably the scheme began with Wilkinson, but Aaron was the man who could lift it from the realm of barroom whispers to the real. That was the capacity that made him so dangerous. And made so tragic his insistence on throwing away his gifts. It all left her with profoundly conflicted feelings.

Later she supposed it had been those feelings that had led her to stop her carriage when Aaron hailed her on Pennsylvania Avenue a couple of weeks before what proved to be his departure. It was one of those occasional days in the Washington summer when a tide of cool, dry air from the north drives out damp heat and the sun gives hard-edged glitter to everything and people and horses and dogs are in splendid humor. She told Robert, the freeman who served as their groom and driver, to open the landau top before they set out, she with a parasol open overhead since it was an article of faith that nothing destroys a woman's looks more rapidly than direct sunlight. Bound for a whist gathering at Maggie Smith's, she had left early to enjoy the drive.

And there was Aaron, stepping into the roadway waving his stick. She had told Robert to stop but when Aaron made to enter the carriage she had closed her parasol with a little pop and slapped it across his chest.

"No," she had said. Parade around Washington with Aaron Burr in her carriage? Certainly not! She told Robert to step down and hold the horses, which put him out of earshot.

Aaron had a wounded expression. He looked tired, grayer than she remembered, thicker in the waist. His clothes were still good but he lacked that perfect look of a man who dresses for women's inspection. "I'm going abroad," he said, "and I'd hoped I would see you. Didn't want to call, you know, but I thought an accidental encounter would embarrass no one."

Her voice was cool. "Accidental encounters do not include touring about as if we're old friends."

"What do you mean? We *are* old friends."

"We were. Once, long ago. But no longer."

"Dolley, really! Are we to let nasty politics destroy friendship. We were never political, you and I."

But that wasn't going to work. She had had her fill of remembering with gratitude, with defending Aaron for old time's sake. Yet even as she thought this the old memories were strong. He did look as if he had paid a price for his adventures, especially that tightness around his eyes. But otherwise he wore the same easy expression, relaxed and confident, generous and genteel, that she had known so long. But it had none of the old effect, for now all was different. He had made himself indefensible.

She said as much and he grimaced as if he'd been struck.

Then, voice low, apparently in pain, he said, "Please, dear Dolley, this is just politics."

But the momentary weakness had passed. "First," she said, "don't you 'dear Dolley' me. And second, it isn't just politics—it goes to the heart of what you are."

"Really?" His face hardened. "And what am I, in your view?"

"A mountebank," she said. He stared at her with a wild quality she hadn't seen before. She felt a little tremor that she recognized as fear and this made her angry. How well did she really know him, after all? But more importantly, the thoughts flashing through the pause in their talk, what really lay behind this sudden anger that made her want to gore him, hurt him? This was totally different from her attitude of the last dozen years. Was she really ready to write him off as a friend? The answer, she saw abruptly, was that he had written himself off. She was tired of Aaron Burr, tired of defending him, tired of see-

ing Jimmy plagued by him, tired of his antics and his
selfish—

"Yes," she snapped, "that's exactly what I mean. A
man who postures for his country but acts only for himself. Selfish, in love with himself, sure that the world
owes him much for all his gifts and brilliance but not
willing to serve—"

"Not willing! By God, madam, that is unfair, I've
served—"

His voice rose and two men in a passing carriage
turned curiously. There was considerable traffic on Pennsylvania, especially on such a glorious day, and she
thought everyone who passed recognized Aaron and saw
the wife of the secretary of state in deep conversation
with him. Probably it wasn't wise, but so be it. Deep in
the woodsy lowlands lying alongside Pennsylvania Avenue she heard shotguns bang. Presently a man with a
dog, gun over his shoulder, bird dangling from his hand
by the neck, emerged from the woods and crossed Pennsylvania. Looking about, she tried to calm herself without much success. Talking about his service! What
service?

"Aaron, for goodness' sake, you've served no one but
yourself from the beginning. Trying to steal the presidency—"

"Oh, my God, are we going to go back to that?"

"Of course. It set the tone for everything that followed. Killing Alex—tell me you didn't dog him to the
point that he had to duel?"

She saw him color and he didn't answer.

"When I realized what you'd done I saw you might do
the same with Jimmy—"

"No, Dolley! I never had such a thought. Never."

"That's all very well, but I'll tell you something,
Aaron. I thank God in heaven that you have placed

yourself beyond the possibility of killing Jimmy. Because you're disgraced. You have no standing now as a gentleman."

"Oh! That's not true!"

"It is. Think about it. Jimmy wouldn't dignify a challenge with an answer now. I wouldn't let him."

She saw he was angry and that calmed her and she settled back in her seat.

"You assume my guilt, then?"

"Certainly. So does everyone else."

"Everyone but the jury."

"Tut! You weren't proven legally guilty, that's all. And I'm glad—the last thing I wanted was to see you hanged."

"How gracious," he said.

They glared at each other, and again she was struck by the sad knowledge that once they had been friends and now were not. He had placed himself beyond the pale and she could mourn that but she couldn't repair it. She sighed. "Oh, Aaron," she said, softening her voice, "why did you listen to that fat piece of offal?"

"Wilkinson? What makes you think—"

A bird shrilled suddenly in a small oak tree as if reflecting her irritation. "Don't be ridiculous," she snapped. She shook a finger close to his face. "Listen, if you're going to take the position that the verdict gave you anything more than slipping the noose you might as well walk on, for I don't even care to talk to you. Of course, Wilkinson! Who else? You know nothing of the West, you're the most urban man I've ever known. I'll wager you felt like a fish out of water every moment you were there!"

He smiled a little at that, anger seeming to pass a bit. "Somewhat," he said, and added, "trusting Wilkinson was not my wisest move either, I'll give you that."

"A dreadful man," she said.

"Yes." He hesitated, then brightened. "I've known him for years and I admit that once I liked him. A serious mistake. But how insightful of you to see so deeply and clearly. Yes, I suppose I was Wilkinson's victim in a way. You see—"

But she cut him off. "No, no," she said, "we're not going to become old friends again denouncing Wilkinson as your seducer. Reflecting on how poor Aaron has once again been misunderstood and mistreated in his innocence, how his heart was pure, his conduct impeccable—"

"Damn it all, Dolley, I didn't say—"

"You listened to Wilkinson. He fed something in you, that damnable hunger of yours, that unbelievable yearning." He stared at her, not answering. "That *wanting*," she went on, "that's what was at the core of you. Everything revolved around you, what you wanted, what you needed, what you would do and how you would do it and what the profit would be. Steal the presidency, kill Alex when he got in your hair, try to steal the West when the East gave you thumbs-down—and was there ever, *ever* one thought in your head about what might be good for the country?"

"Oh, the country!"

"Exactly! Jimmy says you created the most dangerous moment since the Revolution itself."

"Jimmy! Jimmy's an ass when he says—"

"He is *not!*" she shouted. Unconsciously her arm flew up and she stopped herself just short of slashing the parasol across his face. She was panting and he gazed at her dumbfounded and then she saw something sad flow into his face, as if he recognized love when he saw it and love had fled his own life with the death of Theodosia.

"Aaron," she said slowly, "we're finished. You were kind to me once and I owed you gratitude. I think I've repaid that, and now I call it quits. This latest trick puts you beyond the range of decent folk. I wish you well but I don't expect to see you again, and I hope that will be the case."

His mouth opened as if to answer and she saw defiance mixed with pleading but he didn't speak. His mouth closed, lips in a firm line. He stepped back and bowed. "Good day, madam," he said.

"Good day, sir." She nodded to Robert, who swung up into the box. "Drive on," she said.

THIRTY-TWO

Late in the fall of 1808 as vote tallies poured in from the Maine district of Massachusetts to the western end of Tennessee it became evident that James Madison had been elected president of the United States. Madison was a modest man, prided himself on lacking undue pride, kept a quiet demeanor, and would no more have jumped into the air to click his heels than he would have tried to fly. But with all that modesty of manner he still had to admit that winning the presidency was the goddamnedest sensation he'd ever experienced, and if it got any better the top of his head might blow off!

Why, he felt more satisfaction than he had (in, of course, his quiet way) the day Dolley came home and told him she'd seen Aaron Burr on the street just before he exiled himself off to Europe and out of their hair once and for all. And then she had said that she had perceived him at last to be a self-centered monster who would sacrifice his country for his own gain without a second thought. And, the part that had struck Madison like fine wine, she had told Burr so and dismissed him from her life. Madison hadn't been jealous, really, she had given him no cause for jealousy, and to have owned up to such emotion would have demeaned her, but just the same . . . Well, put it just that he had, after all, noticed her tendency to stand up for this scoundrel whom women pursued with mattresses on their backs.

President of the United States! He emerged with 122 electoral votes. The Federalist candidate had 47. That was approaching a three-to-one lead. Old George Clinton, who'd replaced Burr as vice president and hoped to elevate himself, took a bare six votes, a minor share of New York's count. And James Monroe, running hard and planning a triumph, won not one electoral vote, none, zero, not a jot or a scrap or a lick, not hide nor hair nor tittle!

Of course Madison didn't express himself with such exuberance, he being a man of quiet demeanor, but triumph is sweet to even the most modest man. And Jim Monroe, darling of the radical Democrats led by John Randolph of Roanoke, he of the pissing hounds and the crackling rhetoric, had done his best to demolish Madison's hopes. Poor Monroe might well make a president someday, but not this day. Madison and Jefferson had warned him again and again that the treaty he was negotiating with the British must deal with impressment. We couldn't tolerate the Royal Navy stealing our men at will. Well, Madison could see Monroe's point, too—Jim knew that the British would not yield on impressment and we had no way of forcing them, so he took the best treaty he could get. But, as Madison counseled the president, better no treaty than that! So no treaty it was, which enraged Monroe, who then listened eagerly to Randolph's wild whispers that the whole point of the exercise had been to position him for failure.

But Monroe and the radicals were small cogs in the British imbroglio. The Royal Navy defending the nation against Napoleon continued to handle Americans without gloves. Madison could understand the British position if he really tried, Napoleon an implacable enemy controlling the Continent and determined to strangle the island nation. But what about *our* position? That's what mattered to Madison. Especially since he was convinced that Britain was living in a dream world. If it understood the extent to which it actually depended on its American trade it would draw in its horns—and Madison was ready to give it a demonstration if it didn't mend its ways!

The unpleasant Mr. Merry, Britain's ambassador, and his even more unpleasant missus were replaced by a handsome young man of impeccable manners named David Erskine, and for a while Madison thought things would look up. Then, as if determined to slap our faces, a British warship opened fire on an American frigate in the Chesapeake Bay within sight of Norfolk! Any nation's warship has all the rights of sovereignty inherent in native soil—it was an act of war. Caught unaware, the American ship with three dead and twenty-three wounded was forced to strike its colors and submit to a search for British deserters.

Orators mounted their boxes on every corner to say if we wouldn't fight over a clear act of war we wouldn't fight over anything. All right! It was time to implement the ultimate weapon, the economic weapon! He and Jefferson pushed an embargo bill through Congress; ships could ply coastwise trade but neither exports nor imports to Britain would be allowed. Let Britain try to get along without the American market. Trade collapsed. Grass grew in the streets of American seaport towns. Borders, especially that with Canada, proved remarkably porous. Britain hardly seemed to notice and certainly didn't soften its position. We might be punishing them but we were punishing ourselves more. Cutting off our nose to spite our face, opponents kept insisting. Madison began to have the uncomfortable feeling that they were right—

and that Dolley was right when she said this miserable embargo that was throwing everyone into bankruptcy might be just the trick to put a Federalist back in office!

But he held the line and by God, Americans held it with him. Still, it was a failure, solved nothing and nearly broke the economy. It was only repealed after the election as if it might be undue pandering to give people what they wanted *before* the election, though Dolley argued that might not be a bad idea.

And *still* the vote went three to one for Madison, for the second revolution, for the new democracy!

That was triumph!

Nothing accidental about it, Dolley was saying, nothing, nothing, nothing! Madison had said something to the effect that this or that had been a lucky break, and she had snapped that luck had nothing to do with it. They had fought a great fight and they had won. They were lingering over breakfast on a Sunday.

"I suppose," he said, "though there wasn't much opposition, way it turned out."

"Oh, Jimmy," she cried, "that wasn't the fight." He gazed at her; she was in a blue dressing gown of a shade close to the color of her eyes, her cheeks were flushed and rosy from sleep, her black hair a little tousled—what a beautiful picture! He started to say as much but she waved him aside.

"Be serious! On what do you think people—voters—based their judgment? Not the British outrages. Firing on our ship angered us, granted. Royal Navy seizing our ships and stealing our men irritates us, of course. But sailor pay has gone up four hundred percent, didn't you tell me?"

He nodded. "A full twenty dollars a month now."

"And ship owners are getting rich?"

"Yes."

"And irritation aside, most people don't really give a fig for what Britain does? True, isn't it?"

He laughed. "I suppose so."

"So," she said, smiling broadly, "what won the election was Louisiana. Isn't that so? Devised the means of keeping it out of that selfish beast's hands, Aaron with his insane greed."

She folded her napkin and jumped up. My, she did have a way of lifting his spirits! She was already full of plans if not dreams for making the President's House, or the White House as a few people were calling it now, a national treasure, what she called a great building to exemplify a great nation. She and Mr. Latrobe had been drawing plans for weeks and Tom had turned her loose to do as she liked even before he left office. She bustled off to dress and rush out to examine fabric for the cushions she wanted made for the great oval room.

Sukey brought more tea and he lighted a cigar and shook out a copy of the *Intelligencer* but in the end he didn't read. He sat with his feet up on a window seat looking out into trees now giving up the last of their golden leaves on a warm fall day when the air still had a faint touch of summer's softness.

The Second Revolution was over, he thought, revolutionary victory set with this election. Three to one! That meant profound satisfaction with the way things were going despite the British trade embargo. When they had voted in the Jefferson administration eight years before, it had had a definite ring of a trial. All right, we like what you're saying, we'll try it, give it a shot, give you a chance. But you'd better make good!

If Napoleon had put himself astride the Mississippi River that would have been a disastrous failure labeling the new democracy as fatally weak and spelling its end at the next election. Had Burr succeeded in carving out the whole center portion of the continent for his private empire, had Wilkinson kept his nerve and stayed the course, had they subverted the army and seized Mexico's gold and set up a new empire, the new democracy would have been finished. Madison didn't doubt that the scamp had placed the nation in its greatest peril since the Revolution itself. Had Burr succeeded, chances were good that New England Federalists would have insisted on writing off the challenge and forgetting the West, and then the United States would have been reduced to the little seaboard power, which seemed to appeal most to New Englanders anyway.

Now that it was over the very thought of what might have resulted gave Madison chills. We could forget the burgeoning West. Forget the idea of a continental nation. Abandon the magnificent trek that young Meriwether Lewis and his friend Captain Clark and their intrepid men had just made across the continent and back. In the end, forget even Kentucky and Tennessee and Ohio, and finally, everything west of the Appalachians. Forget the nation as we know it if Aaron Burr's terrible plans had succeeded.

For look at it, after all. Would we have reestablished an army and gone west to fight the new power and reclaim the continent? Maybe. But maybe not, too. Britain wanted North America split; certainly it would have allied with and put the Royal Navy at the service of the new empire. Tennessee and Kentucky folk were patriots, but with a new country offering economic bounty and the old country helpless, their allegiance might have shifted. Already the fact that the new territory strengthened the slavery bloc was alienating the North still further. New England saw its vote diluted, its once preeminent role in the country deteriorating. Would it send its sons to fight for slavery of which it disapproved wholeheartedly?

And somehow, without it ever clearly being stated, the people knew that. They understood what the new democracy had given them just as they would have understood and acted if it had failed.

For the premise was utterly simple. It said that free men have the capacity, the restraint, the self-discipline, the power to govern themselves. That's what the new democracy meant; that's what its success said, and that explained three-to-one voting in support.

That this magnificent reception spilling out before his eyes was all in his honor struck Madison as almost eerie. In deference Tom had gone off to Monticello. Being the center of attention left Madison feeling strange and uncertain. The affair was splendid, though, which was all Dolley's doing. There must be a hundred guests already with more pouring in to wander through the rooms of the President's House. Men of every stripe came with their ladies, servants with trays of Champagne in crystal flutes and savory tidbits, tiny sandwiches and bite-sized morsels from the ovens all stacked in heaps. The long table in the state dining room was heavy with platters of food, gold-imprinted plates ready at each end with little silver forks. Two vast punch bowls anchored a table under the windows, ice floating in a bath that was mostly corn liquor to which rural congressmen flocked, a footman opening new bottles of the gentleman's choice, Madeira, as fast as they emptied, which was fast indeed. The clatter and buzz and laughter grew louder until the whole house seemed to shake with pleasure.

The receiving line had held him fast for more than an hour. Congratulations, Mr. President-elect, we're happy for you, we want to work with you, disagreements may arise but you know how highly we regard you, on and on, his hand sore, responding in platitudes and inanities in a voice that seemed to sink down into his chest as if it wanted to disappear. He had to laugh at the thought. It wasn't just his voice, *he* wanted to disappear, and at the sight of his laughter everyone around him laughed with him. He was the president-elect of the United States, and with a start he realized that everything in his life would be different. Everything.

Now he had maneuvered himself to the wall in the oval drawing room with the tattered blue furniture and stood with a glass of Madeira untouched in his hand. Albert and Hannah Gallatin had joined him and were fending off the talkers; he was touched that they so well understood the tumult of his feelings. He saw Dolley at the other end of the room, by the windows. She was talking to Mr. Latrobe, who gestured toward the window framing, and she shook her head. There was a small crash as a tray fell somewhere and she turned from Mr. Latrobe to survey the damage. She was very much in command and it struck him that this would be her last big entertainment as mere hostess for the president. Already she was slipping into her role as president's wife with joy. Borrowing servants and tableware and all the accoutrements, she would make this great house hum, though he thought if it hummed much more than it was humming now it might explode. It was magnificent, he whispered to her as she paused momentarily at his side. And still a bit frightening.

Congressional leaders were here in numbers too great to count, ardent Federalists, radical Democrats, and the solid middle all mingling, drinking, hurling barbs at each other that stayed carefully within the range of civility, to be met with laughter and counterbarbs.

Young Adams bowed in that grave way of his. The Adamses were patriots of the old school, standing for what was right and good and never mind political advantage. Madison doubted they much liked what the Federalist party had become. Might even be ready to join the right party. Madison asked after his parents.

"They're quite well, thank you, Mr. President-elect. You know that Mrs. Madison was kind enough to offer insights that might facilitate rapprochement with Mr. Jefferson."

"She told me. So how was it received?"

"They listened with real attention. Didn't say much, but it took effect. They'll come around to a healing in time. I believe both sides want it."

"Be a blessing for both sides. But what of you? Do I understand Massachusetts didn't return you to the Senate?"

He saw a sadness in the younger man's expression. "Mr. Pickering said they would get me," he said, "and indeed they did. I suppose I was a bit cavalier too and I thought I wouldn't care, but it's rather surprising how much it turns out to hurt."

"I thought you were wasted in the Senate and needed abroad," Madison said. The young man laughed abruptly and said that mirrored his feelings precisely. He had spent ten years in American legations under General Washington and his father.

"I want to open an embassy in Russia," Madison said. "Think you'd be interested?"

"Ambassador to Russia?" Adams's grip on his hand tightened. "Yes, *sir*!"

"We'll talk about it soon."

David Erskine, the new British envoy replacing the unmerry Mr. Merry and his even less merry wife, saluted Madison graciously. Things were more pleasant under him if no better in fact, but at least he wouldn't be flirting with the likes of Aaron Burr.

The ambassador drifted away after further pleasantries and Sam Smith stepped up to take Madison's hand. Sam, a Baltimore merchant of considerable power, represented Maryland in the Senate. A solid and highly decisive man with a direct gaze under beetle brows, he was an ardent Democrat and an old friend.

"That youngster," Sam said, nodding toward Erskine, "he's another Merry, really. We'll have to fight 'em, sooner or later, you know."

"Yes," Madison said. "But better later."

"I'll make you a wager, Mr. President-elect. Inside of four years we'll be at war with them. Four years, say sometime in 1812, I'll put up fifty pounds on that."

Madison laughed. "I'd rather wager on a horse race, but I don't doubt you're right . ... 1812."

Oh, yes, it was coming, for before long Europe must be brought to recognize America as a new nation standing equal in the family of nations. Rough times lay ahead, but it was time for European designs on America to fade and die. That was the lesson of the Louisiana Purchase—they had made Napoleon see that he couldn't hold out against the future power of America. Captain Lewis's magnificent trek to the Pacific told the British that their hopes of dominating the West must collapse.

He saw that young Adams had fallen into conversation with a French legation secretary, no doubt probing the realities of the Russian situation even now. The whole diplomatic corps stood in a small group, from France and Britain and Denmark and Russia, all watching the president-elect of the United States. As was everyone else. The reflexive thought that it was alarming passed. It struck him that he might be getting used to it already, even to liking it.

Think about it, he said to himself. It's a fact that you aren't comfortable in big gatherings, but how distasteful is it really for three hundred national leaders to be here honoring you? To move into this magnificent house? To run this magnificent country? Maybe not so distasteful. He had to smile suddenly as he saw plainly that in fact he loved it. Some very rough days lay ahead and there would be problems before which any normal man must feel trepidation. But in fact, he knew no one whom he felt might make a better president as Tom left the scene. War was coming and Tom had felt Madison might be the better president at war.

In other words, Tom's magnetic personality, his image still strong from the Declaration of Independence, was no longer required to hold the new democracy together. Tom's landslide election four years before might have spoken to his popularity; Madison's landslide now spoke to democracy's popularity. Testimony to the power of free men holding their fate in their own hands.

Yet it was vulnerable, too, and he supposed it always would be vulnerable. Sometimes he wondered if things happened because they needed to happen, the way Lewis and Clark's expedition so recently and gloriously knit the country together and assured it a continental future. The way the outcome of Burr's plot told all the old western conspirators that their day was done. Of course, there were great dangers. Burr could have succeeded; Madison never doubted that the Burr conspiracy was the most dangerous moment in American history since the Revolution itself. That it didn't succeed anchored the future. The coming war would be dangerous, too, but he knew Britain could never really crush us. Napoleon had been wise enough to withdraw gracefully; perhaps because Britain once had owned us, we would have to give it a bloody nose to persuade it, which was about all we could manage anyway. But we would emerge from that encounter as a full member of the family of nations.

He saw Dolley coming across the room, all heads turning, she clasping hands with both of hers, kissing cheeks, laughing and chatting and wishing them well but never stopping. She came close and he caught both her hands and wanted to kiss her.

"Don't you love it—don't you just *love* it?" she whispered.

"Yes," he said, surprising himself. "Yes, I really do."

She was glowing, more beautiful than ever, a tendril of her black hair fallen over one eye, and he felt a sudden surge of desire. Her arm was around him. "We must go," she said. "You're the guest of honor. They won't leave till we do." Again that startled awareness of attention focused on him stirring something wary in his nature.

She took his arm. He started toward the nearest door but she pulled him to the right and they promenaded through all the rooms, taking the crowd's salute. When they reached the front door he wheeled about on impulse and raised her hand in a triumphant gesture, and she leaned against him to kiss his cheek. There was a roar of laughter and applause, whistles and cheers from westerners well along on corn-liquor punch. They stepped out the door to their carriage with the applause still ringing. The crowd might hate him tomorrow but it loved him today.

It was a good ending.

And a good beginning.

★　　★　　★　　★　　★

NOTE ON METHODS AND SOURCES

The series of novels making The American Story 1800–1860 are, of course, fiction. But they are historically accurate, unusually heavily grounded in fact. They undertake to tell the historical elements of the period so that history itself—what happened and why it happened and how it happened—provides the story line. I don't have fictional main characters who live in or are affected by history but have their own story as well; in my novels, the characters are the figures of history themselves as they deal with the events of history, struggling to bring to successful conclusion the problems and perils most immediately faced.

In making central characters of men and women who were real, who lived and breathed and loved and fought as do all the rest of us, I have been at great pains to present them accurately as they are reflected in biographies, their letters, their memoirs and the memoirs and reminiscences of the men and women who knew them and dealt with them, both friends and enemies. I have tried generally to place them where they were known to have been in the particular times. I never ask them to do or say anything that is inconsistent with their character as they have come down to us over the years or that is inconsistent with the history of the period. As I examine their aims, motives, reasoning and pressures faced, consistent with their natures and attitudes, I look to what reasonable men and women might reasonably say and do under those circumstances. Indeed, that goes to the whole point of what I'm about; my conviction that figures now frozen in history really were living, breathing people with all the pressures, angers, fears, hopes that you and I know in our lives today. The same is true, I think, for national leaders today.

In the case of *Treason*, however, I have had to delve much more deeply into speculation than in other books. This is the story of the Burr Conspiracy, which conspiracy Burr never admitted. There was much evidence of conspiracy, but Burr was a facile explainer and his modern partisans insist that he has explained everything satisfactorily. In essence, they assert that he was just fooling around, maybe trying to cheat the British, believed his frontier property was workable and all his young men were settlers and so forth and so on.

Burr's biographers tend to fall under the man's spell but to laud Burr one must denounce Jefferson, which Burr authors usually do. I personally find Jefferson a more substantial figure than Burr by a wide margin. Madison, now widely recognized as perhaps the most substantial figure of all, firmly believed that Burr had put the new republic in the greatest danger it had known since the revolution itself.

There is no middle ground. Burr was guilty or he wasn't. No one thought his rigged trial proved anything but that it was rigged. Guilty or innocent: take your pick. As I see the story I believe he was guilty of the treason that I describe. I think he was desperate to recover from the depths to which rage and failure had plunged him and that he tried a scheme that had it worked would have meant a United States vastly different from the continental nation we know today. To offer that conviction in story form I must invent an interior that matches it, and that is what I have done.

Everything that I have Burr say and do is consistent with the record, or with one interpretation of the record. Of course, his intentions in doing what he did are everything as to his guilt or innocence. I offer fictional intentions that make him guilty because I believe he was guilty. If my aim had been to establish that Jefferson and Madison united in unholy unity to destroy poor Burr in order to advance Madison, I suppose I would have seen his intentions differently.

With that caveat, I offer a look at the Burr Conspiracy that follows the factual record as carefully as I can. Burr did go where and when I say he went. His actions were as I describe them. The part that is open to the reader's questioning and possible disagreement is why he did what he did.

The other large area open to question is exactly how the conspiracy was defeated. It is historical fact that Wilkinson turned on Burr; the letter from Burr that Wilkinson described but couldn't produce and Burr couldn't describe without admitting his own role, clearly implicated both men. Further, it was obvious to everyone that if there was a conspiracy, Wilkinson had to be involved. Burr could not have turned the West and conquered Mexico with a thousand men recruited along the Mohawk. Wilkinson as traitor was widely rumored then; in modern times Spanish archives make clear that the commanding general of the U.S. Army was Agent #13 at $2,000 a year for a couple of decades, a fortune in those days. A thoroughly slippery character.

But why did Wilkinson turn on Burr? As the plot unfolded it became obvious that something was going on and it was the State Department that was required to answer. In those days, State was not the foreign affairs center we know today; it was the only cabinet post not anchored to a specific (war, navy, treasury, etc.) and it was much more involved in domestic than in international affairs. I think it must have been entirely clear that if Burr's aims were real then Wilkinson must have been involved. If Wilkinson were involved the danger multiplied and the question becomes how to turn him? We know that he did turn and the often accepted supposition is that he lost his nerve. But why did he lose his nerve?

That brings us to the letter that I have Madison pressuring Daniel Clark to send playing on the estimate of Wilkinson as coward. This letter is speculation but I think there must have been something that triggered Wilkinson's actions. Clark, the merchant prince of New Orleans, is a real figure, as is his mistress, Zulie. In my fictional letter from Clark to Wilkinson, there is a reference to a letter Clark had in fact written a year before; this is historically accurate, Clark sent exactly such a letter to Wilkinson in the prior year. My speculation that Madison was the intellect that precipitated Wilkinson's terror (instead of Burr's letter saying we're ready to go) is my fictional approach but is consistent with all known facts and attitudes and with Madison's way of doing business.

Coming at the story from another viewpoint, the tension between Madison and Dolley over their estimates of Burr is fictional but consistent with the facts. That Dolley and Burr were friends, his assistance in the terrible period when her husband died and she feared she would follow him, the multiple street encounters that encouraged him to feel they remained friends all are accurate. The extent to which she might have supported Burr with her husband, her fear that Burr might push Madison into a duel, and the sense of an ongoing relationship arise from the situation and from my estimate of how people operate but is not documented.

My main characters, obviously, are the figures of history. But one or two fictional characters who can move about and deliver parts of the story are quite essential. Danny Mobry and Jaycee Barlow are fictional figures. Danny gives us the New Orleans picture and lets us see Burr in a different way from that of other characters. All the figures directly associated with Danny are perforce fictional—Captain Mac, Clinch Johnson, the British officer, Henri Broussard and others.

Barlow is useful in various ways, including putting into words the general dismay at Jefferson and Madison making a hero of Wilkinson, clearly a co-conspirator, in order to convict Burr. This was widely condemned at the time.

The New Orleans figures, Governor Claiborne and Ed Livingston and his wife are all accurately drawn. Livingston went on to serve as Secretary of State under President Jackson.

The most unusual figures in the novel are entirely factual. Harman and Margaret Blennerhassett did have an incestuous marriage, did sell the estate in Ireland, did come to the island in the Ohio and build the incredible house and did sweep it all into the Burr conspiracy. In recent years the house has been completely restored and now is a state park. Harman clearly was a fool; my estimate that Margaret was not a fool is my own but seems reasonable.

I have tried to place historical figures only where and when I know them to have been. The exception to this is General Wilkinson, who operated from New Orleans to St. Louis to Washington and even New York. In his case I have moved him as needed to convey his meetings with Burr. Both of Burr's trips down the Ohio and the Mississippi are accurately drawn. His time and performance in New Orleans follows the record. Dolley's boil which threatened her with amputation, that being the state of the medicine of the day, is accurately presented including the trip to Philadelphia.

John Quincy Adams is accurately drawn, including his conflict with his family, his distaste for the legal profession, his hunger for assignments abroad, his appointment as envoy to Russia. The confrontation with his father is based on his and the family's feelings and interaction and is conceptually accurate but such a specific trip is not known. Travel was brutal and exhausting in that day and I have moved people about in some cases to accomplish what probably was done by letter.

Obviously *Treason* is based on extensive research but I am not an historian and I do not undertake original research nor do I feel that is what I can bring to the work. I read extensively in histories, biographies, memoirs and period material. I must express appreciation to the Butler Library of Columbia University, the New York Public Library and the Library of Congress for an historical education over the years.

For the Conspiracy itself I relied heavily on *The Burr Conspiracy* by the distinguished southern historian Thomas Perkins Abernethy which was published in 1954 and makes a powerful case.

For Madison, I turned to Irving Brant's six volumes on the Madisons, plus Ralph Ketcham's single volume and numerous treatments of Dolley Madison. Dumas Malone's six volumes on Jefferson are powerful, as is Merrill Peterson's single volume. *American Sphinx* and *Founding Brothers* by Joseph I. Ellis offer important looks at my characters. I relied heavily on Milton Lomask's two volumes on Burr though my conclusions are very different from his. Thomas Fleming's *Duel* which treats the tragic Burr-Hamilton duel is excellent. Paul Nagle's *John Quincy Adams* offers a more personal view of his subject that well supplements Samuel F. Bemis' powerful work and earlier biographies. Henry Adams's magnificent *History of the United States During the Administrations of Thomas Jefferson and Henry Adams,* ten original volumes now available in a fine two-volume set from the Library of America. Adams is splendid, sometimes biased, occasionally off-base in the view of modern scholars but always interesting and often very wise.

Finally, however, I must say that I based much of my estimates of how politics and human nature intertwine, then and now, on my own substantial experience with politics, Washington, and the White House as a national journalist.

—DN